MESTACLOCAN

R Lawson Gamble

This is a work of fiction. Although the author has described actual locations, any resemblance to events or persons living or dead is entirely coincidental.

Rich Gamble Associates

First Paperback Printing 2013

ISBN-13: 978-1493680191

ISBN-10: 1493680196

To Matt and Stef

When they introduced me to the city they love,

they didn't know what I would set loose upon it.

"We have two brains; one of our brains spends the whole of its life in denial of what the other brain knows."

Prologue

Arizona 1854

Firelight danced on the old shaman's stretched leather cheeks and the fire's pulsating flames leapt and glowed in his eyes. He stared into the undulating red-yellow heart of the blaze as if the words he would speak were scribed there. A silent circle of soft-cheeked buckskin-clad boys watched the old man and waited, crowding close to the welcome warmth of the campfire to escape the snapping cold lurking in the darkness behind them. The ancient one swayed and then began to speak and his age-rusted voice crackled like the snap of the burning logs. He told the story they had come to hear, drawing the words from his memory one by one, slowly and carefully like a splinter from flesh.

"My children. At a time before memory, when our people had not lived long upon this earth, they had no fire to warm them and protect them and to cook their food as we have now. Then one day a band of hunters caught by the sudden darkness and fury of a storm took shelter beneath a cliff overhang. The pelts they wore were little use against the slashing winds and stabbing rain and they huddled together for warmth. The darkening clouds rumbled and writhed above them and thunder cracked and sudden spears of white light ripped through the blackness and stabbed earthward. At the height of the tumult came a blinding light and a tall tree nearby exploded into flame. It creaked and groaned and split apart with the roar of a wounded bear, dying slowly and agonizingly. Fiery limbs fell from the heights showering sparks and spreading flame. The men cowered in fear.

But eventually the storm passed and the grumbling grew

distant. Then a brave young hunter seized by sudden impulse ran to the engulfed tree and in a reckless display of courage seized a burning branch by its end. Whirling his flaming trophy high above his head he walked toward his companions. They scattered and ran. But when the heat reached the young hunter's hand he was forced to drop the branch and stood defenseless to face the wrath of his companions.

My children, from unexpected moments come lasting lessons. The hunters learned well from what they had witnessed. Their people would overcome the fear of fire and learned to control it and from that time forward their lives would be changed. When they wielded this fierce weapon no enemy could withstand them and none of the animals could face them. Their fire lit the darkness and gave them comfort and safety such as they had never before known. And the people who did not possess this fearsome weapon were soon overcome."

The old man stopped abruptly as if memory had failed him and he closed his eyes and swayed gently. The young men waited. Then the ancient one lifted his head once more and resumed his story.

"But a few beings without fire did survive, hidden deep in the forests. They lived through cunning and guile and they made the night their habitat and darkness their protective veil. Over the years their senses grew strong so that when the curtain of night descended upon the land it became their world. But our people relied upon the fire's light to hold back the darkness and so their senses were diminished. And it remained so down through the ages.

But our people prospered and their numbers became great and before long they had forgotten the people of the night. Yet some of the night people still existed. Highly evolved for their dark world they had grown powerful and agile and cruel. No longer did they hide in the forest's depth but hid instead among their daytime cousins, living undetected alongside our people by day but preying upon them at night..."

The ancient one's voice trailed off. His rheumy eyes studied each intent face through half-closed lids. When he spoke again it was in a whisper.

"It is the shaman who remembers and preserves the stories of our people and it is he who is responsible for telling them when the time is right, as I do now. You will soon become warriors and so it is fitting that you know what warriors know; that when a baby disappears from its blanket, or a hunter does not return from the hunt, or when the howl of an unknown beast sounds in the darkness, the night people are near."

The Shaman's gaze turned away from the fire and searched the darkness beyond. His next words were barely audible. "Our fathers had a name for these hunters of the night," he whispered. "They called them...Mestaclocan."

ONE

The smell of her came to him: sensual, intoxicating. It came sharp to his nose and he savored it on his tongue and felt his passions rise. The fire in him was kindled and he struggled to hold it back, to slow the raging sweet darkness that would soon transform him. He sensed her growing fear and it ignited in him a sharp edge of anticipation. He saw that she understood what was to come. Her understanding was his foreplay and he would make it last.

Arizona

Present Day

FBI Supervisory Special Agent Zack Tolliver heard a phone ring in some distant place and he swam toward it through rising consciousness. His arm groped out of the covers and he fumbled for it, found it, and clamped it to his ear.

“Yeah?” he mumbled.

"There was another one last night." The words sounded sad, resigned, world weary in the manner of one who has seen too much and no longer feels shock. "Same thing,” the voice continued, “throat torn open, mid-thirties. She’s even got red hair like the last one."

Zack rolled toward his night table and cradled the phone against his ear with his right elbow while he used the other hand to turn on the bedside lamp. He looked at the clock: six AM.

"Where'd you find her?"

"Night patrol found her up at the Presidio while shaking druggies out of the old bunkers up there. She was behind one crumpled up against it on this tiny goat path of a trail."

Zack mentally subtracted an hour. The Navajo Reservation didn't observe Daylight Savings Time so it would be five AM in San Francisco. "Are you at the scene?"

"Yeah. Lucky me," Marty said. Lieutenant Marty O'Bannon was a homicide detective with the Richmond Police District of San Francisco and Zack's old friend and colleague. "We moved her outta here just a few minutes ago. We're trying to keep a low profile with this. Just another dead junkie hooker, ya know?"

"You've got pictures…?"

"Oh, sure, a whole battery of 'em. You've got 'em already. I sent 'em from my phone a few minutes ago."

"I'll take a look after my shower. Guess I'm up now," Zack sighed.

"My heart bleeds."

"Listen, Marty, any prints on the path near the body? Any blood splatter, cigarette butts, anything to tell you whether she was killed there or dumped later?"

"Pretty certain she was killed right here. Like I said, her throat was torn out - not cut, torn. Her blood's all over the ground here."

"Any idea what she was doing there?"

"No, not yet. We're just gettin' started with the investigation. I'll call you when we've got more, after the lab guys have had a look. I gotta go now."

"Okay, Marty. Thanks for keeping me in the loop."

"Yeah, well, I hope all this means something to you."

The line went dead.

Zack turned off his phone and lay on his back, his fingers entwined across his forehead, thinking. Libby rolled toward him and a strand of her auburn hair draped itself across the pillow and down one sleep-softened cheek. She peeped up through half open eyes without lifting her head.

"What is it?"

"Cop consulting me on a case. No reason for you to wake up."

"Do you really have to go?"

"Yeah, I guess I should." Zack smiled at her. "I'm awake now, but you don't have to be. Get some more sleep. I'm gonna shower and then sit down with the pictures Marty sent me before I go to work."

Libby smiled sleepily and stretched, arching her back cat-like, then cuddled back into the warmth of the bedclothes.

Zack swung his legs out of the blankets and onto the cold hardwood floor. He immediately felt a chill. It was late April in Arizona; they'd been getting some real hot days, but the nights were still plenty cold. Zack hopped one-legged across the floor to the bathroom, shaking off his boxers as he went, and turned on the hot water in the tub. While he waited for the water to heat he leaned on the sink and studied himself in the mirror. A little over medium height with thick brown hair, he had bright blue eyes and his body was lanky and long muscled. A small pucker of red skin on his shoulder was all that was left to mark where the bullet had entered over a year ago. In an unconscious morning ritual he found he could pinch considerably more than an inch at his waist and grunted with dissatisfaction. *Got to work out more*, he thought. He turned away from the mirror and stepped into the steaming shower. While he soaped up he thought about things.

He knew he shouldn't get ahead of himself. In a big city like San Francisco hookers get killed all the time. It could be coincidence, or it could be a serial killer. Yet all these victims had their throats torn open - not slashed, torn - that's the piece that grabbed him.

Zack dried quickly and vigorously and wrapping the towel around his waist walked back into the cold bedroom. He saw that Libby was fast asleep already and he was glad, especially with this unofficial investigation he was involved in. It had taken her months to recover from the nightmarish conclusion to the last case they had worked together, and most of a year to learn to sleep through the entire night and even then her dreams were filled with nightmares. He didn't want to see her sleeplessness start up all over again. Zack felt a surge of affection as he looked down at her sleeping form, the luxurious dark hair with those burnished red highlights, the long oval face with high cheekbones, the dark almost black eyebrows above soft lids hiding those huge brown eyes: all relaxed, all at rest.

Zack dropped his towel and stretched into his jeans. He pulled a sweatshirt over his head and shuffled across the hall in his wool socks to his tiny office and sank into the desk chair. He sat still for a moment, reluctant. Then he sighed and pushed open the laptop and clicked into his e-mail. Immediately several rows of thumbnail photos marched across his screen. Zack filled the monitor with each of them, one by one.

Marty did good, he thought. There were several close-ups of a ragged gaping wound, followed by full figure shots of the girl. He'd have called her attractive under any other circumstance, even lying there slumped against the concrete bunker with her head drooped over and her long red hair hanging to the ground. And all that blood: down the blouse, down the concrete, pooling on the ground. There were shots of the path itself. Marty was right, it really was a goat path, just a narrow rocky trough at the seam of the bunker wall.

Zack flipped back to the full figure shots. The girl was fully clothed; one pink short-heeled shoe on, one missing, a short pleated skirt showing a lot of thigh from the way she'd fallen, some sort of fluffy blouse with tiny yellow flowers on it and even a brown leather vest. He'd find out later if there'd been a sexual assault, but from these photos it didn't look like it. And that bothered him. Neither of the other two girls had been assaulted sexually; just killed, throats ravaged, left there. Nothing more.

We don't know if the three deaths are related, Zack reminded himself. He had no time of death for this one yet, but of the other two one had died in the early morning, the other in the late evening, which seemed a likely timeframe for this one, too. Again, he'd know soon enough. But the throat wound...there was no doubt about that. And they'd all been youngish women: mid-thirties, healthy, strong - a blonde and two redheads.

Zack sighed and pushed away from the computer and then headed over to the kitchen to start up a pot of coffee. As much as he'd like to study the girls' deaths further, he had his own work to do today. He'd go check in with Luke Forrestal at the Tuba City FBI Office first to see what was on the duty schedule, then maybe stop to chat with Jimmy Chaparral on the reservation at the Elk Springs Police Station. After that, he'd see what was what.

Zack Tolliver's first assignment after graduating from the Academy was to the FBI Liaison Office responsible for the Four Corners Navajo Indian Reservation. That had been almost a dozen years ago now. It was not a glamorous posting nor had he sought it. But once he'd arrived, despite its heat and vast emptiness, the place had begun to grow on him. Long and short, he'd never left.

Back in the bedroom he pulled on his boots. When he reached for his handgun in the bedside drawer he made sure the alarm was still set for eight AM. Libby had plans to go over to her own ranch for a couple of days, what with the big mare ready to foal. Her hired hands could handle it fine but Libby always wanted to be right there during all the births on her ranch, whether horse, dog or human. Zack chuckled to himself. Libby was real big on renewal.

Zack's truck keys were on the hall table and he patted his butt to be sure he had his wallet. He was almost out the door when he remembered he'd promised Libby to mail her letter. He found it on the counter in the kitchen right next to his coffee. He'd forgotten that, too.

I'm sure as hell not a morning guy, Zack thought to

himself. He was hungry now but he decided he would wait and have an egg over easy on hash at the diner in Tuba City. The less noise he made in the house now with Libby asleep the better.

As he walked out through the closed-in porch and down the steps, he pushed a button on his phone.

"Wake you up?"

"That'll be the day, White Man."

"I thought you'd like to know we'll likely take a field trip soon."

"Another body?"

"Yeah. Just like the last."

"Same MO?"

"Yup. Just the throat; torn, not cut. I was just looking at the photos; could've been done by long canines. Or not."

Eagle Feather went back to the first news. "How soon?"

"I feel like we should wait to see if there's another body. Forrester won't want me hopping all over the country every time there's a suspicious murder."

"You comin' to town?"

"I'm on my way now."

"Meet you at Julia's?"

"Done."

After Zack rang off he touched the Weather App on his phone and checked it while walking over to his truck. *Cold to start, heating up, then clear*, he read. No surprise; a typical Arizona high, it wouldn't change much. Then he checked the weather for San Francisco. It was in the 60's there, damp and foggy; again, no surprise. *Up at the Presidio it must be extra soggy*, he thought and he wondered how that might affect any signs left at the crime scene.

Zack's assigned territory was the Western Region of the Navajo Indian Reservation, working out of Tuba City. He was responsible to Luke Forrester, Agent in Charge. Luke hadn't been out here long. He'd been enjoying a cushy posting in Washington D.C. when Zack's former supervisor and mentor, Ben Brewster, had decided to retire following the Roundtree case, a brutal murder investigation that had been splashed across the national media. That was the case that so traumatized Libby. But Zack had identified the real killer and connected him to serial murders here and in Palm Springs and the case had gained him immediate notoriety within the Bureau; to some a success story, to others a rogue agent - take your pick.

Zack grunted as he thought about it. The case had taken its toll on pretty much everyone except Ben, who had retired with accolades - courtesy of Zack. Then Luke Forrester had come to fill the vacancy and he'd filled it well, Zack thought. It took a special personality to last out here; you had to have patience and you had to respect the Navajo, even if you didn't understand 'em. Luke seemed to know that. And he allowed Zack freedom to work in his own way and in his own time. But Luke did have a limit to his patience and Zack might be getting close to it because of the time he was spending on this unofficial investigation. He hadn't spoken to Luke about it yet, but he knew Luke was aware of the calls Zack was getting from San Francisco. He must know something was going on. Hey, the man was an investigator, wasn't he?

Zack quietly resolved to be more careful not to upset the apple cart. When the time was right he'd bring Luke in on it, but he needed a whole lot more evidence than he had right now. He emerged from his thoughts surprised to see he had arrived at the outskirts of Tuba City - the half-hour trip had flashed by. He pulled in at Julia's Diner and noted with pleasure the rust-red 1963 Ford pickup with its boxy old cab parked near the entrance. So Eagle Feather was here already. Zack's stomach growled. He hadn't realized how hungry he was getting.

Inside it was cold; the AC was working hard to get a head start on the day. Zack glanced along the counter until he saw a thick black braid hanging under a black felt hat adorned with a single feather. He slid onto a stool next to the man under the hat. Eagle Feather spoke without looking up.

"Julia's hash is extra fine this morning."

Zack grinned. "That's just what I've been dreaming about all the way over here." He raised a single finger to the waitress, then glanced at Eagle Feather. "Keepin' busy?"

"Two clients yesterday. Only one of 'em got his sheep, but both looked happy. Seems all white folk need to gain a whole new outlook on life is to tromp around in the wilderness for a while. "

"Are you a guide, or a shrink?"

"Maybe a little of both, now that you mention it."

Eagle Feather looked up now, showing a rare grin beneath crinkly brown-black eyes. If anyone was capable of on-the-spot psychoanalysis, it was Eagle Feather. He had a natural sense for people to go along with his Masters in Anthropology from ASU and some advanced courses in psychology and neuroscience at UC Davis. Born Elmore Bernstein to a Navajo mother and a Jewish father, he'd been exposed to diverse cultures his whole life. He began guiding at a young age and made good money helping rich white clients bag the *Ovis Canadensis Nelsoni*, Nelson's Mountain Sheep, the most populous of the Bighorn sheep that roamed the area. His clients nicknamed him Eagle Feather for the solitary feather rising from the band of his battered felt hat. When he found he could draw more clients using that moniker, he'd kept it.

Zack rattled off his order to the counter girl when she brought his coffee. She refilled Eagle Feather's cup and bustled away while both men sipped the hot liquid.

After he'd rattled his cup back in its saucer, Eagle Feather stared into the murky brown liquid as if looking for a sign. "Give me your gut," he said, not looking up. "Do you think it's him?"

Zack grimaced. "I just don't know. I can't get a feeling about it, one way or another. Remember Los Angeles?"

"Yeah."

"Well, it's like that. It could be him, or it could be some lunatic with a garden tool. I just don't know."

"Three attacks, three different places, but all wooded areas, all parks inside the city. I mean, no dark alleys, no vacant lots, no city streets. He seems to prefer real trees in real forests."

Zack nodded his agreement and listed them on his fingers, "Golden Gate Park, Buena Vista Park, the Presidio."

"Exactly. All wooded, all natural. That tell you anything?"

"That the guy likes to murder girls in isolated places?"

"It tells me it could be spiritual, a connection to deeper roots, the call of ancient instincts."

"Maybe. Or maybe just some homeless guy living out of his grocery cart."

Both men sipped their coffees. Zack broke the silence.

"You think we ought to get up there right away, don't you?"

"You're reading my mind."

"So go."

"What do you mean?"

"Look. You know I can't just up and leave, not without something more definite than what we've got right now. Forrestal would have my head, and maybe my badge, and I couldn't blame him. I can't pull another Los Angeles on him. But you can, right? You could just go up there, sniff around the crime scenes, get a feel. Then if something breaks, you'd be right there. Even better, you'd know if it's something important enough that I should come up."

"And how am I supposed to make a living in the meantime, White Man?"

"Even if I can't go up there myself, I can authorize compensatory pay for you, like I would for a snitch or a private investigator. That'll at least pay your bills."

Eagle Feather thought about it.

Zack pressed. "And I'll set it up with Marty O'Bannon so they don't pick you up as a suspect while hanging around up there. You do look kinda suspicious to me."

Eagle Feather ignored him. "I may be crazy, but I've got a feeling about these murders. I'd keep thinking about them even if I didn't go up there..." Then he said, "Okay, I'll do it."

"Great. Go pack. I'll get you a cash advance."

Zack slapped some bills down on the counter. "Least I can do is get your breakfast."

"Least is what you usually do, White Man."

Zack laughed. Eagle Feather slid off his stool and started toward the door of the diner.

Zack called after him. "You be careful up there. If your gut is right, you'll be in danger the minute you hit those streets.

TWO

He woke feeling tired but satiated...and regretful. The dried blood smeared sticky dark on the carpet and spotted on his sheets and pillow told him all he needed to know. He thought of Los Angeles and groaned. He hadn't wanted to leave there, but he'd been careless. Now he was growing fond of San Francisco. But he'd end up having to leave here too if he wasn't more cautious in the future....

Jim Snyder pulled the flat copy pencil from its habitual nook behind his ear and crossed out a word in the manuscript, then read on. The clickety-click of keys and the constant drone of voices around him was a pleasant, even necessary background hum, not the distraction it had been for him when he was a cub reporter. He stroked out another word and wrote a better one above it. Jim was aware that he was considered old fashioned by the young pups of the office - no one used pencil and hard copy anymore – but the proof, as they say, was in the pudding: his copy never needed editorial review. They couldn't say the same.

But Jim's thoughts at the moment were not on the mechanical task of revising. He was thinking about the content of the piece. Jim knew the article couldn't go to print just yet; he'd have to put it aside and wait. As an old dog journalist his nose was telling him there was another chapter yet to come. But it was close - real close.

He picked up the copy and walked along the busy rows of computer-laden desks to the glassed-in editor offices and rapped on the door that said Editor-in-Chief, San Francisco Chronicle, etched in the glass. The door itself was oak, probably the original door from the last century, considering the age of the Mission Street building. But the glass panes that surrounded it were modern, constructed of tempered impact resistant glass in response to an incident with an angry reader who had smashed the old plate glass with a paperweight. That projectile was only the most recent of a long, historic and varied list of earlier missiles hurled at the office, including a brick, a baseball, and even a gilded cane.

Jim rapped on the door and walked in without pausing. George Henderson looked up from his computer monitor and stared at him and waited.

Without preamble, Jim laid it out. "Last night at the Presidio over behind the old concrete bunkers a thirty-something red-haired hooker: murdered, throat ravaged, nothing more. No molestation, clothes not even disturbed except by her fall. No bruises, no cuts; no other signs of violence on her body- "

"How-da-ya know that?" Henderson demanded.

Jim grinned. "Can't reveal my source, but it's solid."

Henderson nodded.

Jim continued. "Nine days before that, up in Buena Vista Park, in the woods; another woman, a redhead, throat torn open, no molestation, nothing disturbed or taken, not even the two hundred bucks in her purse."

Jim glanced down at his copy. "Nine days before that, in Golden Gate Park up on the north side near 12th Street where the dirt footpaths tunnel into the undergrowth: the body of a woman, jogger, about the same age, blond haired, throat torn open, no other signs of violence, no molestation, nothing taken."

Jim glanced at Henderson.

George stared back at Snyder.

Jim went on. "George, these murders lay out like tintypes of one another. Each had the external carotid artery severed resulting in huge blood loss all over the place. But that's all, no other wounds." He stared at Henderson and demanded pugnaciously, "Tell me they aren't connected."

"You tell me. That's your job."

"I think they are and I think the cops think they are, but they're keeping mum. George, I got a hunch. I think there's gonna be another one on" -Snyder glanced at the date calendar on his watch- "Tuesday next week. That's why I got this piece ready. I want it to go to print the moment I hear about the next victim."

"You got it." Henderson's attention was already back on his computer screen.

Jim turned away and for just a split second a look of quiet satisfaction softened his craggy features.

Marty O'Bannon kicked at a tuft of grass at the edge of the path in disgust. He'd been up and down it and found nothing, no sign at all beyond the girl's footprints. The marine layer had moved in last night and it had misted heavily here, leaving the place effectively irrigated. The path was cobbled with rock, but in the mud patches in between he saw the girl's prints, as clear in the damp mud as if they'd been drawn on a blackboard. He could see she'd been running through here - running hard, up high on her toes. She'd even lost one of her pink square-heeled shoes back there and gone on with one stocking foot. Running like hell, poor broad; must've been terrified.

O'Bannon pulled out a pack of Winstons and started to tap one out, then caught himself and pushed the cigarette back in. Not yet. He was down to four a day and if he had this one now his skin would be crawling by this afternoon.

A burly Park Police sergeant came tromping down the path toward him obliterating footprints as he came. *Good thing I checked for prints there already*, Marty thought. *They're fucked now.*

He called out to the man.

"Sergeant, stop where you are and go back the way you came. You're destroying evidence."

The man looked down at his large shoes and then stared at O'Bannon with opaque eyes, his neck beginning to flame red. "Sorry, sir. Wasn't thinking...I was sent to give you a message."

O'Bannon gave him his weary seen-it-all look. "What's your name, Sergeant?"

"Kelly, sir."

"Alright, Sergeant Kelly. Just don't come any further

toward me, please. I don't need a bigger mystery than what I already got here."

"Yes, sir. They said to tell you that an FBI guy named Tolliver called. Left you a message" -Kelly looked at a notebook in his hand- "some guy named Eagle Feather..." The sergeant looked up and grinned. "Really?" Then at O'Bannon's quick look of impatience went on. "This guy Eagle Feather is coming up here and you shouldn't think he's a suspect and lock him up." The sergeant smirked again despite himself. "I swear! That's what it says."

"Sergeant, you've delivered your message. Now turn around, go back, and stay in the prints you made coming here so's not to destroy any more evidence."

But O'Bannon couldn't help grinning to himself as he watched the over-fed Park Policeman balance like a ballerina, arms out horizontal trying to find his original footprints and stay in them.

After the man had gone Marty thought about the message and grunted. So Zack must have a stronger feeling about these murders than he let on this morning. Marty had heard about this Eagle Feather guy but never met him. He'd been mentioned a lot in that Roundtree business that got so much press, the case that apparently put the burr on Zack's ass about these killings. So now he'd have another amateur underfoot. Great!

O'Bannon's cell phone rang. Sighing, he pulled it out. Had to be the captain. O'Bannon had been assigned as the lead homicide investigator for this case, mostly because of the two other murders. He'd been investigating the murder in Golden Gate Park when he'd learned of the Buena Vista Park murder, and now this. But his captain wasn't about to let that stand in the way of his regular workload.

"Lieutenant O'Bannon...?"

"Yeah."

"Got to be a connection, right?"

O'Bannon was startled. "Who's this?"

"Jim Snyder from the Chronicle."

"Where'd you get this number? No, never mind that! Lose this number!"

"I promise, right after this serial killer is found."

"What're ya talkin' about?"

"Don't be coy, Lieutenant. You know what I'm talking about, the three women with their throats cut open. They've all got to be connected."

"Where'd you get three?"

"Golden Gate Park, Buena Vista Park, and now the Presidio."

"Who told you anything happened at the Presidio?"

"I monitor all the police frequencies. The U.S. Police up there aren't particularly subtle. I can give you in-depth detail of the murder victim if you want it."

"Look, Jim. I know you, right? You've been around the playground. We've got nothing to connect these killings, no reason to think serial killer or anything else. We're going a step at a time. That's all."

"So you're involved why? Just to help out on your day off?"

"Look, wise guy, I've got to get back to work. I'll be honest with you; I don't know what we got yet. But when I do, I'll call you first."

"Yeah, right you will."

"Look. You print anything now you're more likely to be wrong than right. And you'll do a whole lot of harm."

"I'll be honest with you, too. I'm not going to print now. You know why? There's gonna be another one, somewhere about next Tuesday. And when that happens, I'll go to print. You got 'til then." The line went dead.

"Balls," O'Bannon muttered as he hung up.

THREE

It had been tough today, tough to keep up the usual dull daily pretense; acting out the charade, blending in, going through the motions. And all the time his senses alive and his need growing in him, the blood scent coming sharper and more intoxicating while in his mind the recurring image of each of these posturing, strutting, over-confident people around him becoming suddenly fawn-like, frightened, eyes bulging, hearts pounding, then running, running... No, no. Push it back. Be cautious...

Eagle Feather finally found a place to park his battered truck between a Beemer and a Mini Cooper almost a block away from the red brick Romanesque Revival Police Station on Sixth Avenue. He parked and walked back to it. He went up a short set of steps and pushed open the big door in the white stone archway and found himself in a reception hall. The desk sergeant was writing on a clipboard and didn't look up. Eagle Feather stood quietly in front of the desk and his eye ran down the office directory on the wall behind it. He found the name listed under homicide: Lieutenant Martin O'Bannon. When the desk sergeant finally looked up, Eagle Feather was gone. He looked around, scratched his head and turned back to his work.

Eagle Feather went down the corridor that led to

the back of the building and followed it around to the left. A line of oak doorways with snow-glassed windows marched along the hall, each with the occupant's title painted in black block letters. He walked along until he came to a door with *Homicide* on the glass and several names listed beneath. He saw O'Bannon's name there. The door was open and he walked in. Several desks lined the far wall beneath small square windows. All had chairs on either side and grey paper trays and black telephones. A large whiteboard with messages scrawled on it in blue marker hung on the back wall and several photos were stapled next to it. One had a dart stuck in it. Two men were in the room; one sitting at a desk and the other perched on its corner. They were both in jeans and T-shirts. When Eagle Feather entered the room they stopped their chatter and turned to look.

"I'm looking for Lieutenant O'Bannon."

"So are a lot of people."

"He's not here?"

"Who's asking?"

"Mind leaving him a message? Tell him Eagle Feather is here."

"Sure, Chief. Would you like to leave the telephone number of your teepee?"

The other cop laughed at that.

Eagle Feather's expression didn't changed. "I'll send him a smoke signal," he said. Then he turned and walked out, waving his hand above his head as he left, calling out, "Thanks."

O'Bannon drove his black Toyota Celica up the alley next to the Richmond District Station and looped around to the back and pulled into his assigned parking place. He sat for a moment after he'd killed the engine, thinking. Old Snyder at the Chronicle was probably right about the connections. But what made him so certain about next Tuesday? Was there something he'd missed? Or did Snyder know something that O'Bannon didn't? It pissed him off when the media knew more about his case than he did.

He climbed out and walked to the back door of the station, flipping through his notepad as he walked. He'd stopped to interview the husband of the jogger they'd found in Golden Gate Park. No help there. The lady had gone out to run in the early morning from their home on 12th Street before hubby was up. When he came down to breakfast and didn't find her there he'd assumed she'd gone to work at the marketing office where she was a partner. Didn't even miss her until that night. *Working couples*, he thought derisively. *How can you even call them couples?*

He walked directly to his desk in the homicide office and glanced at his telephone light. It was blinking with messages as usual. Harrar was at the next desk, shuffling paper. He grinned as he watched O'Bannon stare reluctantly at the phone.

"Hey, some Indian Chief was in here looking for you. Where you been all day?"

"Up at the Presidio trying to learn everything I could before those rent-a-cops destroyed the crime scene. After that I stopped to chat with the jogger's hubby on 12th." O'Bannon slumped down in his chair. He spoke over his shoulder without looking. "Say his name was Eagle Feather?"

"Yeah, that's it. Tried to get a number but he blew smoke up my ass."

"Hope you treated him with respect. He's famous, you know."

"He a movie star or somethin'?"

"He helped solve that Navajo murder case, the Roundtree pedophile deal."

"What's he doing here?"

"Gonna try to get in my way, is my guess." O'Bannon sighed and reached for the phone, then punched the blinking button. He pulled a notepad closer and started jotting down the long list of messages.

Eagle Feather stood by his truck on the cinder-paved berm near the pathway down to the old concrete bunkers of the Presidio and stared at the red bridge towers rising up and then disappearing into the clouds like Jack's beanstalk. He understood why tourists flocked here; it really was impressive. Then he looked down at the park map in his hand to orient himself. He had decided to approach the crime scene from the south. He looked around again. Seemed kind of remote. Why would a working girl be way up here, anyway? They had their personal lives too, he guessed.

He walked up along the narrow road, stepping off the pavement whenever a car hurtled by with almost no room to spare. After about a quarter mile he came to a dirt parking area with a couple of cars in it: hikers, likely.

Paths led off in several directions among the trees and way down below he could catch glimpses of the grey Pacific swells. The trees here were weather-gnarled and old. The ever-damp debris-laden forest floor was quiet-footed beneath.

After another glance at the map Eagle Feather took a path that bore to the right back in the direction of the Golden Gate Bridge. The path sloped gently downhill through the trees before leveling off in a northerly direction, back toward the bunkers. Eagle Feather was satisfied that this must be the path the girl would have taken. That was more than two days ago but marks in the moisture-laden soil tended to stay. There'd been a lot of foot traffic since then, he noticed. He organized each individual set of prints in his mind and separated them out as he progressed: ripple sole man, worn inside leather guy, lady sneaker. And among them, a woman's narrow square-heeled shoes. Unusual footwear for this path, he thought. Then about a hundred yards along square heels abruptly disappeared. Eagle Feather pulled up short. He backtracked and tried again. No doubt, they were gone. But a different set of tracks had appeared; diamond shaped smudged prints with a longer stride. Of course! It was the same woman's low-heeled shoes, but running now, up on her toes.

Eagle Feather backtracked again. This time he wasn't looking for the woman's shoes but for the reason she started running. But he found no new prints or anything at all that was different on the muddy surface. So what had made her suddenly sprint like that? He continued along the path. It rose slightly and became rockier in substance, making prints harder to see. Ahead, he could see the outline of large concrete structures through the trees. Then he came to a yellow police tape stretched across the path. At the tape, ripple sole man, worn inside leather man and the others stopped and took a fork in the trail that led downhill, back in the other direction. They were obviously dissuaded by the police tape. But the lady's prints kept going. So did Eagle Feather.

Snyder pulled his aged Mercedes into the small parking lot of the Presidio Travelodge on Lombard Street. He double parked next to the courtesy van at Registration and climbed out, looking up at the green awning that shaded the third floor rooms. He found the exterior stairway and climbed up three flights then walked down the breezeway until he found room 315. He rapped loudly three times.

Beyond the thick white door Snyder heard sounds of movement and then a shrill voice called out, "Who is it?"

"Jim Snyder, the guy who called you an hour ago."

"What'd we talk about?"

"We made an appointment for six PM to discuss my tunnel plans for your infrastructure."

"Oh, yeah, the engineer."

Jim heard bolts slide and the safety chain clatter. The door opened a crack and a blue eye regarded him through it.

"Sure, come on in."

The door swung wide and Snyder stepped in. He found himself in a simple room with a single king bed, a tiny white microwave on a white mini-fridge, and an old style TV inside a laminated plastic wooden cabinet.

The woman who stood looking at him had white-blonde hair showing black roots and was in a flowered kimono that hung open to expose the curves of artificially rejuvenated but well-rounded breasts. She poked a shapely knee out from under the kimono as Snyder stared back.

"It'll be a hundred fifty bucks for the hour."

"We agreed to a hundred bucks over the phone."

"I don't remember that, but you're here now, so take it or leave it." She undraped the curves of her breasts a bit more.

"Okay, fine." Snyder pulled the bills out of his wallet and passed them to her, then looked at his watch. "One hour".

"That's right, lover boy. Hope you got the stamina."

"For what I want, I think I do."

"So what do you want? I don't do bondage, you know."

"I just want to talk." Snyder pulled out his notebook.

"Whoa, wait a minute. What are you, a reporter or something?"

"Actually, yes. But I'm not interested in you or your business. I'm barking up another tree. Your name and location will never be mentioned."

"Well, I dunno."

"That's pretty good pay just for an interview, but I can take it back and go somewhere else for my info."

"Okay, Okay. Hold your horses." She pulled the kimono back tight around herself and flopped back in the barrel-backed over-stuffed chair. "What do you want to know?"

Jim sat on the edge of the bed. "How long you worked out of this motel, Ms....?"

"Lana, call me Lana. I've been here about a year now."

"Do you know a red-headed professional girl, about five foot seven, light freckles, blue eyes like yours?"

"Might. Why?"

"If I wanted to hook up with her, what would you tell me?"

"I wouldn't believe you," Lana snickered.

"Pretend you do."

"Look, I don't want to get my associates in trouble."

"This one can't get into much more trouble - she's dead."

Lana gulped and turned white. "Cindy's dead? Whatta ya mean, dead?"

"I mean dead like not alive any more. Was Cindy working two nights ago?"

Lana sat shocked, her eyes wide. Finally she responded in a whisper.

"Yeah, right here in this room. We both were working."

"But she never came back from her last trick?"

"I didn't expect her to, she lucked into a full nighter for solid cash. She went out to meet the guy in his car."

"How'd the appointment get arranged?"

"Just like you - the guy called the number, made the deal, and gave her the directions."

"He wanted her, particularly?"

"Yeah, knew her working name and all, asked for her specifically."

"Hmmm." Jim wrote something in his notebook. "So tell me, did she tell you any details, like the car make, or anything about the arrangement?"

"No, just that she was going out to Lombard Street and he'd be along and not to wait up. That's all."

"How was she dressed?"

"I remember clearly, she had her Versace top, mini wrap-around skirt, hose, and the leather vest."

"What'd she have on her feet?"

"Not sure, but I think the pink square heels." Then

in a burst, "What's going on? What happened to her?"

"Nobody knows yet, but this client didn't work out too well for her."

Lana's lip trembled. "Murdered?"

"Looks like it. Take my advice, work out of a different place for a while until they find this guy."

Snyder stood up on stiff legs with a groan and put away his notebook. "I still got thirty-five minutes on the clock. I might call you later. I'll let myself out."

As he closed the door he caught a glimpse of her slouched in the barrel chair, staring after him.

FOUR

He knew not to return to the same place. He must keep moving, be unpredictable. But when his senses sharpened, when the call grew strong in him he was drawn to that wild place where the wind was heavy with the sea-salt smell, where ancient trees stirred and swayed, where fog hid the world in its cold blanket of dampness. And so he returned, drawn almost against his will. But it was a mistake. His nose told him that. The ones from Los Angeles had been here. They hunted him still...

Zack's cell phone rang just as he started to change for dinner. He was tired. It'd been a long day. He thought about pretending not to hear it but decided he couldn't risk missing something important. He was glad he didn't.

"Zack? Eagle Feather here."

"You settled in up there?"

"You could say. I haven't met up with your buddy Marty yet but he knows I'm around."

"So?"

"I poked around at the scene up at the Presidio.

They've strung tape but no one is up there to keep people out. There's already a bunch of footprints from curious on-lookers. Good thing I went up right away."

"What'd you find?"

"Well, nothing."

"Nothing?"

"Yeah, there's nothing on the path but the girl's prints, walking brisk then running hard. The conditions are perfect for finding tracks, almost like working in clay. It's muddy and damp but never rains hard enough to wash anything away. Everything that was on that path that night is still there. And that's the problem...there's nothing there."

"But she must have been running from someone or something..."

"Yeah, I know, believe me."

"How about where her body fell - nothing there?"

"It's a mess up there, Zack. Everyone and their uncle have been milling around and the rockiness of the path just makes things harder. But if someone had been there who didn't belong, if even the slightest bit of shoe print had poked out from under another print or if there had been an ash from a cigarette where no one else was smoking, that sort of thing? I'd of seen it. If it's there, I usually find it. But I didn't. There was nothing there."

"Well, I'm pretty sure she didn't tear her own throat out. You've worked out a theory, I'm sure."

"Yeah, but not a good one. Here it is: whoever, whatever killed her leapt off the bunker fifteen feet above her and somehow caught her by the throat - maybe as she looked up just at the wrong time - and ripped her throat open with some kind of jagged edged tool, all without ever landing on the path. Then she's in shock from the wound and falls and crumples back against the wall and bleeds out."

"That's a pretty amazing hypothesis."

"That's what I'm saying. But that's not the worst part. Where does the killer land? On the ocean side of the path there's maybe a yard of berm and bushes and then the cliff; a sheer cliff straight down to the rocks some seven, eight hundred feet down. No way."

"You checked the berm and the bushes..."

"Oh, yeah. No sign of him landing there; nothin' at all."

There was silence while both men thought about it.

"And Zack, here's the other thing. What makes her run like that all of a sudden? I mean, she's just walking along, easy like, then she walks a little faster, and then suddenly she's in a dead run - sorry about the pun."

"And no other tracks on the path, no one chasing her?"

"Right."

"How about in the trees just off the path, running parallel to her."

"I worked both sides of the path three to four yards out on each side. There's thick gooseberry bush all around there, almost impossible to get through. On the seaward side, there are some scary drop-offs right near the path. But the main thing is there is no trace of anyone or anything going through there. No prints, no sign. I guarantee you, nobody went through there."

"That's good enough for me."

"It's always been before, White Man. But it leaves us with a problem. I'm curious to see what your friend Marty makes of it. I saw his tracks where he came along, checking it out."

"You gonna see him soon?"

"Yeah. He left a message on my phone. We're gonna meet in a bar near the station tonight."

"Well, keep me informed. And..."

"Yeah?"

"Thanks, Eagle Feather."

"Gonna cost you a few beers, White Man."

The call ended.

O'Bannon looked up at the man in the wide-brimmed felt hat with a solitary bedraggled feather tucked in a silver hatband. Around his neck was a turquoise necklace that draped low across his shirtfront.

"How'd you know it was me?" he asked.

"Cop sticks out all over you."

"Funny. And here I never would of guessed you for an Indian."

"Now I see where Zack gets his pathetic sense of humor."

O'Bannon chuckled and held out his hand. "Call me Marty. I know Zack sets a lot of store by you."

"Eagle Feather. Zack's a good man."

"What do I call you for short?"

"Eagle Feather."

"You're gonna take some ribbing around here with that moniker."

"Probably will anyway. But most times, no one will know I'm here."

"Oh?"

"Let's set the bounds for our relationship. First, I'm not a cop. Second, I'm working the same case as you but I work for Zack. It's up to him how much I tell you about what I've learned. Third, I work how, when and where I want."

"So what's in it for me, besides a pain in the ass?"

"I'm unofficial. I can go places you can't, talk to

people who wouldn't ever talk to you. It's a dimension you don't get otherwise. I learn something, I give you a hint."

"And what do you need from me?"

"Not much. Just keep your guys off me, allow me into the crime scenes, let me see some files now and then, that kind of thing."

Eagle Feather motioned to the bartender who was working his way toward them down the long mahogany bar. It was crowded and he came slowly. When he got close, Eagle Feather wiggled two inverted fingers.

"What do you think you'll be able to do here?" O'Bannon asked. "You're not on the reservation, you know. No rocks or bushes to look behind."

Eagle Feather chuckled. "There's more sign to follow in the city than there is in the desert. And plenty of rocks to look under."

Thc barkeep arrived with two glasses of scotch. Eagle Feather reached for one.

"Oh, thank God. I was beginning to think they didn't serve Indians here," he said. He took a long sip.

O'Bannon was thinking he might get to like this guy. Marty O'Bannon didn't have a lot of friends. His relationship with Zack Tolliver had come about before he'd come to San Francisco, back when he'd worked as an assistant deputy in Page, Arizona, in Zack's jurisdiction. Neither of them had been the one giving orders at the time, but each had found the other to be hard working and practical, willing to share the results of an investigation, ready to cut through the bull shit. Now, three wives and four kids later he was a homicide investigator, a lieutenant here with the San Francisco police. He'd stayed in touch with Zack; they'd had a beer or two when Zack lost his own wife. Now he felt Eagle Feather eyeing him.

"Saw where you were checking out the prints up at the Presidio. Who was the big-foot who stomped all over the sign?"

O'Bannon grimaced. "A Park Policeman. Didn't mean any harm, just didn't know any better." He went on. "Something you better know to go with all the rules and regulations you spouted earlier. I don't own San Francisco, more's the pity. I've got to share it with a bunch of other police districts. And none of us have jurisdiction up at the Presidio; that belongs to the U.S. Park Police. So for me to go there, I've got to be invited and then play nice."

"What about Golden Gate Park?"

"That's not a problem. Most of that's in my district - at least the crime scene is."

"And Buena Vista Park?"

"That's in the next police district, the Park District. We work real close with them. But I still gotta tell them when I'm there."

"That's where I have an advantage. I want to check something out, I just go."

"Maybe. But you may find that the San Francisco police are a bit sharper than the Park Police."

Eagle Feather changed the subject; it was starting to

feel like a pissing match. "What's your take on the Presidio murder?"

"Ripped out her throat."

"Yeah, duh."

"Just like the other two murders."

"Stop playing games, I'm not with the press. You tracked the girl, just like I did. You saw how her prints went suddenly from walking to running. Why?"

"I don't know. I couldn't figure that out."

"Right. And how'd he kill her without leaving any footprints?"

"I don't know that either. I was toying with the idea that some kind of throwing weapon - like one of those Chinese thingies? - sliced open her throat and kept going. But that's crazy."

"He was on top of the bunker."

"How do you know?"

"Process of elimination. Only place he could've been."

"I looked up there. I didn't see anything; no fresh scratches in the concrete or anything like that. And there's always gonna be tracks around the front of those bunkers, from tourists and dog walkers and stuff. Hard to tell anything from that."

"Yeah, that's what I figured. What about the other

crime scenes?"

"Same deal. No meaningful tracks other than what the girls left in both cases. The jogger in Golden Gate? You could see her prints real clear in the dirt once she left the cinder path. And that's weird, come to think of it. Those tracks were all up on the toes, like sprinting. I was impressed when I looked at them, thinking she must have been in some kind of good shape, sprinting up the hill like that."

"No prints in the cinders?"

"No, but I didn't expect to find any. Hard to leave prints there."

"But what if you run hard in the cinders, you know, really dig in your forefoot. Wouldn't you see that?"

"Well, yeah, I suppose."

"So that tells us something, doesn't it? She wasn't running hard until she went onto the dirt path. She changed her stride all of a sudden, just like the Presidio girl. That wasn't her usual route, was it? The dirt path, I mean? Something made her do two things at the same time; turn onto that dirt path and start running hard."

"And no sign of anyone chasing her."

"Right. How about the one up at Buena Vista Park?"

"That's the hardest one to tell anything about. That park is just a hilltop with lots of old growth, really big old live oaks and pines with deep forest litter underfoot. We found the girl at the base of one of those great big trees, crumpled against it kinda like the Presidio girl. Her throat was torn open in an identical manner to the other two: no other injuries, no sign of assault. She had red hair very much like Presidio girl, which might be a connection. But that's the end to any similarities. Buena Vista girl was the youngest of them all, twenty-two years old and healthy, very fit like the others. But she didn't come from that neighborhood, not even close. She lived over in the Mission, over in the Harrison and 24th Street area. Lived all alone, was last seen by a downstairs neighbor when she stepped out for some groceries around six that night. That was it, nobody saw her after that. Guy in the store where she usually shops says he never saw her that night, said he'd remember 'cause she's cute. So how does she end up all the way over at the top of Buena Vista?"

"How did a working girl get to the Presidio?"

"We don't know that, either."

"Well, thanks." Eagle Feather stood up and signaled the bartender for the tab. "I got this. It's on Zack."

"What have you got in mind now?"

"Well, maybe I'll scout around Golden Gate Park. She's the only victim who wasn't transported to the place she died. She had a routine and somebody knew it, which means that somebody was hanging around there long enough to watch her for a while. Might be he's living around there."

At O'Bannon's shrug, Eagle Feather grinned.

"Haven't got much else." He walked out

FIVE

He must prepare better. He shouldn't have to leave the city just because they *were here - not if he planned well. The urge would come again soon and overpower him and all conscious thought would cease and he would be in the moment, that delicious moment. When that happened, when it overcame him, it must be at the time and place of his choosing...and the prey must one* they *wouldn't suspect.*

Two days later when Zack came to dinner Libby was waiting in ambush for him.

"Zack, what's going on?"

"What do you mean?" Zack sat down and slipped his napkin into his lap.

"Don't you think I know when you're on the phone for official FBI business, or when it's something else?"

"I'm sure you do."

"Ever since you and Eagle Feather took that trip to Los Angeles, the two of you have been like little junior high buddies on the phone every night. So what's going on?"

Zack was startled. He looked at Libby. "Eagle Feather is helping me with a case."

"It's not a case that Luke Forrester assigned you, is it?" she demanded.

Zack gave her a long appraising look. He spoke reluctantly. "No," he admitted. "The situation hasn't clarified itself enough for me to propose an official investigation. So I've asked Eagle Feather to take a preliminary look."

"Is it the same thing that took you to Los Angeles for three days? When you said you were going for the Laker's game?"

Zack put down his fork and gave her an embarrassed grin. "Is this an official inquiry, Ms. Whitestone?"

"Yes it is. I don't like for you to keep secrets from me, Zack. And the way you drop your voice when you take those calls, going off to another room - it makes me think it's something you don't want me to know." Libby screwed her lips in a dramatic pout. "Have you got another girlfriend, Zachariah Tolliver?"

Zack reached across the table and took Libby's hand. "I know you're kidding, but maybe not entirely. So the answer is, no! Never! You're all that I want."

Libby's voice was softer, but plaintive. "Then what?"

"Libby, I've been trying to protect you, to be honest." He raised his palm as she started to object. "I know, I know, you don't need to be protected from anything. I know you're a strong woman. But listen for a minute - let me explain."

Libby waited.

"In a way, this is about the Roundtree case. I-"

"I knew it! You've never really gotten beyond that case."

"Well...no, maybe not. But not for the reasons you think. I learned something during that investigation, something about that kind of killer and his patterns - patterns we haven't come across before, patterns that are not the typical serial killer profile. It was brand new to everyone. And as lead investigator in that case and the agent who ultimately worked it all out, I get the calls when some police department somewhere thinks they might have a pedophile killer on their hands and are stuck and need advice."

"So Los Angeles...?"

Zack grinned sheepishly. "We did go to that Lakers' game. I didn't lie about that."

"But you hid the real reason from me. Why couldn't I know the real reason?"

Zack's grin went away. "Libby, we haven't talked much about that night up on the butte, when the man who abducted you- "

"The man who tried to kill *you*. I'll never forget that."

"Yes, and then Eagle Feather was there and distracted him and we drove him away-"

"You killed him. That's what you said." Libby stared back at Zack, puzzlement in her brown eyes.

"Yes, but you don't remember any of it."

"No, you know that. It was the drugs...it was all hazy, misty, kind of..."

"Right. And it's best left that way. It was a terrible moment for each of us; each believing the other was going to die. The last thing I want to do now is force you to relive that moment."

"Hold on, Zack Tolliver. Are you telling me that man - that terrible person - didn't die? That he's back?"

"No, I'm not saying that. That man is dead and gone. But there are other men like him, men who think like him, act like him. That's what we didn't know before the Roundtree case; that they were there, what they did, how they behaved. We didn't know to look for certain patterns, certain connections that we found in that case. Now we do...I do."

"And you saw those patterns in Los Angeles?"

"Yes. That's why we went there. We thought that several of the killings that occurred there over a period of months might be linked, but in ways that the LA police couldn't see."

"Were they?"

"Like I said, we thought so. But then they stopped.

There were other killings, but they didn't fit. Then the LA cops figured there wasn't a connection after all and decided to treat each of those cases individually, so we really ended up doing more harm than good."

"What do you think happened?"

"I think he simply left, went away, went somewhere else."

"Do you know where?"

"Well, that's why all the calls lately. There've been several killings in San Francisco that seem similar and might be connected. The murders are forming a pattern that suggests it could be him. Eagle Feather is there now to take a look."

"And you'll be going soon."

"Well, it's possible, but only if we're sure - and if I can convince Luke that it's necessary."

"And you'll put yourself right back in the same danger again." Libby's mouth pursed in the petulant way that Zack always found irresistible. He felt a surge of fondness.

"Libby, I won't be reckless, I've got too much to live for. Yes, it's important to me to catch this killer but it's more important to come back again, to be here with you. If I go - and that's not at all certain - I'll have lots of help up there. And I'll have Eagle Feather."

Libby was not mollified. "Well, you shouldn't have to go. Why can't they solve it themselves?"

Zack knew better than to respond to that. Instead, he raised his eyebrows and grinned and changed the subject. "So here you've been gone for two days and now you're back and I don't even know if there's a new foal or not."

Libby's face softened and then brightened gradually as she told Zack all about her past two days at the ranch.

That night when Eagle Feather called, he'd been to visit the other two murder scenes. He started talking about Buena Vista Park.

"Ever been there?" he asked Zack.

"No. It's pretty small, isn't it?"

"Yeah, it's maybe thirty-five acres covering the top of a steep hill. It didn't seem to fit with the other locations because it's so small, but once I got there I understood."

"You understood what?"

"Why he went there. Yeah, it's small, but the trees are even older and taller than at Golden Gate Park and there's just as much a sense of age, you know, an old forest kind of thing? Just like at Golden Gate Park and the Presidio."

"You think that's important?"

"Yeah, I do. I think he's instinctively drawn to the old forests, the places where he can get a whiff of how things were before people covered it all up."

"So what'd you find?"

"Not much, at first glance. There are little trails weaving everywhere through the trees, all interwoven and all connecting to larger paved pathways that kind of circle up the hill. It's like a labyrinth. You could be fifty feet from the main walkway and never know it. Underfoot there's about six inches of litter from the shedding of the eucalyptus trees and cypress leaves and pine needles and it's amazingly overgrown for a place in the middle of the city. Its about the worst place to track anything you could imagine."

"What about the crime scene? Anything unusual?"

"Much like the others. The police tape was stretched about a hundred yards downslope from the top of the hill on the south side, on a little side trail. There was blood, a lot of it, on the ground at the base of a large cypress. From descriptions it sounds like they found her leaning up against the tree in a sitting position. I checked the area from all around the tree and out a good twenty yards and found nothing. Well, nothing but scuffed areas from police, rescue teams, and the curious. Whether she'd been running hard like the other two, there was no way to tell."

"So that's all?"

"Well, maybe. Not too far from where the body was found is one of several small clearings in the park, places with openings in the trees with great views out over the city. It's the closest place to the crime scene where a track could possibly be detected but it's so far away that even if you found one, it'd be meaningless. And yeah, there was a bunch of tracks there all right, where people had jogged through or sat on their butts, walked dogs, all of that. But there was something else there, something I didn't expect to find in a park in the middle of the city."

Eagle Feather paused for effect.

"Okay, wise guy, cut the suspense."

"Well, right near the edge of the clearing on the side closest to the crime scene was one single footprint of a large wolf."

Zack sucked in his breath. He knew the answer, but had to ask the question anyway.

"Not a coyote, not a large dog?"

"Don't insult me, White Man."

"How far would you say that print was from where they found the body?"

"A long way, maybe four hundred yards. I mean, if it was Arizona or Utah I wouldn't think a thing about it. But here..."

"Could you tell anything from the print?"

"No, just that is was made by a wolf, a large one, standing still, not walking or running, its weight evenly distributed."

"How old was the track?"

"Would have been made a while ago, maybe two weeks. Not fresh, but there haven't been any significant rains in that time, so it hadn't eroded much."

"Any other sign near it?"

"No, just that track. If it had just come out from the trees I couldn't tell, there's just no way to find any sign on that forest floor."

"What do you think?"

"I just don't know. One print isn't enough to conclude anything. When you consider all the wild animals that start out as pets and get away from private owners in a city like this - otters, alligators, pythons, whatever - a wolf, in a wooded area, doesn't seem so strange."

"Yeah, guess you're right. What about the Golden Gate Park crime scene?"

"Yeah, Golden Gate. It's just like the other two with the old growth, the huge trees, the dirt paths winding everywhere. But it's larger, much larger than the other two. You can literally get lost in that place, and people do. Lots of homeless live there, the shopping carts, the cardboard box houses, the whole deal. But I'll tell you, Zack, if it weren't for the identical cause of death, according to O'Bannon, I'd never think this death was related to the others. There's no other common ground."

Zack was silent, so Eagle Feather went ahead.

"Okay, first the victim. She was a working mom with a good job and a husband with a good job, a nice house and kids. She was out for an early evening jog, like she always does. O'Bannon told me the route she always takes - the husband showed him. It's all paved or cinder pathways. She'd strayed at the very end of her route, just before arriving back at Fulton Street. She'd suddenly gone off into the woods on a dirt path; running hard, not jogging."

"Were the tracks still there?"

"Some, yeah. But O'Bannon had already found them; he does pretty well for a city guy. She was running hard, all right, straight up a pretty steep hill and into dense bushes; just where you'd not want to go if you were afraid you might get mugged. That's where her body was found, slumped against a large redwood."

"All the bodies were slumped up against something," Zack mused.

"Yup. True enough."

"Any other markings on the body beyond the throat, did O'Bannon say?"

"Nope. No molestation, no beating, nothing but the throat ripped out."

The line was silent for a moment or two.

"Did O'Bannon find a way to connect any of the victims?"

"Not yet. I don't think he will."

"Oh...why?"

"Because I think the victims are more random than we thought, selected for their availability, or some other appeal."

"But you said the Buena Vista girl was last seen all the way down in the Mission. She didn't jog all the way up there. How'd she get there if the killer didn't take her?"

"I haven't got an answer for that one yet, but I'll let you know when I do."

Zack was disappointed but practical. "We haven't got enough. I can't take this to Luke and tell him I need to go up there. You could argue that these crimes are not connected at all, that the wounds to the throat are coincidence. Unless O'Bannon can link them, no one will see them for serial killings."

"And I'm saying the link is the randomness, like the Los Angeles guy."

"Eagle Feather, you know that and I know that, but who else is going to buy it?"

Zack paused, then he asked the most important question.

"Eagle Feather, tell me your gut. Is it our killer?"

"My gut says yes."

"In that case, stay on it. Something will break, sooner or later. Agreed?"

"Okay, White Man. It's your dime. I do think it's him, so I'll push hard. Besides, they've got some pretty good ales up here and you're buying." Eagle Feather chuckled and rang off.

SIX

He felt the anger rise in him and he pushed it back. It came from his human side, his weak side. He wondered if spending so much time with people who expressed emotion tended to trigger it in him. The anger came on him suddenly, born of frustration. They kept pushing him; pushing him away from the places he wanted to be, where he wanted to hunt - the musky earth smells, the dense stands of ancient sheltering trees shrouded by fog and mystery. There are no trees here. Here it's barren and craggy, windblown, featureless. And that's why it had to be here. They wouldn't expect him to come here. They won't think it was him...

Lance Pimmel, age twelve, climbed on his blue Huffy Boy's Pro Thunder bike and wished for the hundredth time that the bike had more than one gear. It wasn't fun thrashing up the steep hill where he lived at the far west edge of the Castro. His home was large and spacious and had a really cool view out over San Francisco but its location half way up north peak of Twin Peaks meant that if he decided to ride down to Market Street for candy bars he had to work hard to get back home, and when he went to his friend Mike's house, like he was doing now, he had to pedal hard to get up there, which was a bummer even if it was a great ride back down. But he'd say this for the Huffy: it had great coaster brakes, which was pretty important around here.

Dinner was done. It was late, around nine. Mom never let him go out at this hour. But he'd left his iPad up at Mike's house after play this afternoon and all his notes and homework assignments were on it. Mom didn't want to let him go but she didn't want him to get a zero, either, and when he reminded her that he's gone up that road a million times she reluctantly agreed...but no dawdling!

It was very dark on the narrow winding road up to Mike's place. A car came by and its headlights blinded him for a few seconds and he became disoriented and his balance got shaky. That scared him for a moment and he was glad there weren't many cars tonight. He didn't want to ride off the side of the mountain.

Lance couldn't see the houses along the road, only their garages that faced onto it. The living areas were set back behind them and the only light came from their single bulb lampposts, not enough light in the ever-present fog. But in truth, Lance was enjoying himself. This was a rare after-dinner excursion and an even rarer after-dark adventure. He loved how the familiar world disappeared in the dark and was replaced by another world he hardly knew. The trees looked different somehow; he saw only dark shapes until he was close and then their leaves and branches became visible and they became familiar for an instant but grew mysterious again the moment he had passed. His tiny headlamp beam was a small pool of light on the road surface directly in front of him as he pedaled laboriously up the steep hill.

Mike's house was at the end of the row of houses perched along this side of the mountain just before the road forked. One branch switched back and climbed up to an overlook just below the summit of North Peak and the other leveled off and continued back down to the neighborhoods on the other side of the mountain. In the dark Lance found it hard to judge his progress and was surprised to find himself in front of Mike's driveway so soon. He wasn't ready to end his adventure just yet and without really making a decision he pedaled on. Just a couple minutes more, he thought, because really it would take no time at all to coast back down again once he turned around. When the road branched he kept climbing up toward the summit. It would be a great ride back down, really fast and kinda scary here where the road was less familiar to him.

The way grew even steeper and then suddenly he broke free of the fog. Off to the east an amazing view became visible in front of him: a zillion twinkling lights filtered through thin ribbons of fog that floated in space like wisps of smoke. Lance was fascinated. The drifting fog created an ever-changing kaleidoscope of multi-colored lights that spread all the way to the very end of Market Street and then climbed vertically up the spear-like skyscrapers to their red and green tipped needlepoints. And beyond them, cutting through the dark bay waters, the curved luminous ribbon that was the Bay Bridge led toward the distant blur of lights that was Oakland.

Lance stopped pedaling and planted his feet with the bike between his thighs to gape. The moon was bright above the fog that now blanketed the slope just below him. The profile of the mountain rising on above him was crystal clear and somewhere up there was the overlook parking area. The road beyond where he stood was in shadow but he remembered that it crept back along the mountainside to a switchback that redirected it up to the overlook. In front of him the mountain fell away steeply, and back behind him, sloping toward the reservoir, was a moonscape of rock ledge and coyote bush blurred together by shadows.

A sudden chill took Lance. It was cold here; the breeze was stiffer and the warmth and exhilaration from his brave uphill ride were both fading. Time to go. Lance lifted his Pro Thunder with his hands while still straddling it and incrementally shuffled his feet to face it back the way he'd come. He couldn't wait to tell Mike about all of this, but he'd play it kinda cool when he did.

A rock thunked down the steep face somewhere behind him in the shadows, bounding and smacking other rocks once, twice, then thudding on dirt and finally thumping on the road surface. Startled, Lance whipped his head around and stared in that direction. He couldn't see into the shadowed portion of the mountainside. There was no further sound, but his heart pounded so much it felt like it would escape his chest. Must be an animal up there, he thought, a little annoyed at himself for being so spooked. He climbed up onto his seat and started to pedal.

When the howl came it felt as if it was right next to him, almost inside him, and the sudden enveloping loudness of it froze his blood. His body lost all control and he wet himself. He fell and his feet got entangled in his bike and he had no chance to arrest his fall. Down he went, Huffy Pro Thunder and all, crashing to the road. His head came last, slamming hard against the pavement.

Mercifully, everything went black.

Snyder pushed the doorbell button next to the gated portico of the huge stucco mansion in Palo Alto and listened to the deep gong sound within. At least it seemed like a mansion to him compared to the neighborhood where he lived in Soma, a few blocks from the Chronicle Building. I'll bet my first townhouse cost more, though, he thought idly.

The man who opened the door and peered through the grill at him did not look professorial - for good reason, as it turned out, for the man announced himself as the professor's secretary.

"Yes, Mr. Snyder, I remember your call. Dr. Westfield is expecting you. Please come through."

The secretary opened the gate and stepped to the side to allow him in. The spacious entry hall was huge and ornate with a sweeping central staircase leading to some other level and the space where he stood soared up to a sky-lighted ceiling far above. Tall vases framed the corridors on either side of the stairway. Glancing up the stairs, Snyder glimpsed the outline of several full size pine trees in a glass atrium of some sort.

I take it back, he thought. This place cost a lot more than my townhouse.

The male secretary, a ruddy dark-bearded fellow who looked a bit like the mad Hungarian from *My Fair Lady* asked him to wait there while he summoned the professor.

Jim was not kept waiting long. After the Hungarian disappeared, another man came walking in from the back somewhere and approached him with outstretched hand. He didn't look professorial either; he actually looked rather normal, his face freckled, sandy hair uncombed, dressed in jeans and a T-shirt with Stanford University Drinking Club written across the chest.

"Hope I didn't keep you waiting," he said, and ignoring Jim's protestation went on to say, "Follow me. The patio should be very pleasant for our little chat."

They passed the staircase and walked down a short oak paneled hall to a screen door. Once through it Snyder found himself out in the sunshine again on a wide patio that led to a pool, the entire area enclosed by an eight-foot yew hedge. A young woman was in the pool swimming laps. They sat at a round glass table shaded by a partial awning.

The professor saw Snyder's glance. "Not what you think," he grinned, nodding toward the pool. "One of my Grad students. This is like a second home to them."

Jim swept an encompassing arm. "All this on a Stanford professor's salary?"

"Not just a professor; a full professor. And I'm the Anthropology Department Chair. I've got my Ph.D. and several other degrees, and I'm at the top of the pay scale." Then he looked sheepish. "And yeah, my parents are loaded."

Snyder laughed. "Good to know you earned it all, Professor."

Westfield grinned in turn. "Please call mc Andy. Everybody does." Then he dropped his grin. "You have an interest in mammal predation practices, I understand? I'm not sure how that ties into my speciality of ethnoarchaeology."

"If I got it right, Professor...I mean Andy, you study the way people lived in the past from evidence you find at archaeological digs, yes?"

Andy raised his eyebrows. "That's pretty close. My particular interest is in paleoenvironmental reconstruction from chemical signatures at archaeological sites."

"But you also draw conclusions from artifacts found at these sites, like pottery, old bones, and the like?"

"Well, yes, although that's not my precise area of study."

"Okay, but you're knowledgeable enough to read evidence from, say, scratches or teeth marks on bones or on old hides, that kind of thing?"

"Yes, my background is comprehensive enough, if that's what you mean."

"Let me cut to the chase, Professor...Andy. If I showed you a wound on an animal, would you be able to tell me what weapon or creature made that wound?"

"It sounds to me like you need a forensic pathologist."

"That would only get me part way there. I'm looking for a broader spectrum, a less directed analysis, should I say? In other words, I want to avoid presumptions."

"You certainly won't encounter any presumptions here, since I'm still confused about what you need, but in the interests of trying to understand what you want, let's go ahead."

"Fine. Please take a look at this."

Snyder pulled a photo with crumpled edges out of the breast pocket of his vest and handed it to the professor. Westfield turned it this way and that before deciding upon an orientation, as he gradually understood what he was seeing.

"And this wound was found on...?"

"Can you make an analysis based purely upon what

you are looking at first? And we can fill in the detail after that?"

"Well, first off, when doing a necropsy study one would usually investigate surrounding circumstances; for instance, was the animal alone or in a herd, was it pounced upon or chased for some time, what was the severity of the struggle, was the carcass moved after the kill, that sort of thing. After that, one would study the carcass itself, its external appearance, size, age of the animal, its external parasite load, any older injuries, blood or fluids in body openings, any other fresh injuries, any predator hair on the carcass, were the nose, ears, or eyes eaten. Then you'd skin the carcass and-"

"Whoa, Professor, way too much information. We can't do all that. What can you tell me just from that picture?"

"Well, I believe the wound I'm seeing is in a throat, a large portion of a throat. Can I assume it was a morbidity causing wound?"

"Yes. In fact, I can tell you it was the only wound present."

"Okay, I'll start out by telling you what it wasn't. It wasn't one of the skull crushers, those animals with jaws so powerful they kill by biting and crushing the skull, which includes the Brown Hyena and the Mountain Lion, nor was it any of the predators that don't leave neck wounds, which includes the Spotted Hyena, the feral dog, baboon, otter and mongoose" -Snyder rolled his eyes but Dr. Westfield went on pretending not to notice- "or the wolf."

Snyder sat up. "Not the wolf?"

"Not the wolf. The wolf kills by slashing its victim's tendons from behind and then disemboweling it."

Snyder stared.

The professor went on. "So let's talk about some animals that do kill by attacking the throat. These are the Caracal, the Black Bear, Grizzly, Bobcat or Lynx, and Cheetah, among others. But every one of these animals necessarily leaves other wounds or markings on their kill, either claw marks on the shoulders or back, or dewclaws on the rump, or in the case of the bear, slap marks. These additional wounds are signatures left from the animal's method of attack."

"Can they vary?"

"Really not. The method of attack for a particular predator has evolved over its history to fit particular physical characteristics. It's instinctive."

"Go on."

"Okay, let's talk about the predators that kill by the throat that might not necessarily leave other wounds before feeding. I'm assuming the feeding in this case was interrupted?"

"Let's assume that."

"In that case, we're left with some members of the jackal family, the fox, possibly the leopard, and the coyote. Judging from the size of this wound, I think we can eliminate the fox. The jackal bite tends to be toward the side of the throat - so much so that it often involves the eye. The bite in this photo is very much centered, so let's put the jackal aside. That leaves us with the leopard and the coyote. The leopard attacks the neck and is very capable of ripping out the throat of a mammal the size of the one in this picture. But its teeth are forty to fifty millimeters long. It's hard to tell in this photo, but I don't see indications of teeth of that length. That leaves us with the coyote. The coyote will often kill with a solitary bite to the throat. And the tooth length and the bite size are a better fit to this wound. Although the coyote seldom demonstrates the power to rip a throat out completely in this particular way, it could."

Andy's eyebrows lowered and he looked questioningly at Snyder. "This, of course, is a picture of a human throat. Coyotes almost never attack humans. What are you involving me in here?"

"That's what I'm trying to find out. I'm following a series of deaths...murders of women in San Francisco. I'm trying to understand if they're related. They've all had their throats torn out, more or less like this. I was able to obtain this image from a source in the coroner's office. I haven't seen the wounds on the other two women, but I've heard descriptions and they sound similar."

"So no doubt your first question is whether there's a wild canid loose on the streets of San Francisco."

"That would be one part of it."

"And the other part?"

"Is there some weapon or device that a human is using to kill these women, something that can rip out their throats without leaving any other sign on the body or any prints near it."

"Even a coyote or leopard would have to leave prints."

"Yeah, I thought that too."

"What else?"

Snyder hesitated, staring off over the yew hedge toward the Palo Alto hills. Then he seemed to change his mind and shrugged. "Well, nothing, I guess. Maybe I could take a Mulligan here and come back if I need to?"

Dr. Westfield stood and extended his hand. "Of course, any time. But be sure to contact my secretary first so you don't waste a trip."

"You're calling me because you've got nothing new to tell me?" Zack stood next to his king cab pickup truck parked on the street outside the Tuba City FBI offices. "Are you telling me you want to come home now?"

There was a quiet chuckle on the line. "You don't get it, White Man. What's new is there's nothing new. It's been two weeks since the last kill. Even O'Bannon has been thinking there should've been another one by now. The kills seemed to be escalating but now - nothing."

"Maybe you scared him away."

"You and I both know that's not likely."

"Thinking back to Los Angeles I remember those kills were about eight, nine days apart. That's how we knew he was gone, when they stopped completely. There was nothing other than accidental shootings and gang knifings anywhere in the entire city for the next month. Could that be true now?"

"It could be," acknowledged Eagle Feather. "But it doesn't feel the same to me. Something else is going on."

"What's O'Bannon doing about it?"

"Nothing to do, just sit and wait. Meanwhile, the cops up here are starting to doubt there's a connection between these kills, just like in Los Angeles. Each murder here occurred in a different jurisdiction and the only thing holding them together now is O'Bannon himself. Once they decide there's no connection, they'll each go their own way, which means the investigation will go stale."

Zack chirped his remote key and opened his truck door. "Okay, I'll give O'Bannon a call and try to get him to hang on. That's what you want, I'm guessing. What will you do?"

"I'll wait. And look around, maybe a bit further away. I think he's here and I don't believe he can go this long without a kill."

SEVEN

Snyder stared at the coyote. It was large, far larger than he'd thought it would be from the quick glimpses he'd had of these animals flashing across the road or standing far off in a field. They always seemed dog-like to him and so he'd never felt afraid of them. But this fellow was big, lanky and strong looking, its gray-brown pelt uneven and a bit scraggly. Its long jaw was slightly open with its big white incisors exposed and it was looking right at him. Yeah, that jaw looked capable of ripping out a human throat.

He looked up at the sign on the fence: *Canis Latrans.* Hmm. Evolved in North America during the Pleistocene...lived side by side with the Dire Wolf...can reach speeds up to forty-five miles per hour and jump thirteen feet...communicates with howls, yips, yelps, and barks...adaptable, versatile predator, been known to shadow human joggers and even attack a small dog on a leash. Hmm. Here we go: coyotes will typically bite the throat just behind the jaw and below the ear but will adjust their killing technique to the size and strength of their prey...

Snyder walked away from the coyote cage and out through the gates of the zoo lost in thought. Smart, strong jawed, fast, able to leap great distances: sure. But to tear out a human throat in one bite and leave no other evidence of its presence - not once but three times: that's what he couldn't get his head around. There had to be another explanation.

When he got back to his desk, Snyder pulled out a map of the city. His finger moved from the Presidio down to Golden Gate Park and then east to Buena Vista Park. If it *had* been a large coyote, just for the sake of argument, it could live somewhere in the huge confines of Golden Gate Park and still make sorties up to the Presidio and over to Buena Vista Park without being seen very easily, especially at night.

Snyder groaned. A human killer could do exactly the same thing, so he still had nothing. He'd just have to wait, maybe take another look at the crime scenes in the meantime.

Eagle Feather was thinking similar thoughts where he sat on a natural earth bench at the summit of the rounded hill that was Buena Vista Park and looked out over the city. He didn't doubt his own identification of the wolf paw print - he'd seen hundreds of them - but Zack had questioned that and he'd come back just to make sure. He wasn't surprised to find the track partially obliterated by other footprints, but enough of it remained to confirm his initial identification. A dog, no matter how large, didn't make that print - it was too compact. A dog's paw print spread more at the toes. That and the lack of toenail impressions meant a wolf. Too bad there weren't other prints to learn how it walked, but that didn't matter. He was sure.

But then he thought about a coyote. He had dismissed the coyote from his original thinking because of the size difference. A wolf is much larger and stronger than a coyote and coyote tracks tend to be at least an inch smaller than the one he'd found, not to speak of the fact he'd never heard of one that would attack and kill an adult human - not in this way, for sure. So he'd dismissed coyotes from his thinking.

But now he thought again. It would be unusual, yes. But let's face it; everything about this case was unusual. So suppose you had an unnaturally large coyote, maybe some sort of cross breed. Here in the city, every species of canine wandered about and a coyote could breed with any of them. So combine the greater size of the dog with the natural cunning and opportunism of the coyote, then add a dash of just plain meanness from whatever it had bred with, and who knows?

Eagle Feather chuckled to himself, imagining his next telephone conversation with Zack. *Hey, Zack, I've just decided the serial killer is a large coyote. I've turned it over to the animal warden and I'm coming home.* Yeah, sure!

He was ready to leave when he noticed a man in a crumpled jacket and baggy trousers looking down at him from up on the hill. The man wore bifocals and was looking over the top of them at Eagle Feather.

When he caught Eagle Feather's eye he ambled toward him with an engaging smile. "Hope you don't take offense at this but I'm going to ask it anyway. Do you wear that feather for show or are you really Native American?"

"Who wants to know?" Eagle Feather could never quite adjust to the nuts in the city.

"Name's Snyder, Jim Snyder. I'm a reporter but that's not why I'm asking."

Eagle Feather just stared.

"Mind if I sit?"

"Sit all you want. I was leaving anyway."

"Can I ask you a question?" Snyder plumped down next to Eagle Feather.

"I'm guessing you will. The real test is, will I bother to answer?"

Snyder laughed. "Fair enough. I'll ask and you decide."

He pulled out a notebook and flipped back a page.

"I've seen you around twice before this, once in Golden Gate Park and once walking into the Richmond District Police Station."

"Maybe you saw two other fellows wearing hats with eagle feathers in the band."

"You're a real funny guy. But that wasn't my question. When I saw you in Golden Gate, you were studying the ground, like you were looking at tracks or something. Now here you are in a park again. You a wildlife expert of some kind?"

"I guide hunters for a living."

"Ahhh. Perfect. So here's my question. Could a coyote kill a human with one bite?"

Eagle Feather turned and stared hard at Snyder. The man was slightly overweight, late sixties maybe, soft hands, neatly combed gray hair but balding in front and in back. His pale blue eyes twinkled back at Eagle Feather.

"I guess maybe we do need to talk," Eagle Feather said.

"I thought we might. I was just at the San Francisco Zoo standing in front of the coyote pen. I can tell you, they're bigger than I thought. And their jaws look plenty strong."

"Let's be plain." Eagle Feather leveled his gaze at Snyder. "You're talking about the murders, the women."

"Aren't you?"

"You said you're a reporter. So I get the interest. But how'd you make the leap to a coyote?"

Snyder pulled the crumpled photo out of his pocket. "This. I got it from a contact. It's a picture of the dead girl at the Presidio. I showed it to a professor down at Stanford. He told me this kind of predation - throat, no other marks - could be either a leopard or a coyote."

"And you decided against leopard?"

"Not altogether. But you see a coyote skulking around the city; you think nothin' of it. You see a leopard, it's big news."

Eagle Feather studied the photo. "No matter what made this, it's strange," he said. "This wound was made in one motion, with one impact. See how the edges of the wound are neat, not torn or frayed? The killer, man or beast, didn't need to re-grip. Know how an animal, say a dog like a mastiff or terrier, will bite the throat of its victim and then bite quickly again for a better grip and to try to bite deeper? That's because their jaw muscles aren't strong enough to bite right through the first time for the instant kill. So they re-grip several times and hang on; some species choke the victim this way. That leaves a messy wound, ripped and torn. That didn't happen here. Whatever killed this girl did it with one powerful snap of its jaws, ripping away that whole piece of the throat in one fast movement. See, if it had been any slower the victim's weight hanging by the neck would have caused some tearing. That never had time to happen."

"Jesus. You mean like some sort of robotic arm that could just reach out and take away a big chunk of throat?"

"That's the idea."

"So how could an animal do that? I mean, without using some sort of leverage that would leave marks on the victim's body, or at the scene?"

"Good question."

Snyder was quiet, thinking about it. Then he offered his hand to Eagle Feather. "I told you I'm Jim Snyder, with the Chronicle. So who are you, and how'd you get involved?"

"Call me Eagle Feather. I'm up from Arizona. We've had some murders down our way that bear a resemblance to these. That grabbed our interest, so I came up to have a better look."

"We?"

"I work with an FBI agent down there." He turned to stare at Snyder. "And none of that, reporter, is for print."

"As you say. But we should compare notes from time to time. How can I reach you?"

Eagle Feather dug into his pocket and pulled out a

card. "That's my cell. You can get me on that any time."

Snyder started to reach into a vest pocket for his own card but Eagle Feather put up a hand. "Don't bother. I can find you when I want."

Snyder stood. He looked out over the city, now infused with bright sunlight causing reflective twinkles from thousands of windows. "Did you know that this park was a refuge for San Francisco residents during the Great Quake and fire of 1906? Fifteen hundred people crowded together on this very knoll to watch their city burn." He glanced down at Eagle Feather. "I'm feeling a little bit that way right now. I look out over that great jumble of houses and buildings and I know that something is hiding in there right now, watching, listening. And when the curtain of night falls it will come out to hunt its unsuspecting prey."

"It hasn't done that for over two weeks now."

"What do you make of that? The kills were nine days apart, regular as clockwork before that."

"What do I think? I think he has killed and we just don't know who, what, or where." Eagle Feather squinted up at Snyder. "Here's something you can do, newspaper man. Go through your back copies and look for any death we might have missed. I'd say anything involving wounds to the throat; that's really all we've got that connects the murders."

Snyder sighed. "Yeah, that does make sense. It always comes back down to desk work."

"Why so downhearted? Shouldn't take you long. You only need to check one issue, the paper printed nine days after the Presidio kill."

Kelly came out of the dark cave that was O'Keefe's Bar on Balboa Street feeling nervous as a cat, despite several pints of good stout. He always felt this way after these meetings - jumpy and anxious.

His hand felt for the thick envelope in his back pocket. It's the only thing that made it worth it, the only thing that kept him from quitting. The guy definitely paid well, and let's face it, the things he asked him to do weren't all that bad. Like stamping around on some footprints. Or like this new job. He could handle this job without changing his work schedule or working up a sweat, even.

Kelly worked for the United States Police. They'd trained him and eventually assigned him to the Presidio but the pay was minimal and the hours short, almost like a part-time job. So he'd had to take on some rent-a-cop type jobs here and there: watching construction sites, doing store security, that sort of thing, just to make ends meet. But after he'd met this Donny, or whatever the guy's real name was, he'd moved up to another level of living, one that involved not having to worry about paying his bills. He liked that.

But Donny scared him. Let's face it - he scared the crap out of him. The worst part about working for him wasn't doing the jobs; it was having these meetings, sitting across from him in the same booth. Kelly didn't know what it was about the guy that was so frightening, maybe his breath, which was pukey bad, or his eyes, which Kelly never looked at - he just couldn't - or maybe it was simply the size of him. Kelly wasn't small, tipping the scales at two-seventy and well over six feet, but he felt like Donny could lift him up in the air with one hand, if he wanted. Not that the guy ever threatened to do anything like that, he never even raised his voice. And that was the other thing, his voice... Kelly shuddered.

Well, enough of that. The point is he didn't have to think about the guy for another two or three weeks now. And the money in his pocket would help him forget his fear, no doubt about it. He thought about Lucia, the little Mexican number at Adult Friendfinder. No way he could have paid her so-called tip fee of four hundred dollars without a thick envelope every couple of weeks, and he definitely wanted to keep meeting her.

In fact, maybe he'd give the service a call right now. She knew just what to do to settle his nerves. And right after that, he'd take care of the little chore he'd been assigned.

EIGHT

It's been a week now. They don't seem to have noticed. They haven't visited the scene; only the local district cops have been there. Another careless child death, a sudden roll down a steep hillside, he'd made certain that's how it looked. It was disappointing, the prey too young, too easy, all over too quickly. It did not bring the fulfillment of other kills. But it would hold him, at least for a time…

Libby pretended sleep for Zack's sake, but her thoughts swirled relentlessly. It was starting up all over again: the hushed telephone conversations, the early morning hours in front of his computer screen, the distracted behavior – just like Los Angeles. And the worse part was, he was excluding her. She felt a wave of helplessness sweep over her. He thought he was protecting her, of course. It was his nature, his nobility. And so she must play her role, the role of unwitting innocence in order to protect him in return. Irony upon irony, she thought.

Libby Haddeford Whitestone was a self-reliant woman; she'd had to be. When she was thirteen her father stood up from the breakfast table at the family ranch near Cameron, Arizona and walked out the door and was never seen again. After that her mother fell to pieces. It was left to Libby to raise her three younger siblings and keep the family ranch going. Any other thirteen-year-old girl with her head full of boys and her body changing alarmingly couldn't have managed, but Libby was not that girl. By the time she was twelve she had shown she could handle any chore on the ranch. Her dad treated her like the boy he'd never had; she'd been included in all the morning meetings with the foreman to plan the work for the day. She was never told she couldn't do something because she was a girl. But she couldn't remember when she'd last worn a dress, either.

After her father disappeared, her authority at the morning meetings was assumed. All the hands from the foreman on down worked hard for her, maybe even harder than for her father. But along with supervising the ranch, Libby had to raise three children who needed to be fed, clothed, comforted and educated. Libby's strength was in motivating and delegating and she soon had the ranch chef cooking for the family as well as for the bunkhouse. She hired a housekeeper to care for Libby's distraught mother and keep an eye on the kids around the house. But Libby herself saw the kids off on the school bus every day.

When Libby was sixteen, she introduced a new element to the family business. She began to train dogs. It all started when a neighbor couldn't handle his German Shepherd and threatened to shoot it. Libby intervened, brought it home, and trained it and when she returned the animal it was so obedient that the man handed her three more dogs to train. Libby had a gift for working with animals, not just dogs, but horses too. Her reputation grew. She was highly sought after and she began to dedicate her time to training dogs and breaking horses, leaving the foreman to oversee the rest of the ranch chores. Her business grew, the ranch prospered and the hardships of the early days became a distant memory.

Then came the suitors, a constant stream of them

down the long tree-lined drive, one after the other. Her tomboy nature, her utter disregard for her appearance, her natural grace and athleticism all conspired to mold a woman of stunning physical beauty and unconscious magnetism. When Libby sat on the top rail of a fence with a wild-hearted stallion nuzzling her hand, her wavy chestnut hair cascading down under her wide-brimmed straw hat, she unknowingly created an image that stopped hearts at mid-beat.

But Libby's thoughts were for her family and for the ranch and she fended off all suitors until the children were grown and gone, one after another; two to college and the third to wed a local farmer. Then after her mother passed away, Libby faced something she had never known before: loneliness. She couldn't tolerate it, couldn't tolerate the silence, the slower pace, not being needed. So one day, the day that Raymond Whitestone arrived at her door, she said yes.

Libby smiled at the thought of Raymond. He was a veterinarian, the perfect yin to Libby's yang. He set up shop at the ranch and Libby learned a new set of skills watching him work. Libby especially loved to assist in the birthing; she never grew tired of watching this miracle. Perhaps there was some irony in this, for it turned out Libby herself had difficulty in conceiving. The two boys arrived only after a struggle, seven long years apart. But the wait was worth it. Libby's soul was renewed by the sound of rapid footfalls echoing on hardwood floors. She set about raising the boys as she herself had been raised, fully involved in all the ranch routines.

But children seldom fulfill parental expectations and her boys were no exception. Neither of them showed any interest in the ranch or the animals and turned instead to scholarly pursuits and computer analytics. Then Raymond was taken from her by the kick of a horse and Libby threw herself fully into training her beloved dogs and horses.

Now Libby stared at Zack as he slept, thinking that life never went where you expected. Zack was not nearly so handsome as Raymond and, unlike Raymond, was not one to favor home and hearth. His face was sunburnt in layers, like seasons, up to the sudden blanched whiteness where his hat covered his forehead. Zack's attractiveness was in his energy, Libby decided, in his animated features and his personality that reached out and excited you while his blue eyes held you.

But he had his secrets and he kept himself to himself, and Libby struggled to understand that. They lived independent lives together, each with a calling that often kept them from home long hours at a time. But Zack's ranch was their haven, a place just for the two of them and their horses and the miles and miles of unspoiled wilderness. By mutual agreement they left a space, a sort of buffer between themselves to preserve the autonomy of their independent lives and their accustomed way of living.

For that reason Libby anguished before demanding to know what Zack was keeping from her. She would insist upon knowing only out of fear for Zack's personal safety. It was the single reason he might keep a case from her: that he knew it was dangerous and that she would worry.

Libby thought back to the night on the mesa when the man-creature had put his spell on her - hypnotic, maybe, or drugs - but sufficient to destroy her memory of most of that day until the moment she awoke as if from a dream to find Zack and Eagle Feather by her side. The men were reluctant to talk about any of it and she'd had to content herself with the knowledge that the killer they had sought across two states was finally dead, gone.

Libby let her head fall back on her pillow and closed her eyes. She trusted Zack to care for her and to protect her, but she did not trust him to take care of himself. She might have to take a hand.

Another woman lay sleepless this night. Her bed was in one of the better apartments in the Tenderloin District of San Francisco. Just six weeks ago, Meg could not have imagined the luxury of sleeping during the night, certainly not in her own bed. She was more likely to be in Raphael House seeking refuge when all the cash from her night's work, work that was increasingly hard to come by as her looks faded, had been spent on delicious, forget-the-world, crystalline meth highs.

Thirty-six days ago she'd suddenly and unexpectedly been rescued from this destructive cycle by a stranger, a man she knew only as Max. He offered her money, a lot of it, not for sex but to run errands for him or to procure the occasional companion for him. Now she could sleep each night in the luxurious comfort of her own bed in her own apartment off Geary Street. But on this night she lay awake. Her ears were unconsciously tuned to the familiar cadences of the street outside her window as she watched the light and shadow from a neon sign play across her wall.

It was said the Tenderloin District got its name when police officers transferring here from other districts found that the bribes they received from drug dealers and hookers allowed them to upgrade their evening meals from hamburger to tenderloin. But others said the name came from the working girls with their tender loins who serviced the area. But few who lived there knew or cared about the long history of the district; not about the old Indian trail buried beneath its streets leading across the peninsula to the great bay and its plentiful shellfish, a trail later buried beneath the El Camino Real which resounded to the hooves of Spanish horses traveling to and from Mission Dolores just to the south near a now disappeared marsh of a lake the Spanish had named Laguna de Nuestra Senora de los Dolores. Few cared that the Spanish road was in its turn repaved to suit the needs of the invading Americans, or that all of that history was buried beneath Market Street which led straight as an arrow from Twin Peaks through commercial downtown San Francisco all the way to the Embarcadero - an arrow shot right through the heart of the Tenderloin District.

Megan neither knew nor cared about the rich history of the district in which she now lay. Her mind was solely on the mysterious stranger and the most recent task he had assigned her. She didn't know how she would manage it, but she knew she must. Failure wasn't an option. She shuddered to think what might happen if she failed.

She thought about the night over a month ago when Max first approached her. Despite the drug-induced cobwebs that dulled her otherwise capable brain her street-savvy warning-bell rang when Max reached inside his coat and brought out an envelope stuffed with cash. Somewhere in the far reaches of her mind she knew that so much money was for a purpose beyond the usual services. But avarice overcame caution. She reached for the envelope and her soul was sealed and delivered right then and there.

But when Max outlined his requirements they seemed simple enough. Harmless even. He told her to find an apartment for rent in the district and to stay there and always be available. She was no longer to turn tricks and she must modify her drug habit. When he called, she was to drop everything and meet with him. He would have occasional tasks for her to do.

In the thirty-six days that followed Max had called her only once. She was to walk down the street and find a Zip Car left there for her and drive it south through the city to the Mission District to a particular address and wait there for a certain woman to leave the building. She was to give the woman an envelope containing a message and wait for her to get into the car. And it happened just that way, exactly as Max had laid it out. She drove the woman to Buena Vista Park and left her at the southwest corner of the park on Masonic Avenue near a paved park path. That was it. She returned the Zip Car to its original place and went home. Nothing could have been simpler.

Megan was street savvy enough to realize that there was more going on than that. But she had no intention of looking any closer. In her experience she had learned two things: always be attuned to what was going on in the street and close your mind to anything that didn't concern you. So the next night when the TV in her favorite bar blared out the news that a young woman had been murdered in Buena Vista Park, she heard it, filtered it away and forgot it. Her life was vastly improved lately and she intended to keep it just that way.

Until now, that is. This last task that Max assigned her was not so simple. His stare had been cold. She had agreed without question. Somehow, she would have to find a way to accomplish it.

NINE

This was a different kind of excitement. This was a chess match and he was ahead by one move. He had another move in mind, one that would stalemate his pursuers. He'd wait until the need grew strong again. He'd take his time and plan well. Then he'd set the drama in motion. He had the perfect cover and a worthy quarry. And best of all, they would never know...

Captain Finney stood in the morgue of the Park District Police Station on Waller Street and stared down at the boy's body. With all those injuries: the contusions, the broken bones, the jagged cuts to the head, throat, shoulder and buttocks, he certainly looked the part of a kid who had fallen off a mountain. He must have rolled hundreds of feet, bouncing off sharp rocks over and over again, just as the morgue attendant had surmised. He'd been found at the bottom of a steep pitch below the northern most summit of Twin Peaks. His bike was by the road at the switchback, undamaged. He must have left it there and walked toward the edge of the cliff and then lost his footing in the dark. Hard to imagine, though. The kid looked agile and the drop-off wasn't that abrupt. But once you got some momentum up, once you really got rolling, this could happen.

Finney walked around the body. The boy lay on his back. He had a nasty throat tear, maybe from a sharp rock or something like that. Finney looked at his watch. The meat wagon was due to pick up the body and transport it to 850 Bryant Street, the Medical Examiner's office downtown. Accident, suicide, murder - it didn't matter, the body had to go there to establish cause of death. That was okay with Finney. It took the pressure off the individual police districts.

And speaking of pressure the boy's parents were hovering out at the reception desk. Really upset - and who could blame them? Their only child, a nice looking little boy, and mom eating herself up because she'd let him go out after dark on his bike just this once to get something at a friend's house just up the street. The kid never came back. Shame.

Finney sighed and walked out of the morgue. Just an accident on a cliff in the dark, a very boy-like adventure gone south. He took a deep breath and steeled himself for the meeting with the parents.

The FBI Navajo Nation Liaison Office, that unofficial but necessary presence of the FBI at the west end of the Four Corners Navajo Indian Reservation was in a small building on a dusty street in a town named Tuba City. Zack knocked on the door labeled *Supervisory Agent in Charge* and waited for a voice to respond and then entered.

When Zack first arrived in Arizona as a raw recruit fresh out of the Academy this office had belonged to Forrester's predecessor, Ben Brewster. A dozen years had passed and Zack was now well seasoned and respected and he worked for a different boss, a man named Luke Forrester. Luke was as unlike Ben Brewster as salt and pepper. Zack liked Ben; he'd been his mentor. But he also liked Luke, who had become more of a colleague than a boss to him. Where Ben had been an organized man with lists and specific orders and notes written in a tiny precise hand, Luke was all about stream of consciousness and reworking ideas and shaping his thoughts out loud. And he let Zack use his own initiative.

Luke looked up and smiled as Zack entered.

"Things are quiet here on the reservation, but off it, not so much. There's been another shooting up in Page. We don't need to get involved yet but there's the possibility it's linked to a shipment of guns that crossed the state line from California. That's up your way. Why not stop by and see Sergeant Ruffey, listen to his story, take some notes and then go home and catch up on paperwork today?"

Zack slid into the mahogany chair next to Luke's desk. "That sounds just fine to me," he said, and then he paused. "Got time for a quick word?"

"Sure, Zack. What's on your mind?"

Zack shifted his position slightly to avoid a shaft of bright sun peeking through the shade. "I've had some calls from Martin O'Bannon up in San Francisco. He's worried they may have a serial killer."

"What's his evidence?"

"Identical wounds to the throat; a tearing or ripping apart, is how they describe it."

"How many victims?"

"Three so far."

"Hmm. What's the interval between crimes?"

"Every seven to nine days, they think."

"And how long since the last one?"

"Well, that's in question. They seem to have overrun the interval by almost a week now. But it's a big city."

"Meaning there might have been one but they haven't found it yet." Luke pondered this for a moment. "Have they anything else to go on?"

"Just indicators, like footprints that suggest the victims became frightened suddenly and ran for their lives. In each case the cause of death was a single slash wound to the throat. There were no other wounds. The killer left no tracks or evidence of any kind at the scene. And all the victims were women."

"Something about it interests you, I can tell. Do you see similarities to the Roundtree case?"

"It's sketchy, too early to tell. But something in my gut..."

"Mmm." Luke stared back at Zack. "I get it. You'd like to go take a quick look, just to be sure."

"Well, yeah...if things here are slow enough. I could fly right up there and then if things begin to stir up down here I could be back within a few hours. In any case, I wouldn't plan to be more than a few days" -he glanced quickly at Luke- "and on my own dime, of course."

Luke sighed. "Zack, you gotta do what you gotta do. But have you considered that you might be developing an obsession out of the trauma you experienced with the Roundtree case? You might want to slow down and consider whether you could possibly be reading things into cases like this. You haven't told me anything to make me think there's more than a plain old serial killer up there."

"Like I said, it's more my gut right now. We were right about the Los Angeles murders, I'm sure of it. We knew he had to have gone somewhere, and most likely a big city."

"We?"

"Well, Eagle Feather is-"

"So Eagle Feather is involved. And no doubt he's up there already?"

"Well, yeah, but-"

"And no doubt we're paying for his visit?"

"Well, yeah, but-"

Luke began to laugh. "Well, at least you didn't rent a helicopter on a whim like you did the last time. Okay, Zack. I know you have to follow your hunches and right now things are calm enough around here. This won't be official - San Francisco has its own FBI division. Just take care of that little matter in Page before you go, please. And Zack, when I call you back, you come running, right?"

"Yes, sir."

Zack climbed to his feet with an appreciative grin on his face.

"And Zack, you don't need to spend your own

money. I'll call up there and see what we can squeeze out of the San Francisco office. We'll call it a consulting fee."

Zack smiled again. "Thanks, Luke. I really appreciate it."

But when the office door had closed, Luke's smile went away. The possible outcomes to Zack's involvement with this case in San Francisco were limited - and none of them good.

Mary Benham, Ph.D., forensic autopsy technician, sat at her desk in her tiny cubicle adjoining the huge morgue at the Office of the Chief Medical Examiner at 850 Bryant Street, San Francisco, and stared back at the spectacled man in the chair opposite her. Snyder was an old pain in her ass and always had been, with his poking around and continual questions, most of which she wasn't at liberty to discuss, let alone answer - as he well knew. But he kept coming back like a bad penny. Sometimes, though, like now, he actually had something amusing to say.

"You're talking about the three women with the slashed throats? You want me to check for what?"

"I want you to check the throat wounds for evidence of tooth or fang marks."

"Are you kidding me? What are you looking for, vampires?"

Snyder laughed. "I'm thinking of another kind of creature. Don't you ever get wild animal bites here in the city?"

"Sure. But they don't come my way. There's seldom

a fatality from animal bites. We get about fifty-five homicides in a good year and about ten of them are from sharp instrument injuries, knives or whatever. That's how we're looking at the three women you mentioned."

"That's what I wondered. You called them 'slashed' throats just now, not torn or mangled. Is there forensic evidence to support that word usage?"

"Okay, dammit, you're going to make me pull files after all, aren't you? Hang on." Mary wheeled her chair around to face the large file case behind her and pulled open a drawer. She found a file and removed it and then reached into another section and took out a second one.

"You seem to think these deaths are connected in some way? They come from three different districts."

"You didn't see any similarities?"

"Not my job. But yes, I do recall a similarity to the wounds."

"And the fact that there was only one wound, the fatal wound?"

"I'll need the files to recall that much...there, that's the third one. Now let's see..." Mary flipped all three open on her desk and her eyes flitted among them, comparing. "Yes, I see what you mean. Some contusions and scrapes consistent with falling down in the one case, absolutely no other marks on this one..."

"What notes were made about the nature of the fatal wounds?"

"This one suggests a sharp narrow instrument, like a stiletto. This one here suggests a knitting needle-type weapon. Both cases propose a possible weapon based upon the markings left around the wound: an insertion and then a ripping. This last one doesn't speculate - the damage is too great."

"Okay, so my question is, could the stiletto or the knitting needle have in fact been a long tooth, like a canine?"

"A dog kill? That's what you think?"

"Something like that."

"Well, that's pretty far from the conclusions reached by the Medical Examiner Investigator. Homicides, yes. Dog kills, no."

"Look, Mary, if I needed a trained parrot to repeat the results, I'd go to a pet store. I'm asking what *you* think after re-reading those files."

Mary sent Snyder an irritated look. "Could it have been an animal with exceptionally long canines biting and then ripping out the throats of each of these women? Yes. The marks around two of the three throat wounds are consistent with that. And they're also consistent with aliens using long poles and reaching down from their hovercrafts up in the sky. Where in the city do you expect to find a large wolf-like dog with super long canines agile and strong enough to leap at some young active women - in this last case quite a strong woman - and rip out their throats without leaving any other marks? C'mon, now."

"So you'll stick with knitting needles and stilettos."

"Until something better comes along. Look, Snyder, this kind of investigation requires a study to determine the nature, dimensions, depth of penetration, and direction and power of the weapon used - and it's based strictly upon specific criteria. There's no room for fantasies or wild speculation. If you hope to propose a dog-like perpetrator, you'll need data much more convincing than what I see in these wounds. Many tearing wounds manifest marks similar to one another around the edges. In fact, I'm just now setting up a young boy for the examiner who has a throat wound very similar to this; that's along with all the other gashes and slashes the poor kid got falling off a cliff."

Snyder stood up. "Okay, I take your point. That kind of wound is pretty common."

"I didn't say it was exactly common, just that there can be similarities."

"Well then, how common?"

"This little boy has the only other wound that I've seen so far this year that shows this same tearing at the throat. Throat gashes like this are relatively rare. In fact, accidental ones like this kid suffered are quite rare."

Snyder sat down again. "What do you think happened to the kid?"

"Remember, the body hasn't been formally examined yet. I can only tell you what I saw setting him up and what I was told happened to him. He fell off a mountain. He must have snagged his throat on a sharp rock while tumbling down."

Snyder laughed. "That's right up there with your alien story."

Mary became defensive. "Look, Snyder, you've

taken up enough of the city's time. Come see me when you really have a case. Or better yet, don't come see me at all."

"Okay, okay, I'm going. Just one last question. Where did this boy take his tumble?"

"He came in from the Park Station. I think they said he fell on North Peak."

Snyder stood again. "Thanks, Mary. You're a gem."

"Yeah, hard, old, cold and transparent. Get out of here, Snyder."

Snyder walked out the door, chuckling.

TEN

Jan Olson was an ultra runner - a good one. At his last race, the American River Fifty-Mile Endurance Run, he'd placed tenth overall and fifth in his age group - that difficult thirty to thirty-five bracket - and he was pretty pleased with himself. He'd powered up the Hazel Bluffs and felt pretty good climbing the infamous Dam Wall at mile forty-six. He'd seen the admiration in the eyes of his competitors, most especially in the blue eyes of Thurma Wilson standing at the finish line as he came in. Yeah, so Thurma had beaten him again. But that was expected, she was that good. But he'd come in just a minute and thirty-five seconds behind her and in good form. Jan knew that's what separated the true endurance runner from the wanna-be: how you finished, what reserves you had. She'd given him a slight smile as he crossed the timing strip, just standing there watching, her own sweet little chest hardly moving from the race she'd just run. She'd ended up sixth overall and first among the women. He'd hoped to see her at the party but she'd hung out with her sponsors - she had to, he guessed - and taped one interview after another. They would use only a quarter of that footage, probably. But she glanced his way more than once, throwing him a couple of wan smiles as if to say, "Don't you know I'd be over there with you if I didn't have to do this?" Then she'd turn to look perky for the camera.

Jan rattled the ice cubes around in his Jameson's and watched the glass fog near the rim. He swiveled around on the bar stool to check out the tables. He didn't expect much at a hotel bar but he was tired and didn't want to stray too far from his room. He thought again about Thurma. He'd see her at the next race, he knew, probably the PCT fifty miler in San Diego in a few weeks. Then he'd make his move. There wouldn't be so many sponsors at the PCT; there never were.

Jan looked around the room again. Let's face it, he was horny. He'd gotten his expectations up that night in Sacramento and then ended up in his hotel room all by himself. Now here he was at the Hotel Adagio in San Francisco one night later. He always stayed here after the American River Run to treat himself to a nice meal and some time in the steam room before heading home the next day.

Movement caught his eye across the lounge. The woman at a table there had just crossed her legs, flashing shapely thighs under her sequined taffeta skirt. There'd been a man with her last time he looked over there, Jan was sure of that. He'd been a big guy, formidable looking. Both were dressed like they'd come from a formal party. Jan hadn't given her a second thought. But there she was alone. And now she saw him looking, caught his eye, and deliberately switched her legs again.

Jan felt himself become aroused. Just when he was ready to give up, it was game on. He picked up his drink and walked slowly over to her table.

O'Bannon answered after the third ring, his voice gruff and irritable.

"Yeah?"

"It's Zack Tolliver. I've cleared my schedule for a

while. I'm coming up."

"You'll be wasting all that free time. Nothin's goin' on here."

"That's what I heard. That's why I'm coming now."

"Wadda ya mean?"

"It's the pattern. Three kills and then nothing. There are only three possibilities: that it's not him, that he's gone away, or that he's made a kill and you guys can't find it."

"Not for lack of looking. And I've got other cases to work on up here - not like you G-men who can take a few days off whenever you want."

Zack ignored that. "That's why I'm coming, to help you and Eagle Feather look for kills. The way I see it, either we'll find one and get back on his trail, or we won't find a thing and then we'll get out of your hair."

"That sounds good, Zack. And listen, I really appreciate your help on this."

"No problem."

Zack put away his cell phone. He was just turning on to Interstate 15 on his way south to Las Vegas. He'd catch a San Francisco flight from there. As his truck whirred along the highway through St. George, Utah, and then down into the beautiful Virgin River Canyon area, he wondered for the tenth time if he was being rash in his decision to go to San Francisco right now. He'd tried to explain it to Libby, telling her he had a hunch; that he had to follow it. She'd been patient, tried to understand, but he could tell she didn't get it. He told her this was his last best chance to figure it all out and then he'd put it behind him. Libby didn't judge - he liked that about her - but he could tell she didn't believe that he would actually stop looking for this killer, this ghost, even if he found nothing in San Francisco. Maybe she was right.

The night wind tousled Jan's hair and blew cold on his face. He felt the engine vibrations through the deck beneath his feet. Stars hung like lanterns in the black sky, so close he could see them twinkling. The ever-present bank of fog near the Golden Gate Bridge obscured the stars in a single patch like an invisible blanket.

He still couldn't believe his luck. The girl Meg had accepted his offer of a drink, they had chatted amiably and then more suggestively and she had followed him to his room where they had immediately intertwined. Jan had learned delicious things he hadn't known were possible. But the adventure didn't end there. Meg knew people, it seemed, and here they were on a private yacht converted from a tugboat plowing through the bay swells on the way to Alcatraz Island for their own midnight tour of The Rock. Jan had been to San Francisco many times but had never been to visit the famous prison. But tonight - tonight he would have it all to himself with his own tour guide, a friend of Meg who would meet them on the island. It just didn't get much better than this.

The dark mass that was the island grew large and Jan began to see a vague outline of the blacker than black cliff and the great cell house, and the needle point light house perched high above that sent reflecting splashes of light off the white foam. The tugboat turned and throttling down, purred slowly around the island. Meg came to stand by Jan at the rail, abandoning the warmth of the pilothouse. She cuddled up. The adventure had been so spontaneous that all she wore over the maroon taffeta skirt and thin blouse was a thin embroidered scarf. It was always cool out here on the Bay, no matter the season.

A large pier rushed up and Jan felt the boat throttle down to a crawl and the stern eased slowly around to slide perfectly up against the worn tire buffers. The tugboat held there, its burbling engine keeping it tight against the pilings.

"C'mon."

Meg pulled his arm in a spontaneous burst of enthusiasm and climbed quickly over the rail, her skirt billowing back to reveal all the special places that Jan had visited not so long before. To his amazement, he found himself becoming aroused yet again. He quickly followed her over the rail, landing lightly on his feet, and ran after her across the dock toward the dark of the building beyond. He caught up to her at the arched entrance beneath a black-on-white lettered sign he could barely read: *United States Penitentiary*. He hugged her against him, nudging his hardness against her responding thighs, somehow driven to an even greater urge by the feel of her warmth in the cool of the night, by the evil nature of their surroundings, by their aloneness on this mysterious island.

"Wait," Meg whispered. "I'll tell my friend to come back in an hour, and then we can..." She pushed her pelvis tighter against him to underscore her intentions. Then she broke away and ran back across the dock to the tugboat.

Jan turned to look at the old building that faced him where the bleary spotlights created more mysteries than they exposed. Looking straight up he saw a sparse wooden balcony that ran the length of the building. To his right a watchtower looked down on him, a metal frame structure with peeling paint that enclosed a precarious looking circular staircase. The floodlights on the tower illuminated the tops of the buildings and shown on areas out of his sight somewhere up the steep island face. He shivered involuntarily at the bleak unvarnished purpose of the place and turned to look for Meg.

The tugboat was motoring away, its gentle wake a lengthening white road leading away from the dock. His eyes searched the dock's shadowy surface for Meg.

It was empty. Meg was gone.

Jan was shocked. Disbelief rooted him in place. Then, slowly, he understood. He laughed in spite of his unease. The little minx! She was just one continual tease! He'd show her something when she came back. Grinning, he waited for the boat to turn around...any minute now.

But it didn't. It just kept going until he couldn't tell it from the other dark clumps and dull pinpoint lights on the water's surface. It was gone.

Jan stood there with no idea what to do. The realization crawled over him slowly that he had been had, that Meg had intended to abandon him here all along. He slapped his pockets for his phone. Oh, no! He'd left it in his room, wait, no, *she'd* left it in his room he remembered now, having borrowed it to call the boatman. Let's be impulsive, she'd said. He groaned and patted his pockets again. He had nothing. No phone, no wallet, nothing. Think, now. There had to be a public phone here. This was a National Park, after all. He looked at the building in front of him. To the left of the arches he saw a sign but couldn't quite read the large letters...wait! It said *Museum and Book Store.* There must be a phone there. He walked over and tried the door. Locked. On the door's glass pane he saw the international emblem for phone. It was inside, of course. He looked at the door. It was made of thick wood and wired glass and the hinges were huge. Any thoughts of breaking in quickly faded. This was a fucking prison, after all.

Jan slumped down next to the door. Anger swept over him: anger at Meg, anger at himself for his childlike naiveté. Then after a while came acceptance. Okay, so he'd gotten himself into this mess with his desire for pussy. He deserved it. The sex had been good, after all, real good. Was it worth it? Maybe it was, actually. And think of the story he could tell later - what an adventure! Abandoned overnight on Alcatraz Island. Who could match that tale?

So, what next? It was cold and it would get colder. He had on a light jacket, nothing more. He'd have to find a warm place to hole up for the night. Then he'd wait for morning, for a tour to come along bright and early. He'd laugh with the tour guide, tell him what happened, maybe a little shamefaced; the joke was on him. Then he'd hitch a ride back to town.

Jan stood up, his confidence restored. He looked each way along the walkway. To his right a surfaced roadway ramped up to a large arched entrance in a stone building and seemed to tunnel on through it. To his left the road ran beyond the buildings and on along the island shore as far as he could see into the shadows. It looked like open ground out there, unsheltered. He'd be better off the other way. He turned and started toward the stone underpass.

The howl came like a physical blow, a tremulous vibrating force that exploded in his head and lashed against him like a blast of wintry air. It stopped his heart mid-beat, emptied him of all thought and filled him with horror. His muscles froze, every hair stood on end. He gasped, swallowed, grabbed his chest, shivered.

What the *fuck* was that!

Somewhere in the darkest part of his reptilian brain in some deep forgotten corridor a part of him recognized the sound. His fear was absolute. His brain reverted to another time and place, to another age when survival depended purely upon reflex. He ran. He ran away from the origins of the sound, away from the darkness of that arched tunnel. He ran along the pavement toward the far end of the island, on his toes, sprinting, every one of his well-trained muscles straining, every fiber of his being focused on escape.

The cold air whipped his face, burned his eyes, and made them tear. His toes caught on chunks of broken pavement and he stumbled, nearly fell, and caught himself. He felt loose gravel under his feet, slipping, churning, then hard pavement once again. He caught his stride and ran as fast as he could. The illuminating spotlights faded behind him, the darkness closed in. He felt the path gradually turn to the right, then climb. He was circling the end of the island, he realized. Where could he go? It was an island. Eventually he'd have to circle right back to whatever had made that sound.

Then the roadway switched back again and now it climbed more steeply and he found himself high above the black glistening bay waters. He had circled above the road he'd just run down and he looked for a pursuer but saw nothing. He ran on and a shadowy mound materialized on his left and then became a pile of rubble. The path flattened out now. He could see that it opened onto a wide expanse. It was an open place, probably an exercise area for the prisoners. The tower spotlight where it reached over the buildings cast a pool of light at the far end.

Jan ran into the light and on flat open ground at the very center of its beam where it offered the best possible visibility, he stopped finally, heaving and gulping for breath, still on his toes, wary as a frightened deer.

He waited there; eyes open wider than wide trying to pierce the shadows around him. He gasped at every slight sound. He heard a sob, spun toward it, but then realized it was his own. But there...was that a pebble that clicked behind him? He spun around. Nothing. He whipped his head back again and from the corner of his eye he saw it. It moved from shadow to shadow, incredibly fast, beyond what was possible. It was nearer now. His fear reduced him to tremulous Jell-O. There it was again, just over to his left. He spun around. He caught a glimpse of red eyes in a large shadowy form behind him. Before he could turn again a smell descended on him like a foul damp tissue, a smell of fetid breath, decay, rotting flesh.

He didn't hear the howl this time. He didn't hear the rising triumphant primal cry of the successful hunter, for his senses were frozen and his nerve endings mercifully numbed as his brain shut down.

He never felt the fangs tear into his throat.

ELEVEN

Kelly bent over and puked his guts out. He hadn't expected this. Donny said there'd be a mess for him to clean up before the Park Rangers came in this morning and Kelly thought he was ready for anything. After all, the guy was paying good money and would be expecting more than a custodial service. But not this, not these sticky pools of drying scummy blood spread all over the Parade Ground, big pools of it soaking into the porous concrete squares, mixing with the dust and dirt, sticking like day-old chewing gum in the cracks in between. And those little chunks, what the hell were they, anyway? Meat? Flesh? Kelley really didn't want to know. And then those marks, the red skid marks over to the ramp where something big had been dragged. He'd be lucky to have this all done by the time the first Ranger arrived.

Kelly stood up again, disgusted, and looked at his pool of vomit. Now he had more to clean up. He picked up the mop. He'd better get at it; he wasn't feeling any better and he needed to finish before he made another contribution. Kelly wasn't really worried about being found here, just so long as the mess was cleaned up. As a member of the Park Police his presence wouldn't be questioned. He'd left the service runabout tied up in the space assigned to the Park Police down at the dock. It was often tied there for various reasons and Kelly didn't need to explain himself to some Ranger Rick.

Kelly didn't know what Donny was up to, what his gig was or anything, but he did know that he'd made a good choice in hiring him because he could go places no one else could go without being noticed. Like the task he'd done up at the Presidio a few weeks ago. Donny had told him simply to walk along the dirt path below the bunkers. Just that. And he paid him damn well for the stroll. He realized now that he was the only one who could have crossed the police tape in order to take that stroll without being questioned, even though that homicide cop he ran into had struck an attitude. He wouldn't be questioned here, either. But he'd sure as shit better finish this job. After that he'd walk down the slope to the souvenir shop and have a chat with the sales girl, casual like. Then he'd mosey on back to the launch and go home. Easy.

"Hey, you wanna come get me?"

"Where are you?"

"The airport." Zack dodged a little kid playing on the people mover. "I'm on my way to baggage claim right now."

Eagle Feather laughed. "My truck's farther away than you are. I'll jump on the Bart and meet you. Wait for me at the airport Bart station."

Twenty minutes later the two friends greeted one another warmly, then climbed on the Bart to head back to the city. They didn't try to talk about the investigation right away, not wanting to shout details of the case over the noise of the train. So they sat in silence and watched the buildings flash by until the tunnel enveloped the train in darkness.

"Next stop is ours," Eagle Feather said.

They hauled Zack's luggage up the long steep steps and out of the Mission Station to the streets.

"I've taken a little place just up the hill to the right," Eagle Feather said.

They walked slowly up the hill and talked in quiet tones.

"Still nothing?" Zack asked.

"Still nothing. Haven't found a thing that fits our man's modus operandi."

"How widely have you looked?"

"Everywhere - North to Sausalito and south as far as San Mateo. There's plenty of crime, believe me, but not a thing matching what our guy likes to do."

"What do you think? Is he gone? Or was he never here? Have we been trying to make connections where they just don't exist?" Zack sounded discouraged.

"Oh, I'm sure enough it's him. And I'm not quite ready to say he's gone. He wouldn't quit that easy. But if we don't find evidence that he's here soon, I suppose we'll have to pack it in."

"What's O'Bannon say?"

"He's up to his nose in other cases. He'd be just as happy if this thing went away. The other homicide cops in his district aren't happy with him for the time he's already spent on this. They're feeling the extra load."

"Here we are." Eagle Feather stood next to a steep

set of steps that led to the second floor.

Zack hitched his bag higher on his shoulder and followed his friend up, talking as he went. "Let's think about this thing from another angle. Where's he been living? What's he been doing? He's not out killing people every minute so he's got to be doing something during the daytime. How does he find his victims? What connects them? Does he have a job? There must be a way to get a lead."

Eagle Feather laughed. "You sound just like O'Bannon. He's been asking the same questions, looking at new employment rolls, new rental agreements, new checking deposits, anything within the last two months. No dice so far. Don't forget, this guy could simply have joined the homeless and there'd be no way to trace him. I don't think material comforts are exactly his thing. Just a hunch, there."

"Yeah, that's true enough."

Zack looked around the small apartment they had just entered. A kitchen area with a small gas stove, a sink and a tiny refrigerator took up one end of it and a curtained sleep area the other. In the space in between there was a couch, a coffee table with a laptop on it, a folding chair and a tiny TV set.

"Material comforts aren't exactly your thing either, I see."

Eagle Feather grinned. "If you're staying here tonight, you get the couch. It doesn't fold out and it's lumpy as hell, but it's all yours. There's a nice little beanery around the corner where we can eat dinner. Hungry?"

A short time later they sat across from each other at a tiny table, enjoying the best beef burritos Zack had ever tasted. He took a sip of his Pacifico.

"What angle have you been working?" he asked.

"I've been spending your money on hookers." Eagle Feather grinned broadly. Zack waited. "Only one of the three victims was in the Profession. But the killer had to make arrangements with that girl somehow. There's a real grapevine among the working girls; it's how they stay alive. Something like this happens to one, the others hear about it right away and become hyper alert. They spread the word; tell each other what to watch out for. Maybe it's a physical description, maybe some quirky thing he does, how he communicates, whatever. So I've been scanning the papers and checking police logs by day and talking to the girls at night. You'll get my bill."

"So? What'd you learn?"

"Bad breath. That's the word on the street. Watch out for bad breath."

"Oh, come on."

"We're talking about seriously bad breath here, the kind that makes you puke. I can't trace it to the exact source, but it's what the girls are saying. There's this guy - accounts differ, but most say he's really big and scary looking - who's been trying to hook up with some girls in the Presidio area. He wanted outcalls only and he'd come for the girls in a limo, real impressive. But none of them would get in the car. Word is they became terrified as soon as the driver opened the door; something about the guy, his eyes, the feel of him, but most talk about the stench of his breath. He's tried to hire girls several times. They keep refusing, and now the word is out."

"So you think..."

"Could be him, you know? If you put that together with the Presidio murder, you can see a connection. A girl working that area gets an outcall on the phone and goes to meet the guy in his car. She never comes back. She's found later behind the Presidio bunkers with her throat ripped out. Maybe Bad Breath Guy finally got his girl."

"Yeah, maybe. So where does that leave us?"

"Well, to me, it confirms our suspect was here. He must have come up from LA. The timing's about right and it sounds like him. Best description we've had."

"Sounds like the LA guy, alright. But now what?"

"Well, that's the question. The prior two victims were different; they weren't in the Profession. I can figure the jogger in Golden Gate Park: he sees her running out there, learns her routine, then simply waits for her one fine morning. But the Buena Vista girl? That's different. She's not from around that area. She lived here in the Mission, worked in the city, never been out to the Buena Vista Park area before, as far as I know. But there she was, dead as a doornail, throat torn, same bit. Her car was still here in the Mission. She'd only left her apartment to go to a nearby market. I can't figure that one."

"So now he's stuck, maybe? No working girls would get into his car, especially after the Presidio murder. Think maybe he's having trouble finding victims?"

"I just can't believe that. It's a big city, chock full of kooks. He'll always find someone out and about."

"And your newspaper search - no murders, nothing that might remotely fit the pattern?"

"Nothing."

"Well, seems my visit might be a short one. I think your bad breath theory is solid. I'm betting he *was* here, but he could be gone already. Maybe he sniffed you out, realized we'd connected the dots from LA. So off he goes, next stop Sacramento or Portland, who knows?"

"What's your plan?"

"I'll go up to the Richmond District and see O'Bannon in the morning. Get his thoughts. I'll decide after that. Meantime, I think I'll just take you up on your offer of the couch. Can't be worse than sleeping in the bed of my pickup truck."

Eagle Feather's cell phone rang around ten that night. It was Jim Snyder.

"I was down at the Medical Examiner's office today to see if their investigator had picked up on the similarity of the wounds that killed our three women."

"Did they?"

"Not at all. They'll take a look now, though."

"That's good news. Maybe they'll find something we don't already know."

"Sure hope so. But along that line, the technician there, Mary, mentioned another body they had down there. It was a kid, sent up by the Park District Police. Seems this kid fell off a cliff somewhere up on Twin Peaks recently. The fall killed him, she says, although they haven't done the formal autopsy yet. But here's what's interesting: she says the kid has a throat wound similar to the wounds on those women. She brought that up to make her point that a jagged throat wound could happen in a lot of ways. She thinks the kid's throat must have caught on a sharp rock edge as he tumbled down the slope. But later I got to thinking about it. How could that happen, really? It would be quite the freak accident."

"Go on."

"Well, being naturally curious I looked up the newspaper accounts. Not much on it, really - freak accident, parents devastated, mom says, "I never should have let him go out" - the usual. It's just a little blurb. But here's why I'm calling you particularly. When I was looking up that story in the police call records I came across another report from the same general location that same night..."

Snyder paused here. Eagle Feather waited.

"Several neighbors complained of howling, a single strange very loud howl from somewhere up on the peak."

"A coyote?"

"They all said no; they'd heard many coyote howls up there before. But this one was different, much louder, rising but not falling. As one caller put it, "blood curdling". So what do you think of that, Mr. Indian Tracker?"

"I think that's real interesting. When did the boy

fall?"

"It would have been Tuesday night, nine days after the Presidio murder." Eagle Feather could almost see Snyder grinning.

There was a long silence. Then Eagle Feather said, "Stay in touch," and hung up. He turned to look at Zack on the couch watching the tiny TV with his legs up.

"What?" Zack asked.

"I think you might want to go over to Twin Peaks with me tomorrow before you visit O'Bannon," Eagle Feather said.

TWELVE

Mary Benham was angry. "I can't do that, you old fool. You ask too much." She started to hang up the phone.

"Wait, wait...!"

Mary dangled the phone in mid-air.

"Hear me out for just a second. You'll be doing the city a greater service than you could possibly know. If you hang on for just a minute more, I'll tell you what I'm working on."

"Why do I care?"

"Because you'll be able to give your boss something she doesn't have already, some evidence regarding those girls with the gashed throats."

Mary let out a great sigh. "Okay, go on."

"I just need a picture of the boy's wound, the kid that tumbled down the mountain. That's all...just fax it to me. I need to compare it to some other pictures I have here. If it matches, we're on to something."

"On to what?"

"I'll tell you as soon as I get the picture."

"You don't even know for sure, do you?"

"I'm ninety-nine percent sure."

"I'll think about it." Mary slammed down the phone.

Back at his desk at the Chronicle, Snyder didn't wait for the fax to arrive. Instead he clicked into the police call archives in the Chronicle's data bank and searched methodically through the Presidio Park Police calls from the night of the girl's murder. But there was nothing. Disappointed, he looked up the Park Police District calls and worked back to the night of the Buena Vista Park murder. Suddenly his pulse raced. There it was. A complaint had come in from a resident living on Upper Terrace near Masonic Avenue, just outside the park. The call complained of a loud, rising, pulsating howl just after ten that night. And here was another from a frightened pedestrian walking along Museum Way. It was called in at eleven-twenty, apparently after he'd gone back home, and it referred to a howl he'd heard just after ten that seemed to be coming out of the park.

Bingo! This couldn't be a coincidence. Snyder scrolled back another nine days and began searching the Richmond District police call log for Golden Gate Park from early that morning. But he found no reports. Nothing at all in the way of animal noise complaints, no barking dogs, nothing. Still, Snyder was satisfied. He guessed that the people who lived along Fulton Street near the park probably were used to all kinds of noise and wouldn't bat an eye at something howling, although from all reports these particular howls were terrifying.

Armed with this new connection, Snyder walked over to the fax machine. There near the top of the pile of recent faxes was one with the seal of the Chief Medical Examiner of San Francisco and one page with a photo. It was from Mary. He grabbed it and walked back to his desk and set the photo down next to the three other photos. He found his magnifying glass under a pile of papers. The pictures in each case were of the neck area and highlighted the gash wound. Jim meticulously examined the edges of each wound, one by one. When he was satisfied he set down the magnifier and sat back and let out a deep breath of satisfaction. His hunch had been right. There was no doubt in his mind that this little boy was the fourth victim of the killer. He picked up the phone to call Mary.

Zack and Eagle Feather stood on the shoulder of the narrow road at the tight curve where it switched back from the precipice and continued on up North Peak. On their right was a steep bluff. The large parking lot for the lookout known as Christmas Tree Point was somewhere on top of that, a hundred feet above them. Fifty feet in front of them yellow police caution tape waved in the breeze. Beyond that the mountain fell away.

"If Snyder got his facts right, the autopsy should prove that the kid was dead before he fell down the mountain. If he was still on his bike when he was attacked, he was away from the cliff, closer to the road." Zack took the hypothesis further. "It must have been pitch black; I don't see any means of illumination here. And the ground is actually higher here at the road than it is closer to the edge. So if the kid stops to take in the view, why would he leave his bike? He can see the city lights just fine from right here."

"Okay. So if your scenario is correct, he would have been knocked off his bike, and the bike would have dropped." Eagle Feather walked slowly along and stared down at the road surface. Then he stopped.

"Right here. Here's a mark and some paint, looks like. And here. That looks like blood."

Zack looked where Eagle Feather pointed and nodded. "That's blood, alright, and more than just a few drops. It's mostly soaked down into the gravel." Zack scratched his head under his hat. "So why didn't the police report mention this?"

"I'll bet they never saw it. They weren't looking for it. They were looking close to the cliff. They figured it was just a simple accident with a careless kid."

Eagle Feather moved toward the cliff, his eyes on the dirt surface. "Here's a trail of blood drops leading toward the cliff edge. But I don't see any drag marks."

"So maybe he picked the kid up after he killed him and carried him to the edge."

"Yeah, but the thing is, it must have happened real fast. You'd expect much more blood on the ground from a ripped carotid artery, even with a kid. These blood droplets are quite far apart and they're not that large, not as large as you'd expect with the carotid severed. The only explanation I can think of is that the guy moved fast. He attacked the kid back there while he was on his bike, went right for the throat, then almost before the kid could fall scooped him up and carried him real quick to the edge."

By now the blood trail had led the two men beyond the tape and all the way to the cliff edge.

"It's not all that steep," Zack mused.

"No," Eagle Feather agreed. "But if you fall here, and especially if you can't use your arms or legs, the momentum would get you rolling real fast." He bent down and studied the ground closely. "He stood right here. I see just a slight impression from a weight greater than the cops' feet. This stony surface doesn't give very much." Eagle Feather's eye kept searching. "There's a drop of blood." He pointed to the stone surface slightly to his right.

"If he dropped the kid here, there should be a lot more blood," Zack observed.

Eagle Feather nodded. "That's what I'm thinking." He looked down the steep slope. "You can see where the rescue guys scrambled down to get the body. They would have been secured with ropes. Their slide marks end right there on that outcrop. Even from here I can see a lot of blood. That must be where the kid bled out."

"He didn't drop the kid, he threw him."

"That's how I see it," Eagle Feather agreed.

Zack spoke slowly. "Strong guy."

"Not too sentimental, either," Eagle Feather said.

The men walked back to the Zip Car. Zack was doing some mental math. "If this was his next kill after the Presidio murder, he's still on his nine day pattern, right to the hour, almost."

"And it's been over nine days since then."

They looked at each other.

"We're missing another kill," Zack said slowly

"Well look-ee here, the Lone Stranger and Tonto. Thought you'd gone back to the reservation by now, Chief." Harrar was sitting with his booted feet up on his desk, talking on the phone. The cop at the desk behind him looked up and guffawed.

"I would have, if you white folks had cleaned up your own mess," Eagle Feather responded mildly.

"Ain't no scalps lying around here. We got 'em all hung neatly outside the teepee." Harrar laughed again, joined by his henchman. He hung up the phone.

Zack cut in quietly. "You expect O'Bannon back any time soon?"

Harrar looked irritated. "We don't expect much from O'Bannon these days. But I'll tell him you were looking for him, if he does bother to come in."

"Know where he went?"

"Well now, that's another mystery, isn't it? He doesn't exactly keep us up to date with his engagement calendar."

Harrar looked at Eagle Feather and grinned evilly.

"Guess you're going to have to send up another smoke signal, Chief." The cop behind him laughed uproariously at that.

Back outside the Richmond District Station, Zack

called O'Bannon. After several rings he was instructed to leave a message. "O'Bannon, it's Zack," he intoned. "I'm here at the Richmond Station looking for you. Your colleagues are looking for you too, it appears. Give me a call back."

Not three minutes later, Zack's phone rang. It was O'Bannon.

"Hey, Zack. Welcome to San Francisco. I'm surprised you decided to come on up. There's not much going on right now."

"That's why I decided to come," Zack said. "But I've learned there's more going on than you might think."

"Okay, then. I'm just now wrapping up a meeting with Captain Marvin of the Park Police. Why don't we meet over at Orgazmica Brewing up on Clement Street - say fifteen minutes?"

O'Bannon was already in a booth when Zack and Eagle Feather arrived. They slid in opposite him.

"Hi, Chief," O'Bannon said. Then, "Zack, it's good to see you. Thanks for getting involved in this."

"It suits my needs, to be honest." Zack signaled to the girl for two more ales. "What've you been working on?"

"I'm trying to establish some kind of connection between all the victims. I mean you just couldn't find three more dissimilar people - the hooker, the jogger, and the software developer. One lived up in the Presidio area, one here in Inner Richmond next to the park, and the third all the way down in the Mission. So I ask myself, were they selected randomly? I just don't believe that. This murderer is too careful. He's much too precise to pick victims at random. So I've been going through the backgrounds of each of the victims with a fine tooth comb, looking for any common ground: church, favorite restaurant, hobbies, anything."

"Any luck?"

"Nothing - nothing at all. But it takes a whole lot of sifting and I've still got a lot of ground to cover." O'Bannon sipped his beer. Then he had another thought. "One bit of good news, though. The Medical Examiner's office called. They found the same DNA on all three victims. It's the same killer, for sure."

Zack's jaw dropped. "Marty, that's huge. It's one thing to speculate there's a connection but it's another to know for sure."

Eagle Feather stared at Marty. "They've got the DNA, so who's the perp?"

"That's the bad news. That DNA isn't in any data bank we've accessed. In fact, the lab tells me it isn't even close to anything in their data banks."

"Why doesn't that surprise me?" Eagle Feather mumbled.

"Maybe we can help." It was Zack's turn to grin. "We can give them another victim."

O'Bannon's jaw dropped this time. "Another victim? I haven't heard of any more victims - and we've checked every report."

"He disguised this one, probably hoped to throw us

off his track. It was a kid, all the way down in the Park District. Everyone down there thought the kid had taken a fall off of one of the Twin Peaks. He had a lot of wounds but the fatal one was a throat wound. It just didn't seem to fit. Turns out his throat had been gashed before he ever fell off the mountain. Eagle Feather and I just came from there. We were able to reconstruct the crime, even after all this time. The guy killed the kid near the road, picked him up and carried him to the cliff edge and literally threw him over. The kid didn't take his first bounce until fifty feet down the slope."

"Jesus!" O'Bannon breathed. "What a monster."

"That may be more apt than you think," Zack commented.

Eagle Feather chimed in. "The guy managed to gash the kid's throat and move him to the edge so quickly that he hardly bled at all before he went over. Even with his carotid severed. He bled out on the shelf where he landed. The time from the kill wound to the toss down the slope couldn't have been much more than ten seconds or there would be a lot more blood."

"Jesus!" O'Bannon repeated.

"So now there's another victim to check for DNA. You'd better get the Examiner's office going on that. And while you're at it, check for reports of howling."

"Of what?"

"Howling. Some sort of primal howl was heard by several neighbors living on North Peak at just about the time the kid was killed."

"Oh, come on!"

"Yeah, seriously. Those people are used to coyote howls up there, but they say it wasn't that. Whatever they heard made them sit up and take notice."

"So waddaya want me to do about that?"

"You could check for similar complaints at the time and place of the other kills. Might've been howls then, too."

O'Bannon looked at Zack. "You two have been calling them kills, not murders. What are we talking about here?"

Eagle Feather showed a tight grin. "Just habit. I'm a hunting guide by trade; it's the way I think."

Zack said nothing.

O'Bannon continued to stare at him. "You've had something in mind right from the start, something you haven't been telling me."

Zack looked back into O'Bannon's accusing eyes. When he spoke, his tone was low but intense. "The man we've been following, the guy we thought we had in LA a few months ago, and this guy; they both act like predators more than murderers. A murderer leaves traces of his motives: passion, theft, prejudice - whatever. But this guy just kills: clean, quick, efficient. If he gets his rocks off doing it, he leaves no sign. They're just like one of Eagle Feather's mountain lion kills: efficient, purposeful; no more, no less."

"Why is this guy different from other killers?"

"If we knew that, we'd know what to do next."

O'Bannon sighed. "Well, that doesn't change my game plan."

"No."

O'Bannon stood up. "You two gentlemen may be men of leisure but I've got to get to work." He pulled out a scuffed, dog-eared notebook and wrote a few notes. "I'll check on the howls, I'll connect with the Park District guys about the kid, I'll have the Medical Examiner's office try to get DNA off the kid and then see if they can match it to the DNA they found on the girls and I'll see if there's anything in this kid's background that could possibly connect him to any of the women." Then he grimaced. "And I'll do all the other work I'm supposed to be doing down at the Richmond Station. Anything else anyone wants to load onto my work day?"

"You'd better see to those district chores," Eagle Feather commented. "Those guys down there are right pissed at you." He followed that up with a broad grin.

THIRTEEN

He was here now, in San Francisco, that other one, the persistent one. Why had he come? He should be thinking it was over, the killings done. But he was here…the smell of him lingered on the heights where the boy died. Had they made that connection? They couldn't know about the one on Alcatraz. So why had he come? The man's actions weren't practical, weren't logical. He seemed driven by some intangible, some emotional element. That might make things more difficult...

"*Monster Loose In The City? (Section B, page 1)*" O'Bannon lowered his steaming coffee and stared at the raised type in the copy of the Chronicle he'd just unfolded. His fried eggs forgotten, he searched through the paper for Section B. There:

"*What manner of creature is attacking people in the dark of night on San Francisco streets? Police are investigating the deaths of three women in three different districts in the city, concerned that a common killer may have done the murders. Each of the women died from a single wound: a large gash to the neck. There were no other wounds on the victims or anything to suggest a motive. Police are now considering the deaths unrelated. But new evidence may call that theory into question. This reporter has learned of another victim, a young boy attacked while on his bicycle on Twin Peaks two weeks ago. The boy was found below a steep face of the mountain, apparently having fallen. He sustained multiple wounds. But he had a gash to his throat identical to those received by the three women. The Medical Examiner determined that the wound occurred prior to his fall. Neighbors in the area reported hearing a bone-chilling howl in the night around the time of the attack. This reporter has learned that similar howls were reported coincident to the murders of at least one of the women victims. Further, the wounds on all four victims have puncture marks that suggest large incisors. Is there a killer in the city imitating a predatory animal? Or is there a dangerous animal loose upon the streets preying on solitary late night pedestrians? What manner of monster is loose upon the streets of San Francisco? When asked to comment, the office of the..."*

"Damn." O'Bannon felt a surge of disbelief and anger. That wily old coot Snyder! Where did he get all of this? But what did that matter now? There will be hell to pay. The whole city could go into a panic.

O'Bannon grabbed his cell phone and dialed the office of the Medical Examiner. The call went to voice mail, but the official message was interrupted by a woman's voice - a very strident voice.

"Is this Lieutenant O'Bannon?"

"Uh, yes, I- "

"Investigating the murdered prostitutes?"

"The three women, yes, but they aren't all- "

"What the hell are you doing talking to the press? And what is this cockamamie story about a serial killer...or an animal, for God's sake?"

"Whoa, just a minute." O'Bannon's voice was sharp. "First of all, to whom am I speaking?"

"This is Madeline Forster, the Chief Medical Examiner. And I'm hopping mad."

"Well I'm hopping mad, too. I was calling you to find out who's been talking to Jim Snyder at the Chronicle from your office. I can guarantee none of this came from my people. We don't even have the details Snyder mentions."

"You better believe I'll soon know if anyone in my office is the leak. But right now we need to do some damage control. I want you here in ten minutes. I've been on the phone with the Mayor who just spoke to the Commissioner. You and I will be holding a press conference in one hour to put all of this to rest. So as you're driving over here, decide how you'll put all this into the correct perspective." The line went dead.

"Shit." O'Bannon immediately dialed another number.

"San Francisco Chronicle, Jim Snyder speaking."

"Snyder, this is O'Bannon. You've just lost all the credibility you ever had with me."

"I've been expecting your call."

"I'll bet you have. You've got the Mayor and the Chief Medical Examiner all over my butt and I just can't wait to hear from the Commissioner."

"For what it's worth, I'm sorry about that. I did what I had to do. The people of San Francisco are in danger and they need to know that."

"You can't be sure of that. You don't know who's doing this. All you're managing to do is terrorize the entire city."

"Or maybe prevent more murders by keeping people inside at night, or watching their backs, at least."

"Okay, Okay. We could go round and round about this. But at least tell me where you got the bit about the marks on the wounds. You know, the fang thing."

"Of course I can't reveal my sources, but I have photos of the wounds on all four of the victims. I studied them very carefully. There is no doubt that all four were made by the same weapon...or teeth. You can't have that kind of consistency unless it's the same perpetrator, or the exact same weapon."

"Say it's an animal. What's your guess?"

"A very large coyote."

"Aw, c'mon."

"You asked me."

"I've never heard of a coyote attacking a full grown human. Nor one that large."

"Me neither, but that doesn't mean it hasn't happened, or couldn't happen."

"Well, whatever it is, I'm on my way to a press conference where I'll be doing my best to downplay the panic you just caused. And Snyder?"

"Yeah?"

"If you want to get back on my good side and keep

getting those little morsels ahead of the rest of the hacks, you'd best do me a favor."

"What's that?"

"Warn me before you go to print next time."

O'Bannon hung up.

Zack sat in the breakfast nook of his boutique hotel near Union Square on Geary Street, reading the same article. He had decided to stay in a place central to the pattern of the murder locations that seemed to be emerging. He'd noticed when looking at a city map that the crime scenes described a sort of irregular arc, particularly if you included the Mission home of the second victim. The killer apparently didn't lack mobility. And if that arc meant anything, he wanted to be near the center of the circle it represented.

As he read Snyder's article he chuckled, thinking how upset O'Bannon must be. This reporter James Snyder was getting very close to the truth, as Zack saw it. At first Zack was concerned the article might drive the killer further underground. But then he realized he was there already; the change in his *modus operandi* suggested that much. When killing the boy he had obviously tried to avoid similarities to his previous three kills. Maybe the warning sounded by this reporter would make it more difficult for him. He might start making mistakes.

Zack put down the paper and took a sip of his coffee. For hotel coffee, it wasn't bad. In fact everything about this little hotel pleased him, even the price. Sure, the room was tiny. But it had a window, and the bed was comfortable. He rubbed his lower back, thinking of

Eagle Feather's couch.

Zack picked up the city map and opened it again, wondering what the kill patterns meant, if anything. Obviously, they had occurred in open spaces rather than on city streets. This didn't surprise him. He'd seen the same pattern with the Los Angeles murders, a sort of hopscotch from park to park. Zack's finger extended along the arc he'd drawn on the map. There were a lot of possibilities. At the northern end it pointed to any part of Crissy Field and beyond it to Fort Mason. At the southern end, if continued, it reached down to Mount Davidson or Glen Canyon Park, or maybe across to the Mission Dolores Park. Zack sighed and folded up the map. Even if the emerging circle meant something, there was no way to predict the next murder scene. And now Snyder's article might force a change and make it less likely that the killer would return to the scene of his former kills. Worse, he might change his MO even more dramatically.

Zack stood and stretched, shaking his head. This might not be his man at all. Maybe it was all a coincidence. It'd been a dozen days since the boy was killed. He'd scanned all the police reports in the entire city with O'Bannon. There'd been no incidents since the boy - nothing at all. So maybe it wasn't the same man...or maybe he was gone. Zack felt guilt grow in him, guilt that he'd left his work, guilt that he was wasting department money. And guilt that he'd left Libby at a critical time in their relationship, a time when she seemed to be questioning his actions and his motives.

What had made him come here at this particular time, he asked himself? There'd been no real reason to come, no fresh kill, no new evidence. Was he reading too much into it? Was he still feeling the effects of the Roundtree case? Maybe he was traumatized without even knowing it. Was he creating a bogeyman where none existed? If so, it was time to give up police work for good.

I'll give it two more days, he decided. Two more days and if nothing more happens, if there's no new evidence, I'll go home and drop the whole thing. No excuses.

Feeling better, he squared his shoulders and walked across the foyer to the elevator.

After hanging up from O'Bannon, Snyder dialed a number on a torn scrap of paper that Westfield, the Stanford professor, had given him. It was the number of one of his colleagues, a guy up at UC Davis, an animal guy.

"Wildlife Health Center, UC Davis. How may I direct your call?"

"I'd like to speak to Dr. Philip Morgan, please. I'm Jim Snyder. I'm a friend of a friend."

"One moment, please."

Snyder listened to the light classical Muzak and drummed his fingers on his desk. After a minute or two there was a click and a practiced voice asked, "Mr. Snyder? May I ask who our mutual friend is?"

"Is this Dr. Morgan? Dr. Westfield sends his regards."

"Oh, yes of course, Andy Westfield. Well, how may I be of service?"

"I'm investigating a rather unusual set of circumstances for my paper, the Chronicle. Dr. Westfield tells me you're an expert in animal necropsy. If I faxed you pictures of some bite wounds could you tell me what animal made the bites?"

"Were these bites made into muscle tissue?"

"Yes, human in fact."

"Ah...and you believe these to be animal bites?"

"I'm not sure. That's part of what I hope to resolve."

"Oh, I see...uh, sure. Send them along to my attention. I've a rather tight schedule right now but I'll take a look and get back to you as soon as I can. Fair enough?"

"I appreciate this, Dr. Morgan."

Snyder hung up and went to get the pictures from his file.

Meg was not a reader of newspapers. She cared little for politics and current events, preferring to curl up with a dime store novel and let the world pass her by. But someone had left a newspaper in the booth where she sat sipping her coffee, waiting for her eggs over easy to arrive. It was left open to the 'B' section and when she glanced at it the header caught her eye.

"*What manner of creature is...?*" Meg read, and her world was suddenly reduced to the printed page, the cafe background noises were diminished, her mind raced. "*Deaths of three women...a young boy...*" Meg gasped aloud.

She scanned the article, looking for dates and places. There! Buena Vista Park…yes, that was it, the very day. That poor girl, so sweet, she chattered all the way to the park, happy with something in the contents of the note Max had sent her, smiling when she left the car, smiling when she walked into the park. And then...? Sure, she knew Max wasn't likely to be canonized any day soon - he was a sleaze-ball of the first order...but this?

Sure, she'd closed her mind to thoughts of what might follow after she did the things he asked her to do. She needed the money, didn't she? She loved the comfort and security it brought her...but this?

Meg devoured the details. Incisor marks? Throat ripped open? She shuddered. Was this Max's doing or could this be a coincidence? She hoped so, but she knew better. But maybe Max was simply following directions, just as she was - another errand runner, another go-fer. But no, in her heart she knew Max was capable of great violence, capable of this very thing. It was why she feared him. And that was why she knew she couldn't follow her first instinct and run away; he would find her and do something horrible to her.

Meg shuddered and set the paper aside. Her mind was already doing what it always did to protect her, shutting down. By the time her eggs arrived all thoughts generated by the newspaper article had vanished. As she scooped up the runny yolk with the crisp buttered toast her memory was blank. She took a bite and sighed with pleasure.

FOURTEEN

They were beginning to understand, to connect the dots. Who was this reporter, this snooping Snyder? He didn't know anyone with that name, but for the man to know so much he must have gone to the kill sites. If so, the man's scent would be familiar to him, he just needed a human to go with it. He'd go over to the Chronicle offices and sniff around and see if he could connect his own dots…

It was a total accident, a complete chance. Zack had gone to the front desk to check for messages and the clerk had looked strangely at him and asked, "Are you the police officer investigating the disappearance of Mr. Olson? Your boss would like you to call him."

"Pardon me?"

"The police investigator. Is that you?"

"Uh, yeah, I guess so, but I'm not..."

The clerk read from a slip of paper. "Captain Tom Garret of the Central District Station would like you to call him."

"I don't know a Tom Garret. Are you sure this is

for me?"

The clerk started to sound annoyed. "Are you the officer investigating the Olson disappearance, or not?"

"Not."

"Oh, I'm sorry, sir. I thought you were a police investigator."

"I'm an FBI agent."

The clerk's eyes widened. "They've called in the FBI?"

"No, no! I'm here on my own, a vacation, if you will."

"Oh, that would explain the confusion. I'm sorry, sir."

"Well, I'm glad that's settled. Now, are there any messages for Zack Tolliver?"

"Oh, yes, I believe so...here you are, sir."

A stocky man in a Giants windbreaker approached the counter. "Any messages for Pete Clark? San Francisco police."

"Yes, sir, your boss would like you to call in. Oh, by the way, sir, this is Mr. Tolliver of the FBI."

Zack had started to walk away from the counter. He turned back.

The policeman offered his hand. “Pete Clark. What brings you here?”

“Just a vacation. Sounds like you have a missing person case?”

“Yeah. A man, an ultra-runner. He disappeared from the hotel a couple of nights ago, hasn’t been seen since. It’s standard procedure for us to ask a few questions. Usually, though, they’re just skipping out on the bill. Strange thing here, though, he’s a fairly regular guest. And his bed was never slept in.”

Clark started to turn away. Zack put a hand on his arm.

“You said he disappeared a couple of nights ago?”

“Yeah...let’s see” -Clark checked his iPhone- ”the night of the 16th, to be exact.”

“Ah...” Zack thought a moment. “Listen, I may be able to help you with this one. Here’s my card. How can I reach you?”

“Here’s a number.” The detective scribbled a number on a card. “That’s the number I actually answer,” he said, grinning. “How do you figure you can help?”

“To be honest, I don’t know yet. Might be nothing. But I’ll be in touch.”

The two men nodded to each other. Zack walked out of the hotel. As soon as he hit the sidewalk he called Eagle Feather.

"E.F., hey, its Zack. I just had a thought. What if the killer is looking specifically for athletic types...you know, physically fit people who can run and make the killing sporting for him? What do you think?"

"Could be. So where's that leave the kid?"

"He was on a bike. If he'd gotten started downhill in time he could've got up good speed."

"True."

"Listen." Zack spoke almost in a whisper, as if the killer was in the same street with him. "I just stumbled on to something. There may be a kill that we don't know about."

"Tell me."

Zack told him about his encounter with the police detective.

"C'mon, Zack, there's got to be a score of those missing persons every week. You know that."

"Sure, but get this. He was an athlete...an ultra-runner."

Eagle Feather was silent. Zack went on. "And, get this. He disappeared on the night of May 16. I don't have to do the math for you, do I?"

There was a sharp intake of breath from Eagle Feather. "What have the cops got so far?"

"Nothing yet, but I've got the detective's number."

After Zack rang off he punched O'Bannon's number on his cell. After listening to Zack's idea, O'Bannon promised to contact the Central District and stay on top of any developments in the case.

Zack pulled out his city map. So, if the killer had abducted this guy, where did he take him? Zack thought about the Buena Vista girl. She had come all the way from the Mission. He must have abducted her, too. Then he thought, but why her? She was young and strong looking, not an invalid, certainly, but nothing in her background suggested she was necessarily an athlete.

Zack swatted the folded map against his thigh in frustration. *Something* must connect all these victims, something he couldn't see. The victims were not selected at random; each one of these kills had been carefully planned.

Libby heard Zack's call tone and grabbed her cell at the first ring.

"Well hello, stranger. Are you calling to tell me you're coming home?"

"Not yet." There was a tremor in Zack's voice. "I think he's still here, this killer. I just got a new lead so I'm gonna stay here and work it through. A couple more days, maybe."

Libby couldn't conceal her disappointed. They'd made plans for the coming weekend, a real nice dinner in a place they both liked a lot. Now Zack seemed more excited about chasing criminals around San Francisco than that special date with her.

"Look, Zack, don't let your desire to catch this guy color your judgment. You need to ask yourself if you're possibly seeing something that isn't really there."

"I know you're right, Libby. If this lead fades out, I'll head home. I promise. I'll know for sure in a day or two."

After the call, Libby tucked her cell phone away in its holster and picked up a pitchfork. She forked fresh hay into the stall and thought about her secret and just how and when she'd reveal it to Zack. She felt annoyance with him, then with herself. She should have been more assertive, but she didn't want any unpleasantness to color her special news. He'd be back soon. Then she'd tell him.

O'Bannon called Zack later that morning. He'd been on the phone with the Central District and had the facts of the case, few as they were.

"Not much here. The barkeep saw the guy around eight PM.

He was a loner, drinking whisky and looking for action. The barkeep got busy for a while and next thing he saw the guy at a table with a woman, dark hair, real dressed up, like a party outfit. Then they were gone. That was it. Nobody ever saw the guy again. They pressed the barkeep for a description of the woman, but the only thing he could add was she had an old-young face, you know? Like she was young and kinda pretty but had seen too much and done too much - old before her time, if you know what I mean."

"Um, yeah. Could they ID her? Was she staying at

the hotel?"

"No, not a guest. But sometimes hookers do come in to the bar on occasion, just the classy ones. He was guessin' she might be one of those."

"Thanks."

"How does she fit in to this?"

"I'm not sure, Marty, to be honest. Just kind of a gut thing."

Zack thought about it after he hung up. Could the killer be using an intermediary in some way? Seemed unlikely - he'd not want any witnesses, any links back to him. But if he was using one - say this girl, for instance - he wouldn't plan to leave her around to talk about it when he was done.

Zack thought some more, then he decided to call Eagle Feather.

"Two times in one morning? What's wrong, white man, you lost?"

"Yes, metaphorically speaking. I've got a job for you. I just learned that this ultra-runner who's missing was seen that night with a girl at a table in the hotel lounge, probably a hooker."

"Okay."

"So here's what I'm thinking. We need to track this girl down and get some answers. If our killer had nothing to do with this Jan guy, then no harm, no foul. But if he sent this girl to get him, if in fact he's using the girl to run errands for him, he's not going to let her live when he's done with her. You with me?"

"Makes sense."

"If we can find her, she might lead us to him."

There was an appreciative chuckle. "Not bad, white man. Not bad at all. Are you going to put O'Bannon on this?"

"No, you."

"Keeping it close to the chest, eh?"

"You never know who's listening to whom out there. If our killer catches on, he won't go near her. Or more likely, she'll be dead before we can find her."

"Makes sense. Have you anything more to go on besides Adagio lounge bar, May 16, party dress, old looking young hooker?"

"That's it," Zack responded cheerily. "You might be able to get more out of the barkeep, name of Jurgins."

"I'm on my way."

A very harried Dr. Philip Morgan stopped at the fax machine on his way to buy a sandwich to eat while he worked. His project at the Wildlife Health Center at UC Davis had gone into overdrive, with a new rash of pet kills and episodes of mauling by the bears and mountain lions that increasingly encroached on the residential backyards of northern California. Wildlife encroachment was already escalating due to climate and habitat change but now with the out-of-control wildfires in the Sierras, the animals had no where else to go to find food, and his team spent every working hour responding to calls to capture or kill predators making a meal of whatever they could find, small pets included. One glance at the fax machine smothered by incoming documents told him that their work was far from over.

Dr. Morgan scooped up the pile of faxes and leafed through them on his way to the vending machine, mentally filing them according to urgency. He noticed the fax from Jim Snyder, that nut case reporter with the Chronicle who said Westfield had referred him. He'd have to remember to ask Andrew to stop doing that; he seemed to think that anyone with an animal issue should be sent his way. He glanced at the photo on the second page and stopped in his tracks. What was this? It was a picture of a gash in a human neck, tearing half of it away. This should have gone to the cops, not him. It looked like murder by garden tool. He studied the wound closely. It must have been fatal, he thought, surprised he hadn't already heard something about it. But there *was* something about this wound...

Morgan popped a couple of dollar bills into the vending machine and took his sandwich. Then he walked back to his desk and picked up his magnifier and studied the photo. Whoa, hold your horses! Maybe this *was* an animal bite - those looked like incisor marks, very deep with a slight inward turn. It *was* a bite, he was sure of that now; a weapon hadn't caused it. And whatever made the bite must have had very strong jaws because this bite was made in a single motion. The lack of fraying at the edges meant that it was done quickly, almost instantly. There had been no weight suspension from the wound site - no pulling, no ripping. How could that happen? The creature must have supported its prey somehow during the attack. There must have been deep claw marks on the body. But if so, they would have known it was a lion

- why come to him? A lion attacks from the rear quarter and most often bites the back of the neck, although on occasion it might swing its head under and bite from that position. But in that scenario the angle of the wound would be toward the chin; this wound was straight across the neck as if the predator were at right angles to the victim. To manage that, it needed arms, very strong arms to support the body during the bite. Maybe a gorilla? Gorillas will bite when fighting among themselves but it's never a first option. They're more likely to maul and pound their opponent with their huge strong arms. But they do have large mouths and long incisors and strong jaws.

He slumped back and took up the second photo. My God, the same exact wound, but on a second victim, apparently, and delivered the same way as the first. He compared the wounds in the two photos with his magnifier. No doubt about it, they were made by the same creature, whatever it was. Morgan hurriedly glanced at the remaining photos. All four wounds were exactly the same and each wound was on a different victim.

Dr. Morgan turned to the next desk where his associate was working at his computer.

"Clem, you got a minute? I'd like you to look at something."

FIFTEEN

Snyder snapped his head up and looked around. It was dark in the room except for the pool of blue light from his computer screen. All the other desks were empty. His focus on the archived article had been so complete he'd never noticed. It wasn't the first time this had happened. He'd nod and murmur "Good night" to his associates as they left and then forget all about it. He didn't know if his concentration was that good, or if his memory was that bad.

Snyder shrugged and glanced at his watch. Well, it was time to wrap it up anyway. His neck was stiff from holding the same position and hell, he hadn't really learned anything. He'd hoped to find archived references to strange howls or murder victims with neck wounds to see if this killer might have been active before the Golden Gate Park murder, but no dice. So the killer or whatever this thing was had either just arrived or just become active for that killing. Tomorrow maybe he'd check the archive back to the first week of April or so but this time he'd look for animals escaping from shipping crates or zoos, that kind of thing.

Oh, well. Snyder stretched and stood, knees creaking, and reached for his jacket on the coat rack. He settled his hat on his head and looked around again. The place had emptied out completely. That was somewhat unusual; there was usually someone working on a deadline, typing away far into the night. It must be an easy news week.

Snyder walked among the empty desks and out into the stairwell. His heels on the granite stairs echoed eerily off the walls and then clattered on down the stairs ahead of him, like a stone dropped into a well. The building had a creaky old elevator but Snyder never used it; he needed the exercise to offset all his bad habits.

Somewhere below he heard the muffled but resonant click of a door being carefully closed. The sound came hollow to his ear, like a car door closing in a tunnel. The silence was vibrant, the clack of his footfalls too loud. Snyder felt uncomfortable. The entire building seemed empty. When had he ever noticed that before? What time was it, anyway? Where was the night shift? He had glanced at a clock just a short while ago but couldn't remember what it had said. Talk about getting old.

Snyder stopped where he was on the stair and pushed in the tiny light button on his watch but it wasn't very effective. He'd already put away his reading glasses. No way he could see that tiny barely illuminated digital readout. Why didn't they make real watches anymore with big clunky numbers and hands that glowed in the dark?

And it was very dark where he stood in the stairwell. The landing just below was barely brushed by a dust-filtered beam from a bulb somewhere below. The next flight down was obscured by inky blackness. What happened to all the safety lights? Why did he feel so nervous? Was he so old he was afraid of the dark?

Annoyed with himself, Snyder clamored on down the stairs, purposefully making just as much noise as he usually did when he left. He stomped down the last flight and landed heavily on the marble floor. Crossing to the lobby door he stepped out into the well-lit lobby. The security officer sat at the central desk wrapped up in his newspaper, as usual. Beyond him out beyond the heavy iron and glass doors were the lights of the city. Snyder felt a strange sense of relief.

As he passed the security desk the officer looked up from his newspaper. "Good night, Mr. Snyder."

"Good night, Louie," Snyder replied and started to walk on but then stopped as his curiosity took over. "Did someone come out of the stairwell just now?"

"Only you."

"Mmm. Well thanks. See you tomorrow."

Snyder pushed through the glass doors and stood for a moment on the terraced step above the street. It was dark and the usual late evening pedestrians passed to and fro before him, the jackets and sweaters that had been draped stylishly over their shoulders during the day now worn fully against the foggy chill. In the street, cars jerked into motion and stopped again as the lights changed. Everything was as it always was. So why was he so jumpy?

Snyder respected his instincts. A newspaperman's second sense is what keeps him in the game. Snyder's seldom let him down. He listened to it now, but he wasn't sure what it was trying to tell him.

Jim Snyder was a holdout bachelor. He'd never intended to get married, thinking it would get in the way of his career as a journalist. The job was his life: his work, hobby, recreation, and relaxation all rolled into one. There'd been moments, temptations, times when he'd found his mouth about to shape the words that would take him down the aisle but he'd stopped himself in time. And he never regretted it, as he told himself often. But his lonely apartment just down Howard Street with the rickety fire escape that led to the single pane window of his bedroom seemed vulnerable somehow. It just didn't seem inviting right now.

Snyder shivered. Something different was in the air tonight and he intended to respect the warning signs. He took a determined step opposite his usual nightly path that would take him to his apartment and headed instead to the busy streets and crowded bars near Union Square. Soon he was swiveling comfortably on a cushy bar stool, a chilled mug of Sierra Pale Ale on the slick bar in front of him, feeling warm and safe. The small taproom was packed with the usual weeknight crowd. They'd have a glass or two or three and later trudge home to wife and kids or to a live-in girl or guy, or simply to four walls that enclosed an empty space, like Snyder.

At times like this, it might have been nice to have someone waiting for him at home, maybe even a kid or two bustling with energy, eager to tell him all about their day, firing questions at him. It might have been...

Nah! Snyder let a sip of ale linger in his mouth. Who was he kidding? He looked again and saw that same someone with a contorted angry face, demanding to know where he'd been, and didn't he know dinner was getting cold? And the little kid crying, snot running down his chin, a teenage girl yelling that she hated him because he wouldn't let her go out on a school night...!

Snyder smiled grimly to himself. Nah! He'd got it right. This was the life for him - the only life.

"I'm not going to hunt down old receipts for every Tom, Dick, and Harry who wants to see 'em. Who're you?"

The reaction didn't surprise Eagle Feather. He pulled out a letter. "This is my authority, signed by the Police Commissioner of the City of San Francisco. I'm here as a consultant with the department, following up on several murders."

The hotel manager looked at the letter, the official city stamp and stamped signature of the Commissioner, the counter-signature of a Lieutenant Martin O'Bannon, and shrugged. "Well, okay. You said you wanted them for just a certain night?"

"Yeah, the night of May 16. I'll need everything you've got from the lounge starting around five PM."

"The beginning of Happy Hour. Okay, give me a minute." The manager disappeared into his little office area beyond the counter. When he emerged several minutes later he had sheaves of tissue-thin receipts in one hand and cash register printouts in the other.

"These are the credit receipts and these are the cash receipts. You're not going to learn much from the cash transactions." The manager smiled slightly. "Some will be a bit hard to read; in the lounge they tend to get wet and then smear."

Eagle Feather smiled his thanks and took the bundles to a table. He wasn't expecting much but he might get lucky. He didn't know where else to start.

Twenty minutes later Eagle Feather sat with four piles of paper. Two were the credit and cash receipts that he had disqualified for one reason or another, the other two stacks were the possibles. And those stacks were still way too large. Directly in front of him was a single credit receipt. It was a room charge, for room 212, to Jan Olson, the missing Ultra Runner. It didn't tell him much but it raised a possible new avenue of investigation.

Eagle Feather looked at the remaining cash receipts again, spreading them out side by side on the table. Some were crinkled from getting wet and a few were tainted and colored by food and drink stains.

He'd already interviewed the bar keeper from the night of the sixteenth. The man didn't remember much, not even as much as he'd remembered for the cops; it had been many nights and hundreds of customers ago. But one thing the man did remember: who had what drink. It was uncanny, his ability to match drinks to customers. And he'd remembered the drink he made for the girl that night: Blue Curacao. Now Eagle Feather's eye caught a bluish tint on a cash receipt: diluted, dried, but definitely blue. He picked it up, studied it. There was something written in pencil across the top, a series of numbers. Some were indecipherable, some he could read.

Eagle Feather walked over to the front desk and showed it to the manager. "What are these numbers here?"

"That? That's an ID, looks like a driver's license. Whenever a barkeep is suspicious of someone's age or intent he asks for a form of identification and writes it on the receipt. That way, if the customer turns out to be underage, for instance, he has proof that he asked the question if the authorities come knocking. This person showed a driver's license to him."

"Thanks. May I have a photocopy of this?"

The manager disappeared into his office with it and Eagle Feather called O'Bannon. "Can you look up a driver's license for me? A partial number?"

"Have you got the beginning and ending numbers?"

"Yeah, a letter and some digits. I think there are three characters missing from the middle."

"Well, that'll narrow it down to a few thousand."

"But then we can narrow it further by gender, age, and appearance in the photo, am I right?"

"Maybe. Is this the girl in the bar?"

"Yea, I think so. I'll text the number to you when I get my copy." Eagle Feather hung up, pleased. It had seemed an impossible search but he just might have a thread to pull after all.

Zack opened up a Tour Guide map of the city and spread it out on his bed. He picked up a yellow marker but put it down again. Too optimistic, he told himself. He couldn't be sure that a new yellow circle was ready to join the other four on the map yet, circles at the location of each kill.

The girl in the lounge presented new difficulties. If the killer was using an intermediary (as in this case if Zack's suspicions were correct) he could no longer assume that the murderer was present when each victim was abducted. But if the disappearance of the ultra runner was not related to the murders, Zack was right back where he started when he got up this morning: with nothing. So he couldn't assume that, either. Which brought him right back to the present and the urgent need to find this mystery girl. I'll follow this one lead, he told himself, and if it goes poof, like that runner, I'll go home.

Zack looked at the map again and studied the arc

that connected the murder sites. He mentally projected the arc into a full circle. He saw again that Twin Peaks was outside the emerging pattern. Too far outside, he thought. And in more ways than one: not just that the location was outside the circle but the obvious fact that the victim was a small boy, not a grown woman. And then there was the environment: rough, rugged, and barren, not at all like the other thickly forested sites along the arc. Then there was the murder itself, the fatal wound followed by all the additional injuries that came from throwing the boy off the precipice, as if to disguise that telltale wound. Yet the other three victims had been left where they fell after receiving the throat slash, their bodies untouched and unblemished - almost as if demonstrating a grotesque pride in his workmanship, Zack thought.

Why was the boy's murder so different? And what might that mean for future kills? Most serial killers proved unable to change their Modus Operandi, a fact that often led to their capture. Could this monster be different? Was he capable of changing his ways entirely just to throw law enforcement off the track? Worse, was he able to change permanently? If so, Zack thought with despair, they'd never catch him. Further, it must mean he wasn't subject to the usual deep-seated psychological disturbances that drove serial killers. It made him unusual. It made him unusually dangerous.

Now I'm just speculating, Zack thought. He had no doubt that the same killer had done the kid but that kill might have had a different purpose, to be a red herring, just this once. Maybe he's gone back to his old pattern now. Maybe he really is responsible for the missing runner; if so, Zack felt sure they'd find the victim somewhere along the circumference of the circle he'd drawn on the map. He picked up the marker. This time he ignored Twin Peaks and drew an arc from Buena Vista Park through the murder site at Golden Gate park and up through the murder site at the Presidio. When he had done that he stared at it for a moment, then continued the arc to complete a circle all the way around and back to Buena Vista Park again. Without Twin Peaks, the arc departing from the Presidio was steeper and took him farther up into San Francisco Bay. There was nothing there but water until he reached Alcatraz Island and after that nothing but water until he reached the Embarcadero at a place called Sydney G. Walton Park. It was the only green area before returning to where the circle started.

How could this be? Zack was stumped. Neither place, Alcatraz nor this Sydney G. Walton Park, seemed likely. The first was too remote and too inaccessible and where could he find a victim out there anyway? And the other was too open, too busy, and too well illuminated by the surrounding city lights even at the darkest hour. The chronological order of the murders, excluding the Twin Peaks murder, took you clockwise around the circle, which meant that the next site in the pattern would have to be Alcatraz. There simply was nowhere else. Discouraged, Zack folded up the map. He must be on a completely wrong track. The kills were probably random after all. He was reading patterns that didn't exist.

Zack hoped Eagle Feather was having better luck.

SIXTEEN

"It's good news, bad news," O'Bannon was saying. "The state of California issues an eight character alpha-numeric driver's license, a letter followed by eight numbers, and uses the Soundex code. Good news, the girl's first name is short with just two vowels, so Soundex required only the first letter and two numbers. We have that. Her first name is probably Megan. The bad news, we can't read anything else from the remaining numbers because in California the date of birth, initials, special code, and so on are jumbled up in the rest of the license number. No way to read it with the center three numbers missing."

"Did you do a computer search of the number to narrow it down?" Eagle Feather asked.

"Sure. And we did narrow it down, to over a hundred thousand Megan's in the state of California. Then we narrowed it further, to 1856 licensed Megan's in San Francisco, if indeed she lives in town. We eliminated everyone over fifty years of age, which brought us down to 1,250. We uploaded the license pictures for those women and now we're visually eliminating all but the dark haired Megan's, assuming she hasn't dyed her hair recently. Maybe that will get us down to around 800 or so."

Eagle Feather groaned. "Thanks for trying."

O'Bannon chuckled. "Welcome to big city police work. But it's not as bad as it sounds. We'll keep these search results and wait for more data to cross reference with it. You never know..."

After ending the call, Eagle Feather decided to ask the staff at the Adagio if they knew the name Megan. Maybe this wasn't her first time here.

The next morning Jim Snyder had a return call from Philip Morgan at the Wildlife Center. Snyder sat up and became fully focused when he heard what Morgan was saying.

"Before I get into this with you, I need to know if the police are aware of the deaths of these people...they are dead, of course."

"Yes, yes, the police certainly know. This is an ongoing investigation."

"Okay. Next. Shouldn't I be giving my information to the police directly, not to a journalist?"

"Sure, you can try that. If you're about to tell me that a criminal killed these victims with some kind of strange weapon, you should hang up and call the cops. But if you have something else to say, think about it for a moment. Do you really want to call the police to tell them the wound wasn't made by a human?"

Dr. Morgan didn't reply.

Snyder went on. "And while you're thinking about it, remember that it's in everybody's best interest to catch this killer, man or beast. As a reporter, my story can force the issue if the cops are reluctant to act on your information - whatever it is."

Dr. Morgan had made up his mind. "Well, here it is, like it or not. I consulted with a colleague with expertise in this area and he agrees with my findings. The wounds were not made by a human...exactly. I mean, these are definitely bite wounds from a mouth with long incisors and a very strong jaw; much stronger and larger than yours or mine. But the perpetrator had to be human-like, in some way able to support his victim while inflicting the wound because there was no tearing along the edge of the wounds. I'd need answers to several questions to go any further. For instance, were there other markings on the body, like bruises, for example, or cuts or slashes? An animal would leave more markings, like claw marks from seizing its prey, or other bites from attempting to feed. Something, anything?"

"Those throat wounds were the only wounds on three of the four victims," Snyder said. "The fourth was a young boy who fell down a cliff face and so had cuts and gashes from that. But the coroner insists all his wounds, other than the throat wound, were post-mortem."

"Do you know what signs or tracks the police found near the bodies?"

"Nothing - absolutely nothing."

"Remarkable." Dr. Morgan was silent for a moment. "I can't help any more than this, I'm afraid. I suppose I've just made your quandary worse. Maybe if I had a little more data..." Then more briskly, "Well, I certainly will help more if I can, and I'm interested to learn the outcome of the police investigation. Call me if you get more, would you? And please keep me informed."

Snyder stared at the telephone after he'd hung up. My God. What were they dealing with? Could there possibly be a large ape of some sort loose in the city? Snyder picked up the phone and began calling zoos.

Detective Harry Harrar watched Martin O'Bannon finish his conversation with Eagle Feather on the phone. He cranked up a grin and yelled over to him.

"Hey, O'Bannon, you been talking to the Chief? He doing your job for you now?"

O'Bannon responded calmly. "He's doing a little checking for me."

"Sounded more like you two are playing the numbers game. You his bookie?"

O'Bannon remained unruffled. "We've got six out of nine figures for a telephone number. Wouldn't be so bad, but the missing numbers are right in the middle."

"What's the number for?"

O'Bannon felt annoyance at the questions. Although a seasoned cop, Harry Harrar was new to the Richmond District. He'd been transferred recently from the Tenderloin. But from what O'Bannon had heard they didn't much mind losing him over there.

"If you must know, it's a lead to a possible accomplice of the killer we're tracking. Haven't you got your own work?"

"Hey, take it easy, I'm just busting your chops a

little."

Then Harrar sounded irritated. "And yeah, I got plenty of work, some of it yours, by all rights."

O'Bannon felt a surge of guilt. "Hey, I'm sorry about that, Harry, I really am. I just didn't expect these murders to blow up into a full-fledged serial killer investigation. I'm on a serious timeline now, thanks to pressure from the Mayor."

Harrar relaxed a bit. "No problem, really, O'Bannon. I don't mind helping out. In fact, if you need some work done, like this license number search, I'll handle it. I'm desk bound for quite a while anyway, with the stuff I have to do."

O'Bannon felt more guilt. "That's real nice of you, Harry. I might just take you up on that."

"No problem. Say, doesn't that Indian friend of yours have his own life someplace? Where's he get all this time?"

Back came the annoyance. "He's a friend of a friend who likes to help out and I'm damn grateful, to tell you the truth. And now that I think of it, I do have a task you can help me with right now. I need to put every dark-haired girl from this group of license photos into this special folder. Do you mind?"

"Send it on over," Harrar said.

Maybe he's not such a bad guy after all, O'Bannon thought to himself.

The Indian in question was feeling pretty good about himself. Luck had played a part. The lounge barkeep from the night Olson had gone missing had walked in while Eagle Feather was still interviewing a housekeeping maid in the lounge. The closed lounge made a good place to have a secluded talk.

And the barkeep knew Megan. Or at least knew who she was - and had seen her in the lounge on several occasions.

"I saw her more frequently about eight months ago," he remembered, "and then she stopped coming for a while."

But yes, he'd seen her that night and noticed that the missing man had gone to her table. "The guy was looking for action, you could tell by the way he scanned the room from his stool."

"Could he have known Megan was a professional?"

"You know, I doubt he cared, one way or the other. I mean, she started out with another guy, but then that guy left. I remember because he didn't buy a drink. The Olson guy must have gone over after he left."

Eagle Feather leaned toward him. "This first guy - what'd he look like?"

The barkeep wiped a glass with his towel. "I didn't pay him much attention, to tell you the truth. Big guy is my impression, formidable; I remember hoping I wouldn't have to bounce him."

"Why would you think you might?"

The barkeep reached down for another glass. "Guy

comes in here and doesn't drink - sometimes he's got something else in mind."

The bartender was beginning to look annoyed at all the questions but Eagle Feather pressed on regardless. "How was he dressed? Any memorable characteristics, that kind of thing?"

"Seriously, man, I only got a general impression. I don't remember any details at all."

Eagle Feather leaned back in his chair. "You've been a lot of help - more than you know. Thanks." He walked out to the hotel foyer. While he stood there gathering his thoughts his cell phone rang.

"Jim Snyder here. In the interests of full disclosure, like we agreed, I've got some information for you."

"Shoot."

"I sent the photos of the victims' wounds over to the Wildlife Center at UC Davis, to an expert named Morgan."

"And...?"

"He says they're not human."

Eagle Feather stood perfectly still. When he next spoke his voice quavered with intensity. "What does he think it was?"

"He doesn't know, says he's never seen anything like it. Said only a gorilla could have the strength of jaw and length of incisors to make those wounds along with the strength to support the victim in the air while he did it."

"So...first a coyote, now a gorilla."

Snyder ignored the jibe. "I've called every zoo in the northern half of the state," he said. "No one is missing a gorilla."

"I'm not surprised."

"No. I didn't expect you would be," Snyder said. "In fact, I don't think you've told me everything you know. What are you holding back?"

"What makes you think I'm holding anything back?"

"Answer me this, then. Why did you *really* come here, all the way up from Arizona? Not just to help out the San Francisco police, I'm sure."

"I told you when we met, we had some similar killings back in Arizona. I'm just helping out the FBI agent."

"No, it's more than that. I'd say it's personal, from the way you're going at it. Tell me I'm wrong."

Eagle Feather hesitated. How much should he tell Snyder? He owed him something for sharing. And he owed him enough information to keep him from harm. But on the other hand, he already showed that he intended to use all of it in his story. Full disclosure to the public would be a very bad idea.

"Okay, you got me," he said finally. "Here it is. Zack - Zack Tolliver, the FBI agent I'm assisting? A killer in Arizona threatened his wife. Similar MO. So it's personal to him. He's my friend, I know his wife, and I helped track the guy in Arizona. So when Zack heard about these killings up here he took an interest. He asked me to come up and get started on it; he had to wrap up some things. So that's it, you've dragged it all out of me."

"So you didn't catch the killer in Arizona?"

"Well, yes and no. Put it this way; we're pretty sure we got the guy down there but he seems to have a colleague or two, and we think one of them is here now."

Snyder was quiet, digesting it all.

"You keep saying 'he'," Snyder pointed out next. "You still think we're chasing a human, not an animal, despite my expert."

"Look, Jim, I don't know who or what this killer really is any more than you do. But do you honestly think an animal could have done all the things this killer's done? How'd it manage to abduct that girl from the Mission District and get her all the way up to Buena Vista, for instance? At the very least, your animal would have to have a human enabler, but even that doesn't make much sense. No, despite your expert, I'm convinced we have a human killer on our hands; a very skilled and clever human." Eagle Feather paused, searching for the right words. "Jim, I've been wanting to say this for a while. The killer we're chasing is very dangerous, much more dangerous than anybody might imagine. Don't stick your neck out. In fact, I think you've already stuck it out too far. How much is a story worth in the end?"

Quiet laughter came back over the phone. "Hey, Eagle Feather, I never expected to hear those words from you, of all people. This is San Francisco, man. I've chased the worst the human race has to offer for a story, from serial killer to psychotic nut. I think I can handle myself."

Later, Eagle Feather wondered if he should have told Snyder everything. But what was everything, exactly? No, he'd told him what it was necessary for him to know. Now it was up to Snyder to heed the warning.

SEVENTEEN

Harry Harrar felt pretty darn good as he walked down Eighth Street toward Geary. Another couple of jobs and he'd be out from under, he figured. Each job he finished, Mick took another grand off his debt, which by now he'd whittled down to a bit under ten grand: not too bad for just five weeks' work. This last job, one that he'd thought impossible, had turned out easy. Hell, O'Bannon had simply handed it over to him. No sweat.

Just two months ago Harry was a desperate man, right at the edge of suicide. He just couldn't win for losing. Everything he touched turned to shit; his marriage over, his career shaky. He'd transferred out of the Tenderloin just ahead of Internal Affairs. They'd keep on snooping, he knew that; and sooner or later they'd figure out he was bribing those girls big time. And so what? Everybody down there was taking bribes. But with Harry's shit luck, he'd be the one they nailed.

Not as if bribing the whores did him any good. Money flowed through him like shit through a duck. He still couldn't figure how he'd managed to get himself down two hundred G's to the mob. Betting on the horses hadn't helped. Each bet he'd made had been a sure thing. But one after another turned sour and instead of erasing his debt, added on to it. And hadn't he been assured each time that the fix was in, that he couldn't lose? Never trust a bookie.

But then miracle of miracles, along comes this guy

Mick and buys up his entire debt - the whole bloody thing. After that, all Harry had to do was meet with him occasionally; maybe do a couple jobs for him, nothing so difficult. Even the transfer to the Richmond District that Mick wanted him to make hadn't been so hard. It wasn't like people were lining up to come here, and that move alone knocked fifty grand off his debt - just like that. But that little surprise had pretty much put the kibosh on his marriage once and for all. His old lady wouldn't budge, even for the extra money. She'd had it. But he'd gone ahead and made the move anyway.

Now he was on his way to pick up payment for his last job. They had arranged a dead drop on Geary Street; a mailbox attached to the door of a walkup. Mick was a busy man; he couldn't meet personally with everyone who owed him money, could he? And Harrar was just as happy not to meet with him; the meeting places were always dark and grim, the man's breath was incredibly foul and his voice, though never loud, was totally intimidating. Besides, Harry couldn't be seen meeting with guys like that too often, being a cop and all. If the captain knew he was so deeply in debt there'd probably be an investigation. The dead drop idea worked just fine for Harrar.

He'd left a note there yesterday saying the job was done, that the girl's name had been removed from the list O'Bannon was compiling and the lieutenant was none the wiser. Clean as a whistle. So what if it was easy? Mick didn't need to know that; for all he knew it had been real risky. Maybe he'd even knock a couple of grand off the debt for that one. Harry was excited to find out. He turned the corner and walked along Geary Street to the third door. Sure enough, the flag was up on the mailbox. Harry reached in and removed the slip of paper he found inside. He unfolded it and stared at it. There was nothing written on it about money: no debt reduction, no words of praise - just two words scrawled across the paper: "*Kill Her*".

"Special Agent in charge Luke Forrester. How can I help you?"

"Hello. My name is Jim Snyder. I work for the Chronicle in San Francisco."

"And how may I be of service to the press this morning?" Luke's voice remained calm but his mind raced. He knew immediately it wasn't simply coincidence that a reporter was calling from the same distant city where Zack was involved in an investigation. Luke knew that Zack believed that these murders, first those in Los Angeles a year ago and now in San Francisco, were all related somehow, and something was driving Zack to see the investigation through to the end. He needed it settled one way or the other. Luke allowed Zack to go on both occasions but each time he worried that he would live to regret that decision. He worried that Zack might be slowly derailing, that he was no longer making sound choices in his single-minded pursuit of this mystic super killer, an entity that Luke, quite frankly, was not convinced even existed. Zack was a good agent - one of the best - and Luke had tremendous faith in him, but this time...

"I'm doing some back story on a series of murders here in the city. You're aware of the situation?"

"A series of murders? Have you substantiated that they are connected?"

"To my satisfaction, yes. And more important, to the satisfaction of your people up here."

Luke spoke very carefully. "First, I have no people up there in any official capacity. One of my agents requested leave to pursue a matter of personal interest. You used the plural. I have no other agents there."

There was quiet laughter. "No, that's true. The other person is not from the FBI. He's from the Reservation."

"Eagle Feather."

"Yes."

Luke sighed. "I have no official relationship with Eagle Feather. He goes where he wants."

Snyder laughed again. "Yes, he does. But the important thing here is that both Zack Tolliver, whom I've yet to have the pleasure of meeting, and Eagle Feather both believe beyond a doubt that the several murders here were committed by the same individual. Further, Eagle Feather has indicated to me that their interest was sparked by a similar series of murders in Los Angeles, and before that, right there in your district. Can you confirm that?"

"I will not confirm the musings of every private citizen, and I'll say this, emphatically: I am not aware of any serial murders that are connected in any way to past murders in my district - period. As I am sure you are aware, we did have a series of child murders here some years ago which eventually led us to the Palm Springs area of California. There were two perpetrators in that case, one who died here on the Reservation and another who was killed by an FBI task force in Palm Springs. That case is closed. There were no loose ends. If you suspect some connection to that case from this current one, you are mistaken. Of course, the Navajo people have their own myths and beliefs, but don't confuse those with real FBI investigations."

"Please let me be clear," Snyder said. "I'm not asking if they are connected; I am inquiring about the similarities."

"You'll need to be more specific."

"Were the victims in your child murders killed by a large bite-like wound to the throat?"

"No."

"Hmmm." With Luke's response the steam went out of Snyder's inquiry. "Well, thank you for your time. I appreciate your candid responses."

After the call, Luke sat musing for a few minutes. Then he picked up his phone and called Zack's cell. It rang for a while and his recorded message came on. Luke left his number. After another moment, he called Libby.

"Luke?" Libby sounded surprised. "Are you looking for Zack?"

"Well, yes...and no. I tried his cell a moment ago but couldn't reach him. I thought maybe you were in touch with him."

Libby laughed. "I'm not sure I'll have any more success than you in that regard. Zack calls when he remembers, but he gets involved and forgets to call for days at a time."

"Well, I'm sorry to trouble you," Luke said. "I just had a call from a reporter up there working for the San Francisco Chronicle, and I'm a little concerned that Zack may not realize how much he is stirring things up."

“Oh...”

“Nothing to worry about, we both know that Zack is sensible and won’t leap to any conclusions, but I want to get his sense of things. I wouldn’t bother you if we weren’t friends. But if he calls you, would you see that he gets in touch with me right away?”

“Oh, yes, of course, Luke.”

“Thanks, Libby. Louisa’s been asking after you. Let’s get together soon.”

Libby stared at her phone for several long moments after the call concluded. Zack was clinging to his suspicions like a Pit Bull, as usual. Libby didn’t share the optimistic view that Zack’s dogged pursuit of this killer wouldn’t over-ride his good sense. Ever since his confession that his trip to LA with Eagle Feather had not been just to see a ball game, she had become more concerned about his obsession.

Let’s face it, Libby thought. She wanted Zack to give it all up and come home more than just about anything. She wanted all those suspicions swept out of his mind. She wanted him here, relaxed and happy, so that she could tell him her secret. Sure, she could force the issue and try to lever him into coming home but she knew it wouldn’t work. The only thing to do was wait for him to decide on his own that it was time to give it up. Maybe Luke would help with that.

Libby called Zack’s cell and when his recording came on she left Luke’s message.

Jim Snyder was taken aback. He had been sure he would

find that the victims in the Arizona case had suffered similar injuries. Why else would Eagle Feather seem so certain of a connection? Snyder had called Agent Forrester hoping to gain a sense of this whole business, to see these murders through Eagle Feather's eyes from the very beginning. He wanted to know what had gone on there, what had made such an impression on him and the FBI agent that they had chased murder cases from LA all the way to San Francisco, even after the original case was solved. What was Forrester not saying? Was there something he didn't know? Could it be that Tolliver and Eagle Feather had kept something from Forrester?

Snyder remembered what Forrester had said about the Navajo having their own myths and beliefs. What did he mean by that? Had something happened, maybe something mystical that he had dismissed out of hand?

Or maybe I'm just trying to read between the lines where nothing is written, Snyder thought, chastising himself. But a lifetime of reporting compelled him to be thorough. He did a quick Google search and dialed a number.

"Navajo Nation Police, Lieutenant Jim Chaparral speaking. How may I help you?"

Snyder's discussion with the Navajo Police Lieutenant was brief and discouraging. As soon as the man learned that Snyder was a reporter he clammed up, telling him the case was a matter of public record, that the newspapers had all the facts of the matter...and good day.

Funny. Snyder had gone deep into the Chronicle archives but found no mention of the case. It must only have received local coverage. That was surprising, given the nature of it. Of course, the FBI is always secretive and usually releases only the most necessary information. And the Navajo Nation Police tended to keep to themselves as well. Usually no one knew or cared what was happening on the reservation.

Snyder checked a list of the Chronicle affiliates in western Arizona. He found a paper in Flagstaff, Arizona, called the Arizona Daily Sun and went to its website. He found the archive section and began to search it. This time he found an article.

"The tiny reservation town of Elk Springs was in an uproar last night when combined forces from the FBI and the Navajo Nation Police surrounded a local resident's home. A shoot-out ensued and two men, the suspect and a reporter for a local television news team, were killed. An FBI agent was wounded. According to sources, this was the culmination of an investigation into the murder of a child found dead in a remote area of the reservation. The local population was much relieved to learn that the suspect, John Roundtree, had died in his home. Few details were made available but this reporter has learned that some local residents feared that he was a 'Skinwalker', a mythical being reputed to have witch-like powers. When questioned, the FBI Agent in charge, Ben Brewster, dismissed those concerns as 'culturally based superstition' but was pleased that the investigation had concluded successfully, despite..."

No wonder the FBI put a lid on this case. A Skinwalker? A mystical creature with strange powers? And Eagle Feather? He would naturally be inclined to take this seriously, given his cultural background. But what about Zack Tolliver? Was he some kind of rogue agent? Did he give credence to this? Or was there more to it?

Snyder realized that his research raised more questions than it answered. He thought about the killings here in San Francisco, their clockwork regularity, the strange wounds, the terrifying howls. Then he remembered his discomfort working alone at his desk the other night and the strong instinct that told him not to go home alone but to seek safety in numbers. He felt a chill. Then he laughed at himself. Look at me, a seasoned reporter. If this bothers me, no wonder the reservation was in an uproar.

But the next moment he was on Google, searching with the key words ethnology, ethnography, mythological studies, Navajo, and cultural history. Then he picked up his phone and dialed a number at the University of California, San Berkely.

EIGHTEEN

Once again they had taken his hunting grounds away from him as they and their kind had always done. He knew now they would force him to leave San Francisco, just as they had forced him to leave Los Angeles. But not right away. First, he would have his way. First, he would hunt in the primeval forests of his deepest memories one more time; it was his birthright. And he would have his revenge…

Zack stood in front of the obelisk and read the inscription, "*Sydney G. Walton Square*". Immediately below it was a sign that read "*No skateboards, roller skates, roller blades, motorcycles, bicycles, alcohol or pets allowed in the park*". This isn't a park, Zack thought; this is a corridor for business people to pass from one building to another. He glanced around at all the light fixtures; the place must light up like a billboard at night.

Zack shook his head. This did not feel like the stalking ground of a primitive predator. It was too open, too well illuminated, too small. But this was the only park south of Alcatraz along the circle he had drawn on the map, the only green grass and trees. Next came Buena Vista Park and that closed the circle. But he had killed there already. Zack didn't think he would repeat himself, for that was his pattern so far in San Francisco and it had been his pattern in Los Angeles. Would he move from his pattern, perhaps with the purpose of concealing the kill, as he had done at Twin Peaks? Maybe. But the other more immediate question was, where was his last kill, the kill of May 16, now three days past?

Zack thought about the murder victim at Buena Vista Park. She had been abducted miles away in the Mission and then transported a long way to fit into the circle. That couldn't be a coincidence. If the killer simply needed a park for his kill, he could have enticed her over to Mission Dolores Park, which was practically next door to where the girl lived. No. Clearly he wanted her within the circle. Had he also abducted the ultra-runner and brought him into the circle somehow? If so, it certainly wasn't here in Sydney G. Walton Park. Zack pulled out his marked map and looked again. He saw no other possibility except Alcatraz, unless...

Maybe he was being too literal. Maybe the circle was not as perfect as the placement of the first three kills suggested. Maybe the killer was constructing a less perfect circle, one intended to include Twin Peaks, for instance. A circle that vague might include many additional areas, maybe even Crissy Park. Zack felt discouragement sweep over him in a wave. Widening the circle meant going back to police files and news reports for the night of May 16 to investigate every conceivable possibility. Maybe this ultra runner, this Olson guy, had nothing to do with it at all; maybe he was at home right now soaking his feet.

Zack's iPhone sounded.

"We found the girl." It was O'Bannon.

"What g...Oh, the girl with Olson!"

"That's right."

"Are you with her now? Can I talk to her?"

"Yes...uh, no. She's dead."

Zack felt the air go out of him like a flat tire. "Where did you find her?"

"We're in the Tenderloin. Seems she had an apartment here. We're about to go there and take a look. Wanna join us?"

Zack hailed a cab. He found O'Bannon at the corner of Hyde and Geary. He was easy to find; police and emergency vehicles were everywhere with lights flashing. Zack identified himself to the cop guarding the scene. The man glanced at his ID and lifted the tape to let him in. He found O'Bannon standing with a group of Tenderloin District cops. O'Bannon waved him over.

"She was right here, slumped up against the building. The boys took her away already."

"Was her throat...?"

"Naw. Bullet hole, close up, execution style, neatly placed in her temple."

"Professional?"

"Yeah, looks like it. We recovered the bullet out of that brick wall behind her. We won't know for sure until the lab does their test, but it looks to me like a 40 caliber."

"Your handgun is 40 caliber."

"Yes, it is. It's a Smith & Wesson SIG-Sauer P226 pistol; standard issue for all San Francisco cops. But I didn't shoot her - at least I don't remember doing it."

Zack grinned at him. "I won't tell anybody. Was there anything else?"

O'Bannon thought a minute. "No, not much. She was dressed up like for a date, a well paid date: slinky, revealing. Had a wrap. I'd guess it must have happened around two or three in the morning."

"Was the pistol suppressed?"

"Seems like it, although at that hour you could set off fireworks here and nobody would even look out their window."

"What makes you so sure it was our girl from the Adagio Lounge?"

"Description fits, attractive but old before her time, had a drug habit. Dark hair. And we recovered her wallet and driver's license - the number fits. So..."

Zack slowly nodded his head. It had to be her. "You said you have an address?"

O'Bannon led Zack to a patrol car and they drove a short distance down Hyde and around the block to Leavenworth. They parked part way up the block toward Geary and walked up the street. O'Bannon stopped at a locked iron gate.

"There we are, 550 Leavenworth, Apartment A. Not bad digs for a hooker: lots of space, a couple of sweet bay windows onto the street. Wish I could afford something like this."

O'Bannon rang the bell. After a short while the intercom crackled to life and an old woman's voice asked their business. O'Bannon identified himself. A long while later a grey-haired lady leaning heavily on a cane shuffled up to slide back the gate.

"We need to see Apartment A, belonging to a Megan McMitchell," O'Bannon said, showing his identification.

The woman led them slowly and painfully up narrow stairs, all the while making sure they understood that she ran a respectable house, that she checked every renter's background, that she evicted any tenant exhibiting the slightest criminal or disruptive behavior. When they reached the next level the landlady turned the key to an apartment and O'Bannon pushed past her. Zack followed closely. The place looked neat, feminine, cared for: a home. It didn't look like a professional girl's place of business. There were pictures on the walls, stuffed animals on the bed, knick-knacks on the bureau. O'Bannon began pulling open drawers while Zack walked about, trying to gather an impression. He looked in the closet. The clothes that were hung neatly inside weren't hooker's clothes, they were average everyday clothing: slacks, conservative dresses, sweaters. He looked at the pile of clothing growing on the floor near O'Bannon: cotton undies, shorts, T-shirts. No silks, no sheer bras, no low-cut blouses. Again, not the dress of a professional. It just didn't make sense.

"Our Megan doesn't seem in need of any cash," Zack commented.

"No." By now O'Bannon was tearing through the small writing desk. "And if she's in the business, she's not keeping a record of it."

"This place reflects order, pride even. There's a

book on the nightstand, an alarm clock set for...uh, seven AM. What girl in the escort business is able to read herself to sleep at night and get up with the birds?"

O'Bannon only grunted. He had a small computer open now and was pushing keys. "Can't get in. We'll take this to the lab."

A deep voice came from the doorway. "You're out of your district, aren't you, O'Bannon?"

Zack had his hand under the pillow of the neatly made bed. He felt something hard. His fingers closed around it and he slipped it quickly under his jacket while he looked up at the newcomer.

O'Bannon was rising from a crouch near the desk. "Oh, hey, Lester. We decided to come ahead of you and get started."

"Nice mess you've made of it. How'm I to know what's what?"

"Don't worry, I'll tell you all about it. Nothing there or there..." O'Bannon pointed first to the bureau and then to the desk. "This" - he held up the small computer notebook - "needs to be opened at the lab. She's got it protected."

Lester took it from O'Bannon's hand.

"Let me know what you find," O'Bannon went on. "You all set, Zack? I think we can go now."

Zack nodded and the two men shouldered past the policemen at the doorway. As they walked back to the car, O'Bannon pulled a piece of paper out of his pocket. "Bank cash withdrawal receipt," he said. "She's got a tidy sum here."

Zack reached under his jacket and removed the object his fingers had found under the pillow. He stopped in his tracks.

"A diary? You've got to be kidding." He opened the small book and flicked through pages. "It's a diary, all right, but of what, I don't know. It's very cryptic. Here's some numbers, there's a time: it's the only thing written on that page. Here's a name...Max, I think, and some more numbers. This is going to require some study."

"Let me see." O'Bannon flicked through the pages and then handed it back to Zack. "Why don't you take first crack at it, then give it back to me. I'll need to pass it on to Lester eventually along with some excuse for taking it away." He grinned. "But only after we've finished with it."

Zack dropped the small book into his pocket.

O'Bannon left Zack at the Bart station. Zack took the train to Union Square and walked from there to the Adagio. Once in his room he shrugged off his jacket and took Megan's book out of his pocket. Then he threw himself on the bed and began to work his way through the diary, page by page

"Anthropology Department, University of California Berkeley. How may I direct your call?" came a soft female voice.

"Hi, Sugar, would you please connect me to someone in Anthropology?"

"This is Dr. Susan Apgar, Department Chair speaking. Perhaps I can help you, *Honey Buns*?"

" Uh...right, that was rude. This is Jim Snyder from the San Francisco Chronicle. I didn't expect the department chair to answer the phone...but that's no excuse, is it?"

"The person who usually directs the calls is at lunch, as it happens. That's a nasty habit you have. However, apology accepted. How can I help?"

Snyder paused. "My problem is complex and difficult to talk about over the phone because it also requires a degree of show and tell. If I were to jump in my car, could you possibly meet with me sometime in the next twenty-four hours?"

"Mr. Snyder, I don't know you from Adam and I have a very busy schedule. What's this about?"

"Again, Dr. Apgar, it is not something I can discuss over the phone. But I can say that it is a life or death matter and that I am working in concert with the FBI."

There was a long sigh. "Well, okay. If you promise to bring better manners, I could manage it, I think. I have a Geoarchaeology class at eight this evening and an Archaeometry class at nine AM tomorrow morning. And I do try to sleep between ten PM and eight AM, like most people. Can you work around that?"

"I could be there today for a five o'clock meeting, if that suits you. But tell me, what are your specialties?" It had suddenly occurred to him to ask after hearing the classes she named.

"My areas of study are Settlement pattern studies,

Geoarchaeology, lithic production and technology, Archaeometry, mathematical methods, the emergence of complex society and economic systems, and alternative models of social and political systems with emphasis on the Maya and Mesoamerica in general."

There was a long silence at Snyder's end, then, "Oh, that will do fine...I think. Dr. Apgar, thank you for seeing me with so little notice. I think what I have to say will interest you."

When Snyder next glanced up at the huge round clock over the editor's office it said 4:00 PM. He slapped an ending on his sentence, grabbed his sweater and ran down the stairs to the parking garage. He presented himself in the foyer of the Department of Anthropology Berkeley at precisely five.

A few minutes later a blonde woman wearing owl-eyed glasses and a pencil stuck over her ear bustled in and said, "Hello, I'm Susan Apgar. You must be Jim Snyder...?"

"Yes, I am. Thank you again for seeing me on such short notice." Snyder was surprised by her youth and attractiveness, but resisted the temptation to comment on it.

They were soon seated in a comfortable office, surrounded by exotic statues, strange tools, and a wall covered with aerial photos, maps and graphs. Snyder didn't know how to begin so he simply blurted it out.

"I'm investigating a series of murders that seem to have been committed by a creature that can't possibly exist."

Dr. Apgar's blue eyes, magnified through her

glasses, widened slightly. "Do go on."

"The mortal wounds on each victim were to the neck. They appear to be bite marks caused by a set of teeth with very prominent incisors. We thought at first..."

"We?"

"I'm collaborating with an FBI associate, a private investigator who happens to be a Navajo Indian."

Susan Apgar's eyebrows rose at that.

"So at first we thought it was a wild animal of some sort. The manner of attack seemed to suggest a very large coyote but after a closer look and the assistance of some experts it appears more likely we are dealing with either a human with a very unusual murder weapon or a beast of some sort, a gorilla-like creature that shouldn't exist."

Dr. Apgar raised a hand. "May I ask some questions before you go any further?" At Snyder's nod she asked, "First, is this an active investigation by the police?"

"Yes, it is."

"And what have they concluded? Surely they aren't inclined to suspect some mythical beast?"

Snyder grinned. "No, true enough. They're plodding along, gathering evidence as they go. At this juncture, I don't believe they're seriously considering a connection between all the murders, even though the wounds are identical."

"And the private investigator?"

"Eagle Feather is more inclined to attribute them all to the same perpetrator. He'd been thinking of a wolf-like creature; he even found a track at one of the scenes. But he had a previous experience that he won't share which brought him to San Francisco in the first place, and he hasn't seemed surprised by what we've found."

"What about the FBI? You mentioned they were involved?"

Snyder shook his head. "I've not met the agent so it's hard to say. But he's working very closely with Eagle Feather and they seem to have shared the same prior experience."

"Hmmm. I see." Susan sat deep in thought. Finally she asked, "Have you any pictures of the victims?"

"I thought you'd never ask." Snyder opened his briefcase and brought out the pictures of the neck wounds and handed them over. She took them and studied them carefully, comparing one to the other. "Who else have you consulted about these wounds?"

"I first consulted Dr. Andrew Westfield, at Stanford." Susan nodded knowingly. "He sent me to Dr. Philip- "

"Philip Morgan at UC Davis." Susan finished for him.

"Yes, exactly."

"And he suggested me?"

"Uh, no, that was my idea. He didn't seem eager to take it any further."

"I can see why," Susan said dryly. She thought for another moment. "Let me give you an ethnological perspective, if I may. It comes from Mayan studies and involves native mythology. Now I'm not proposing any solutions here, simply offering background from the perspective of my area of study."

Snyder nodded. "That's exactly what I want."

NINETEEN

Susan Apgar rolled her chair back away from her desk, leaned back, and crossed her legs: quite shapely ones, Snyder couldn't help noticing.

"Every culture known to man has stories and legends about those things that they don't understand to try to explain them. But while it is generally accepted that all of these myths and legends are fictitious, sometimes there is an element of truth to them, usually the very element that caused the myths to come into being in the first place. For example, many cultures describe great floods in their oral histories, floods that wiped out entire countries. These legends and stories are not widely accepted, or at least, verification has been limited. But increasingly, scientists are finding evidence of universal catastrophic flooding at a particular period of time in history. We now understand that the melting of the great ice sheets that enveloped the northern latitudes of the earth during the glacial periods did not melt as gradually as we had supposed, but in fact gained momentum in many places causing flash floods and sea rise for which some populations would not have been prepared. Hence, the great flood mythology contains an element of truth. That being the case, why then are we so hasty to discredit the stories of some individuals - Noah comes to mind - whose actions in the face of these events were handed down similarly?"

"Go on."

"Okay. Now instead of great floods think about the legends of mysterious human-like creatures. Even today, we hear persistent stories about them from every culture; some part of our hindbrain clings to them."

Snyder laughed. "Point taken. But you're talking to the wrong guy. I'm a newspaperman: hard-boiled, facts only. And I'll discredit those stories if I can. In my view, such mythological creatures were all created to scare children into staying in bed at night."

It was Susan's turn to laugh now. "Precisely. Yet the stories persist. Grown men, men with reputations to protect, have mounted extensive expeditions to track down these mythological creatures. The myths are powerful."

"I know the myths are powerful. But again, they're only myths."

"But remember my opening argument." Susan spoke earnestly now. "Many of these myths - the existence of Atlantis, the white gods of the Mayans, even the star of Bethlehem - are gaining credence because of new scientific discoveries. And with each new bit of evidence that emerges we find we must adjust our thinking about that particular myth. To my mind, it is time to reconsider our views on the veracity of myths in general to avoid being hoisted on the petard of our own hubris."

"Again, point taken."

Susan smiled. "Thank you. Since you've awarded me that point, I'll build upon it. You have just acceded to the view that the stories of man-like creatures unknown to us should not be dismissed out of hand."

"I suppose..."

"If we accept that, we must accept that some element of fact probably exists within the myth somewhere, that these seemingly preternatural beings described in every culture may well have a basis in reality. Certainly the stories are very similar; most describe a larger-than-average human-like mammal, ape-like, fur covered, capable of some degree of reasoning, furtive, strong, usually vegetarian, afraid of or hostile to man. Yes?"

"Often seen by individuals with great imaginations or those seeking notoriety," Snyder retorted.

"Often, no doubt. But as with UFO's, some very steady down-to-earth professional people claim to have seen the same thing."

"Okay, Okay. But what does all of this have to do with the series of murders I've described? Surely you're not suggesting that they were all committed by Bigfoot?"

"What I am suggesting is that we should not dismiss out of hand the possibility that your killer could be a human predator evolved somewhat differently from most of us. I'm sure you've read of Jacko, the young human-like fur covered creature captured in British Columbia in 1884? And the story retold by Teddy Roosevelt from his life in the Badlands of North Dakota of the human-like creature that killed a man's partner, leaving four great fang marks in his throat?" Susan held up a restraining hand. "Now I'm not suggesting by any means that the police should completely change their methodology and begin looking for a large hairy creature around town, but I *am* suggesting that investigators should not automatically discount any possibility. This reasoning may constitute an apostasy of traditional police methodology but such a multifarious approach ensures that all evidence is given equal consideration and that nothing is overlooked." Susan powered a high wattage smile at Snyder. "So don't ignore evidence."

"Is that all you have for me?"

"That's just the prelude. It's to prepare you for the perspective I would bring to your investigation. But first things first; I need to know everything you've learned so far about these murders."

Snyder pulled out his notebook and began at the beginning.

Eagle Feather slowly digested the news that the woman he had been seeking, the mysterious Megan, was dead. That it was a silenced pistol that killed her surprised him. It raised two new possibilities: that all the murders were actually a part of a conspiracy or that her murder was a coincidence and had nothing whatever to do with the other murders. Neither possibility was particularly helpful.

But Eagle Feather's instincts told him that Megan was involved in some way with the string of murders and that she was also involved in the disappearance of the Olson man. Her murder effectively stopped that line of investigation, and could that really be a coincidence? It made no difference, though. There was nowhere to go with it now...unless...

Acting on a thought, Eagle Feather hailed a cab and directed the driver to the intersection of Hyde and Geary. Two patrol cars were still parked there when he arrived and yellow police tape was strung around an area of sidewalk. There were forensics people working near a chalk outline partly on the building wall and partly on the sidewalk, presumably the outline of Megan's body. Eagle Feather did not attempt to cross the police line but instead knelt and inspected the pavement outside the tape. He knew from long experience that most people tended to look without seeing and that investigators often saw the things they expected to find and did not see the things they did not expect. He worked his way slowly along the entire length of tape searching the surface of the sidewalk as well as the street and the gutter. The street and gutter were extraordinarily clean; apparently the street sweeper had been by before the crime was committed. At the corner he found it, the thing he was not looking for, the unexpected. Two fresh pink Dentine gum wrappers lay six inches apart in the gutter. Eagle Feather found a Ziploc bag in his pocket and used the stiff rim of the bag to nudge the wrappers into it. They might have DNA or fingerprints, but more important, they told a story, which was that the murderer had stood and waited for Megan at this street corner knowing that she would pass. Eagle Feather looked back at the chalk outline. It was several yards down Hyde Street, meaning that the murderer either followed her after she passed or - and this was the more intriguing possibility - had actually walked side by side with her to the murder site. If so, she must have accepted the murderer's presence. This scenario was supported by the fatal wound Zack had described over the phone, a single shot to the temple at close range. Not a head wound from behind.

Was it an unhappy John, maybe...or a friend or an acquaintance? Or possibly someone she felt safe with, like a priest or a cop? The chalk outline indicated a body position of a person who had simply collapsed against the building, not someone who had been running away.

Eagle Feather knew it was useless to look for a shell

casing. This had all the earmarks of a professional hit. Yet the gum wrappers indicated carelessness, or over-confidence: not the action of a highly trained, practiced assassin. So...where did that leave him?

Eagle Feather grunted. Could Megan have had a hit man as her client? No, that would be too coincidental, he answered himself. Not a John. But he was someone who knew firearms, someone who was able to acquire a silenced pistol, someone who appeared familiar or safe to her. Eagle Feather decided it must have been a cop.

Now it was time to try to retrace Megan's last route. The killer had been waiting for her to come along. Assuming she had come from her apartment and was traveling away from it she must have had a specific, routine destination that the killer anticipated.

Eagle Feather walked to Megan's residence at 550 Leavenworth and found a locked iron gate. That explained why the murder didn't occurred in her apartment. It also reinforced his thought that the killer wasn't someone she expected to visit her at home. Eagle Feather turned and retraced his steps up to Geary Street and down to the intersection with Hyde where she had been killed and scanned the pavement along the way. He paused at the intersection to look around, wondering where she might have been going.

There was nothing to see here. There was no store or facility that could have been open late last night. Then he saw the sign on a post just down Geary Street; a bus stop. She was on her way to the bus. Dressed for work. Of course! She had been professionally engaged and probably offered more money than she could turn down. All that the murderer had to do was wait for her to walk to the bus stop. Suppose he was a cop: he simply invents some reason to talk to her, maybe threatens to bust her, walks her out of sight a little ways down Hyde Street, and then "pop"!

So. He might be looking for a cop or a man dressed like a cop. Was it the big man the bartender had described from the lounge, that big guy? No way to know. But the next step was to try to backtrack Megan's life, to try to find where she had gone and what she had done in the days prior to her death. What had she done to get herself killed? Eagle Feather had no idea how to go about this but he was going to try.

After a quick glance Zack realized that the diary he had taken from beneath Megan's pillow was her little black book, the record of her clients and professional engagements. At the beginning of the journal, names and times marched regularly across the pages with an occasional dollar amount appearing in the margin. Many of the names were repeated or were re-entered as initials. But toward the back of the book he began to see fewer repeated names and on some pages entire days were left blank. He began to see entries written in a scrawl as if Megan were writing while drunk or high. It read like business was falling away. Then he came to a stretch of several blank pages in a row. Had she forgotten to make entries? Or was she incapacitated in some way?

But then came a change. The hand making the entries was now firm, confident, and instead of names of Johns and appointment times he read the light-hearted observations and girlish thoughts of a normal young woman's diary. He found only three appointment entries here - all with the name Max, a time, and a series of numbers too short to be a telephone number but not a dollar amount. No other appointments were entered. Had she been holding on to one special John, this fellow Max? And if he was so special, why didn't she write anything about him?

Zack flipped to the rear of the diary and looked for the name Max in the last entries but found no other mention of him. The final entry for Max came on May 16. That was five days ago. The last pages were about things she planned to purchase or to do. They were not inexpensive things, Zack noticed. Her work had apparently paid very well.

He put down the book and thought about what he'd read. Why the sudden change? The journal was a story of her downward spiral, of her gradual decay into alcohol or drugs or maybe both and then oblivion and then...what? She had re-established control somehow. She'd become strong and steady, and judging from her entries, had become optimistic and forward looking. What had caused this amazing turnabout? And who was this Max, this lone client? Had Max been around before this change?

Zack reached over and picked up the journal again. He skimmed the first pages looking for his name. No Max. No Max anywhere prior to her transformation - the only mention came after it in those infrequent, solitary appointment entries.

Zack sat up abruptly. He had a sudden thought. What if...? He took out his own small notebook and opened it. His eyes darted between it and the pages of Megan's journal. There - April 18, on the day of the Buena Vista Park murder. There was an entry for Max at 11 am followed by a set of numbers. He flipped forward in the journal and glanced at his notebook. There - another Max meeting on May 15. Zack swallowed, trying to contain his excitement. After all, it might well be a coincidence. But he didn't think so. What were the odds that Megan would have an appointment with this Max the day of the Buena Vista murder and again the morning of the very day that the ultra-runner disappeared, when she was seen in the lounge with him?

Who was this Max? Could he be the murderer? Or was he a go-between? Megan had written nothing more about him in her journal: no descriptions, no impressions, no meeting locations. It was as if she wanted to stop thinking about him as quickly as she could. Was it fear? And what were those numbers written after the appointment times? A code?

Zack sighed and put down the journal. He rolled over on his back on the bed and tried to put this discovery into some perspective. What did it tell him? What had he learned? One thing he knew for sure: Megan had begun working for someone else, maybe this Max. This person must have given Megan money - a lot of it. That would explain the changes he saw in her journal: her apparent new independence, her new lease on life. It might also explain the brevity of her Max notations. Was she into something she didn't want to think about, maybe a poor moral choice that she was ashamed of? Or was it caution, or fear?

Who was this Max? Was he the killer they sought? Or was he just another messenger? And why hadn't he met with Megan before any of the other murders? And those numbers...? Zack sighed and picked up the journal again. Let's see, the first set of numbers was...

After Snyder had finished, Dr. Susan Apgar sat silent for a very long time; so long in fact, that Snyder began to think her mind was elsewhere. He coughed. She looked up.

"I'm sorry, I'm digesting all of this. I see now why you came to me."

"I guess I had hoped- "

"That I would have a magic answer? Well, I don't. Yet...there are certain elements of this that...tell you what, let's try this: I'll teach you some ethnologically supported mythology to give you some background for my thoughts." Susan shifted to a more comfortable position in her chair. "I've already explained to you that most ancient cultures, regardless of location and differences actually have quite similar oral histories which include several consistent themes: a creation story, a great flood, god figures, and so on. One theme common to most but discussed less is a creature with the ability to transform in some way or other. Ethnologists believe this particular mythology results from the very human desire to escape difficult or tenuous situations by becoming someone or something else." Susan smiled. "I think we've all experienced this desire at one time or another. But regardless of the psychology of the origins, the stories persist. We've already talked about certain cultural beliefs that involve a man-like hair-covered creature. From what you've described, the perpetrator of these murders, whether man or beast or myth, is able to live among humans without fear of discovery. It follows, then, that he or she blends in with the population." Susan laughed. "That's not so difficult in San Francisco no matter what you look like. But I think we can both agree that a large hairy ape-like creature would be noticed, even there." Susan paused to gather her thoughts.

Snyder leaned forward in his seat. "Go on."

"So, let's visit some ancient cultures around the world. The topic is Therianthropy, the technical term for the metamorphosis of humans into other animals." Susan smiled at Snyder's expression. "Yes, we have a special term for it, as well as Lycanthropy, which is humans changing into werewolves, Cynanthropy if you change to weredogs, Ailuranthropy for changing into werecats and of course, Naguals and Skinwalkers. You've heard of Skinwalkers, I'm sure, from Native American mythology. Well, Naguals are the Mesoamerican version."

Susan took a breath. "Did you know that psychiatrists recognize a condition called clinical lycanthropy, generally associated with severe psychosis wherein the patient believes he or she is part animal? You can see that this subject is taken very seriously in some quarters."

Snyder interrupted her. "Are you saying you think that there could be some psychotic character in San Francisco who thinks he's a bear or something and goes out and preys on random people?"

"Well, that's certainly a possibility, but let me continue. North American indigenous cultural beliefs, as we've said, include bear ancestors and ursine shape shifters wherein the bears are able to shed their skins and take human form and even marry humans in that form and thus bear, excuse the pun, progeny with unusual capabilities, to say the least. Now the Chinese are oriented more toward dogs, with various Chinese legends of a supernatural dog or a dog-headed man. There's even a canine shape shifter that married an emperor's daughter and founded an entire race. As for the Turkic and Mongolian races, the animal of choice is the wolf. My particular area of study is the Mayan culture. They believed that certain humans could change form to become any animal they wished and then could manipulate the minds of other animals. They called this creature a Mestaclocan."

"Now I bring all this up because I culled from your story the following points:" -Susan ticked them off on her fingers- "you are dealing with a clever and stealthy being, one that is unusually strong. It has large extended incisors, it has the strength and ability to lift and hold its victims while administering a fatal bite, and finally - and this is most important - it has the ability to hide among the human population. Have I got it right?"

Snyder nodded.

"The big question is, do you suspect a human being who has these capabilities, or an animal of some sort, or something in between? And before you answer, I will point out to you that you are here, now, with me. That tells *me* something."

"It tells you that I'm at my wits end. I find myself going back and forth from suspecting an animal to suspecting a human. I've not seriously considered the in-between possibility you suggest."

Susan looked hard at Snyder. "Let me ask you this: you're a reporter, yes? Your job is to report, not to analyze. Yet it occurs to me that you are trying to solve this mystery. Why is that?"

Snyder looked away and thought about it. When he looked back at her he said, "I've been asking myself the same question. It began as a story about a murder that soon turned into serial killings. Then I began to notice other interested parties: the FBI agent and his Navajo associate from Arizona and the cop who appears to be abandoning all his other work to concentrate completely on this case. It was as if...it was almost like these guys were a team, that they had worked together before, like maybe they were even chasing this killer from city to city. They deny it, of course, but it seems sort of like a nuclear plant denying a radiation leak so the people won't panic. I did some background work. I checked some back newspaper articles. I found that this Agent Tolliver had headed an investigation on the Navajo Indian Reservation, a big case involving a pedophile. It was a serial murder thing. The local rag went on about some unusual circumstances, even mentioning Skinwalkers and strange animal tracks…whatever. I even called Tolliver's supervisor in Arizona. He denied there was anything unusual about the case. He claimed the native people were simply acting out their fears and superstitions.

And yes, I report the facts; I don't draw my own conclusions. I've already published a story on the San Francisco murders. It stirred up a few people. But no one has any answers. And since I seemed to be the only one with any kind of an angle on the thing, I, well..."

"You just kept going. I get it. But let's get down to brass tacks. How do you believe I can help you?"

"I'll be straight with you. I don't believe in mythology coming to life, I don't believe in creatures with extraordinary powers, men that can fly, caped crusaders with super strength - none of that. Nor do I believe in visitors from other planets, nor witches, nor goblins. But I know that others do believe in these things, at least to a degree, and particularly those with ancient cultures like the Navajo. I don't want to leave any stone unturned here."

"Again, what do you want me to do?"

"Well, you have a different perspective on these sorts of things from your studies. You're an academic with a historic perspective, if nothing else. If this is more than some psychotic getting his jollies, I want you in my corner. I guess I was hoping you'd be curious enough to look into it."

Susan smiled. "On my own time, with my own resources?"

"I could get the paper to offer a stipend of some sort, particularly if you were to co-author an article with me."

"Okay."

"Okay? Just like that?" Snyder's jaw dropped.

"Sure. Your story interests me. It falls along a line similar to my own body of work. I might be of some help. But I'll need as much detail as you can give me. And I'll need to visit each of the murder sites. Let's see" -she looked at her watch- "I have a master class at one that I can't miss. Where can I meet you at, say, two thirty?"

TWENTY

At two-thirty precisely Snyder looked up and saw Susan Apgar walking toward him in the Department reception area. She carried a duffle bag in one hand and a jacket slung over her arm. She grinned at Snyder.

"I'm ready. Let's go."

"You're coming right now?"

"Isn't that what you wanted?"

"But your classes, your responsibilities..."

"All handled. I've got some time coming. Let's go."

Snyder led the way. He opened the passenger door of his battered VW Golf and threw the files and old newspapers into the back seat. He gave the seat a symbolic swipe and stood back for Susan to enter the car. Back behind the wheel, he found his way to Route 80 and headed west. He looked at Susan.

"You got a place to stay in San Francisco?"

"I'll stay with you."

Snyder almost choked. "With me?"

"I don't take up much room. Don't worry. You're not married, are you?" She glanced at his ring finger where his hand rested on the wheel.

"Uh, no."

"Good. Then I don't see a problem, do you?"

Snyder chuckled. "I guess not."

They drove on in silence. When they entered the outskirts of Oakland, Snyder glanced at Susan. "Where to first? Drop your things at my place?"

"I'd like to get right at it, if it's all the same to you. Can we visit the murder sites?"

Snyder glanced at his watch. "Sure. I'll check in at the Chronicle first to arrange your stipend. Then we'll head over to Golden Gate Park, where the first murder occurred. We can take the sites in chronological order. We'll see what we can accomplish before it gets too dark.

Libby's conversation with Luke Forrester festered in her mind. She shared Luke's barely disguised concern that Zack was fixated on the San Francisco killer to the detriment of his duties here in Arizona. She tried several times to reach Zack but each call went to his voice mail. She had left a message after her first call but resisted leaving any more after that, not wanting Zack to feel pressured or nagged - at least not by her. But she was worried. Zack usually got back to her as soon as he could because she so seldom called him when he was on a case. This lack of response was unusual. She listened to his phone ring on and on and felt her anxiety rise. This investigation was consuming Zack like a cancer. She knew that worry and fear were the price of a relationship with a man in law enforcement, but the best possible outcome for everyone right now was for Zack to come home - and soon. Zack was a practical man. He was a responsible, thoughtful man, slow to judgment, almost pedantic in his work. But he was stubborn - bulldog stubborn. He had sunk his teeth into this case and now it was in him. He would never give it up on his own.

Zack smacked himself on the forehead. So simple! Why hadn't he seen it sooner? The numbers weren't a code at all but a kind of shorthand for an address. This number, for instance, next to her first Max entry: 92800. It looked like an area code, but that didn't make sense.

Zack spread his city map out on the bed and stared at it. So assume that Megan was a hooker working the Tenderloin District. Professional girls are territorial, or if not, their pimps certainly are. Meaning that the girls stick relatively close to home so not to risk trespassing on another girl's territory: bad things happened if you were caught doing that. So, if Megan's territory was the Tenderloin District, what if she assigned numbers to the streets in her territory instead of names? For quick reference, possibly, or to keep her assignations secret? If she recognized Market Street as the southern boundary to her territory and Van Ness as her boundary to the west and then if you number each street sequentially...

Zack scratched his head. That only accounted for two digits. But what if the remaining numbers were street addresses? That might work. He looked again at the number next to the first Max entry, 92800, and counted streets south to north from Market Street beginning east of Van Ness. The 9th street was...O'Farrell. Okay. And west to east...? He checked the number again. She must mean two, not twenty-eight:

that would take him out of the Tenderloin. So the second street was...Larkin. Then the house number must be eight hundred. On Larkin or O'Farrell? Well, that should be easy enough to figure out.

Zack sprang up from the bed and grabbed his room key. It was time to take a walk. As he left the hotel he pulled his phone out to call Eagle Feather. To his surprise, he found that his cell phone was off. When had he done that? He turned it back on and saw a score of messages, among them one from Luke Forrester and several from Libby. Zack made a mental note to call Libby as soon as he had the chance and placed a call to Eagle Feather.

Eagle Feather was walking along Geary Street pondering his next move when a call came from Zack asking to meet him at 1081 Post Street. Zack explained briefly about the journal and his idea about the series of numbers that followed the name "Max". Eagle Feather suddenly realized that the problem of how to backtrack Megan through her last days might just been solved for him. He immediately turned and headed north to Post Street, just a block away. He turned west and a few doors before the next street intersection he saw number 1081 on a gold plaque. It was just under the name *Divas* written in simple block letters above a blue and grey paneled storefront. Another sign announced *Karaoke Tonight.*

So. *Divas Nightclub and Bar.* Zack hadn't explained what the address had to do with Megan but this certainly looked interesting. He walked in and found himself in a large room with a very long bar. Several men - business types, older - clustered at the far end. The muffled bass thump of a jukebox throbbed somewhere above his head; apparently there was another floor. A large woman with huge arms and a white bow tie eyed him from behind the bar. Eagle Feather found a stool and sat to wait for Zack. The barkeep came over.

"Hey there, Sweetie, are yuh plannin' tuh tickle me with your feather?" A whiskey baritone laugh accompanied the question.

"Only if you'll pour me a beer - and not one of those near-beers you white folks like so much."

"One IPA coming right up for the Indian. Are yuh here lookin' for a brave, or a squaw? Or mehbe something in between?"

"If you must know, I'm looking for one brave and waiting for another."

"Ah ha! Well if yuh decide yuh want a squaw, just let me know. Ah've started a tab for yuh, honey, so take your time." She laughed again and made her oleaginous way back down the bar toward the group of older men.

Eagle Feather swung the stool around to scan the room. It was semi-dark like most bars but glittery; faux windows were ornamented with colored glass, the ceiling was painted with bright colors and images, and glittering reflective globes hung from the ceiling. The room wasn't very crowded this early but as his eyes adjusted he saw that there were people seated at tables in dark corners that he hadn't noticed before. He imagined what the place must be like at night when it would be overflowing with patrons. A person could disappear in the crowd here, he thought... or lose his wallet.

Light glared in from the doorway, a shadow blocked it, and Zack entered. He stood for a moment letting his eyes adjust. When he saw Eagle Feather he grinned. The androgynous barkeep was back and hovering by the time Zack reached the bar.

"What would your mighty warrior friend like to drink?"

"Whisky, neat, please."

"Put it on my tab," Eagle Feather said.

"Which is coming out of my wallet anyway," Zack observed.

The two friends walked their drinks over to a table in the corner.

"It's been a while," Zack said.

"It has. We've each been busy following our own threads, I guess."

"I think we'll have to work together from here on in," Zack said. "The Megan angle is all we've got, really, and it's going to need both of us."

"Fill me in."

Zack took a sip of his whiskey. "You first."

"As you wish. I visited the murder scene; Megan's, I mean, and read the signs, walked to her place and then back again. I figure she got a call last night or early this morning, maybe. Must have been a client."

"A pretty special one," Zack added. "We haven't liberated her bank account yet, but her room and her journal suggest she had all the money she needed. Yet she went out very late last night in full professional regalia anyway."

Eagle Feather's eyes had been roaming the room and now they came back to Zack. "Interesting." He sipped his drink. "So she's walking down Geary toward the bus stop; I guess whoever hired her was too far away for her to walk there. The local buses through there run every seven or eight minutes after midnight. But she was headed toward the Van Ness stop, not the Powell stop. Since her place is more or less equidistant from both, I think we can assume she was heading out of the district."

Now Zack's eyebrows came up. "Impressive."

"It's in the blood, white man. But that's not all. There were signs that someone was waiting a block away down Geary, someone who knew that she would be along and even knew which bus stop she would head for. It had to be someone she trusted; she went out of her way with that person, down a side street. She never tried to run or even turn away, judging from the angle of her body. She just stood there and was shot."

"Who would she trust like that at two AM? A friend? A fellow professional?"

"I figure a cop," Eagle Feather said.

Zack's eyebrows came up again. "That would fill in a few blanks, alright."

Eagle Feather nodded. "Okay, your turn," he said.

"I spent the last couple of hours reading through Megan's journal. When she started it, she was working long hours professionally and taking drugs or maybe drinking heavily. She was on a pretty serious downward spiral. Then, suddenly, everything changed. Her client appointments stopped abruptly, except for three appointments with some guy named Max. Her attitude turned rosy. It's clear from her entries that she came into money. She moved to her current apartment, the drugs stopped or at least slowed down, and she began thinking girlish thoughts. Quite the transformation."

"And you think-"

"I think this guy Max gave her a whole lot of money, enough to allow her to live comfortably."

"Why?"

"To do work for him, is my guess."

"Doing what?"

"Well, that's the question. And that's the crux of the mystery. She put down dates, his name, and then a series of numbers. The numbers stumped me for a while."

"Telephone numbers? Bank accounts?"

Zack grinned. "Those were my first thoughts, too. But that wasn't it. Then I thought, what would Megan actually need to remember? The Max entries were very brief, like she worried about leaving a tangible record. So she put down only what was necessary. She had the date, which was on the journal page, his name, and the time. So what else did she need?"

"The where."

"Exactly. Looking at it from her point of view, she simply needed the street and the building number. So why didn't she just write an address? Maybe she wanted to keep the entry brief, or maybe this guy Max cautioned her not to write it down. Whatever, I guessed that her frame of reference must be the Tenderloin District, where she worked. With that in mind, I worked out that the first number must be the street counting from east to west and the second number the cross street from south to north. Then the remaining numbers had to be the street address. So...here we are."

"Not too shabby, white man. Not too shabby. So here we are, indeed." Eagle Feather grinned. "But where are we?"

"I'd say one of the places where she met with Max. Now we need to take another walk. I deciphered the three location entries from Megan's journal. We're sitting in the second one, the place they met just before the Buena Vista murder. We need to go find the other two. After that, we can try to find some connection between these particular choices."

Eagle Feather looked around the bar. "Have you got any clues from this place?"

"I've got some thoughts, but I'll need to see the other two and compare them first."

"So...where to next?"

Zack checked his small notebook. "Let's try the very first entry, back on April ninth. That's the morning of the night of the Golden Gate Park murder. The location number for that entry is 92800. According to the code, that's the ninth street north, O'Farrell, and the second street east, or Larkin. The number is 800. Finished with your drink?"

Eagle Feather paid the tab and the two friends went back out into the bright sunshine and headed east toward Larkin Street. They found a grey painted building at 800 Larkin. The *O'Farrell Street Bar* was discreet compared to *Divas*. If not for a small sign on the corner light post that said 800 Larkin and the single word '*cocktails*' they would not have known it was a bar at all. It seemed to be a strictly local drinking hole: quite content with its regulars and not eager to advertise to outsiders.

Inside, the message expressed by the understated exterior was repeated. The room was stark and completely lacking in personality. A jukebox stood by itself on the bare floor, like a lone tree in a large meadow. A fish tank claimed space near one of the walls and a long bar ran along the other. They heard the clack of pool balls through a door to the rear. The bar was completely empty except for the barkeep and one lonely patron.

"This is the first place they met, according to the journal," Zack said, looking around.

Eagle Feather took in the large empty room. "What time was that appointment? It's four PM now and the place is totally empty. They'd have been pretty obvious."

Zack checked his notebook. "Says here eight PM. It must get a lot more crowded by then."

Their voices seemed to echo in the large cave of a room. Zack led Eagle Feather back out into the street.

"Nothing more to see there," he said. "Let's visit the last place." He checked his notebook again. "This is the one where they met the day before the Olson guy went missing. It's... hmmm...six streets up, to Turk Street, and six streets across, to Taylor. Ready for a walk?"

Again the two men walked east. After a couple of blocks Eagle Feather looked at the street sign. "Well, look where we are."

"Leavenworth," Zack said. "The home street of our Megan."

"All of these locations are snuggled together," Eagle Feather observed. "Maybe by design? Waddaya bet this Max guy picked out Megan's apartment for her just to keep her handy."

"I didn't think of that." Zack said, nodding approvingly. "I'll bet you're right. Do you think that might mean he's nearby?"

Eagle Feather shrugged. "Maybe. But he seems to be more careful than that. He'll want a few degrees of separation."

They turned the corner at the next block and headed south. After several more blocks they turned east on Turk street and found number 133 several doors down and directly across from the Rescue Mission. They stood in front of a nondescript grey building with a hunter green door. A white sign hanging above it announced *Aunt Charlie's Lounge* in bright red script.

"Our Max likes high class neighborhoods," Eagle Feather remarked dryly.

"There's the Youth Hostel just down a few doors," Zack laughed. "Might be an eye opener for some of them."

It was dark inside, so dark that they had to stand for several moments waiting for their eyes to adjust. The garish glow of red neon hindered the return of their vision but the rows of round black tables and black cushioned stools slowly took shape. Now they could see the owners of the voices they had been hearing seated at tables facing a center aisle, arranged for viewing floorshows. On their left was a large sign with *Aunt Charlie's* glowing in neon lighting. Its bright red glow reflected off a phalanx of banners hanging from the ceiling. The bar beneath was dark as pitch with a mirror that made it difficult to distinguish the real bar from its reflection. The more their eyes grew accustomed to the dark the more there was to see; everywhere they looked was the garish glare of glitz and color. It overwhelmed the senses.

"Max could walk in here and disappear completely," Eagle Feather remarked.

Zack chuckled. "And it's only just after four. Yet it's hard to see how the place could get any busier."

"Even with all these people you can carry on a normal conversation. Sound just seems to die here."

"That would make this a great place to meet," Zack agreed. The darkness would hide you and no one would hear you." He turned back to the door. Out on the street, the friends took stock.

"What have we learned?" Zack asked and answered his own question. "Not a lot."

"We know that this Max seems to know the neighborhood."

"Which tells us either he has lived here long enough to learn it, or has had enough time to explore it - or maybe both."

"Or maybe it was Megan who suggested the meeting places?"

Zack nodded. "That's possible, but none of these three bars seems a particularly good place to ply her trade. So why these?"

"Eagle Feather nodded in agreement. "They meet in a plain bar the first time, and the next two meetings are in gay and tranny bars. Does that tell us anything?"

"I can't think what."

"Maybe we're over-thinking this. Maybe these places are simply convenient and crowded enough to allow privacy."

"You're probably right. So what's next?"

"You tell me, white man."

Zack thought about it. "Maybe there's an angle we can explore from another perspective. Assuming Max is the man we're after, or even if he's just a go-between, how did he find Megan? Suppose you are Max and you're in San Francisco and you need a messenger, someone to run errands for you, someone you can buy, someone who values your money enough to do what you want without question. So you look for someone down in his or her luck, maybe someone who works a shade outside the law. So you think, aha! How about a prostitute? They're used to taking orders from pimps for money, they know not to ask too many questions, and they're close to the streets. So you look for a prostitute, preferably one who has fallen onto tough times. So where do you find her?"

"Yellow pages?" Eagle Feather offered sarcastically.

"Exactly what I mean. There's no place to go for that, no directory. So what do you do? You'd have to ask around, right? You'd need to talk to pimps or other working girls."

"So we need to start asking working girls and pimps."

"I think so. That's what he must have done. He must've talked to some girls, maybe some girls who worked with her around here. I think it's time for us to hire some prostitutes."

TWENTY-ONE

Lieutenant Martin O'Bannon leaned back in his chair, causing its ancient springs to complain, and said, "Crap!"

Harry Harrar looked up from his computer. "Got a problem?"

"Where do I begin?" O'Bannon moaned. "It was bad enough to have to solve four murders at the same time but now I've got another one, an execution - I don't know what else to call it - of some girl who might have a connection in some bizarre way to the other murders. And I don't know how, or why, or even for sure *if* there's a connection. And of course the Mayor is barking up my backside."

"I found all those dark haired girls for you, if that helps. I sent the folder to you; it should be on your desk top."

"Thanks, Harry, and I really mean that. But it seems the dark haired girl we were looking for is the one in the morgue right now."

Harry looked crestfallen. "All that work." Then he grinned. "Oh, well. Carry on. Have you got anything else for me?"

"You're a peach, Harry, you really are. I take back all those things I was thinking about you." O'Bannon laughed. "So yeah, I could use some help. I need to find this girl's assassin. Forensics tells me the gun was a Smith & Wesson SIG-Sauer P226. We're all pretty familiar with that one, since they're issued to cops. Let's check our lists of hired guns and see who's in town and who fancies that weapon. A former cop, likely as not."

"I'm on it," Harrar said and began clicking away with his mouse.

O'Bannon picked up his phone and dialed the forensics lab. "What can you tell me about my deceased?" he asked. He listened for a few minutes, then said dryly, "Thanks" and hung up. Annoyed, he muttered, "Like I didn't already know she was a hooker, had a hard life, took drugs, yada-yada."

Harry peered over his computer. "Learn anything?"

"Nothing I didn't already know. Except maybe the fact that she was well fed and fairly healthy at the time she died, kinda unusual considering her life-style."

"Must've had a nice list of Johns."

O'Bannon shot a quick look over his shoulder at him. "Did I tell you she was a hooker?"

Harrar's eyebrows flickered momentarily. He said, "Seemed a reasonable assumption, that part of town."

O'Bannon stared for a second and turned back to his desk. "Yeah, I suppose," he said.

Harrar looked at his computer screen. "Interpol thinks three guys are in town who fit our description. One is a former cop, but he favors the Ruger Mark I .22LR autoloader with a built in suppressor. The other two have reputedly used the Sig-Sauer but not in clandestine shoots. They're not guns that are customarily suppressed."

"Well, it's a start," O'Bannon said. "How about you see if you can locate those guys and I'll have a chat with 'em."

Susan stood in the center of Jim Snyder's apartment and looked around and smiled to herself. It was pretty much what she'd expected from a bachelor newspaperman; stuff scattered everywhere, books piled up, a MacBook open on the desk with old newspaper clippings littered across it. Right now he was pulling several layers of sports coats and sweaters off a smelly overstuffed couch, its faded design obliterated here and there by coffee stains. Funny how life is so unpredictable, she thought. A year ago, she would never have imagined she'd be bunking in with some guy she just met as casually as going out for coffee. But a year ago, she had a husband to go home to.

Snyder looked up and saw her watching him. "I told you it wasn't the Ritz."

Susan laughed. "I knew pretty much what to expect. I'll be just fine here."

Snyder went to a narrow closet and pulled down a pile of bedding from a high shelf. "I think there's a pillow in there somewhere. And here's a comforter. It's been chilly at night lately."

"Thanks. I think I have everything I need."

Already Susan's thoughts were going back to the

crime scenes they had just visited. They never did get to the Twin Peaks crime scene; darkness came just as they were leaving the third murder site at the Presidio. She'd asked Jim to take her to each in chronological order, thinking that might help her to understand the mind of the killer.

Snyder clumsily attempted to stretch a bottom sheet over the couch pillows but the sheet was much too large for the cushions.

"Leave that be, Jim. I'll take care of it. Let's talk for a moment about those crime scenes."

Snyder looked relieved. "What are your impressions?"

Susan sat down on the crumpled sheet on the couch. "I've not got much just yet, but I did notice a couple of things."

"Go on."

"The trees, for one thing. In each of those three locations there are old forest trees, real old growth."

"No surprise. The killer could conceal himself among them."

"I think it may be more than that," Susan said. There was no hint of a smile now. "It might not be just *any* trees that draw him, it might be specifically those trees."

Snyder stared at her. "Waddaya mean?"

"Really old trees, like I said. Eucalyptus, huge oaks

hundreds of years old, Spanish moss, the smell of the place."

"I don't get it."

"It's just an impression," Susan said. "Remember, I'm coming from the perspective of ancient peoples; you brought me here for that point of view. If we just for a moment suppose the killer you're hunting is more animal than human, then we must consider habitat. And Jim, there seems to be a consistent theme in that regard."

"Old growth? What else?"

"Height. Altitude. Each crime scene is on higher ground than the land surrounding it."

Snyder was still confused. "So what does that mean?"

"It suggests primitive instincts. Keep to the high ground, stay within the safety of the forest primeval. The smells, the ground underfoot, the forest, the accustomed killing ground."

"Couldn't a human have those instincts? A hunter, even a native American?"

Susan nodded. "Of course that's possible. But I'm suggesting that this killer's need to bring his prey to this environment seems exceedingly strong. How did he manage it? You told me that the girl killed up on Buena Vista Park lived all the way down in the Mission. And the woman killed at the Presidio spent all her time in hotels, not out in the woods. Only the jogger at Golden Gate Park went there of her own accord but even she was coaxed or maybe driven to a place in the park she didn't usually go."

"We assumed the intent of the killer was to avoid being seen."

"Maybe. But that far up the path? It doesn't seem necessary." Susan searched for a way to explain her thoughts. "Consider a wild animal, a leopard, for instance. A creature like that takes its kill into the bush, or up a tree. Just like this."

Snyder didn't look convinced. "Tomorrow we'll go to the scene of the fourth murder. You may think differently after you see that environment."

Susan's face broke into a grin. "I can't wait," she said. "But tell me this: did any of the murders take place in the city streets?"

"Uh, no."

"Well, that's really my point, I think. This killer went to great pains to avoid the streets, the very place where it would have been easiest to find victims."

"I hadn't thought of that."

"Here's the other thing that struck me. In all three of the locations you showed me - and tell me if I'm wrong - it looked like the victims were encouraged to move about, maybe even try to escape. At the very least they were given lots of room to run."

"So you think- "

"That the killer was looking for sport? Yes. He wanted the chase. These murders weren't just about killing, they were about the hunt."

"That doesn't rule out a human."

"Oh, not at all. Don't get me wrong, Jim, I'm not advocating for some beastie here. I'm simply offering you another pair of eyes, eyes to look at these murders from an anthropological perspective. Imagine that we're in our tent on the veldt of Africa discussing a dead antelope we found today, dismembered, torn and chewed. Would our first thought be a human killer? Probably not. I bring that perspective to the table."

Snyder went to the fridge and found a coke. "Soda?"

"No thanks," said Susan. "It would keep me awake. I'll just have water, please."

While Snyder poured the water, he worked on how to phrase his next question. When he handed it to her he said, "You wouldn't have come with me if you didn't think something of interest to your line of studies was happening here. Fair to say?"

"Okay..." Susan said, a little apprehensive about where Snyder was going with this.

"Therefore, in your mind you've not completely eliminated the possibility that something not human could be doing all this."

"Are you telling me or asking me?"

Snyder laughed. "You sound like my third grade teacher."

"Well, I *am* a teacher. And fair enough, the answer is yes. I know that opens up a whole lot of doors that most people don't want to open. Yet it intrigues everybody regardless. We want to believe that just beyond the shade of our perception strange creatures lurk; the Abominable Snowman, the Loch Ness Monster, Big Foot, the Jersey Devil, and countless other mystery monsters. This fascination isn't new, it's been part of every culture since man evolved from the ape, or since Eve bit the apple, whichever you prefer." Susan's voice dropped. "I've spent years and years studying these legends, these stories, these myths. And I've come to understand two things: that the people in those cultures who preserve these myths *do* believe them, and that with that belief comes a perceived reality. In other words, if your entire culture revolves around the Sun God, then the Sun God becomes quite real and you offer human sacrifices to keep it happy." Susan grinned. "There were explorers not so very long ago who denied the existence of cannibals and they ended up in the pot. Let's not end up in the pot here."

"That's a good segue to bring up something I haven't mentioned to anybody," Snyder said quietly. "The other night, alone at the Chronicle, I had a strong feeling of being observed, or watched...no, I really mean *stalked*. I don't get feelings like that much; years as a newspaperman tend to limit the imagination. But that night it was so strong that instead of coming home to this apartment, which was what I really wanted to do, I went to a bar where there were lots of people. And I didn't leave there until the feeling had gone away."

Snyder suddenly looked embarrassed. "Now I wish I hadn't confessed that. Saying it out loud, it sounds ridiculous."

"That's such a twenty-first century reaction you're having," Susan chuckled. "You want to deny your instincts, but they happen anyway, the unaccountable feelings, the deja-vu experiences, the sense of being watched. It takes a long time for a human being to evolve. We'd like to think that all of our primal instincts and fears have fallen away by now, but they haven't. And in your case, it may be that they served you well."

"You're saying maybe someone - maybe *something* - was actually stalking me?"

"I wouldn't dismiss it out of hand." Susan stretched and yawned. "But suddenly I feel totally wiped. Can I use your bathroom? I'd like to brush my teeth and then crash."

Twenty-four hours! Twenty-four hours with no word from Zack, no response to the message she had left. That wasn't like him. He didn't usually ignore her messages completely. Libby felt her anxiety torque up a notch. In the past she might have let it go, but now her concern was heightened by Forrester's call. Was Zack endangering his career by ignoring his duties here at home? And what about her secret? Was she ever going to get to tell him?

With Zack gone, Libby was spending all of her time at her old ranch and there was plenty to do here. And working hard took her mind off her worries about him, at least for a little while. But her new condition changed things, changed everything. The independent relationship they had enjoyed wouldn't be possible anymore; they'd need to team up now, be more supportive of one another, more available, more *responsible.*

Then the anxiety would come over her. Would Zack want that? Would he be willing to do his share at home, reign in his impulses to chase all over the country? What if he refused to change? What then?

Libby needed to talk to Zack. She needed to tell him

of her condition, she needed to know what to do. She looked up the number Zack had left when he first went to San Francisco. It was the number for a Martin O'Bannon of the San Francisco police.

Her call was answered on the second ring.

"San Francisco police, Richmond district."

"Is this Lieutenant Martin O'Bannon?"

"Lieutenant O'Bannon is not here right now. Can I help you?"

"I hope so. This is Libby Whitestone. My husband, Zack Tolliver, is an FBI agent working with Lieutenant O'Bannon on a case there. I'm trying to locate him."

"Why hello, Ms. Whitestone. This is Harry Harrar. I'm a homicide detective working very closely with the Lieutenant. Let me see if I can help you. I'll need just a little more information about the case your husband is working on..."

It was first thing in the morning and Snyder had forgotten about Susan when he stumbled through the tiny study on his way to the kitchen and a cup of coffee, or at least until his eye caught a glimpse of shapely white thigh flung over the top of the comforter and tousled blonde hair on the pillow. He paused momentarily while his brain caught up with his eyes and he found himself thinking thoughts that perhaps should have been reserved for a younger man. When he became aware that steady blue eyes were regarding him, he almost blushed.

"If you're on your way to get some coffee, would

you make it two, please?" Susan's slightly amused expression suggested she had read his thoughts.

Snyder coughed self-consciously. "Coming right up. Do you use milk or sugar?"

"Both, please." Susan stretched and yawned, exposing a glimpse of firm white breast.

Flustered, Snyder hurried off to the kitchen. By the time he returned with a coffee in each hand Susan was just coming out of the bathroom, dressed and ready to go.

They sat with their coffees to plan their day.

"One last murder scene to visit then?" Susan asked.

"That's all we know about," Snyder said.

"You think there could be more?"

Snyder told her about the missing ultra-runner. He then went on to reveal the nine-day interval between kills and his suspicion that Olson had been the fifth victim of this serial killer.

"But nobody has found a body."

"The man disappeared into thin air. We know he left the lounge of his hotel with a hooker. That's all we know."

"Did you ask the girl?"

"We haven't been able to locate her."

Susan looked surprised. "She's gone too?"

"We can't know that, she's just hard to locate out of all the girls working the downtown area. I'm sure they'll find her eventually, and then we should learn more."

Susan looked puzzled. "We? You seem confident about being in the loop..."

Snyder grinned. "I have an arrangement with an Indian."

He went on to tell her about Eagle Feather and their meeting on top of Buena Vista Park.

"He sounds like quite a character. And the FBI man? What's he like?"

"Strangely, through all of this, I have yet to meet the man." Snyder stood up. "I'm not much of a cook. I always stop for a bite before work at a little place around the corner. Shall we adjourn there?"

As they thumped down the narrow wooden steps Susan had another question. "You mentioned a nine day interval between kills. How do you figure that?"

Snyder's reply floated down from behind her on the stairs. "It's the pattern. The first kill we are aware of is the Golden Gate jogger murder on April 9. Nine days later the Buena Vista kill occurred. Nine days after that, on April 27, the girl is murdered up at the Presidio. And the little boy at Twin Peaks on May 7, exactly nine days later."

They came through the door onto the sidewalk and walked together toward the corner. "Then the ultra-runner...?"

Snyder looked at Susan. "He disappeared on the evening of May 16, right on schedule."

Susan was quiet as they walked along. They came to a little coffee shop and Snyder held the door for her to enter. When they were seated she asked, "Is the time interval your only reason to believe the ultra-runner is another victim of the same murderer? Isn't it strange that he first kills three women of similar description, then suddenly it's a young boy, and now, you think, a grown, athletic man? Isn't that inconsistent?"

Snyder grunted his dissatisfaction. "Yes, it is. That's why I'm looking for help here. There are too many bits that don't add up. I keep finding reasons to believe this killer isn't human. But then there are too many reasons to think it can't be an animal. So that leaves me with something in between, as much as I resist that conclusion." Snyder's phone rang. "Snyder."

Susan watched Jim's expression change from relaxed to incredulity. He listened and said, "Thank you" quietly and folded his phone and put it away and looked at Susan.

"That was Eagle Feather. He was catching me up on the latest news. They found the girl."

"The hooker with the ultra-guy?"

"Yes." Snyder did not look as pleased as he should.

"Well? What have they learned from her?"

Snyder stared back at her. "Nothing. They found her dead with a bullet in her brain."

TWENTY-TWO

"Got something!"

Zack swung a leg off the bed and went to peer over Eagle Feather's shoulder.

Eagle Feather tilted the laptop around so Zack could read it. "Look here, this add: *Maven Megan. Paid companion, your escort for any occasion,* (blah, blah) *Geary Street location, Tenderloin.*"

Zack's mouth moved as he read the ad.

"How do we know this is Megan McMitchell and not some other Megan?"

Eagle Feather grinned. "Didn't you tell me you found the word "Yohan" when you read her diary? And you thought it was the name of one of her clients? Well, in a way it is. It's Yiddish for John."

"Yiddish? How do you know?"

Eagle Feather looked at Zack in amusement. "With a name like Elmore Bernstein I shouldn't know some Yiddish words?"

"Oh, right. You are part Jewish. But what's being Jewish got to do with it?"

"The name 'Maven' is Yiddish, too. It means "one who understands". Maven Megan. The understanding escort."

"You think a girl named Megan McMitchell is Jewish?"

"White man, you've been in the country too long. Do you really think girls in the profession keep their own names? In the Tenderloin, the best thing is to be Irish."

Zack looked sheepish. "Well, this should help. Now we might be able to find people that knew her, maybe even some girls that worked with her."

"Better than that," Eagle Feather said, "as a good Jewish girl, she might even have gone to temple."

Zack's eyes opened wide. "Your talents are wasted on mountain sheep," he said. He grabbed his key card from the tiny desk. "Let's go."

Fifteen minutes later Zack and Eagle Feather were on Sutter Street looking for Number 873. The number was not displayed but by a process of elimination they decided it must be the white stucco building with the heart-shaped gold filigree windows on a heavy wooden door and two Torah shaped columns on either side, ornately wrought in gold.

"This must be it," Zack said. "But they don't seem to want to announce themselves."

"Would you, in this neighborhood?"

Zack rapped on the door. It was so thick that no sound seemed to penetrate to the inside. He looked around for a bell but before he could find one the door swung open. A short man with a heavy beard and a white yarmulke woven with blue and gold threads resting on his dark curly hair smiled at them from the doorway and offered his hand.

"You must be Mr. Tolliver?"

"Yes, Rabbi. I'm pleased to meet you. This is my associate Eagle Feather."

The Rabbi looked at Eagle Feather. "An interesting name. Not your given name, I surmise."

Eagle Feather shook the Rabbi's hand. "You are correct. My real name is Elmore Bernstein."

"Ah. Welcome. I am Rabbi Pogrowski."

The Rabbi led the way into a tiled foyer and then through a door into a small office. A much worn oriental carpet covered most of the old wood floor and a towering pile of books leaned against a small desk where yet another book lay open. Bookshelves covered the rear wall. The Rabbi waved his guests toward two mahogany and leather chairs and took his own seat behind the desk.

"Do you take tea?"

"Thank you, yes," Zack said. Eagle Feather nodded and the Rabbi picked up a small bell and tinkled it.

"Now, gentlemen, how may I help you?"

Zack spoke up. "Rabbi, as I mentioned during our phone conversation we're trying to learn about a young woman who unfortunately was murdered near here."

"Ah, yes, I heard about that."

"You probably are not aware that there has been a series of murders in this city, all connected we believe, all possibly perpetrated by the same person. This woman's murder is associated with those murders. We need to understand how and why."

"And how can I help you to do that?"

At that moment a woman stepped through the study door and looked inquiringly at the Rabbi.

"Ah, Mrs. Rasti, these gentlemen would like some tea if you would be so kind."

She smiled at the guests and was gone.

After she left Zack said, "We think it possible that the young woman was part of this congregation, or might at least have come here."

"What is her name?"

"Megan McMitchell, or possibly Maven Megan?"

The Rabbi smiled gently. "We've had several Megan's here in past years, as I recall. You must understand that this is a more transient congregation than most. We are the only congregation of Orthodox faith in downtown San Francisco, and we are nearest the business centers and tourist attractions. May I give you some history?"

"Of course," Zack said.

"Our congregation was not always located here.

Prior to 1905, we were one of the only orthodox Shuls - that's a synagogue - in the entire city. Our congregation at that time was made up largely of Lithuanian and Russian Jews. Then came the earthquake of 1905. In the shambles that followed, we moved to the 'Western Addition' or what is now Fillmore. But as fewer and fewer Jews came to the area we moved yet again until we came to our present quarters. As you can see, just as our congregation is transient, so too is this Shul." The Rabbi grinned. "We are well suited for each other."

In the doorway the ghost-like Mrs. Rasti appeared, tray in hand. The next minutes were occupied with distributing cups and saucers and taking sugar and milk. The question "Do you need anything else, gentlemen?" and the answering negative nod from the Rabbi caused the disappearance of Mrs. Rasti, like a wisp of fog.

The Rabbi took a sip of tea and sighed. "So you see, people come and people go. I have wished for a more settled congregation, to perhaps delve more deeply into issues and to develop character as other temples have done. Yet I have the rare opportunity to offer succor to strangers, to be an island of comfort in a tumultuous sea of the unfamiliar. It is my lot."

"Have any of those Megans you mentioned come here within the last year or so? Perhaps for a service, or for counseling? What might bring a stranger here?"

"On Friday evenings we have a Minchah twenty minutes before sundown, followed by Kabalos Shabos and Mah'ariv. Then there is Shabbos each morning at 9:30 and Minchah at four PM followed by She'uda Shlishis and Ma'ariv. We try to make a minyan - that is, a required quorum - on Shabbos and holidays. Davening starts promptly at whatever time we decide to call it, usually about 15 minutes before shkiah on Fridays. We host people for meals on Friday night and Shabbos during the day if you reserve in advance, which is nice for the tourists, I think. We get a lot of business travelers and tourists and transients."

Rabbi Pogrowski paused to think. "Yes, if memory serves me, there was a Megan, but not the name you mentioned. Let me see...yes, I remember her now, quite down in her luck, probably homeless or nearly so, fighting drug addiction, I'm sure. Pity. She was quite young and potentially quite attractive. The street ages people."

"You don't recall her name?" Eagle Feather asked.

"It was definitely Megan, but...wait! I remember now. Greenberg, that was it. Megan Greenberg. Her family was in the Midwest somewhere."

Zack leaned forward. "Can you describe her?"

"I think so. As I said, attractive but aged beyond her years, auburn hair, maybe more toward a red hue, dimples, teasing smile but not often enough...uh, green-blue eyes, I think, skinny, too skinny, medium height, maybe 5'7" or so..."

"Did she ever refer to herself as Maven Megan?"

"Very cute, but no. I don't recall hearing that."

Eagle Feather asked, "Did you know her occupation?"

Rabbi Pogrowski's eyes flicked to him. "Oh, I'm quite certain she was a prostitute."

Zack took up the questioning. "You mentioned her

family was from the Midwest. Did you learn anything else about her?"

"Not really. She didn't want to talk about her roots. She did say she'd been here in the city about three years; a runaway, I suspect."

"When was the last time you saw her?"

The Rabbi turned to his desk and began flipping pages in an engagement book. "Let's see, it was at a Minchah, I'm sure of that, so...I think it was the first week of April."

"You've been very helpful," Zack said. "Thank you for taking so much time with us."

The men stood to leave.

Eagle Feather asked, "Was there anything else about her that you can remember? Anything at all?"

The Rabbi stood up. "Really nothing of consequence. You might try the priest, though."

"Priest?" Zack's extended hand froze part way. "What priest?"

"Well, when she spoke to me the first time, when she first introduced herself as being Jewish, she mentioned that she had spoken with a priest."

"What priest?" Eagle Feather asked.

"She didn't say, probably didn't know - it was during confession. She had decided to confess her sins; she was desperate to turn her life around and wanted absolution.

She never saw the priest, just heard his voice."

"Did she say which church she was in?" Zack asked.

"Unfortunately, no, it didn't come up. She never went back, apparently. I guess confession didn't help."

"Was it high church? Episcopal? Catholic?"

"Again, she didn't say."

The colleagues thanked Rabbi Pogrowski once again. Out on the sidewalk Eagle Feather turned to Zack. "You think the priest bit is important?"

"I don't know. It's possible. Megan doesn't appear to have had many friends or close colleagues. She never mentioned any, not in her journal, not to the Rabbi. I think she was a loner and so every connection she had is important."

"There's not much to go on to find this priest..."

Zack grinned at Eagle Feather. "It's just as much as we had when we found the Rabbi. Let's go comb the yellow pages again."

"Here's what I think you should do," Harry Harrar was saying. "And I'm being completely unselfish about this. Your husband has been helpful here in his way but right now you need him more than we do. So get yourself on a plane and come get him."

"Go to San Francisco?" Libby asked.

"Exactly. He's not going to respond to your calls or texts; you know that. Like you say, he's intent on solving this case, so much so that I'm afraid he's blown it out of proportion. This is a big city, Libby, and whether we like it or not, people get killed here all the time, often in ways that seem similar to one another. Your husband is creating a serial killer where I very much doubt one exists."

"That's the very thing I was afraid of," Libby said. "He gets these ideas in his head and won't let them go."

"All of us cops get like that from time to time." Harrar chuckled sympathetically. "But you need him at home this time. So come get him. He can ignore your calls but when you're here in person, he'll get it and come home, I promise you."

"You are very kind to help me through this. In my heart I know you're right. Zack will never come home unless I go get him. I'll do as you suggest."

A few hours later when Zack remembered to return Libby's call, he heard only her recorded message.

TWENTY-THREE

Jim Snyder stood on the asphalt road surface at the overlook and watched Susan study the landscape. He had driven her to the site of the boy's murder, the switchback on Peak Boulevard just below them but she had insisted on coming on up here. Fog climbed toward them from the north and threatened the homes just below on the ridge.

"You're right," Susan said at last.

"Right about what?"

"This terrain is not consistent with the first three murder sites. It's too barren, too bleak."

"So why here?"

"I don't know," Susan replied with a frown. "It feels contrived, like he did it against his will."

Snyder looked down into the wispinging fog. "Why would he murder someone when doing it was against his will?"

"No, no, I don't mean the murder was against his will, I mean the place." Susan swept her arm across the vista. "Look at this. You can see everything that moves for miles in every direction. Not a tree, hardly a bush.

There could not be more of an antithesis to his preferred hunting ground."

"Are you saying you think he wasn't responsible for this killing? How do you explain the exact same wound, the precise nine day interval, the- "?

"No, I *do* believe he killed the boy. I don't know *why* he did it here."

They stood not speaking and then Snyder said, "Would you like to go down and see the place where the boy- "

"No," Susan said quietly. "It won't be necessary." Then she turned and took Snyder by the arm and walked with him back to the car. "I want you to tell me everything you know about the ultra-runner Olson's disappearance."

They drove the winding way back down Peak Boulevard and Snyder told Susan about Olson and the girl in the lounge and the coincidence of Agent Tolliver taking a room in the same hotel where Olson vanished. Susan listened intently without interrupting.

When he had finished she said, "He's using intermediaries."

"So it would seem."

"*If* it's him," she pointed out.

"Yes, there isn't much evidence to connect him; no body, therefore no neck wound and no murder site. All we have is the interval between kills, nine days exactly."

"No other murders on that day that might fit?"

"That's right."

"But tenuous as your evidence is, all of you are pursuing leads from that disappearance, almost as if you had more." Susan looked inquiringly at Snyder.

"It's an intuitive thing with us, I think, and really, we have nothing else."

Susan smiled at Snyder. "You see, it comes down to that primitive part of your brain, the brainstem, with its ancient memories and survival instincts. Is it such a stretch to think there could be a human hunter out there, a creature whose brain more closely resembles an animal predator?" When Snyder didn't respond Susan quickly added, "And for what it's worth, I think you're right. The Olson disappearance does fit. I believe this creature lured him to a hunting ground of his choosing and killed him there. You just need to find where that was; some place with ancient roots, where old forest is or had been, where this creature's ancestors once hunted."

Snyder grimaced. "Now you've gone too far for me to stay with you. I'll accept that this is some psycho who has fallen back on his primitive instincts to hunt and kill for pleasure, but seeking the land of his ancestors who were some ancient species of hunters? I'm a newspaperman - give me facts."

Susan laughed gaily at that. "I'm just giving you the perspective that you wanted. Take only what you can swallow." Staring ahead down the road, she added, "But the thing you need to take away is that Olson *is* the fifth kill and you'll find his body at a place such as I described. He changed all of his habits to kill that boy back there and I don't know why. But I *do* know that he wouldn't do that again, not for any reason."

Snyder grinned sheepishly at her. "Okay, I'll take that much under consideration. But until Eagle Feather and Agent Tolliver learn more about this Megan and why she was killed and what she had been up to before meeting Olson, there's just not much to go on."

Zack sighed and put down the phone. He was in his undershorts on the bed in his hotel room searching his laptop for any church that could possibly require a priest anywhere in the vicinity of the Tenderloin and Downtown area. He'd just taken a call from O'Bannon who was looking into the professional assassin angle. Zack had no faith in that line of investigation; he didn't believe a killer had been hired just to off Megan. He thought they needed to look closer to home for the killer but he knew that O'Bannon had to investigate every possibility, no matter how tedious, just as Zack was doing now.

Eagle Feather had spent the night on Zack's floor and left early to explore Megan's neighborhood on foot and see what churches were within range of her likely daily pattern. He'd check in if he found anything.

Churches were popping up on Zack's screen in response to his query. There were many, but the closest one seemed to be St. Boniface Church on Golden Gate Avenue, just a couple of blocks from Megan's apartment. He'd start there and then search an ever-widening circle.

But questions remained. How would he know if he was in the right church? Priests were not big on revealing the content of confessions or who had done the confessing, for that matter. The Priest might not be willing to talk about Megan.

Zack shrugged and picked up his phone. Subtlety would be required. He might as well get started. He'd call Eagle Feather and ask him to meet him at St. Boniface.

Jim Snyder took Susan to a cafe he knew for an early lunch. It was a place where newspapermen congregated to share tips and question reports and generally enjoy one another's company in a relaxed moment, all too few in this profession. He led Susan to a booth in the back and they lingered over soup and sandwiches. Snyder would check in with Eagle Feather after lunch but he didn't expect much, so they could take their time.

Snyder took a bite of his sandwich and looked at Susan. "What caused you to go into your line of study?"

She looked up from her soup. "Wow! That's a large question to come out of the blue. How much do you really want to hear?"

Snyder was apologetic. "I was just curious. I don't mean to pry. You'd be the same age as my granddaughter, if I had a granddaughter, and here you are chairperson of your department and obviously keen on this ethnology anthropology thing."

"First, Mr. Snyder, if you had a granddaughter she'd be more like three or four years old, in all likelihood. You're not that old."

Snyder shrugged and grinned.

"But to answer your question as briefly as possible, I've always been fascinated by the thought that other people have been here before me. As a child I'd ride in the family car along El Camino Real and where the others saw boring grass hills and fences and cattle I'd see in my mind's eye a Mexican boy walking next to a carreta loaded with hides and pulled by oxen, or maybe it would be a band of Chumash Indians traveling north to their fishing ground, or I'd see vaqueros rearing back on their horses, herding cattle to sell to the miners. And I'd try to imagine their thoughts and their feelings as they lived their lives, just as I was thinking and feeling and living mine. Every old road or swale along the way had a message for me; any broken down shack had a story, even old fence posts held secrets I wanted to know."

"You were very imaginative."

"Yes, I was. And quite the romantic, I suppose. Those people I saw were very vivid and I'd sometimes see myself among them, living as they did. Other times I'd imagine that I'd be walking along some old road or Indian path and find a relic of an earlier time, something real that I could hold in my hands and feel connected to those people back in history." Susan suddenly stopped and looked away. "I didn't expect to open up quite like this. I guess I feel very comfortable around you."

Snyder smiled. "And so you decided to study..."

"It wasn't quite that simple. My father was keen on me becoming a doctor, just like him. I'm an only child; I didn't want to disappoint him. I went into pre-med and was plugging along and then one day I attended a lecture by an archaeologist just back from a dig in Mexico. His description of the ruin he was excavating and his re-creation of the people who had lived their was so compelling, so much like what I had imagined as a child that I was completely captivated. And that's about it. I changed my major the next day, wrote a letter of apology to my father, who it turns out wasn't as set on me becoming a doctor as I had thought...and here I am." Susan lifted her hands palm up indicating her presence.

Snyder laughed. “You certainly are. And I’m glad of it.” He quickly added, “It’s great to have the company, I mean. Pursuing a story can be a lonely affair.”

Susan tilted her head and looked at him. “And in this case, maybe dangerous. I’m still concerned about your experience in your office the other night. Man or beast, the killer you are hunting is pure predator.”

Snyder grinned again. “I think this is my cue to change the subject and see what Eagle Feather is up to.”

Eagle Feather had two phone calls, one right after the other. The first was from Zack. “There’s a Catholic church, named St. Boniface, just a couple of blocks from Megan’s apartment over on Golden Gate Avenue. Just go up Leavenworth and turn right. Meet me there?”

Eagle Feather agreed and started walking in that direction. His phone rang again. This time the call was from Snyder.

“What’ve you got? Anything new?”

Eagle Feather told him about their visit with the Rabbi. “It was our Megan - there’s no doubt in my mind. So now we’re trying to locate that priest she mentioned.”

“What about the forensics?”

“No word from O’Bannon yet. He’s looking into the possibility of an assassin. He has the bullet. The gun that fired it was a Smith & Wesson, just like police issue, but it was suppressed. I’m not thinking a hired gun but there was certainly the intent to keep her quiet permanently.”

"Hmmm," Snyder said.

"Well, that's helpful," Eagle Feather responded. "What are you up to now?"

"Right now I'm eating some really delicious soup with a lovely young woman, if you must know." Snyder paused. "No, really. I have the distinguished chairperson of the Anthropology Department at UC Davis here with me. She's helping me from a cultural angle and we're about to head to the Chronicle to do some research." Snyder hesitated for a moment and then spoke firmly. "Perhaps you should know that I did some research down your way. I read the newspaper accounts from the Roundtree case and I know about the suspected Skinwalker and all that. You've kept that part pretty close to the vest."

"Wouldn't you? Who's going to take you seriously if you mention such creatures? Would you have?"

Snyder chuckled. "You got me there. I'm having difficulty with that very thing just at the moment."

Libby disembarked among a sweaty line of passengers from a Southwest 737-300 airliner and passed through the gate into the San Francisco International Airport pulling a wheeled carry-on. She didn't intend to stay long. She made her way to the Bart station and looked at the route map on the wall and checked it against the address she had in her hand. Officer Harrar, that very accommodating policeman, had supplied it. She must remember to send him a note of thanks. She boarded the train for Union Station and found a seat next to an older woman immersed in a book.

Libby's mind was whirring. Was this a mistake? Could she be doing more harm than good by approaching Zack during a case, something she'd never even thought to do before? Yet, as Officer Harrar had pointed out, the circumstances were different now. This time there was something Zack didn't know, something she needed to tell him in person, something compelling that would influence his decision - she was sure of that. She rubbed her tummy. No, she was right to do this. She'd surprise him; she'd go to his hotel and meet him there. She leaned back and let the clickety-clacking and tunnel roar envelop her.

O'Bannon slumped back in his chair. He rubbed his forehead and stared at his computer screen. He was bone weary in a way that comes from too much to do and too little time to do it, all with pressure from above.

"How do you suppress a Smith & Wesson SIG-Saur P226 pistol?" he called over his shoulder to Harrar.

"Do what?"

"Suppress it. I didn't think you could do it."

Harrar stopped sifting through lists of known killers for hire and looked past his computer screen at O'Bannon. "You can suppress any gun if you want to badly enough."

"Sure, but why? Why not just use something that's built for it, a kill gun, like a Ruger Pac-lite that has a barrel that's already threaded? I mean, why go to all that trouble?"

"I've got no idea. Maybe it was just a matter of

weight or handling characteristics, maybe just personal preference. A man uses one weapon long enough, he wants to stick with it for a really important shoot."

"Ah!" O'Bannon turned to look back at Harrar. "That's exactly what I was getting at. You'd use the gun you're used to. Maybe we're going the wrong way around looking for a hired gun; maybe we should look for someone used to using that particular weapon."

Harrar looked puzzled. "How would we know that?"

"Let's look up trades that train with the Sig-Saur or use it regularly, maybe security forces or one of the big mercenary outfits, like Blackwater."

Eyes wide, Harrar added, "Or cops..."

"Right! Or cops. Let's put together a list and see what we get."

Harrar turned back to his keyboard. "You want I should give up on this list of hired killers?"

"Keep it handy, I suppose. I had the most likely of them picked up and they're in a holding cell waiting for me to talk to 'em. But I don't expect much. Let's concentrate on this new angle." O'Bannon kicked back his chair and stood up.

"What are you planning to do now?" Harrar wanted to know.

"I'm going over to see Tenderloin District dispatch. I'd like to know what cops were in the area that night and which ones responded to the call. Maybe I can learn something.

After lunch Jim Snyder and Susan went back to his apartment to plan their next steps. Susan parked herself on top of her rumpled bedding on the couch and Snyder slid into a well-worn armchair across from her.

"What do you intend to do next?" Susan asked.

"Me? I thought you were the expert."

Susan's eyes twinkled a challenge. "You're the reporter doing an investigation. What would you normally do next?"

"Well, let's see. I'd first consider that the evidence connecting this Megan woman to our serial killer is tenuous at best. Yet the local constabulary seems to think she is their best lead. They're pursuing that. Fine. But I've begun to think that my real story is not the how but the what. What is stalking the nighttime green places of San Francisco? Is it a serial killer? A homicidal maniac? Or something else? What is it that ties the four murders to each other? Its just one thing: those fatal neck wounds. But for them, we'd be looking at four random murders committed by four different murderers in four different locations in the city, with no discernible motive. Three women and a child, all with quite different life situations and not connected in any way. Nothing in any of their backgrounds has revealed any common ground at all. So where does that leave us?"

"Go on," Susan said, watching him through half closed lids, her chin resting on her clasped hands.

"But what if I view these deaths not as murders but as kills? Kills by a predator: human or beast. Kills not for personal gain: not robbery, not a ritual, not revenge or any other emotional satisfaction. Not even for consumption. Just for sport. Then the motive is self-explanatory, the randomness of the victims is explained. Now the circumstance of their deaths makes sense. But it's sport for whom...or what? The murder weapon is either a very sophisticated tool or the long incisors of some mysterious beast. In the case of either, the killer possesses great stalking skill and amazing flexibility and strength. So we're down to the question, is this killer human or animal?" Snyder peeked at Susan's expression to read her reaction to his logic.

Susan smiled. "I'm with you so far. But how do you determine which it is, animal or human?"

Snyder threw up his hands. "I think that's why I found you. I need someone with the training and knowledge to help me figure that out." He looked at Susan. "Your turn."

Susan sat up straight. "Okay, here's my take. I think you need to create a hypothetical and then build upon it and see where it leaves you. For instance, let's hypothesize that our killer is an animal. We won't try to determine what kind of animal yet; we don't have enough to go on. But we'll say it's an animal. What do we know, then? We know it's large, strong, can move swiftly and silently, yes? And probably has excellent night vision. Agreed so far?"

"I'll concur with all of that."

"Great. Now things get a little shaky. I'll propose it's a biped with very strong arms for lifting its victims while it administers a fatal bite." Susan glanced at Snyder.

"Okay," he said. "But what about the lack of prints or sign?"

Susan smiled wickedly. "Try this on. We've already established it has very strong arms. What if they are strong enough to allow the beast to move monkey-like through the trees?" She looked triumphantly at Snyder. "Its victims would never see it coming. Not until it reaches down for them, not until it's too late."

Snyder stared at Susan and his mind raced. "Jesus! And the trees...that would explain its preference for forested places instead of the streets for its kills."

Susan giggled. "Let's not get ahead of ourselves. The problem is, there are very few known animals that fit that description - only a few of the larger monkeys. Think Primata, Sub-order Haplorrhini, and we'd have to say Infraorder Catarrhini and Superfamily Hominoidea to find the physical attributes we've deduced. And I'd say Family Hominidae for the size we need- "

"Whoa, hold on. Let's speak English here."

Susan smiled at him. "That leaves us with the Orang-utan, Common Chimpanzee, and Gorilla. My thought is that both the Orang-utan and Gorilla are a possibility and a preternaturally large Chimpanzee maybe has an outside chance. But let's consider the length of the incisors of each. Despite what you might tend to think, both Orang-utans and Chimpanzees have longer incisors than the Gorilla. The evolvement of incisor length is attributed to the necessity of eating larger and tougher-skinned fruits, which has not been an evolutionary necessity for the Gorilla. Now we see that our hypothesized animal predator could be an unusually large Chimp or Orang-utan and of course both do have exceptional strength, so that fits. But let's set all that aside for a moment and consider where the animal could hide itself. The obvious answer is in the trees. But we must consider that all of the parks where these murders took place are well populated by visitors all through the day.

Snyder looked puzzled. "Aren't Chimps and Orang-utans primarily vegetarians?"

"But remember, nobody has been eaten here," Susan said. "These kills were not made for food but for some other reason involving anger or fear or- "

"Sport."

Susan was thoughtful. "Animals seldom kill for what we would know as sport, although it *can* occur. But they commonly kill to protect their territory."

"Where could this creature have come from? How'd it get here?"

"I don't know," Susan admitted. "And I don't know how it gets from place to place around the city without being noticed. I mean, from the Presidio to Twin Peaks is a long way through city streets - and there's no other way to go."

"Maybe it could stay up in the trees and then move along the tops of buildings," Snyder offered doubtfully.

"But why? Why go to all of that effort and risk? It doesn't make sense."

They both sat silent for a while, thinking. Then Snyder said, "Well, we can take one thing out of this exercise - we better look up in the trees when we hunt this brute."

TWENTY-FOUR

The priest looked up from his desk. Several large volumes lay open in front him. He was ruddy cheeked and fair and his surplice was tousled as if he had not left his desk for a very long time. He smiled wearily at the two men, his eyes large through the thick glasses.

"Welcome to St. Boniface," he said. "I am Father O'Rourke. Please, please, take a seat." His arm swept toward two carved wood chairs with maroon cushions. "What can I do for you today?" he asked as Zack and Eagle Feather seated themselves.

"I hope we didn't catch you at a bad time." Zack looked at the littered desk.

"Oh, no, not at all." The priest nodded toward his desk. "This is how you'll find me most of the time. My scholastic pursuits occupy me almost as much as my service to my parish."

"Father, we have come for your help. My associate and I are looking for a young woman, originally a runaway. We recently learned she lives in this neighborhood and might have attended St. Boniface on occasion."

Eagle Feather picked up the thread. "She ran away from a small mid-western town five years ago," he said. "The parents had nearly given up hope of finding her when they received news that suggested she might be here in San Francisco."

"And they hired us to find her," Zack broke in. "We found her apartment nearby on Leavenworth. Her clothes and possessions are all there but she apparently hasn't been home for several days. She appears to have been working the street. We thought perhaps you might have some information to help us reunite her with her parents."

"What is her name, then?" the priest asked.

"She has called herself Megan McMitchell and Maven Megan. Her real name is Megan Greenberg but she never uses it. She's Jewish, you see, and has actually attended the Sutter Street Fellowship once or twice. The Rabbi there told us she mentioned talking with a priest and your church is the closest one to her apartment and, well, here we are."

"May I ask what you intend to do once you find her?"

Eagle Feather said, "Our job is to inform her that her parents love her and want to see her. And to mention, by the way, that there is a large inheritance involved."

"I see. Well, there are many young women who attend mass here and avail themselves of the social organizations at St. Boniface. But no Megan's come to mind, particularly. Can you describe her?"

Zack reached into his pocket. "I can do better than that. Here is her picture." He handed it across to Father O'Rourke.

The priest glanced at the picture for barely a moment before saying, "Well, sure. I know this girl. This is Mattie."

"Mattie?" Zack echoed.

"Yes, she was here just once, not more than a week ago. But I remember her well because she was quite distressed."

"What about?"

The priest shook a finger at Zack. "You know I can't reveal anything said in confession."

"But maybe you can steer us a little to help us find her?" Eagle Feather suggested.

"I have precious little to add to what you already know. In fact, I don't seem to know as much as you gentlemen do."

"Did she give you any indication of where she might go after seeing you, or mention any friends or acquaintances?"

Zack asked.

Father O'Rourke thought for a moment. "I can't remember her mentioning any names or places. I'm sorry."

"Nothing?" Zack looked disappointed.

"I'm sorry, gentlemen. I wish I could help you." Father O'Rourke rose. "Please allow me to show you out."

They left the priest's study and walked down a long corridor where portraits hung the entire length of the hall on both walls. Father O'Rourke gestured toward the framed pictures.

"We call this Priest's Walk," he said. "There is a picture here of every priest currently serving in San Francisco. My staff does a fine job of keeping it current." He paused. "But that does bring something to mind. When Mattie - or Megan, as you say - was walking along this corridor with me as we are doing now she stopped suddenly and stared at one particular portrait. It was quite a reaction, as I remember."

"Which picture was it?" Eagle Feather asked.

"It was this one right here," the priest said, pointing to a picture to his left. "Seeing it brought the incident to mind."

Zack and Eagle Feather crowded in to see it. It was a picture of a man's head and shoulders. He was dressed in a priest's collar and a black hooded robe. He was looking obliquely at the camera as if caught unawares and his face was partially shadowed by his hood. But his features were clearly visible. The man's face was formidable. His eyes were dark and piercing, his jaw was set and his mouth fixed in a grimace.

"This man doesn't look like your standard kindly priest," Zack observed.

Father O'Rourke laughed. "I've known Father Gilligan for many years, but I would never have recognized him from this picture. He was caught at a bad moment, it would appear, completely unawares."

"Father Gilligan," Eagle Feather repeated.

Father O'Rourke turned and continued on down the corridor. "Yes, he is one of two priests at the Star of the Sea parish. He is the secular monsignor, as we say."

"Did Megan say anything to explain why the picture had so effected her?" Zack asked.

Father O'Rourke turned to look back at him. "No, she did not. In fact, her reaction was so abrupt that I stopped in my tracks. But she offered no explanation and so we moved on. I'd guess that she knows him somehow."

"She might've lived in Richmond before she came here," Eagle Feather suggested.

Zack turned to the priest. "Would you be willing to arrange a meeting for us? You said you know the man?"

"Of course," the priest said. 'I'll give him a call and tell him to expect you."

Back out on the sidewalk Zack felt excitement. "This is a good lead. I figure Megan must have lived or at least worked in the Richmond area. Who knows? This Father Gilligan may have some useful information."

"Okay, boss, do we go there now?"

"We'd better give Father O'Rourke time to call him. What have you heard from your buddy at the Chronicle?"

Eagle Feather chuckled. "He's pure journalist, alright. He did a back check on us. He found out about the Roundtree case and that entire hullabaloo. So he knows about the Skinwalker angle."

"I'll bet he's getting a laugh out of that."

"Maybe not. He's dug up an anthropologist from U.C. Davis. He's got her here right now. That's not the response of a man who's thinking the killer is necessarily human."

Zack's eyes widened at that. "Is she buying it?"

"Dunno. He didn't say. Want I should call him?"

"Yeah, let's make sure we're all in sync from now on. I have this sense that we're getting close and I don't want someone to go off half-cocked and spoil our surprise."

Eagle Feather looked at Zack in amusement. "So Mister Logic has a feeling, eh?"

"Just because I've got a gut feeling doesn't mean I believe in Skinwalkers," Zack retorted.

Eagle Feather continued to chuckle while he took out his cell phone.

Zack shot him a dark look. "I'll give O'Bannon a call to see where he stands. Then we'll put it all together."

O'Bannon answered on the first ring.

"What's up?"

"Thought I'd better check in. What have you got?"

"Well, let's see. I'm almost convinced that the guy who offed Megan was either a cop or a guy dressed like a cop right down to the preferred weapon, a Sig-Saur like we carry. You don't usually suppress that weapon so I thought I'd take a look at how and where that could be done. But right now I'm driving to the Tenderloin to talk to a cop I know in that district to see if I can get hold of the watch records. I'd like to know what cops were in the area at that time."

"You don't think it was a hired gun?"

"Not any of our known professionals. I've interviewed the known hit men in the city and they all have ironclad alibis. Besides, this doesn't smell like a pro to me."

Zack chronicled his conversation with the priest and what they had learned. "We're going to Richmond to see the priest at the Star of the Sea Church in Inner Richmond to see if he can add anything to the picture. I'm hoping that by backtracking Megan we might find where the killer crossed her path. It's a long shot, but it's all we've got."

O'Bannon sighed. "Yeah, all we've got is a bunch of long shots. Seems like that's all we've ever had."

When Zack ended his call Eagle Feather was just putting away his phone. "Got something kinda interesting," he said. "Snyder's developed a theory with the help of his professor. He thinks we better look up more."

"Do what...?"

"He's suggesting that the killer might strike from above, from tree branches or the like. That he leans down and grabs the victim, holds her up, and tears out her throat with some sort of weapon."

"Oh, come on."

"Well, it does explain a couple of things."

"But it creates new problems. How does the killer manage to get directly above the victim at just the right time and place? The victims were running, remember? Even then, how can he pick up a woman weighing over a hundred pounds reaching down from above? And what then? Hold her there with one arm and cut out her throat with the other? We'd be talking about someone with incredible strength, amazing speed and monkey-like agility."

Eagle Feather stared back at Zack.

"That's right," he said.

Libby climbed the two long sections of steps up out of the Powell Bart Station and checked her bearings. The cable car bell clanged nearby. She stopped to look at her street map. She found the Hotel Adagio and checked the address: 550 Geary Street. She could hike up Stockton the two blocks and then go west four blocks on Geary. She sighed at the prospect and extended the handle on her carryon. Pushing through the crowd of tourists she began the steep climb up the hill next to the cable car tracks, her bag trundling along behind her.

The Star of the Sea Church was imposing. A white marble edifice towered high above the street and branched into twin towers that reached even higher toward the Divine Being. On the sidewalk two minaret-like mini towers stood to either side of an impressive central door. Zack and Eagle Feather walked up 8th Avenue next to the sanctuary looking for a less ostentatious door to enter but found only an eight-foot high wall running the length of the block. Signs on the wall announced the presence of a private Catholic school somewhere behind it. There was no egress. They retraced their steps to Geary Street and there found a side door. Inside was all gloom dispelled here and there by rays of dim filtered light from the large stained glass windows that highlighted suspended dust particles with rainbow colors. The echo of their footfalls clattered off the walls and re-echoed in the large sanctuary. Its domed and highly decorated ceiling towered far above. Parallel pews lined up like freight cars in a train yard, all facing an ornately carved altar. They saw no indication of a way to the administrative offices. Several worshippers knelt in pews or were lighting candles. The men had decided to try to find another entrance when a voice came to them from somewhere in the sanctuary.

"What do you seek?" it boomed.

They looked for the origins of the voice as Zack said, "We are looking for Father Gilligan. We have arranged to meet him."

"The Father would be in the parish offices." The mysterious voice was deep and vibrant and echoed around the room. They looked all around but could not see who was speaking.

"We're strangers here," Eagle Feather said into the void. "We couldn't find the administrative offices."

"Strangers to The Way, is it, then?"

"Uh, yes."

“Seek and ye shall find,” the voice replied enigmatically.

Zack and Eagle Feather traded glances and stood in confusion. A worshipper rose from a kneeling position in a rear pew and came toward them.

“Let me show you.” This was not the god-like voice but the softer sound of a woman. She was young looking but with a face creased and lined beyond her years. With surprisingly graceful movements she led them toward a side door. The two men followed. Outside the church they found themselves in a small greensward filled with ritual sculptures and well tended plants.

“Do you work for this parish?” Zack asked.

“Only as a volunteer on occasion,” she replied. “Father Gilligan has helped me to find myself and I try to repay my debt by helping out.”

“He sounds like a good man,” Eagle Feather probed.

“He is.”

“Was that Father Gilligan speaking to us in the church?”

The woman smiled but didn’t respond. She led them across the green and up some steps into a neighboring building. They found themselves in a traditional office suite. Their guide led them to a door inscribed with the name Monsignor Gilligan and left them there with no further words.

Zack rapped on the door. They waited. He glanced at Eagle Feather and rapped again. Still they waited.

"If that was Father Gilligan in there he can't be in here," Eagle Feather observed.

"Then why would that girl bring us here instead of taking us to him in the sanctuary?"

Eagle Feather shrugged. "It seems silly to be knocking on the door of an empty office."

Zack reached over and tried the door handle. It clicked open. He hesitated and then gently touched the door wider. With a groan it swung stiffly inward.

"He must not use this office much," Eagle Feather observed, referring to the hesitant hinges.

Zack didn't reply. He took in the partially exposed room, the heavy carved icons on the wall, the thick cloth-covered books on the shelf, the richly upholstered armchair, the smell of dust and old leather. Hazy sunlight hung heavily in the room.

"There's a layer of dust over everything," Zack whispered. He nudged the door open a bit more.

A melodious voice sounded directly behind them. "The Lord helps those who help themselves, but don't you think you gentlemen are overdoing it?"

Startled, the two men turned. There stood a man in clerical garb with round cheeks and crinkly blue eyes. He had a smile of amusement on his face.

"I beg your pardon," Zack said. "We had arranged to see you and we expected you to be in your office. When you didn't reply to our knock, we thought-"

"Forgive my perverse sense of humor," the priest said. "I never could resist capitalizing on a situation for the sake of a laugh. Were you looking for Father Gilligan?"

"You're not Father Gilligan?"

He chuckled again. Each time the man laughed his entire body participated in his mirth; his face wrinkled and his round tummy quaked above his belt. "Oh, Good Lord no. I am Father Arturo Gonzales. This is my parish. I take it you do not know Father Gilligan?"

"No. He was suggested to us by Father O'Rourke at St. Boniface," Eagle Feather said.

"Ah, Father O'Rourke. Yes. And what is the nature of your business, may I ask?"

"We are trying to locate a lost girl, a runaway of almost five years now. She is thought to have consulted with Father Gilligan recently," Zack added.

Father Gonzales smiled somewhat sadly. "I'm afraid you won't find Father Gilligan very helpful. If the young woman you seek consulted with him, it had to have been several months ago." He gestured to them to follow him. "Please, come to my office. Let me see if I can assist you."

The room Father Gonzales ushered them into contrasted starkly to the office they had just visited. Here it was bright and colorful. A child stick-figure drawing was taped to the white wall and a large trophy with a basketball etched into it sat on a shelf. Leaning in a corner was a lacrosse stick and a glove. A large grey metal industrial desk commanded the center of the room.

Father Gonzales watched them and smiled. "We're not just a church," he explained. "We're a school as well." He removed a sport's helmet from one of a pair of folding chairs and asked them to sit down.

"Is Father Gilligan indisposed, then?" Zack asked.

"In a manner of speaking, yes. But I may possibly be of assistance to you."

"But it is Father Gilligan to whom this girl spoke, most likely in confidence," Zack said. "I don't see how you-"

"You won't get much from Father Gilligan even if he were to see you, which he won't. I myself have not spoken to him for almost two months now. We communicate solely by hand-written notes which we leave for one another." Father Gonzales chuckled at their looks. "Let me explain. Or try to, anyway. I'm not sure I completely understand all of this myself. You see Father Gilligan has been my associate and friend and a valued cleric in this parish for many years. His service to the school has been invaluable. But he is an uncommonly sensitive man, prone to chastise himself for even the slightest perceived misstep. He is a flagellant, you see, a very conservative Christian. Every time he considers himself to have sinned in the eyes of the lord, no matter how insignificant it might appear to you or me, he retreats from the public eye to flagellate and to pray, sometimes for days." Father Gonzales rolled his eyes and his smile appeared a bit strained. "He's not much help to me in those circumstances, as you can imagine. But of course I sympathize and we manage to carry on and usually within twenty-four hours there he is, back again, his usual helpful, capable, responsible self."

Father Gonzales laughed and his whole body jiggled in his chair. "But then almost two months ago a young woman suffered a grievous injury here at the sanctuary. She apparently fell down those long parish steps in the dark and somehow impaled herself on a gardening tool that had been carelessly left there by the caretaker. It was a freak accident, a completely unforeseeable circumstance, but the girl almost died. The sharp tool penetrated her throat, its sharp hooked tines actually protruded out the other side." Father Gonzales grimaced at the memory. "By some miracle she survived but her larynx was destroyed. Its unlikely she'll ever speak again. She is terrified of those steps now and won't come near the church or the school anymore. But the impact on Father Gilligan was possibly even worse. He had been with the young lady that evening and had taken her confession in the church at her request. There had been something that had caused her to want to confess and receive absolution urgently and of course he complied. In normal circumstances after dark he would have escorted her from the sanctuary."

Father Rodriguez looked apologetic. "It's not as well lit as it should be. But on this particular night he stayed to pray and didn't see her out. When he later found her bleeding and unconscious at the bottom of the steps he felt an overwhelming guilt. So with all that self-recrimination, withdrawal and flagellation followed immediately. This time, however, he hasn't been able to recover. He hasn't spoken since then. Knowing Father Gilligan, he may well have taken a vow of silence in atonement for the fact that the poor girl had been rendered speechless by his own carelessness. In any case, he has not participated in any church or school functions since. I glimpse him flitting by in the church now and then in a hood and robe, a sackcloth and ashes sort of thing. He is silent and unresponsive. I have no idea what he does now. As I said, we communicate only by notes."

Father Gonzales raised his palms and turned a benign eye on them as if to say, "So you see..."

Zack looked quizzically at the priest. "But someone spoke to us in the church. A male voice, deep and resonant."

"And he didn't show himself," Eagle Feather said. "Whoever he was, he spoke as if he belonged here."

Father Gonzales leaned forward. "Now that's strange. I would not have described Father Gilligan's voice as deep and resonant; it's much more high pitched and, well...for lack of a better word, squeaky."

"So it could not have been him," Zack said.

"I think not. However, I've distracted you from your business long enough, I think. You say you are seeking a young woman who had run away...?"

Zack responded. "Yes, she ran away from a small town and came to the city and her parents lost any trace of her. We've been able to determine that she lived most recently in the Tenderloin District where she apparently survived by walking the streets. We located her apartment but she's gone and has not returned there since."

"And how did you expect Father Gilligan to assist you?"

"As we said, Father O'Rourke at St. Boniface Church has seen her and spoken to her. When they were walking by some portraits of priests Megan appeared to react to the picture of Father Gilligan. We hoped to find a connection."

"I see. That is something only Father Gilligan could answer. I understand now why you need him in particular."

The two men nodded.

"So you see, we really do have to talk to him," Eagle Feather said. "Maybe you...?"

"Yes." Father Gonzales replied to the unfinished question. "I'll leave him a note. What is the exact question you wish me to put to him?"

Zack thought for a minute before dictating. "What was your relationship with Megan McMitchell aka Maven Megan? What can you tell us about her? Where did she live when- ?"

Father Gonzales interrupted him. "I'll tell you what. Why don't you write down your own questions on this paper and I'll see that he gets it."

TWENTY-FIVE

Libby curled up in an over-stuffed chair in the lobby of the Hotel Adagio in San Francisco. She didn't expect that the clerk would give her the key to Zack's room and decided not to put the woman in an awkward position by asking. She learned that Zack was not in his room and decided to park in a chair with a view to the lobby door and wait for him to return. The clerk had graciously offered her a bottle of water and volunteered to keep her luggage safe behind the counter. Libby had a copy of USA Today and could not have been more comfortable. Somewhere between the Bart station and the hotel she had settled her mind about her decision. She had been right to come, she now believed. Zack needed to hear her news and have an opportunity to decide what to do. And if he didn't return to the hotel within a reasonable time she would call him. And if he didn't answer his phone she would call Harry Harrar and see if he could tell her where to find him. Libby smiled and rubbed her tummy and flipped to the next page of the newspaper.

Martin O'Bannon leaned in to look over the shoulder of the police dispatcher. They both stared at the long list of names and times on the computer screen. Sure enough, no police officers had been dispatched to anyplace that was anywhere near the corner of Hyde and Geary the morning that Megan McMitchell died.

"A detective could have been there without us

knowing," the dispatcher suggested. "We don't keep track of them."

O'Bannon scratched his chin. "They'd have been in plain clothes, though. Megan wouldn't have reacted to them like she would to a uniform. No, she saw someone who made her feel safe enough to stop and talk and walk with him. That means a uniform."

"Hookers don't exactly like to see policemen coming when they're on the job," the dispatcher remarked. "Not unless they already know 'em," he added.

O'Bannon looked from the screen to the dispatcher. "Unless she knew him," he repeated slowly. "You may be on to something."

"But we didn't dispatch anyone there."

"No, but a policeman could wear his uniform off duty and who's to know? A policeman looks like a policeman. And if she already knew him..." O'Bannon was lost in thought for a moment before he continued. "If he was in uniform, that would include his dispatch radio receiver, wouldn't it? If he was trying to fool Megan into thinking he was there legitimately, he'd know she might notice that the radio was missing and sense something was wrong. No, he likely had the radio on his shoulder." O'Bannon turned to the dispatcher. "You can access the GPS info for each assigned radio, can't you? There's a citywide database; it should include every beat cop who's been assigned one. How long would it take the computer to identify a radio from the date and time and some GPS coordinates?"

The dispatcher looked at O'Bannon. "That's actually quite possible," he said. "It'd take a while to gain access and I'd have to have authorization but once I'm in, it should be a snap."

"Then what are we waiting for?"

The dispatcher grinned. "Not for me." He called across to another officer who was reading a paper. "Hey, Evans. Would you mind taking the helm for a while?"

Jim Snyder considered himself a tough reporter, hardened by experience, seen it all. He had chronicled some of the most appalling crime stories the human mind could invent. But the thought of an incredibly strong sadistic creature that could lean down from a tree limb and slash the throat and life out of his victim before the body could hit the ground terrified him. He thought about that night in his office when he sensed that he was being watched, followed, even stalked. He had never thought to look up at any time, not up the stairs, not at the exposed heat ducts along the ceiling... A shudder ran through him at the thought.

Susan noticed from across the room and guessed what was going on in his mind. "You don't have anybody, do you? I mean, no one to talk to about things, no one to comfort you?" Without waiting for his answer she patted the rumpled bedding on the couch next to her. "Come over here, old man. You had a close call the other night, I think. But I'm here now; we'll tackle this thing together."

Snyder stood and shuffled child-like across to the couch and sat down next to her. "I don't consider myself a coward," he said, "but this thing, this killer beast that we're unveiling isn't like anything I've ever known. I mean, if this thing exists, how does anyone stop it? You wouldn't even see it."

Susan swung a knee up on the couch and half turned to face Snyder. "Our deductions are based on the assumption that this is some kind of animal and so our conclusion left us with a hybrid animal of fearful proportions, as you say. But if we begin with the assumption that the killer is human, where does that take us?"

Snyder grinned ruefully. "It takes us to a preternaturally strong person with a very effective killing tool who knows how to hide all signs and tracks."

Susan smiled kindly. "That's a bit of an over-simplification, isn't it? Let's break it down a little more. First, must it be just one killer, or could it be two? That proposal helps out with the strength consideration. One perpetrator could hold the victim while the other dispatches her, for instance. And rather than one monster that moves rapidly through the branches you now have one person driving the victim toward a waiting partner who is already up in the tree."

Snyder looked at Susan appreciatively. "That's pretty good. But what about the lack of footprints?"

Susan stared at the far wall, still thinking. "What if something was said or done that struck deep fear in the victim, something to make the victim run along a set path in a panic, a path that would bring the victim to the partner waiting in the tree while the killer follows a parallel path somehow, traveling in a way that would leave no sign near the victim?"

Snyder considered that. "It could work, alright." Then he looked at Susan. "You don't believe it though, do you?"

She giggled. "No, not really."

"Can it actually be one person? I mean, is there a way for one person to manage all of that?"

"I can't see how."

Snyder was still musing. "We know that intermediaries were used. But how were they found? How were they enticed to help?" He looked at Susan. "How can an animal get humans to help it?"

Susan stared back. "I can't see how," she repeated.

They continued staring at one another. Then Snyder said, "It's really out there, isn't it? Some strange hybrid."

Susan took his arm and pulled him toward her. "I can't see how..." she whispered

It was just after two in the afternoon when Libby looked up from her paper and saw Zack walk into the lobby. She waited for him to notice her but he was entirely preoccupied with his thoughts. She knew that look. When he had nearly passed her chair she whispered "Zack?".

Zack stopped and looked blankly at the attractive woman curled up in the large armchair for a split second and then his face broke into a great smile. "Libby!"

She rose in one smooth motion, dropping the paper into the chair and hugged him.

"I've missed you," Zack said, after several moments.

Libby leaned back to look at him. "You wouldn't

know it. You haven't answered any of my calls."

Zack looked sheepish. "I meant to. I was going to just now, in fact. You know how involved these cases can get..." Then he said, "But why are you here? Not that I'm not delighted...I am! But here? Now? All the way to San Francisco?"

"Something important has happened," Libby said. "Or rather, is going to happen." She smiled a mysterious smile. "But I don't want to talk here. Can we go to your room?"

Zack shaped his face into a lecherous look. "Of course, my little chickadee. I'd love to show you my etchings."

Libby smacked him on the shoulder and grinned. "I'm glad you're not so involved in this case that you can't show a girl a good time."

In Zack's tiny room Libby perched on the edge of the bed and Zack dropped into the chair opposite her. Libby looked around.

"Not sparing any expense, I see."

"I wasn't exactly expecting a second honeymoon when I booked."

Libby smiled. "Not a honeymoon maybe, but- "

Zack's phone rang, interrupting her. He held up a hand. "Hold that thought. I've got to take this; it could be important."

Libby looked away so that Zack wouldn't see her

look of frustration.

It was Eagle Feather. "Have you had any word from Father Gonzales yet?"

"No, nothing. But I just arrived at my hotel, so..."

"I've been thinking about that whole deal with Father Gilligan. It doesn't ring true to me."

"You think Father Gonzales might be lying?"

"No, not him. But I think he could have been fooled."

"By Father Gilligan? In what way?"

"I'm not sure, it's just that something doesn't sit right with me about that story. How does a kind, outreaching, community-minded priest like Father Gilligan change his manner so suddenly and dramatically, even if he is experiencing trauma and guilt?"

"He's a flagellant, remember."

"Yes, but he always has been that. It's nothing new. Yet according to Father Gonzales he was always helpful and social and quite visible. Why would his personality suddenly change?"

Zack hesitated. "Uh, look, Eagle Feather, Libby's here, and I- "

"Libby's there? Oh, I'm sorry, man. I interrupted something. But why is Libby...? No, forget that, none of my business. Zack, you catch up with Libby. I'm going to ask some more questions, starting with, "Who took that picture of Father Gilligan in the Priests' Walk and when?"

"Okay," Zack said. "And I'll..."

But Eagle Feather was already gone.

Libby gave Zack a wry smile. "Eagle Feather?"

"Yes. But he's got his own trail to follow at the moment. Now where were we? I'm still wondering why you've come all the way out here."

Libby spoke in a rush before Zack's cell phone could ring again.

"Zack, I'm pregnant."

A triumphant utterance from the dispatcher brought O'Bannon over. On the man's computer screen there was a miniature time zone with each hour of day from 00:01 to 24.00 labeled across the top and names listed down the side. Where each name intersected with a time, a color-coded GPS location with longitude and latitude was printed: red for on-duty, green for off-duty.

"The central office accountants can use this record to help determine our pay," he explained. "If you're not walking around with your radio, you're not on duty. An off-duty officer who wants to claim time and a half or who makes an off duty arrest can have his location verified here."

At the top of the page that was currently displayed on the dispatcher's screen was the date May 20. The man placed his cursor on 12:00 and began to scroll down. He checked the GPS locations next to each officer's name against a list of streets and address numbers in his dispatch notebook.

"I'm not finding anyone in the area of Hyde and Geary so far. But, oh...wait! There, a green GPS location. It's on Geary, wait, let's see...yes, and right near Hyde. That's it!"

"Well? Who is it? What's his name?"

The dispatcher laughed. "It's one of your boys," he said. "It's Sergeant Harry Harrar."

Harry Harrar sat at his desk in the Richmond Station considering his options. He knew full well how dispatch worked and he knew about the data stream from the radios. Harry knew he had taken a chance wearing his radio the night he offed the girl Megan but he had thought the risk worth taking. She was a woman of the streets; she would have noticed the lack of a radio and she would have become suspicious. He had had no choice. He never thought anyone would take particular notice of a dead prostitute. He just never thought matters would get this far.

Harry shrugged. Well, they had, and now he was in a fix. To his mind, there were only two possibilities left him now. He could wait for the inevitable questions from O'Bannon when he became aware that Harry had been in the area of the murder at the critical time or he could be proactive. If he acted quickly enough, only O'Bannon would know that he had been there. And he was pretty sure he knew Marty well enough to know he wasn't likely to share his thinking with anyone. He really was that much of a loner.

Harry stood and reached down to his lower drawer and took out a snub nose .22-caliber throwaway pistol. He slipped it into his pocket. He'd taken it from the scene of a drug bust over a year ago and had kept it for just such an occasion. Every cop needed a gun he could drop to get himself out of trouble at one time in his career. This was Harry's time.

Sergeant Kelly emerged from the dark smoky bar with the fetid smell of rotting meat or decaying teeth or whatever it was that made the man Donny's breath so putrid clinging to his nostrils. The mission he'd been given this time was simple. He would help clean up loose ends for Donny, a loose end in this case named Detective Harry Harrar who worked in Homicide at the Richmond Station. Kelly was to drop a note on the detective's desk without being observed. He was to invent a probable reason for being at the station in case he was noticed. Kelly looked at the note in his hand; it was addressed to Detective Harrar in a strangely attractive rounded cursive. He'd been told not to open it - and he wouldn't, not for all the wealth in the world - but he'd sure love to know what was written inside this small pale pink envelope. He sniffed a corner of it. The tiniest wisp of an alluring perfume reached his nose. The contrast staggered Kelly; such an ill-smelling intimidating man producing this delicately scented, very feminine letter. Donny had assured him the note would bring Detective Harrar to a place where he could be dispatched: easily, quietly, privately. Kelly was surprised at this freely offered disclosure from Donny who usually kept his intentions close to the vest. Maybe the beast-man was learning to trust him. Well, he'd deliver the note as promised, and then he'd check his bank account for the large deposit Donny had promised him.

Father O'Rourke closed the large volume he had been studying and shoved it to the side. He smiled up at Eagle Feather.

"You Americans celebrate 1776 as the year of independence of your country but we in the Diocese of San Francisco celebrate it for the discovery of a small creek southeast of here on the 3rd of April, 1776, which was the Friday of Sorrows. They named that creek Arroyo de los Dolores in honor of that day and it became the site of the first church of the Diocese of San Francisco, ironically a church even older than the Diocese itself. They named the church Mission San Francisco de Asis."

Eagle Feather stared at him. "That's all very interesting but as a Native American whose people were oppressed and minimized by both cultures I personally am not inclined to celebrate its founding year. And I would remind you that the earliest sacred site of my people in America is far older than that."

"Ouch! Touché!" the priest grinned. "I deserved that. Navajo, do I remember correctly?"

Eagle Feather simply smiled.

Father O'Rourke coughed and shifted some papers. "So, to business. What can I do for you today? Have you found the young woman you seek?"

"In fact, no. But in turning over logs we've found some strange tracks." At the Father's puzzled look Eagle Feather smiled and said, "It's a hunting metaphor. We've not found the girl, but we've not found Father Gilligan either."

He saw he had the priest's full attention.

"Please explain," Father O'Rourke said.

"It seems he's unavailable to us due to a vow of silence arising from guilt he is experiencing. It has to do with the death of a young woman."

Father O'Rourke lifted his eyebrows. "Most unusual."

"We thought so. It was frustrating and disappointing. We left a note for Father Gilligan that Father Gonzales promised to deliver. But when and if this will actually occur...?" Eagle Feather shrugged his shoulders.

"And you have come to me because..."

"I've come to you to ask about your Priests' Walk."

Father O'Rourke stood up, pushing his chair back.

"Shall we go see it again?"

Eagle Feather nodded and Father O'Rourke led the way to the hall of portraits.

Eagle Feather stopped at the first picture. "When were these photographs taken?" he asked.

"I believe I told you at your last visit that they are taken as soon as possible after a priest is assigned to a parish within San Francisco. When such a change occurs, we send a photographer to take a picture for our wall. Our oldest photograph is forty years old. It's the picture of Father Benson here."

"And the newest?"

Father O'Rourke scratched his head. "Well, let's see, it must be Father Beneficio, the new intern at Notre Dame des Victoires."

"Do you ever do retakes? Or replacement photos?"

"We don't ask for renewals." Father O'Rourke grinned. "On our wall, priests appear young forever."

Eagle Feather walked down the row and stopped at the portrait of Father Gilligan. "What about this one? You mentioned before that his pose made him look different to you somehow. Is this the same photo that's always been here?"

Father O'Rourke looked surprised at the question and then became apologetic. "You know, I didn't think of that picture. Usually, we send out for our photos. But this one came to us, unsolicited. Father Gilligan asked to have his original replaced by this one, saying he had never been particularly fond of the original."

"Yet this one does not display him in a very complementary light..."

"True. I thought as much. It was a bit surprising."

Eagle Feather turned away.

"You're leaving already?" Father O'Rourke asked.

"I've got the answer I came for," Eagle Feather said.

TWENTY-SIX

They were close, much closer than he expected in such a short time. He'd have to step up his time-line. He'd have to move faster than he intended. It was inconvenient, but it would make his last hunt that much sweeter. In a few more days it would be time. He could wait. He had patience. He had all the patience of the centuries…

Libby's cell phone rang. She looked at the caller ID and saw it was Detective Harrar.

"I should take this call," she told Zack. "It's Detective Harry Harrar. He was very helpful in encouraging me to come here." She spoke in her phone. "Detective Harrar?"

"Hello, Libby. I'm calling to see how it all worked out for you. Are you in the city?"

Libby smiled. "Yes, I am. I'm here with Zack right now." Libby touched her lips and sent a kiss toward Zack.

"In the hotel?"

"Yes. We just connected. We have a lot to talk

about, as you can imagine. You don't mind if I call you back?"

"Oh, no. Not necessary. You carry on. I'm delighted that things seem to be working out. And Libby?"

"Yes?"

"Don't forget, you need to get that big lug to go back with you. He needs to get his head out of this case and back to his family. He wouldn't agree, of course, but this case is going nowhere."

"I'll remember, Detective. And thank you." She hung up.

Zack looked at her with raised eyebrows. "When did you come to know that detective?"

Libby laughed. She felt joyful about everything right now.

"I spoke with him by mistake when I tried to reach your friend, Lieutenant O'Bannon. He was very kind."

Zack looked at her curiously. "What did he want, if you don't mind me asking?"

Libby smiled. "He wanted to know how things are now."

Her joy was contagious. Zack smiled back. "And how are they?"

"Wonderful. Don't you think?"

Zack stood and walked over to Libby and sat on the

bed next to her. He took her in his arms.

"Yes, wonderful," he said.

Jim Snyder raised himself up on an elbow in the narrow bed and looked at Susan asleep next to him and wondered how he had suddenly become so fortunate. She was beautiful, smart, sexy and young and for some unfathomable reason she wanted him. Snyder had long ago dismissed the idea of a passionate encounter with a beautiful young woman. But now...

Susan's mouth was turned upward in a slight smile as she slept, almost as if she understood his thoughts. It did seem that way. She'd seen his fear and she'd understood his terror at the thought that this man-creature might be stalking him. Snyder was not a fearful man but his cynicism was his protective shield. When the realization dawned that such a creature might actually exist and be hunting him that shield had been stripped away. Susan appeared to know this; she'd seen the fear, she'd understood and she'd comforted him in a way that banished the threat and swept it entirely out his mind. But what about her?

Snyder lay down and clasped his hands behind his head. Did Susan have fears, he wondered? Or did the natural optimism and thoughtless courage of her youth protect her from it? She was so impulsive, so deliciously involved in living. That was unusual for an academician of such prominence. She allowed herself to enjoy the moment and was confident that the future would take care of itself.

Snyder's thoughts turned toward his own future. What now? What could they do about their suspicions? No one would believe such a monster could exist. The police would dismiss the story out of hand. And time was growing short. If his calculations were correct, they could expect another kill in four more days. Suddenly Snyder became aware of a pair of blue eyes.

"What are you thinking about so hard with that frown?" Susan asked. "Did I disappoint you?"

Snyder felt his worries melt away once again. "Allow me to show you how much you disappointed me," he said and rolled toward her.

"Meet me at Star of the Sea Parish right away. We may have found our guy." Eagle Feather's voice sounded curt.

Zack froze in place momentarily, phone to ear. He had let his cell phone go to message rather than interrupt his conversation with Libby. Now he regretted it. The message had been left fifteen minutes ago. It sounded urgent.

"I've got to go," he told Libby.

"Why?"

Zack paused. Libby almost never questioned his actions like this. "Libby, this may be our big break. I know the timing couldn't be worse. If it were anything less..."

Libby looked at Zack and her annoyance showed on her face. "Is it really that critical, Zack? Or is it an excuse to run away from your responsibility to your family?"

Zack had already moved toward the door. “I can’t leave Eagle Feather on his own. He could be in danger.”

“I’ve been told that this case is just in your mind...”

Zack’s hand was on the door handle when she said this. He wheeled around and stared at her, his face hard. She instantly regretted her words.

“Who told you that?”

“Zack, I need to know if you’re committed to-”

“Who told you that?”

“It was Detective Harrar.” Her voice was low, chastened. “He believes the killings are not connected.”

“He’s not even involved in the case. Yet you believe him?”

“He told me he was involved. Zack, I didn’t mean any- ”

“I’ve got to go.” Zack rushed through the door and let it slam behind him.

It was another twenty minutes before Zack found a cab and reached the Star of the Sea Parish Church. It was not very long by San Francisco standards but each minute seemed an eternity. He pushed Libby’s accusation to the back of his mind; he’d have to think about that later. During the cab ride he recalled the earlier call from Eagle Feather, something about checking on Father Gilligan’s picture. What had he meant?

When Zack's cab pulled up to the curb on Eighth Street there was no one waiting at the church door. He paid the cabby and ran quickly up the steps to the side door and pushed it open. In the dim light the sanctuary appeared empty. He walked a short way down the center aisle, his footfalls hollow and vibrant. He paused to listen. There was no sound. Zack returned to the narthex and walked to the door that led to the administration building. When he stepped inside the offices he was met by the usual hum of activity: telephone chatter, keyboards clicking, conversations humming in offices. He saw that the door to Father Gilligan's office was ajar. He walked over and peered in. It was empty and looked undisturbed. Down the hall he saw that Father Gonzales' office door was closed. He thought he remembered the priest saying he usually kept it open for his parishioners. Zack walked on down the carpeted corridor and knocked on the door. It was not latched and it yawned open at the impact. Eagle Feather was there, his back to Zack. He was reading something on the priest's desk.

"Come on in, Zack," Eagle Feather said without looking around.

Zack walked into the room. "Must be my aftershave," he said.

Eagle Feather chuckled. "That's it." He turned. In his hand he held a folded note. "This is from Father Gonzales. It says he's doing confessions."

Zack paused for a moment. "That would be in the church," he said.

"Yes."

"But I just came from there. No one was in there. I would have heard a voice."

Eagle Feather looked steadily at Zack. "Yes. The church was empty when I was there also."

"So what's going on?"

Eagle Feather passed the note to Zack. "I don't think Father Gilligan and the man in the portrait at St. Boniface Church are the same man."

"You think he's an impostor?"

"That's my guess."

"So it could be..."

"That's what I'm thinking."

"And Father Gonzales...?"

"He could be in trouble. I think we'd better go to confession."

The men turned as one and walked quickly out of the office and rushed through the administration building. They crossed the sward in a few steps and pushed through the door of the church building. Zack entered first. He held up a hand for silence and quietly removed his shoes. Eagle Feather followed suit. They walked noiselessly through the narthex and into the dusky sanctuary illuminated only faintly by shafts of filtered light. The two men shuffled silently down the center aisle side by side. There was no sound. Two confessionals ornamented in dark wood with thick rich burgundy drapes stood against the western wall. Zack signaled Eagle Feather to the one on the left while he crept toward the other. He reached toward his belt then remembered that he was unarmed. *I'd better start carrying my gun from here on*, he thought. The two men reached the booths at the same time.

Zack leaned toward curtained entrance. "Father Gonzales, are you in there?" he whispered. There was no response. Zack lifted the curtain and peered in. The little room was empty. He stepped inside. He looked through the latticed window to the confessor's side. It was also empty. Zack released the breath he had been holding and stepped out of the booth. He saw Eagle Feather standing at the second booth holding the curtain open. He looked at Zack.

"I've found Father Gonzales," he said.

Lieutenant Marty O'Bannon's fingers gripped the steering wheel so tightly they turned white. He felt his anger continue to rise and he tried to push it down.

I don't really know that Harry is involved in this thing, he thought to himself. *All I know is he was in the same vicinity the night Megan was shot.* But Marty thought of all the other small puzzle pieces that now began to come together. Why had Harry so uncharacteristically offered to help him? O'Bannon did not believe in coincidence nor in sudden personality changes. *Something* was going on with Harrar.

Well, he wasn't going to wait to learn what it was, not with this case poised to go down the toilet and his career with it. The time to confront Harry was right now.

The stop and go traffic on Geary Street was taking forever. Marty flipped on his lights and carved a lane down the center of the road. At the same time he transmitted a call to the station to see if Harrar was still there.

"Would you patch me through to Detective Harrar?" he asked the dispatcher.

"One moment, sir." The moment turned into several long minutes. Then the dispatcher was back. "Sorry, sir, but Detective Harrar does not seem to be here."

"Where'd he go?"

"Uh, he didn't say, sir."

"Well, what does his duty log show?"

"There's no entry in it for this time, sir. Oh, and sir, his radio is still on his desk."

"Okay, listen carefully. I want you to check the men's room, the women's room, the closets, the parking lot, check *everywhere* in and around the station for Detective Harrar and when I get there five minutes from now I want to be told exactly where he is. Got it?"

"Yes, sir!"

O'Bannon slammed his fist down on the steering wheel in frustration. He knew where Harry Harrar had gone. He knew now that Harrar was dirty and was on the run.

Zack looked into the booth. The crumpled figure of a man in clerical clothing lay on the floor. He stepped in and peered at the man's face. It was indeed Father Gonzales. He looked up at the confession window. The sliding curtain that separated the confessional from the priest's booth was raised and the metal filigree screen had been powerfully fisted inward like a huge bullet passing through a sheet of tin. Zack checked the priest's carotid artery. The man was dead all right, but rigor mortis had not yet set in. He looked closer. There was no blood showing and no open wounds on the priest's body. But there were large and very dark bruises on his neck.

Eagle Feather crouched down next to Zack. Their eyes met.

"He grabbed Father Gonzales through that metal screen like it was paper and strangled him," Eagle Feather said.

Zack nodded without speaking. Eagle Feather rose and stepped out of the booth and Zack followed him. They stood for a moment looking around the sanctuary.

"We'd better see if Father Gilligan is still around," Zack said. "And I think we better stay together," he added.

Eagle Feather gave a tense smile. "I'm not going to argue with you, white man."

The dispatcher was waiting at the top of the steps to the Richmond District Station when O'Bannon pulled up and double-parked in the street. The man looked nervous and frustrated.

"I'm sorry, sir, I can't find him anywhere," he said when O'Bannon approached.

"Not your fault." O'Bannon's voice was gruff. "Go

back to your desk. I'll take a look around myself."

The man held the door for O'Bannon.

"Are any patrol cars missing?" O'Bannon asked. It was a sudden thought.

"I'll check, sir."

They walked in together. A large uniformed man passed them on his way out. O'Bannon glanced at him. He felt a stir of recognition. He'd seen the man somewhere before, it was something about the way he walked. No time now, though.

"I'm going back to the homicide office. You check the patrol cars. Make sure every car that is out is correctly assigned."

"Yes sir." The dispatcher sensed that something big was afoot and he scurried into action.

Marty O'Bannon walked through the familiar door of the Homicide Office and went straight to Harrar's desk. The surface was in its usual disarray and the computer monitor was left on. He glanced at the screen and then stopped and stared. The grid on it was familiar; it was the radio GPS results that O'Bannon had just been studying. How had Harrar accessed it? It required layers of passwords. He looked closer. It was the page for the Tenderloin District database, for Hyde and Geary Streets. And there was the name Detective Sergeant Harry Harrar. There could be no doubt now that Harry knew they were on to him. O'Bannon pulled open the bottom desk drawer where he knew Harrar kept a throwaway gun. It was gone.

O'Bannon slumped down in Harry's chair. Harry

was armed and on the run. He would be exceptionally dangerous. He needed to be stopped immediately. Then he had another thought. Could all this be just a fantastic coincidence? Could it be that Harry was at the intersection of Hyde and Geary that night for some other reason?

O'Bannon had to make a choice. If Harry was guilty, a desperate man on the run, he needed to raise the alarm and catch him before he could harm anyone. O'Bannon squirmed in his chair. But what if he was innocent and O'Bannon launched a citywide search for him? He could be shot, killed by mistake...or another policeman could be hurt.

Marty reached for the phone, then pulled his hand away undecided. As he did he noticed an envelope on the desk, a pink envelope that stood out among all the official white papers. He picked it up. It was addressed to Harry Harrar, Richmond District Police Station, in a woman's handwriting with no return address. He turned it over. It was unopened. He caught a scent of perfume when he put up it to his nose. O'Bannon thought about it. The envelope had been on top of Harry's papers, not buried under them. It must have arrived recently. Could it have been the last thing Harry looked at before he ran? But it was unopened. That didn't make any sense.

O'Bannon took his car key and slashed open the envelope. There was a single sheet of folded notepaper inside. There was no salutation and no signature, just two sentences. It read, "*I no what you did. If you dont want me to go to cops, bring $20,000 and meet me at statue in redwood mimorial grove in Goldin Gate Park at ten tonite.*"

Marty O'Bannon stared at the note. Redwood tree? Memorial? In Golden Gate Park? Where the hell was that? Oh, right, it was that World War I memorial. There were redwood trees near the doughboy statue. He'd been there once. He'd found it by mistake while kicking out druggies. It was a small grove of redwood trees that people didn't visit much: a perfect spot.

O'Bannon thought hard. Who could have sent this note? Maybe a witness to something Harrar had done, like the killing of Megan, perhaps? The writing was just barely north of illiterate; it could be one of the girls working the streets with Megan. If she had seen the murder she could be of great value to him. And Harry wouldn't be going to meet her since he hadn't opened the note. Not that it would've mattered to Harry anyway, now that the cat was out of the bag. *I'll attend this meeting*, O'Bannon thought. He glanced at his watch. Almost 5 PM. He reached for the phone. The note made the decision easy. It was time to put out an all points bulletin on Harry Harrar.

Zack attended church services occasionally and had gone fairly regularly with his parents as a child, but he'd never realized how many nooks and crannies were hidden away in a large sanctuary like the Star of the Sea Parish Church. The men searched cautiously, watching each other's backs. After they were completely satisfied that the building was empty Zack called Marty O'Bannon.

The policeman answered on the first ring.

"I've got a dead priest," Zack announced, "strangled in his own confessional."

"Where?"

"The Star of the Sea Catholic Church on Geary and Eighth. We were tracking down a priest who spoke with Megan recently."

"Is he the dead priest?"

"No, it's his colleague. The other one disappeared."

"I'll be right there. But first I gotta tell you I've got an all points out on Harry Harrar."

"The Homicide Detective who works with you?"

"Yeah. If you see him, proceed very cautiously. I have reason to believe he's the one who killed Megan McMitchell."

A sudden thought clutched at Zack. He caught his breath. "He's been talking to Libby. He's the one who talked her into coming to San Francisco." Zack felt a stab of fear.

"You'd better get hold of her and make sure she's safe. She needs to know about Harry and stay away from him."

But Zack had already rung off and was calling Libby. She didn't answer. Zack felt panic begin to take hold. He tried to stay calm.

"I'm going back to my hotel," he said to Eagle Feather. "Harry Harrar has been implicated in this business and he's on the run. He's been in contact with Libby. I've got to go warn her." He was running even as he spoke those last words.

"I'll stay here and check in with O'Bannon," Eagle Feather called after him.

TWENTY-SEVEN

It was dark, but a row of flashing emergency lights along the street in front of the Star of the Sea Catholic Church draped it with a pulsing blue hue. Policemen were evident everywhere: searching the grounds, canvassing neighbors, talking on radios. Inside the sanctuary, O'Bannon watched as a forensics team worked on the body of the late Father Gonzales, still huddled in his confessional. Eagle Feather stood next to him.

O'Bannon had a lot of questions.

"You say that you and Zack think this priest was connected to Megan McMitchell in some way?" he asked.

"Not this priest," Eagle Feather said. "The missing priest, Father Gilligan. She spoke to him before her death, maybe even confessed something to him."

"And where's this missing priest?"

"We can't find him. We think he killed Father Gonzales while pretending to confess and then ran."

"Why would he kill Father Gonzales?"

Eagle Feather sighed. "Probably because he assumed that Father Gonzales had become suspicious of him."

"About what?"

"About not being Father Gilligan."

O'Bannon glared at Eagle Feather. "I've had an awfully long day today. I'm in no mood for solving riddles. I don't suppose you could give me the down and dirty version?"

Eagle Feather shrugged. "I would if there was one. All I can say is we suspect that an impostor took the identity of Father Gilligan several weeks ago and has gotten away with it until now. Once he realized that the game was up he killed Father Gonzales to keep his secret."

It was O'Bannon's turn to sigh. "Okay, here we go again. Why would someone take this priest Gilligan's identity? And what happened to the real Gilligan?"

"Two excellent questions. We don't know. But we suspect this impostor is the killer we've been hunting. And if we're right about that, we need to be searching for the body of another priest."

"The real Father Gilligan."

"Uh-huh."

O'Bannon turned to an officer nearby. "Sergeant, we need to organize a search for another priest. He's been missing a month, so it won't be easy. Check with the neighbors; see if they noticed anything. Check all around the grounds. Take all the help you need."

"Yes, Sir."

"And sergeant, be quick and be thorough I don't want this dragging on. The press is going to have a field day as it is."

O'Bannon turned back to Eagle Feather. "Where's Zack?"

"He went to check on his wife Libby back at the hotel. Apparently she came to San Francisco at the advice of your Dirty Harry. Zack wants to make sure she's safe."

O'Bannon moaned. "Oh God, what next?" He grabbed his radio to dispatch a patrol car to the Adagio Hotel. "I'll set up surveillance there," he said to Eagle Feather. "We'll try to keep Zack's wife safe and at the same time maybe we'll get lucky and catch our fugitive."

He turned to the forensics chief and gave him some instructions and walked a few steps away from the booth with Eagle Feather. "Any more ideas?"

"Just one," Eagle Feather said. "There's a likeness of the impostor in St. Boniface Church, a photo on the wall. It's not a good one, but it might help you identify the guy. Just ask for Father O'Rourke."

"And you?"

"I'm going to call a certain newspaper man to see if he's got any news."

Zack flung a wad of bills on the seat next to the driver

and jumped out of the cab. He'd been trying to call Libby the entire way back from Inner Richmond but always reached her voice mail. He sprinted through the hotel lobby and ignoring the elevator ran to the stairs. At his floor he raced down the corridor to his room and opened the door. He could see the entirety of the small room and its adjacent bathroom in a single sweeping glance. Libby was not there.

Zack slumped against the doorjamb, his legs suddenly weak, his worst fears realized. There were only two reasons for her to leave the room, both of them bad: either to walk away from their relationship, or to meet with Harry Harrar.

Eagle Feather called just as Susan Apgar and Jim Snyder were heading out for dinner.

"Got time for an update?"

"Uh, sure, go ahead." Snyder motioned to Susan to hold up.

Eagle Feather spoke rapidly. "You remember we were looking for the priest that Megan McMitchell had spoken to? Well, we found him. We learned from him that she had also talked with a different priest, one with a parish over in Inner Richmond. We tracked that priest down. He was an impostor. Then things got crazy. We just found the body of his associate priest in that parish on the floor of his confessional, murdered. He was probably killed because of what he knew. The impostor priest has vanished and the cops are now looking for the body of the priest whose identity he stole."

Snyder sat down on a kitchen chair, his head

spinning. “Whoa! Slow down! So you think this impostor priest is...?”

“Father Gonzales was murdered in a way that required incredible strength, so yes, that’s what I think.”

“And now he’s gone...”

“Yes.”

Susan sat in the other kitchen chair and was watching Snyder’s face.

Snyder paused. Now he asked Eagle Feather, “Is there anything else?”

“One other bit of news,” Eagle Feather said. “A detective working with Lieutenant O’Bannon may be involved, a Detective Sergeant Harrar. O’Bannon has reason to believe he’s the one who killed Megan McMitchell.”

“Is he talking?”

“He’s gone too.”

“Vanished?”

“Pretty much. Zack’s wife Libby has just arrived in town. Seems she’d been talking to this Harrar guy; in fact he’d talked her into coming here in the first place. Zack’s gone to check on her. Now that Harrar’s been flushed out, he’s worried about what he might do.” Eagle Feather chuckled wryly. “So that’s about it. What’s new at your end?”

Snyder couldn’t respond for a while as his brain

raced to digest everything he'd just heard. Susan stroked his arm and looked at him questioningly. Snyder looked back at Susan and shrugged. Then he spoke into the phone. "Nothing...everything. After talking it all over with Susan here and after looking all the evidence square in the eye we've begun to think we might be dealing with some creature...I mean this murderer might be more than...well, you know...human."

Snyder heard Eagle Feather's evil chuckle. "So, you finally got there. Does your anthropologist friend know what kind of creature it might be?"

Snyder groaned. "Beyond some mythical beast? No, not really. But I'd have to think he's some sort of genetic aberration."

Eagle Feather chuckled again. "Well, when you two figure out what name to attach to it, you let me know. But in the meantime nothing's changed as far as I'm concerned."

As Snyder ended the call he felt Susan's eyes on him. "Let's go get some food," he said. "It's gonna take all dinner to talk about this.

Marty O'Bannon pulled his car to the curb along John F. Kennedy Drive in Golden Gate Park. He planned to walk to Doughboy Meadow from there. The streetlights along the road lit his way but beyond their bright fluorescence it was darker than dark. An occasional car rolling by illuminated the individual trees at the fringe of the woods for a few seconds and then it all went black again. Worse, fog had crept in and was slowly thickening. O'Bannon took out a tiny LED flashlight and studied his park map. He should find a trail in another hundred yards or so. He looked at his watch. Good, his timing was right on. He wanted to be in place a full half hour before the appointed time.

O'Bannon walked slowly along the road, dependent upon car headlights to help him locate the trailhead. But even those lights, bright as they were, couldn't penetrate into the dark woods but instead bounced off the vaporous wall of creeping fog. The park at night bore no resemblance to the park he knew during the day; distances seemed to change, almost as if some magic happened at dusk to transform the landscape entirely. O'Bannon regretted that he'd not taken time to scout the terrain before dark; he regretted that he hadn't brought the large torch instead of this penlight. Hell, he regretted he hadn't brought someone with him. *It's too late for all that now,* he thought. Then by the light of a passing car he saw a well-trodden passage leading into the trees. It disappeared as soon as the car did but O'Bannon gauged the distance and directed his light that way. He saw a sneaker print leading into the darkness. This might be it.

But the path turned out to be just a trace and after fifty feet of pushing through underbrush it disappeared entirely. He swept his tiny light around but thick brush blocked his way in every direction. He stood still for a moment noticing how muffled the traffic sounds were here, how still the night was, how alone he felt even in the very midst of this large in-somnolent city. He shuddered and walked quickly back to the firmness of the sidewalk. He breathed deeply for a moment and wiped a bead of moisture from his forehead. Another regret had come to mind; that he'd left his hand radio in the car thinking it might give him away - not thinking it might serve him if he needed assistance.

O'Bannon felt annoyance at his own weakness and walked briskly on. Almost immediately he found a narrow asphalt path. There was no doubt this time. It was easy to follow and he walked rapidly, his penlight illuminating the black surface ahead of him. Down the slope the pavement sounded hollow under foot and then it ended in grass. This was a meadow. In the meadow would be the Doughboy Statue. And near it the author of the note would expect to meet him, if he were Harry Harrar.

O'Bannon's not fully formed idea was to conceal himself and keep the statue in view but he now realized his plan couldn't work. It was impossible to see anything beyond the beam of his tiny light. He decided to wait in the meadow near enough to the statue to get to it quickly but far enough to allow the darkness to conceal him. After all, the author of the note would be facing the same difficulties presented by the darkness and would have to use a flashlight as well. He'd wait there with his own light off and watch for it. O'Bannon found his spot and crouched down. He felt for his handgun in his holster and eased the safety off. Then he turned off his light and let the darkness and the silence envelop him.

Eagle Feather's phone vibrated. It was Zack.

"Libby's gone."

"What do you mean, gone?"

"I mean she wasn't there when I got to my room. She's not anywhere in the hotel and there's no note."

"You think Harrar...?"

"I don't know, I don't know what to think."

"Did you call O'Bannon?"

"I tried but he didn't answer."

"Harrar's a wanted man," Eagle Feather pointed out. "He'd be taking a big risk to go through the middle of town to your hotel."

"It might be worth it to him to have a hostage." Zack's voice broke slightly with the word. "He might have called and convinced her to go to him."

"I'll be there in ten minutes," Eagle Feather said.

Zack went back down to the lobby to question the desk clerk and the other hotel personnel. He experienced a horrible sense of deja vu. Libby could be the second person to disappear from this hotel. He'd questioned all these same people before. And they never found the ultra-runner. He tried to put that out of his mind.

But Zack had better luck this time. The concierge clearly remembered noticing a tall and very striking woman with chestnut hair leaving the hotel soon after Zack himself had left. Yes, she'd had her bag; she was pulling it along behind her. No, she didn't look particularly anxious or worried. No, she didn't seem to be in a hurry.

Then the doorman remembered hailing a cab for an attractive, polite lady, a good tipper. Where did she go? Well, she'd asked to be driven to the Fairmont Hotel, as he remembered.

A cab was pulling up while Zack questioned the doorman and Eagle Feather climbed out. Zack saw him and called quickly to him, "Hang on to that cab!" He tipped the doorman and climbed into the seat next to Eagle Feather. "To the Fairmont hotel, please," he told the driver.

Eagle Feather glanced at Zack. "Moving up in the world?"

"No, but apparently Libby is. She's gone there for some reason."

"Why don't you call her and ask?"

Zack grimaced. "Don't you think I've tried? She's not answering her phone."

Eagle Feather grinned. "That spells pissed off to me."

Zack looked at him and his blue eyes were moist. "Let's hope that's all it is."

It took less than ten minutes to reach the Fairmont. Zack knew the hotel. This was where Libby had always stayed when she came to San Francisco before they were married. Zack preferred something a little less ostentatious but when they were here together, he always obliged her.

Zack had his FBI credentials in hand when they approached the desk but the desk clerk recognized him right away.

"Good evening, Mr. Tolliver. Will you be staying with us tonight?"

"No, but I believe Mrs. Tolliver may have taken a room. May I know the number?"

"I'll check for you, Mr. Tolliver, but I don't remember seeing her recently."

"She wasn't here within the last hour?"

"No sir, I'm sure about that."

Zack and Eagle Feather talked it over in the grand foyer near the stairs that led down to the lower shops and restaurants.

Eagle Feather glanced at the sign. "Maybe she went down to the Tonga Room for a bite? She probably hasn't eaten all day."

It was nearly eight PM and the restaurant was very crowded. The men shouldered their way inside. The exotic central pool reflected the fiery light of the torches flickering along its edge. They divided and searched the tables on either side. It was slow going. People stood shoulder-to-shoulder holding drinks, and the decorative palm fronds and deep shadows obscured the view to the second tier of seating. When Zack and Eagle Feather found each other at the far side, Zack was exasperated and increasingly concerned.

"We're just going in circles and wasting time," he said.

Eagle Feather was staring back across the pool. Zack saw his fixed gaze and looked that way.

"Isn't that Libby?" Eagle Feather asked. "I see her reflection. She's seated at a table with someone but I can't see who it is. His head is turned."

Zack followed Eagle Feather's pointing finger. The reflection in the water mirrored the poolside seats and projected a view impossible to see directly. Zack saw Libby. And there was a man with her.

As Zack stared the man turned his head. It was Harry Harrar. They saw each other at the same moment and Harrar instantly jumped up and grabbed Libby's arm and pulled her away from the table. Libby, startled, resisted. Zack could see her mouth shaping words of objection. Suddenly she stopped struggling and went with him, her body rigid.

He's pulled a gun, Zack realized with anguish. He began frantically pushing his way toward them and Eagle Feather followed. It was an impossible task. There was nowhere for people to go and they resisted and became angry. They were getting nowhere. Desperate, Zack used a swimming motion through the crowd, thrusting people aside and sending drinks flying everywhere. People yelled at him but a narrow opening formed through the crowd as others scrambled to get out his way. They reached the table where Libby and Harry had been. Unfinished plates of food and two drinks sat there. Libby's suitcase was under the table. *No time for that now,* Zack thought. They pushed on. When the two men burst out of the restaurant and into the corridor Libby and Harry Harrar were gone.

"Take the stairs to the lobby," Zack yelled at Eagle Feather and turned the opposite way down the corridor toward the meeting rooms and the rear exit door. When he opened the door to the street and looked each way he knew he'd lost them. Libby and her captor were gone.

The minutes crawled by like hours. Marty O'Bannon pushed the illuminator button on his watch yet another time. Only five minutes after ten. He must be more patient. He'd give it a full half hour and then he'd leave. After all, anything could happen. The woman could change her mind, deciding it was too dangerous and not worth the risk.

O'Bannon shivered. The creeping fog sent a chill down his spine and he felt damp even in his jacket. He shifted his legs. The crouching position was difficult but it was better than sitting in the damp grass. He was looking for any glow of light or any movement but it was difficult to focus his eyes in the blackness. He tried to be methodical by sweeping the area before him in a counter-clockwise direction and then returning to the original point and starting again. *Funny how seeing nothing is more difficult than seeing everything,* he thought. He began another sweep and then froze. It wasn't anything he saw or heard; it was something he sensed. Someone or something was near him. Marty trusted his cop intuition and it told him to pull his gun and he did. He strained to listen, tried to see. He caught a scent, more of a stench, really. It was putrid, rotten. Then he felt a touch, something behind him, something brushing the back of his jacket. He spun around. He tried to rise but his legs, bloodless and tired from his long crouch, responded slowly. He slipped and caught himself. He swept his pistol in an arc looking for a target. He saw nothing.

O'Bannon climbed to his feet, swearing. The grass was damp and now his trouser knees were wet and cold and the palm of his hand was slimy. He pivoted in a slow circle, his gun pointing, his eyes searching. He saw nothing.

Well, that's it, he thought. *If anybody was here before, they're gone now. They know I'm here.* He reached for his penlight. It was time to go.

His hand stopped mid-air. A nerve-chilling animal cry rose out of the nearby woods. His blood froze. This wasn't the rising sorrowful howl of the coyote; this was menacing and terrible. It was like nothing he'd ever heard, vibrant with cruel meaning, terrorizing in its intent. It released all the dark primal fears that resided in the deepest part of O'Bannon's brain and his sphincter choked shut and his bladder released. He could not move, could not breathe. Eyes wide with terror, Marty O'Bannon stood rooted to the earth.

Later when describing his experience, O'Bannon would say he had no idea how long he stood frozen by terror in that damp, dark meadow. His pistol dropped from his hand; the policeman who went to the meadow later to investigate found it. His penlight was also abandoned in the tall grass. Once his petrified brain permitted him to move, Marty somehow found his way back to the sidewalk in the darkness and stumbled and ran to his car. His hands shook too much to put the key the ignition and so he sat and waited until he could control them. By the interior light he saw that his pants were filthy and soaked in urine. Another time he'd have been disgusted with himself but now he had no such thoughts. He sat with the car windows closed tight and the doors locked and stared into the pool of light from his headlights in horrified anticipation of what might suddenly appear there.

For the first time in his life Marty O'Bannon understood how it felt to become prey.

TWENTY-EIGHT

"Here's what I can't get my head around," said Jim Snyder. They were in a Starbucks in the Bart station and were sipping coffee and eating scones at a table for two that was tucked back against the tiled wall. "I can't fathom how a branch-hopping killer monster could have human allies. That would infer that this creature is human enough not only to communicate with people but also be able to persuade them to do his bidding. That in turn infers that the creature must appear human to the people he employs so that they aren't too frightened to meet with him. And to be honest, I can't form a mental picture of what I just described." Snyder wiped strawberry jam from his mustache.

Susan was watching Snyder with her elbow on the table and her chin resting on the heel of her hand. Her coffee steamed in front of her. "I love that you can't envision something unless you are able to construct it analytically," she said, grinning. "You could never have been a Grimm Brother."

Snyder smiled back. "I guess you're right," he said. "I'd have been the guy who goes off into the forest with a spy glass and measuring tape and gets eaten by someone else's imaginary dragon."

Susan laughed and took a sip of coffee. "But you do have a point, I'll admit. While I'm able...okay, eager to create in my mind a missing link sort of creature from an anthropological viewpoint, I'm not quite so willing to give it human characteristics or to bestow it with human intelligence. I suppose in my mind's eye I've drawn a Bigfoot sort of creature with tons of animal cunning and survival instincts. But something that enlists the aid of humans? No, that to me seems more like a master criminal: a depraved, mentally ill, psychotic, steroidal individual perhaps, but definitely a human being."

Snyder looked at her with a thoughtful expression. "In your view, then, we must make a choice. If we go for animal, we must call these so-called human intermediaries - the call girl, the bad cop and the priests - coincidences or possibly parallel cases pulled in by mistake: a misinterpretation of the evidence. Think about it: if Megan McMitchell doesn't show up in the lounge of the Adagio Hotel with this big ugly guy right when Agent Tolliver happens to be staying there, and if this ultra athlete never goes missing - if all that never happens, then where are we? I think I'm still out looking for overgrown coyotes."

"That's right. It's a pretty fragile link that takes us into this whole line of investigation."

Snyder waved his hands in frustration. "Okay, so you may be right. But let's look at it from another direction. If we're dealing with a human killer, how does he do it? What human could possibly have the strength to move swiftly from tree to tree and then lean down from a branch and lift a grown woman off the ground with one hand while dispatching her with a powerful gouge to the throat with the other? Or are we wrong about the method? Is there another means of committing these murders that we haven't thought of?"

Susan sat in silence and stared back at Snyder. At last she whispered, "I don't know."

They nibbled their scones and sipped coffee for a

while and avoided one another's eyes until Snyder finally put down his coffee and spoke decisively.

"The way I see it, I brought you into this because of your expertise with every sort of animal including mythological ones. That's the direction my instincts were taking me then and I'm not going to change that now. I vote animal."

Susan smiled teasingly. "You're just trying to find a way to keep me around, aren't you, old man?"

Snyder looked a little sheepish. "That wouldn't be so bad either." He grinned. "But I stand by what I just said."

"Okay, let's stick with that approach. But we'll have to agree to treat the whole Megan thing as a distraction and assume it's an entirely different case" -she raised her eyebrows at Snyder- "whether it is or not. We have to leave all that to Agent Tolliver and Detective O'Bannon."

"What's our next step, then?"

"We'll draw it up."

Snyder looked questioningly at her. She grinned.

"We'll reconstruct the creature from its actions, its abilities, the noises it makes: anything we have. Then we'll see what it looks like on paper and compare it to all other animals, present, past, or mythical."

"You can do that?"

"It's what I do. It's a lot like the way a police artist

recreates a perpetrator from the descriptions of witnesses. All I need is some sketch paper, some Derwent Graphitint pencils, your kitchen table, and all the evidence you've collected so far."

Snyder stood and beckoned. "My kitchen table awaits."

Libby knew she was in trouble. And it was all due to her own carelessness - her own petty annoyance. After Zack left her to go to Eagle Feather she'd felt abandoned. Worse, she'd felt as if he'd also abandoned their unborn child. So she had called Harry Harrar. She wasn't sure why, exactly; possibly because Zack didn't seem to like him or maybe because Harry might know what was going on. And Harry had been completely supportive. He'd reassured her. He'd even tried to excuse Zack and his stubborn dedication to the case. And he'd suggested that she try to be more patient. And yes, he did have information to share. He'd be more than happy to fill her in; she deserved to know, didn't she? When he suggested they meet in the Tonka Room at the Fairmont she readily agreed. She knew the Fairmont; it was familiar ground to her. So she'd met him there. He had a table waiting and they had drinks and she was starved and she was just tearing into a wonderful rack of ribs when Harry underwent a complete change: his face hardened and he said they had to go. Right then. She'd protested. She'd asked what the problem was and then he drew a pistol and she knew she was in trouble.

Harry pushed and shoved her through the crowd, out of the restaurant, out into the corridor and around the corner and up the stairs. Libby half ran and half fell as he dragged her along. His gun was in his other hand inside his jacket pocket. They walked quickly through the lobby and out into the street. Libby didn't dare protest;

she believed Harry when he snarled that he would shoot her. Then he pushed her into the back of a patrol car, leapt in, and started it up. She reached for the door handle to jump out but there wasn't one, and the front seat was caged off. She was imprisoned.

Harry accelerated into the near empty street, weaving expertly around traffic, driving with one hand on the wheel while he searched through the frequency bands on the radio with the other, listening for something.

"Sorry to inconvenience you, Mrs. Tolliver. It seems I need you now. You are my ticket out of here."

"What's going on?" Libby tried to keep her voice calm, reasonable.

"You'll find out soon enough. If you cooperate and do exactly as I say when I say it, you'll get out of this without even a bruise, just slightly inconvenienced."

"I'll cooperate," Libby said. "Anything you say."

Harry smiled a tight smile. "That's wonderful. But for now, just sit back and relax and enjoy our fine city by dusk."

"Can you tell me where we're going, at least?"

"Just sit back and enjoy the ride, Mrs. Tolliver."

Zack ran down Powell Street to the end of the block and then raced up Sacramento. The daytime crowds had thinned out and far off to the east the last rays of the evening sun shimmered on the bay. When he turned up Mason Street to the front of the hotel he saw Eagle Feather already waiting under the hotel's entrance canopy. His friend shrugged his shoulders at Zack.

"They came this way. The doorman noticed them. He said they were walking funny. He saw them climb into a patrol car just over there." Eagle Feather pointed to a red curb area.

"I should never have left her alone in the room," Zack moaned. "I should have stayed. I should have talked to her."

Eagle Feather looked Zack in the eye. "You did what you had to do. You had no choice but to respond to that priest's murder. Libby's a grown woman. You couldn't have prevented what happened."

Zack pulled out his cell phone and called O'Bannon. The phone rang several times before Marty picked up.

"Hello." O'Bannon sounded very tired.

"It's Zack. Where are you?"

"I'm at my apartment. Zack, we need to talk. I think there's something you and Eagle Feather haven't made sufficiently clear to me."

"Sure, sure, we'll talk all about it but right now we need to find Harry Harrar- "

"Yeah, I know. I've got- "

"No, you don't know. He's got Libby, my wife. He just took her away from the Fairmont hotel in a patrol car."

"Libby? What's she doing- "?

"Never mind that for now." Zack was almost shouting. "You need to find that patrol car. You must have some record of which car he's in, don't you? We can't let him out of the city. And remember, he's got a radio in that car. When you find out which one he's in you'll need to exclude it from your calls. And- "

"Okay, Zack. I'm coming in. I've got it from here; I know what to do. We'll get that sleazy bastard." O'Bannon hung up.

"What now?" Eagle Feather wanted to know.

"I'm going over to the Richmond Station to help Marty." Zack looked at Eagle Feather. When he spoke again he seemed a bit calmer. "You look done in. There's nothing more you can do tonight. We've both had a long day, but at least one of us should get some sleep." He paused. "Look, here's my key. My hotel room is close. Go crash there. If anything changes, I'll call you." Zack put his hand on Eagle Feather's arm. "And thanks, old friend, for everything. I can always count on you."

Eagle Feather started to say something, then smiled sympathetically. "I know you wouldn't sleep anyway, so I'll go along with this. But when you've got that bastard cornered, you call me first."

Sergeant Kelly cringed before the cruel animosity in the man's voice. His clipped consonants were like snarls. He faced him in the rear-most booth of the pub where the hazy curl of marijuana smoke and rising hot grease vapors cloyed together in the dim ray of light from a tiny window.

"Did-I-not-tell-you-to-give-that-note-directly-to-Detective-Harry-Harrar?" Donny snarled, nauseating puffs of breath following each syllable.

Kelly shook like an aspen leaf in a stiff breeze. This guy was terrifying in ways that passed his understanding. All he wanted to do right now was exactly what the man wanted.

"I did," he protested. "I put it right on his desk, right on top of his papers. He couldn't have missed it.'

Donny thrust his face across the table to within inches of Kelly's. The man's anger had a life of its own.

"He did miss it."

Kelly quaked. "I...I don't know how..."

Then Donny was back in the shadowed corner of his own bench, suddenly calm, the transformation instantaneous - and equally horrifying. He was reaching into his pocket and he brought out a thick envelope and slid it across the table to Kelly.

"I'm paying you even though you failed."

Kelly tried to thank him but couldn't get a sound to come out.

Donny stared at him for several minutes. Kelly melted and quivered.

"I have another task for you to perform. You will

not fail this time."

Kelly nodded.

Donny slid over another envelope. "There is a newspaperman, a man named James Snyder who writes for the San Francisco Chronicle." Donny separated each word as if teaching a child. "There is a note in this envelope. It is to be delivered to Mr. Jim Snyder, San Francisco Chronicle. Memorize that. I want you to address this envelope in just that way, then put it in the in-box that's on the door of the Chronicle Building on Mission Street." Donny leaned forward across the table again. "Now listen carefully, Sergeant Kelly. This is very important. You are to drop that note in that in-box exactly at 2 pm on May 24th. No sooner. No later. Am I clear?"

Kelly nodded.

"What will you write on the envelope?" Donny prompted gently.

"Jim Snyder, San Francisco Chronicle," Kelly replied.

All at once Donny's face flew forward as if no longer connected to his neck and stopped an inch from Kelly's own. His eyes flamed and his face contorted and his lips foamed. His words were growling bursts of fetid breath.

"*Do...not...fail.*"

Kelly felt himself lifted from his bench and placed on his feet somehow and then he was stumbling toward the door and thrust through it as if propelled by an unseen force. With the envelope clutched in his hand with a dead man's grip he ran as hard and far as he could, his terror driving him to distance himself as much as possible from the pub and from the terrifying monster he knew as Donny.

Marty O'Bannon felt guilty. Zack's wife was in great danger but all O'Bannon could feel was relief at having something to occupy his mind, something to prevent him from thinking about his experience in Golden Gate Park. His brain had already begun to bury the terror he felt there in those dark woods and he didn't want those feelings to return. He knew deep down that Harry was connected in some way to whatever was out there but he'd think about all of that later, he told himself; first things first. Right now, he had a renegade cop with a hostage to deal with. And Harrar wasn't just any hostage taker. He knew all their methods, he knew their protocols, he knew just what to do to avoid the police net that would be drawn tighter than a fat lady's girdle around the city. So O'Bannon would have to think outside the box. First, though, he had to figure out where Harrar might go. He must have an escape hole, a safe house established just for this circumstance. Marty called the dispatcher at the front desk and instructed him to go through all past financial statements recorded for Harry Harrar.

"Get me anything that asks for reimbursement for a rental or a lease of any kind in the city. Anything for surveillance or any similar purpose."

O'Bannon already knew the identity of the patrol car that Harry had taken from the yard and he'd cut off its radio contact first thing, so of course Harry would know right then and there that they were looking for that car. He'd go to ground as soon as possible. He'd ditch the patrol car for another vehicle or else take public transportation. O'Bannon had set up road blocks all around the Knob Hill area far beyond where Harrar could've reached in that short time. But he could be on foot or in a bus or on the cable car; how could they stop him? It was too much to cover. Zack would be along any time. But all O'Bannon could do right now was wait.

And what was Harrar's connection to this Megan McMitchell? It seemed certain now that he was her assassin, otherwise why run? And why take a hostage? And come to think of it, why that particular hostage? How long had Harry been planning this? He clearly knew who Libby Tolliver was and knew how and where to reach her.

O'Bannon's speculations went further. If Harry had planned that far in advance, how deep did this thing go? And who were the players?

Then another thought: was all of this connected? The slashed throat killings, the missing ultra-runner, the dead priest, the missing priest? Could other cops be involved? O'Bannon paled at these thoughts. And what about that thing...? Never mind. He must go about this one step at a time.

Zack's arrival saved O'Bannon from his thoughts in a dramatic way. Marty knew Zack to be a laid back kind of guy who was always calm and thoughtful, always in control - a man who never rushed into action or jumped to conclusions. But the man who exploded into the homicide unit at Richmond District Station demonstrated anything but these qualities. Zack was in a panic. He was demanding answers before he'd even crossed the threshold. O'Bannon answered him calmly. Yes, yes, and yes, that and that and that had been done. Now they had to wait, there was nothing else to do. Have a coffee, it was late; they'd have to stay alert for a long time yet.

After Zack had reluctantly agreed that everything had been done that could be done and after he had calmed down enough to pour a cup of coffee, O'Bannon ventured his own thoughts.

"I didn't mention it before, but we found an unopened note on Harrar's desk."

Zack looked at him over his coffee cup.

Marty went on. "It was a woman's handwriting and had a perfume smell. It must've arrived after Harry left." O'Bannon showed Zack where it had been. "It was just lying there on top of his papers. It'd been dropped there. I remember a guy was leaving just as I came in, a big guy. I didn't recognize him right then but later a bell went off: he was that government cop who came down the mud path up at the Presidio the morning after the murder tromping on the footprints I was following. I'm sure it was the same guy. Big man, powerful looking. I began to wonder why he was here at my station house. Now I'm thinking he was the one who left the note. It must have been dropped there between the time Harry left and I arrived. Coincidence? That he was there in that exact window of time? I doubt it."

"What was the note about?" Zack asked.

"It was a blackmail note, pure and simple, setting up a meet at Golden Gate Park. Anonymous. It demanded twenty grand. It was in a woman's handwriting and it said she'd seen what he'd done." O'Bannon looked at Zack. "So I decided to attend that meeting."

He had Zack's full attention. "You went?"

"Yeah, I did. The appointed place was in a meadow near the Doughboy Statue at the Redwood Memorial

Grove. You know of it?"

"I don't know the park that well."

"Well, it's pretty isolated. There're no lights near it and it's black as pitch when you go there after dark. And with the fog..."

"Go on."

"Well, all I had was this little penlight and my handgun. Not even a radio." Marty caught Zack's look. "I know, not too smart. But all I'm expecting is some woman, probably a prostitute."

"And?"

"It was that dark, I literally couldn't see my hand in front of my face. But I figured this woman would need some sort of light also and I'd see it coming so I hunkered down and turned off my own light and waited."

"And?"

"And nobody came. At least no *person* came. But something did."

Zack stared at Marty. "What do you mean, something?"

O'Bannon watched Zack's face carefully. "Zack, I think you and the chief have been keeping something from me."

Zack raised his eyebrows.

"Something was there," O'Bannon said. "Something that could see in the dark well enough to walk right up behind me without a light and without making a sound, something that could move really quickly. Something that could make a howling sound that turned my blood to ice water."

Zack smiled wryly at O'Bannon. He said, "That's why I didn't say anything to you, Marty. How could I? Would you have believed me?"

O'Bannon stared back. "Just tell me...what the hell is it?"

Zack shrugged. "I don't know. Eagle Feather thinks it's a kind of man-monster from the reservation, a Navajo witch. We thought we'd tracked down this killer in Los Angeles but as soon as we got close, poof! He was gone. Now we think he's here in San Francisco."

"So that's why you called me, why you offered to help me; you read about those other two killings and you thought maybe it was him."

"That's right."

"I wish you'd told me."

"Well, yeah, but- "

"No, you're right - I wouldn't have believed you. But at least the thought would've been in my mind." Marty shook his head ruefully. "Might've saved me a pair of pants." His mind raced on. "But what about Harrar and the McMitchell killing? And what about the priests? What's the connection there?"

"I don't know yet. I don't really know if there is

one. But my guess is that some of these people helped the killer in some way...or maybe they just got in the way. When we get close he tends to get rid of evidence."

"And Harrar? How did he get to Harrar?"

"Who knows? How does he get to any of them? Maybe he sees a weakness and finds a way to use it against them, like that blackmail note."

O'Bannon raised an eyebrow. "You're thinking that thing wrote that note?"

Zack nodded. "He might've written it to entice Harrar out to the park to kill him. Let's say he blackmailed Harrar into killing the McMitchell girl. When we got onto Harrar, the killer had to clean up that loose end. So he sets up the meet in the park. I'd guess you were real lucky you weren't Harrar out there tonight."

"Why didn't he...it...kill me anyway? After all, I'm the cop hunting the killer of these girls; he must know that."

Zack sighed. "I don't know the answers to all these questions. I can only make guesses out of my experience from chasing him all this time." Zack's jaw knotted in frustration. "I don't even know for sure that I really *am* chasing something and not just reacting to thoughts put in my head by the Navajo."

O'Bannon gave Zack a tight grin. "Don't you worry about that, Boy-O! That thing in the park tonight was real, all right."

Zack sent a quick look at O'Bannon. "But you never saw it."

"No, thank God."

"That's just it. We never actually see anything; there's never anything tangible. So we keep on hunting and following the evidence and hoping we'll finally get enough to identify this man-creature and catch him. Or even just know for sure it's the same guy doing it all."

The radio on O'Bannon's desk crackled into life. "Unit 62 here. We've found Patrol Unit 7. It's empty. We're at Polk and Sacramento. Repeat. Patrol Unit 7 found abandoned. Polk and Sacramento. Please advise. Over."

O'Bannon grabbed the radio. "Unit 62, please stay at the scene. Keep all civilians away until we get there. Do you read me?"

"Ten-four."

O'Bannon beckoned to Zack. "We're off," he said.

TWENTY-NINE

The crazed look in the man's eyes could not be misunderstood; Harrar was a desperate man. That fact prevented Libby from signaling the cab driver, even with her eyes. The bulge that was the gun in Harrar's jacket pocket pressed against her side, an unnecessary reminder of her plight. After abandoning the patrol car Harrar had flagged down the cab and pulled her into it. The directions he gave the driver would take them right back into the city center and into what Libby imagined must be the very heart of the police search. Did he plan to release her and give himself up? Libby clung to that hope and her fear subsided slightly.

The cabby looked at them in the mirror. "Are you new in town?" he asked.

Harrar gave no sign that he had even heard the man.

Libby hesitated and then answered. "I've been here before, but I don't come often." She glanced at Harrar but he was staring straight ahead, his jaw set.

The cabby persisted. "It's a beautiful city. If you like, I can suggest some places to visit during your stay."

Libby sent another glance at Harrar before replying. "That's very kind of you, but it seems as if each time I visit all my free time gets hijacked somehow."

The cabby laughed. "I know how that goes," he said.

Still staring straight ahead, Harrar said, "Before you know it all that free time is shot."

Libby froze. Her fear came back in a wave. The cabby laughed again. "Well, I hope you will return some day when you aren't quite so busy."

The cab fell silent and stayed that way for the remainder of the ride. Finally the cabby pulled to the curb. "Here we are; 500 Post Street, the Marriott. Enjoy your stay."

Harrar dragged Libby by the wrist out his side of the cab and gave a large bill to the driver with his free hand. Still holding her wrist, he pulled her toward the hotel entrance. Libby was stiff with fear but she was also puzzled. For a desperate hunted man with a hostage, his actions made no sense. Inside the massive open lobby Harrar turned away from the desk area and went to the elevators. They entered a car and he pressed the button for the twenty-first floor. The elevator ride was as tense and silent as the cab ride had been. The glass sided car hung out over the lobby and heightened Libby's feeling of vulnerability. Did Harrar plan to throw her off the balcony, she wondered? A thousand wild thoughts came into her mind.

The elevator slid to a stop and the door crawled open and Libby heard the tinkle of glass and murmur of many conversations and saw that they were at a lounge. Her confusion grew when Harrar tugged her inside and claimed a table. He gave her a mock bow and pulled a seat out for her. She sat down heavily. He took the seat across from her at the small table and gave her a tight grin.

"The least I can do is show a lady a good time once I've kidnapped her," he said.

Libby tried to keep her voice steady. "What do you intend to do with me?"

Harrar smiled again. "I intend to ply you with alcohol," he said. He waved an arm for the waiter who came over instantly. "The lady will have a gin and tonic and bring me a double malt on the rocks," he said.

Libby stared at him. When the waiter was gone, she asked, "What makes you think I like gin and tonic?"

"Do you?"

"Well, yes, but- "

"So there you go." Harry's fingers began to drum on the table and his face went blank again. Libby resisted the urge to ask any questions. Before long the waiter returned with their drinks. After he was gone Harry raised his glass to her.

"May your soul be in heaven an hour before the devil knows you're dead." He drank. "Mine too," he added.

Libby stared. She didn't pick up her glass.

Harry looked at her. "You'd better drink. You're going to need it."

Libby didn't want to drink but she was afraid not to. She took a careful sip, her hand shaking slightly. Libby knew she must try to avoid upsetting the man.

Harry was staring at some distant place in his mind. "Do you believe in Hell?" he asked.

Libby shuddered. "Uh, yes, I suppose so."

Harry went on as if she hadn't spoken. "I never believed in it before." He was speaking softly. "And then I met one of its creatures. I believe in it now." Harry looked at her as if conscious of her for the very first time. "You don't want to go to hell," he said.

Libby didn't know what to say. She waited.

"I've been wondering what I could do to appease him," Harry went on. "I thought, what if I can get your husband off his back? Maybe I could get him and his Indian pal to go home and leave that monster in peace. I thought maybe that would make him happy, maybe even happy enough not to kill me."

He looked at Libby. "Have you ever thought that it makes a difference how you die?" He answered himself. "Of course not. Dead is dead, right? Why should it matter how you died once you're dead?" Harrar chuckled humorlessly. "Well, it does matter; it matters a whole lot."

Libby felt a cold chill settling around her heart. This was a madman sitting across from her, a madman with a gun. The whole situation was incongruous and terrifying. She was sitting right in the middle of an upscale and very expensive lounge with relaxed and happy people sipping drinks and chatting at tables all around her yet she had never felt in greater fear for her life. Some instinct told her to keep the fear from her face. So she sat still and listened.

Harry continued to speak in a quiet resigned way.

"It was the radio, that damned radio." He grimaced and his eyes flicked to her face. "Do you see how life turns on such very small details? If it hadn't been for that radio, nobody would have known I was anywhere near the Tenderloin District that night. But if I hadn't worn the radio, she'd have been suspicious and she wouldn't have come with me."

Harrar sighed and shrugged. "It's done. Its all over: my marriage, my career, my life." He didn't speak for a moment. Then he said, "I'm a dead man walking. Once that hell spawn knows I was found out, he'll kill me in order to keep them from finding out about him. He'll want to, anyway. He'll enjoy it."

Harrar took a gulp of his scotch but didn't seem to be aware of it sliding down his throat. He glared at Libby. "How do I face that?" he demanded. "Even if I could convince him that he needs me alive, what would I live for?" Harrar continued to glare. Then his face softened and took on an expression of deep sadness. "Nothing," he whispered.

In one fast motion he lifted the gun from under his napkin and jammed the barrel into his mouth and pulled the trigger.

The call came in while they were combing through the abandoned patrol car in a hopeless search for anything that might suggest where Harrar was headed next.

O'Bannon took the call. He listened quietly. After a moment he put his phone away and turned to Zack.

"They found him," he said simply.

"Where?"

"He blew his own head off in the Club Lounge at the Marriott."

"And Libby?" Zack's heart raced so hard he thought it might come out his throat.

"Libby's fine. He didn't hurt her. But she's pretty shaken up."

Zack was already moving toward O'Bannon's car. "Let's go."

As they rode, O'Bannon consoled Zack. "They've got a police shrink with Libby; she'll be just fine."

"We don't know how this might affect the baby," Zack worried.

O'Bannon looked quickly at Zack. "Baby?"

"Yeah. I just learned about it tonight," Zack said.

"Hey, congratulations!"

"Thanks, Marty. But I can see being a father is gonna make me look at things a lot differently from now on."

"Well, I'm sure not the one to help you with that."

"No, I suppose not." Zack remembered that O'Bannon had had two wives and two divorces but mercifully no children.

It was full dark when they pulled up to the front of the JW Marriott. Reflected red and blue flashes of emergency vehicles punctuated the bright white light issuing from the translucent glass canopy. Zack leapt from the car and immediately saw Libby standing by an ambulance wrapped in a blanket, her face pale against her dark hair. She stared vacantly at him as he approached.

"He just put the gun in his mouth and pulled the trigger," she said mechanically. "Just like that. And then his head exploded."

Zack had his arm around her and pulled her close to him. Her stiff and trembling body gradually softened as he held her.

Zack called over to O'Bannon. "I'm taking Libby away," he said. "I'll help the investigators get their statements from her tomorrow, but not now. She's in no shape tonight."

O'Bannon nodded and Zack turned back to Libby.

"Come on," he said gently. "We're going back to the hotel. We can talk about it on the way if you want...or not."

Libby allowed herself to be guided to the curb and into a waiting taxi. She did not talk on the short drive to the hotel, content to snuggle up to Zack. At this moment she wanted nothing more than to feel safe and to forget it all, at least for now.

O'Bannon took the elevator up to the twenty-first floor. He didn't have much time to enjoy the view out through the car's glass side; his phone rang almost immediately. It was the Mayor.

"Is this the way you lower your profile and avoid the press? What the hell is going on?" His Honor demanded.

"Sir, I've just arrived here and I'm in the elevator on my way to the crime scene. I can't tell you anything until I've had a chance to look it over."

"I can tell *you* more than that right now!" The mayor was apoplectic. "First this ridiculous story you're trying to sell of a howling animal-like serial killer that rips out peoples' throats in the middle of the night. And now a homicide detective from your division decides to blow his head off in one of the most prestigious cocktail lounges in one of the most prestigious hotels in the city! What the hell are you trying to do, single handedly drive away every freakin' tourist in town? My god!"

O'Bannon tried get a word in when the Mayor temporarily paused for breath, but he was shouted down immediately.

"I've spoken to the Medical Examiner who says your theory is poppycock! I've spoken to the Police Commissioner who says you're a loose cannon, and I've spoken to your captain, who says you're not following orders. Now I'm talking to you and I'm saying this just once: you clean up that mess, you keep it out of the press, you low-ball it, or by God I'll have *your* balls. If I- "

"Sir, I've lost a colleague tonight- "

"You've lost your job if I- "

O'Bannon turned off his phone before he could

hear the rest of it. I'd better leave it off, he thought. When the elevator doors opened he was greeted by a cacophony of shouts, cries, and clashing china. Yellow tape barred his way. Waiters were trying to clear the tables but the police were preventing them and guests stood in shocked clumps waiting to be questioned. As soon as O'Bannon stepped across the tape the frenzied manager accosted him. He grabbed O'Bannon's sleeve and clung to it.

"Are you in charge?" he screamed. "Do you see what's happened here? There's blood everywhere, bits of that man's...head...brain everywhere, on the ceiling, on my guests, on their plates, *on their food!* We're finished. No one will ever eat here again, we're done- "

O'Bannon shook the man's arm loose and pulled him toward one of the officers near the elevator.

"Sir, you need to go with this policeman and give him a full statement. It's important that he record everything you have to say." He made a gesture at the policeman. "Get him out of here," he intoned.

O'Bannon found his way to the small table where the body of Harry Harrar sat slumped forward. Blood pooled on the table and dripped to the floor. The seat across the table from him was overturned, likely knocked over when Libby leapt to her feet. Poor woman, O'Bannon thought. He was still taking in the scene when he felt a touch on his arm. He turned to find a homicide detective from the Central District, a man he knew slightly.

"Hi, Tom."

"Marty. He was one of yours, I gather?"

"Yeah, he was."

"Didn't you have an all-points out for him tonight? Was he dirty?"

"Yeah, likely he was. But you're gonna need to know a whole lot more than that."

Tom grinned and pointed to a table in a corner across the room. "No time like the present," he said.

Dawn crept across the roofs of the city and fingers of sunlight poked through Jim Snyder's bedroom window. He moaned and hid his face under his pillow, but he was awake now and he could tell by the slight stirring next to him that Susan was awake also. But before acknowledging her, Snyder wanted a minute to think. He needed to consider how things stood after the news that came last night, the news that Detective Harrar was dead by his own hand. What did it mean? What part had the Detective played in all of this, if any?

Snyder went back in his mind to the recent conversation he'd had with Susan. Harrar was part of that whole line of inquiry that hung on one slender thread, but if that thread *did* connect to the killer they hunted, the detective's decision to take his own life had meaning.

There was more stirring next to him and then Susan was sitting upright and stretching luxuriously, her milky white flesh made visible through her nightgown by the probing rays of the sun, totally unconscious of the effect she was having on Snyder until she looked down at the thin blanket that covered him.

"Are you the ramrod of this outfit?" she giggled.

Snyder grinned. He was continually amazed by the rejuvenating effect that Susan had on him, maybe because before she'd come along he'd allowed himself to relegate his older body to the trash-heap of assumptions that are the accepted American views of aging. Well, part of him wasn't having any of it, that's for sure.

"Let's have some coffee and Danish and then do a reconstruction," Susan suggested. She jumped out of bed narrowly avoiding Snyder's reaching hand. "I'll even make the coffee for you."

Thirty minutes later the two of them were at the kitchen table, which had been cleared of breakfast dishes and transformed into an artist's desk with the sketchpad and drawing pencils they had purchased yesterday.

Susan's hand holding the pencil was poised above the paper. "Okay, tell me something you know about this creature."

"Anything? Or do you want me to start with general form."

"No, no, you can't have a predilection for how it looks," she protested. "That's not how this works. Just tell me the first thing that comes to your mind."

"Well, okay. It must be very strong."

"No." Susan shook her head. "You're still making assumptions. Give me *evidence.*"

Jim was frustrated. 'Well, it howls loudly and sounds terrifying," he blurted.

"That's good," Susan said. She began to draw.

Snyder looked over her shoulder. "What can you possibly draw from that?"

Susan giggled. "You'd be amazed." On the paper a mouth took form, and then a throat, quite large and thick. "To howl that loudly, you've got to have a good sized instrument," she explained. She pointed to the couch. "You go sit over there; I don't want your evidence to be influenced by my drawing."

Snyder went and sat down. He thought another moment and said, "It moves through the trees, apparently branch to branch."

Susan stared at him.

"Okay, okay, that was an assumption. How about this: it doesn't leave any footprints."

Susan sketched busily.

"It lifts its victims off the ground with one hand." Jim waited while Susan sketched. Then she nodded.

"It prefers woodland to city streets." He paused.

"It kills in the dark." He was on a roll.

"It snatches out a human throat in a single stroke." And quickly, "It walks among humans without being noticed."

When Snyder opened his mouth to speak again, Susan lifted a hand to stop him. "Give me a minute; you just said a lot there."

Jim waited. Susan sketched busily and then nodded.

"Uh...it uses patterns, specific time intervals between kills, specific environments for the killings..."

Susan paused, her pencil in the air. Then she went busily back to work.

"It's intelligent, on a human scale."

Susan glared.

"Uh...right, that's an assumption. Let's say that it stays a step ahead of the police and appears to anticipate their methodology."

Susan smiled and went to work.

Snyder peered over at her. "You know, a lot depends upon whether we accept the link to Megan McMitchell or not because there's a lot of evidence in that direction."

Susan nodded. "I thought about that. For instance, we could then say for certain that it can communicate with humans; is that what you mean?"

"Yeah, that kind of thing."

"Actually, I can infer that from its ability to hide among humans. What else would that give us?"

"It'd mean it could be very persuasive?"

"Or maybe intimidating," Susan countered. "Anything else?"

"It moves swiftly. It chased down a physically fit jogger."

"Ah, yes." Susan went to work. After a moment she stopped and looked at Snyder.

"Well, I'm stumped," he said. "I can't think of anything else."

"Okay, that's a start," Susan said. "Want to see?"

"You better believe it." Snyder leapt up and came to look over her shoulder. He breathed out softly. "My God, he could have been in the supermarket with me yesterday."

Indeed, the figure that stared back at him from the sketchpad could have been any man one might see on the street.

"Take me through this, would you? I mean, the face, for instance. That's a recognizable person you've drawn."

Susan put up a cautionary finger. "Remember, there are enough missing clues that in some cases I had to invent, but I did try to follow the evidence even then. Shall we start with the top and work down? His hair, for instance: I've decided on brownish black and thick and coarse, purely from the more primal element our evidence evokes. Same goes for the brown eyes. But the head shape is unique. The forehead, which is the location of the prefrontal lobe, is large and high like a human. He makes logical decisions; he *thinks*. He considers before taking an action. I've gifted him with left and right hemispheres like a human because I'm proposing a similar evolution. Now to the knob, that kind of extra area at the rear of his head - that's the unique part. It's partially from a slightly larger occipital lobe, the home of the visual cortex. This creature can see equally well in the day and night. But" - Susan looked up and grinned - "it also comes from an enlarged brain stem, the reptilian brain. It's the primitive brain, the home to animal instincts and survival mechanisms that this creature clearly calls upon to a far greater extent than you or me. I gave him an enlarged limbic system within the cerebellum, which is dominated by the sense of smell. I think we can conclude that this creature has developed that area greatly. Anyway, without boring you, there were several more considerations of the brain that contributed to this head shape. And of course, as we discussed before, the creature's ability to create great sound requires ample sinus, hard palate, throat and larynx space, as I've shown here with the large square face and mouth and the thick throat area. Then there is the facial appearance, those thick dark eyebrows and the heavy beard he probably struggles to keep clean shaved. He would have a swarthy complexion from extended time outdoors and a large nose with wide apertures to complement his enhanced scent capability...you can see all of that, right? And lastly, before leaving the head, I've drawn the mouth closed but the very high cheek bones and thin stretched lips are to suggest the presence of very large incisors." Susan looked at Snyder. "That's how I solved the throat-slashing weapon idea."

Snyder breathed out. "That's amazing. Go on."

"Well, I made the assumption that I wouldn't let you make about moving branch to branch through the trees. That argues for great shoulders, thick biceps, long arms and large strong hands that you would see if they weren't under the sweatshirt I put on him. But you can see the general size. Such muscle power would be necessary to lift a human of a hundred and forty pounds or so with one hand. And the sweatshirt is the ubiquitous apparel worn in San Francisco by almost everyone at one time or another and it could easily hide distinguishing body characteristics such as his. So I put him in one.

Would you agree?"

"I think all of this is fantastic."

"Okay, then, just a few more points. If you could see under the sweatshirt, you'd find a thick waist, indicative of tremendously strong abdominal muscles. Now his lower extremities are less certain, but I'd have to consider somewhat ape-like characteristics in terms of thick muscular thighs for the power to balance in trees and to move so very swiftly. I've given him a pair of Wrangler Comfort-Fit jeans to fit over those legs, and thick high socks to hide the leg hair. Finally, you see the sneakers for very large feet. That is to suggest the possibility that he moves through the trees aided by his feet, which must be wide and have long flexible individuated toes. Overall, he's shorter than average with a torso disproportionate to his legs, but not noticeably so, with prehensile toes. And I saw from your reaction that I've been successful in one aspect, which was to construct him to blend in with the rest of humanity without causing a second glance. So, there you have it."

Snyder stared in wonder. "But this particular look, the personality, his uniqueness? I mean, I could pick him out of a police line-up."

Susan sighed. "Not really, I'm afraid. Although some of his features came together from those traits I've listed, the final facial sketch required a lot of minute decisions by me. He could have ended up looking quite different."

"Maybe, but all the decisions you've made reflect your consideration of the facts, right? So at least intuitively, you stuck to the evidence."

"Well, maybe..." Susan was thoughtful. "So now that you have this, what do you intend to do with it?"

"I'd like to give it to O'Bannon," Snyder said, "but I'm not sure he'd take it seriously." He looked at Susan thoughtfully. "But there's another way. What if I published this? I mean, sure, it would be a hell of a scoop and I could update my last story, but that's not the point. If this picture is even close to accurate, he'd have to lay low, wouldn't he? Maybe even leave town to keep people from pointing him out on the street. Two good things could come out of it, either he'd be seen by someone and caught or he'd be forced to hide away and not be able to kill any more."

Susan looked concerned. "What if someone else, some innocent person, looks just like this drawing? I don't want to be responsible for hurting an innocent person."

Snyder shook his head. "They might be inconvenienced, possibly, but not hurt. Look, we've been trying to find this killer for almost two months now. You've given us our best chance, right here. We've got to take it!"

THIRTY

Zack's phone vibrated and he propped open one eye and saw the faint red-orange of morning sun pooling against the dust of his tiny window. He grabbed for the phone. It was O'Bannon.

Zack looked at his watch. "You're still up?"

"I caught a couple hours sleep, but now I'm back at work."

"You woke me up to tell me that?"

"I'm always waking you up," O'Bannon chuckled. "You sleep a lot."

Zack yawned, ignoring him. "You'll tell me if you find the missing priest?"

"You'll be the first to know," O'Bannon said. "What's next for you?"

Zack looked down at Libby snuggled deep in the covers next to him, sound asleep. "I don't know. I've got some thinking to do. I won't put Libby in danger ever again. Harrar took her because of me, to stop me. I know he's dead now but who else might be out there thinking the same way?"

"What are you saying?"

"I don't know; that's just the point. I do know that I want Libby to leave San Francisco. I want her to be safe. And with the child and all, maybe I should go too."

O'Bannon didn't comment. When he spoke again his voice was serious. "Zack, no one's going to blame you if you go home. You've given more to this case than anyone had any right to expect. We've got enough to go on now; I think we can see it through."

"Thanks, Marty. I haven't decided yet, but that's good to know."

Zack put his phone down on the dresser. He started to think about the dead priest. The killer had taken quite a risk leaving the body of Father Gonzales right there in the confessional. To Zack it felt intentional, planned, almost as if the impostor expected to be unveiled and was purposefully abandoning his cover. But why?

Zack's mind drifted so far away that when Eagle Feather's head suddenly appeared at the end of the bed it made him jump. Last night when he and Libby returned, Eagle Feather had been sound asleep at the foot of the bed wrapped in a blanket. Zack had forgotten all about him.

Eagle Feather looked at Zack. "White man, you should go home," he said.

"Your people have been saying that to my people ever since we first arrived on this continent," Zack replied.

Eagle Feather chuckled. "And I'm saying it again. For Libby's sake." He stretched carefully and rose to his feet. “You shouldn’t risk Libby, you know that. And she won’t be at ease until you’re back in Arizona with her. And when she’s not at ease, your baby’s at risk.”

“So you’re a doctor now.”

Eagle Feather collected his belongings. He went on as if Zack hadn’t said a word. “I’ll stay on to finish this thing with O’Bannon. He’ll need me. There’s no reason for both of us to be here. I’ll keep you updated...and I’ll report my expenses.” Eagle Feather grinned.

“Where are you going now?”

“Somewhere to find some decent coffee. After that, I’m gonna see Snyder and his anthropology expert and see what they’ve got. When Harrar blew his own head off, that particular line of investigation dead-ended.”

Snyder closed the lid of his laptop. “Well, that’s it,” he said. “My article and the sketch will run in the early evening edition of the San Francisco Examiner tonight. That should stir things up.”

“I’m sure it will,” Susan said. “There’ll be panic in the streets.”

Snyder smiled. “Oh, I don’t think so. This is San Francisco, remember, where people walk down the street in weird get-ups and someone is always going Manson on somebody else and the buildings all fall down or burn every century or so. I’ve reported in this town for over thirty years. I’ve seen protests, yes. But panic? Never.”

“Aren’t you worried about the killer-creature’s response?”

"No, I'm not. He'll not be expecting this; it will constrict him. Wherever it is that he passes himself off during the day, he won't be able to do that any more."

"That's if my drawing is accurate," Susan reminded him.

"How different could it be, really? And even if it *isn't* very accurate it will be the first time the residents of this city are adequately warned. It's all spelled out in my article. Of course it won't appear exactly the way I've written it after my editor gets through with it, but it'll be close enough.

The door buzzer sounded. Snyder went to the speaker and pressed the button. "Hello?"

"Hey, Snyder, it's me, Eagle Feather."

Snyder buzzed him in. He looked at Susan and grinned. "You haven't met this guy yet. You're gonna enjoy him."

Moments later Eagle Feather was walking in the door, ducking his head low at the transom to protect his feather. It didn't seem to occur to him to take his hat off. He looked around the room, saw Susan, and nodded to her.

Susan stared.

"I'm Eagle Feather," he said. He raised his eyebrows. "How old are you, sixteen?"

"I'm actually fourteen but I'm particularly precocious," Susan shot back.

"UC Davis, Snyder said?"

"Bachelor's at UC Santa Barbara, Masters ASU and Doctorate at UC Davis."

"Well, in that case, I'll go with seventeen. I got my Masters in Anthropology at ASU. We wouldn't have met, though; I was twelve when I received my degree."

At that, Susan cracked a smile. Snyder broke it up. "Alright, you two, let somebody else join in here."

Eagle Feather cocked an eye at him. "We won't mention what year *you* got your degree."

"Then let's talk about something else. I'm glad you came by. I've got some news that you and Agent Tolliver need to know."

"You tell me, I'll tell him."

Snyder slid the sketch across the table to him. "Know who that is?"

Eagle Feather barely glanced at it before staring back at Snyder. "How'd you get that?"

"You know who it is?"

"It's the guy we're searching for."

Susan was stunned. "How did you know that?"

Eagle Feather swung his gaze over to her. His eyes were like black holes in the frame of his weathered face. "I've seen his kind before," he said.

"His kind?" Susan asked. She looked even more startled.

Eagle Feather nodded. "His kind," he repeated.

Susan stared at Eagle Feather. "I head an Anthropology Department in one of the most prestigious universities in the world. I communicate regularly with scientists in the field, I have access to the latest bulletins and news from the latest digs. But I don't know his kind."

Eagle Feather's mouth tightened in a humorless grin. "You won't find his kind in books or bulletins," he said. "My people have known him since ancient times because we keep our spiritual connections with the past. Not in books, not in scientific papers, but here" -Eagle Feather pointed to his head- "and here" -he pointed to his heart.

"You're talking about mythological creatures," Susan pressed. "Every culture has them."

Eagle Feather's smile was gentle. "Do you believe in ghosts?" he asked.

"No, of course not." Susan's answer was immediate.

"Yet your literature, your TV programs, your newspapers, your histories are all full of ghosts. And you don't believe in them?"

"All that is entertainment; it reflects a need we have to stimulate ourselves, to keep boredom at bay."

Eagle Feather shook his head. "It's denial," he said. "It's the contemporary Caucasian way of dealing with something you don't understand; you rationalize it out of existence."

"So you'd have me understand that my prejudice prevents me from believing that this" -she held up the sketch- "is an unknown species of human living among us? And that there may be more of them?"

Eagle Feather's smile was tolerant. "Exactly. You drew it, didn't you?" He looked at Snyder. "What do you believe? You've followed the evidence all along." He held up the sketch. "Is this real?"

Snyder's face was grim. Suddenly he looked old beyond his years. "It's real enough that I warned an entire city against him," he said.

It was Eagle Feather's turn to look surprised. "What do you mean?"

"I've sent an article in to the paper, along with that sketch. It'll be in tonight's edition."

Eagle Feather sat abruptly and stared at Snyder. "You know what this means?" His voice was a whisper.

"It means the people of San Francisco will be warned, it means this monster won't be able to show his face, it means the killings might at least be postponed."

Eagle Feather shook his head. "It won't stop him. You underestimate his abilities, as humans always have." He saw their frowns. "Let me put it this way: when you go to a house that is reputed to be haunted by a ghost, you experience an edge of fear no matter what you believe, because in the back of your mind there is the worry that it might actually exist after all. It's not the fear that you'll see it; it's the fear that it's there but you won't see it because it has different form. This gives it a power over you. And if in fact you do see it, you then must believe in it which means you must accept a whole lot of things that you'd rather not accept. This creature is that ghost because it's different from you and me. It won't always look like you expect it to look; it may look like something else. As soon as it sees your drawing it will change and it will no longer look like this. This sketch will not deter it. The only difference is, it will no longer look like this."

"You are describing a shape shifter," Susan said.

"Something like that."

Susan shrugged. "I can accept that there is a mutated monster loose in the city, but I can't take the extra step to believe it's a shape shifter with magical powers to transform itself. Of course I've studied this mythology; it resides, like ghosts, in most cultures around the globe, along with various forms of Bigfoot or Nessie. But it's myth, not reality."

Snyder brought them back to his original point. "Someone or something very real is killing people out there and it must be stopped. That's the bottom line. I believe the best way, the *only* way to protect the citizens of this city is to warn them. That's what I've done."

Eagle Feather shook his head. "With a lot of luck he won't read the paper tonight but we can't count on that." He looked at his watch. "According to his past routine, his next kill will be in just 48 hours. Can I get you to compromise? The city should be safe from him until then. If you hold your article until the evening edition of May 24th we'll have two days to find him. With this likeness we'll have an advantage for once, however slight. We know what he looks like and he doesn't know we know. If we don't find him, then go ahead and publish the picture. Can you live with that?"

Snyder thought about it. Finally he nodded.

"That works for me. As you say, the killings have historically followed a regular pattern." He darted a look at Eagle Feather. "But I hope he doesn't change it!" Snyder opened his laptop. "I'll ask if the article can be published in the evening edition of May 24."

"Thanks," Eagle Feather said. "Now all we need is a way to find him in the next 48 hours."

Zack let Libby sleep on, relieved that she could. But he saw that her sleep wasn't peaceful; her forehead creased in a frown from time to time and her breathing became rapid and she'd murmur something unintelligible. But at least she slept.

Zack couldn't believe that this was happening all over again, just like the Roundtree case when Libby was held hostage by that killer. That killer had held her to get at Zack, and now it had happened all over again with another desperate man. He could stop it all now. He could just take her home.

But could he? And wasn't that what the killer wanted? Except for Eagle Feather, who did not have an official capacity, Zack was the only one with any experience with the sort of killer they were pursuing. Zack felt a sense of responsibility, a feeling of ownership that he couldn't relinquish. He sighed. He must be objective. He needed to remove pride from the equation. What was truly important to him? He had changed since he married Libby, but slowly, so slowly that he hadn't noticed. His work had always come first without question. They had agreed to this when they first discussed marriage. They would continue to manage their careers and their lives independently. That's how important it was to each of them.

But now they had a child coming. Things had changed. And Zack knew they'd changed for Libby, too. Otherwise, she'd never have come to San Francisco to ask him to give up the investigation and come home. She'd not actually done that, of course, but that had been her intention, Zack knew. And now he realized what was most important to him: he wanted to do what Libby wanted, what Libby needed.

He'd already made his decision. He had to take Libby home. After that, he'd see.

THIRTY-ONE

Sergeant Kelly stared at the pink envelope leaning against the sugar holder on the table in his barracks room. He'd addressed it to Jim Snyder, San Francisco Chronicle, with a round cursive hand like a woman's writing, just as he'd been told. Kelly was consumed by curiosity but the envelope remained sealed. He'd deliver it in two more days to the Chronicle office just as he'd been ordered. It would be gone, then, and he'd never know what it said. But if he opened it and Donny somehow learned of it...Kelly quaked at the thought. It was too great a risk. Donny seemed to know everything. And he had another, more immediate concern. That Detective, Marty something, had seen him leave the district station. It was just a matter of time before he remembered Kelly from the Presidio and started to put two and two together.

Marty O'Bannon tried to ignore the newspaper someone had flung onto his desk but his curiosity overcame him and he slowly unfolded it. Might as well get it over with, he thought. And there it was, in screaming headlines: "Policeman Ends Life In Public Bloodbath". He scanned the article.

"*Exclusive hotel cocktail lounge...blood, bone and brain matter everywhere...homicide detective sought by police...Lieutenant O'Bannon* -shit- *...his dining companion unidentified* -that's good- *...Mayor says shakeup in San Francisco Police Force coming* -that figures- *...isolated incident* -I wish-..."

Well, no surprises there. He picked up the phone and called Forensics.

"Have you got anything for me on that priest yet?"

"Not much. Just a second while I grab that report...uh, here it is, let's see...oh, yeah, we took a closer look at the neck injuries. There's no doubt death was by strangulation but even if he hadn't suffocated, he'd have died from a broken neck. It wasn't just snapped like a twig - the individual vertebra were fragmented."

"Strong guy..."

"Really strong. That was the only wound by the killer; the other small bruises and contusions probably came from his impact against the wall or floor on his way down."

"Prints? Threads? Any skin under the fingernails? Anything?"

"Afraid not. Sorry."

"Thanks."

The moment he ended the call his cell phone rang. He looked at the number. The Mayor. He turned it off. *I'm on borrowed time anyway*, he thought. *No point in giving any of it to him.*

Libby woke with a start. For a long pleasant moment she didn't know where she was; then it all came streaming back to her - the anxiety, the fear, the horror, the relief. She looked for Zack; he wasn't there. She sat up slowly in the bed and rubbed her temples. She didn't want to think about anything just yet and her body was screaming for a cup of coffee. Strangely, she felt hungry. She hadn't had a thing to eat after lunch yesterday, she realized. Then she heard the whir of a keycard in the door and it pushed open and there was Zack with a cardboard tray in his hand. On it a cup of coffee was steaming and there was a covered plate of something. Libby smiled at Zack.

"You read my mind."

"I wasn't sure if you'd want anything but I guessed you might."

"You guessed right." Libby took the coffee and added the creamer and some sugar. She took a couple of gulps and issued a long sigh. "Fantastic!"

Zack sat on the edge of the bed next to her. "It's from the cafe next door; they make a better than average coffee." He watched Libby take another sip. Then she put the cup down and removed the cover from the eggs. She scooped up a large portion with the plastic fork and ate hungrily. Zack just watched, saying nothing.

After Libby had taken the edge off her appetite, she looked up at Zack.

"Have you eaten?"

"I had a Danish a couple of hours ago."

"You've been up a while, then."

"Yeah. O'Bannon called me pretty early."

"But you're still here?"

"I'm concerned about you. I wanted to be here when you woke up."

She smiled at him. "All I wanted to do was sleep and sleep." She took another sip of coffee.

Zack stared down at his hands for a moment and then he looked up at Libby. "Libby, I've spent a lot of time thinking this morning and I've come to a decision." At Libby's nod he went on. "I've decided we must leave San Francisco."

Libby started to speak but Zack held up a hand.

"No, hold on and let me finish. I realize now that what is most important to me right now is you and my new child. And I don't want to risk endangering you ever again. Eagle Feather will stay on to help Marty. It's about time I recognized that there are people besides me who have the ability to do this job."

Libby was smiling at him, her heart in her eyes. As she spoke tears welled over. "I have wanted to hear those words from you for so long," she said. "It means so much."

Zack took her coffee away from her and set it down and then he took both her hands in his and his eyes spoke for him.

"But...no!" Libby said abruptly. She let go of his hands. "You can't do that. Not now."

Zack's eyes widened. "I can't do that?" he repeated in stunned surprise.

"No, you can't do that," Libby repeated. "Not now. Not after last night."

"Why? I don't understand."

Libby swung her legs under her and sat cross-legged.

"Zack, what you said just now, that you want to start a family with me, that the new baby and I come first, well, that's the most wonderful thing you could have said to me this morning. And part of me says, shut up, Libby, don't say another word, accept what he says and take him home and live happily ever after. But after last night, I know that we can't live happily ever after until this thing, this cloud that hangs over you and me and the entire city, is gone. I understand how fearsome this creature, this killing monster, truly is. Let me tell you what Detective Harrar feared the most: not you, not the San Francisco Police, not any punishment the justice system could bring to bear, not even humiliation in front of his peers. No, what he feared most was this beast of a man who had hold of him. This monster terrified him beyond belief. That's the whole reason he abducted me - did you know that? Harry hoped that by holding me hostage he could get you to back off and stop chasing that killer. He thought that would appease him; that he might then decide not to kill Harry. He was running from this monster, not from the police, don't you see? And when he realized that his desperate act of kidnapping me wasn't going to work, that it wouldn't make any difference at all to that creature, that's when he shot himself. That's how much he feared it."

Libby leaned forward and took Zack's hand.

"The last thing in the world I want is this monster killer to come after you the way it came after Detective Harrar. But I no longer believe that there is anyone in this city who can stop it: not the police, not your friend Marty, not even Eagle Feather. Just you. You dealt with his kind once before, you are the only one who has a chance now."

"*We* dealt." Zack corrected her. "We *all* dealt with it."

"Yes, it took all of us. And it will again."

Zack shook his head. "Oh no. Not you. Not this time."

"No, not me," Libby agreed. "I'll stay safely out of the way. But you must promise to keep Eagle Feather and your friend Marty O'Bannon with you at all times. You can't be a loner any more. This needs a team. You know it does. You must promise me."

Zack nodded and held Libby's gaze. "I promise," he said.

O'Bannon was relieved when Zack called to say he would stay on after all. He needed Zack's experience and intuition at his side; he had very little else. The Mayor wanted his job, the Commissioner wouldn't support him, and no one on the force wanted to be seen with him. Except for Zack and his Indian buddy, O'Bannon was entirely on his own.

He turned his mind to finding any clues that might still lead him to the killer. The forensic inspection of the body of Father Gonzales had revealed very little. The killer had been tremendously strong with great large hands as estimated from the bruises on the Father's neck. But there were no prints, no bits of cloth or threads left at the scene, no hairs, no flesh under the victims' fingernails; nothing. And there were no witnesses to the murder.

And Father Gilligan was nowhere to be found.

The duty sergeant had placed a file on O'Bannon's desk. It contained all records of Harrar's financial requests and expenditures. It also contained Harry's personal financial transactions. Somewhere in all of these documents there had to be something to connect Harrar to the killer, like a large deposit or a cashed check. O'Bannon had two officers with financial expertise he would to set to work on that.

But most intriguing of all was the picture in the Priest's Walk Gallery at St. Boniface Catholic Church. They'd made a copy of the picture of Father Gilligan that hung there and then enlarged it and computer enhanced it. Then they'd sent it through the FBI facial recognition files. Nothing. The photo had been taken from a side angle and showed very little of the face. O'Bannon now felt certain that was an intentional ruse. There was so little face exposed that Father O'Rourke, a man who knew Father Gilligan quite well, had accepted the photo as genuine. It was only after intense scrutiny that O'Rourke admitted the picture might not be of his friend after all.

O'Bannon found the computer file and brought the picture up on his screen and stared at it. There had to be a clue here somewhere, maybe in the background or on the robe the priest was wearing. And what about the photographer? It might have been a camera set with a timer, he supposed. It was frustrating to know he was staring at a picture of the killer but could do nothing about it.

Then there was that note left on Harrar's desk, the

note that sent him to Doughboy Meadow and an experience he wanted very much to forget. Marty had that note inspected in every possible way; the handwriting analyzed, the paper searched for prints and DNA, the paper type and origins researched, an ink analysis done, and everything else forensics could possibly do. No luck. There was nothing to trace it back to the originator.

As O'Bannon thought about the note he remembered the man who had been leaving as he entered the station, the man in the uniform of the Presidio Park Police, the man at the crime scene who had been destroying footprints with his size sixteen shoes the morning after the murder. He sat up and reached for the phone. In the excitement following his terrifying experience at Golden Gate Park he'd forgotten to follow up on that connection. He called Spencer Wilson, the Presidio Park Police Commander.

"Hi. O'Bannon calling."

"Hello, Marty. You've stirred up some excitement around town, I see."

"Yeah, I figure I've got maybe another 48 hours before the pink slip slides under my door. But meanwhile I intend to finish what I started."

"You always were a stubborn bastard."

"Yeah, I know. But I'm calling about one of your guys this time."

"Oh? Who is it?"

"I don't know. He's a really big guy, maybe six foot four and must weigh nearly 300 pounds - dark hair, great huge feet. I can almost remember the name, something Irish."

"An Irish cop. That's a big help. Where did you see him?"

"He was stamping out footprints when I was investigating the crime scene up at the point. He came down the path with a message for me."

"You're saying it was deliberate?"

"Well, that's not out of the question."

"We assigned a big team to that one. I'll have to talk to a couple of my people. What's this about?"

"I won't pull any punches, Spence. This guy may be dirty."

"You can prove that?"

"No, no, I can't. But I've seen him twice now in situations that could be seen as compromising. It's getting to be too much of a coincidence."

"I'll have a look-see and get back to you."

"I'd really appreciate it."

O'Bannon kept thinking about it after he hung up. The guy's name was just on the tip of his tongue - Reilly, Shelly, something like that. And hadn't the man given his rank? He couldn't remember. *Crap*, he thought, *I'm getting too old for this.* But then he grinned as he thought, *that's not gonna be a problem for very long.*

His phone rang. It was Zack, sounding like his old self.

"Have you found Father Gilligan yet?"

"Not yet."

"I'm coming to see you, but first I want to stop at the *Star Of The Sea*. I want to take another look around."

"You're thinking we missed something?"

"No. But sometimes a different perspective..."

"Yeah, hope it helps. We never did find that ultra-runner. While I'm thinking about it, there's another guy I'm checking on. A US Park Police officer I bumped into a couple of times."

"What for?"

"First, for deliberately destroying evidence. Second, he may have delivered that note that was left on Harrar's desk."

"You think he might be working with-?"

"Yeah."

Zack was silent for a second. "Damn," he said. "He's got a whole army working for him."

"Well if he does, one of 'em is gonna slip and lead us to him. The more the merrier, I say."

"Well, I hope so."

Right after Zack hung up the man's name popped into Marty's brain for no particular reason. It was Kelly - Sergeant Kelly. He snatched up the phone.

"Hi, Commander, Marty again. Listen, I just remembered. His name is- "

"Sergeant Sean Kelly."

"Yeah. You found him. How long's he been with the force at the Presidio?"

"Not long, actually. He was transferred up here less than two months ago from the Intelligence Counter-Terrorism unit. He'd been on assignment to the Los Angeles Police, to help with security at the Memorial Coliseum. They'd had some bomb threats. He came with good recs and according to his commanding officer, he's a good man. That's all I've got."

"Mind asking his superior officer one more thing? Had he sent him to my district station house here in Richmond for any reason in the last day or so?"

"I'll ask. Can you tell me any more about your suspicions?"

"I'd rather not just yet. I could be way off base. When I know for sure, I'll call you."

There was yellow tape all around the confessionals in the church but there were no policemen in sight. Zack didn't want to waste time searching places that had already been well covered. But this mammoth church was a large space. During the taxi ride he'd been thinking about places where some small sign might have been missed, like the bell tower, or the organ pipe chambers, or the catacomb cellar areas. If the murder had been done in the building there might still be some clue.

Zack decided to start in the cellar area. He found the heavy oak door near the sacristy that accessed it. Stone steps circled downward to the left, dimly lit by small electric bulbs in sconces on the wall. Zack thought he remembered there was a symbolic reason that catacomb steps circled one way and not the other but he couldn't bring it to mind. Church rituals came very close to mysticism to his thinking. He'd read that "Star of the Sea" was the ancient name for the Virgin Mary, yet it had also been one of the titles of the Egyptian goddess, Isis.

At the bottom of the steps he found himself in half-lit corridor with thick wooden overhead supports. He moved along it cautiously, wondering what direction he was going. West maybe? The circling stairs had disoriented him. Sconces with dust-dimmed bulbs lit his way and presenting a chain of faintly glowing orbs like the guide lights for a runway marching down the tunnel ahead of him. The walls were of stone block, snuggly fitted. Further along, the character of the walls changed to a different type of stone. A bronze plaque on the wall announced that he had now come to an older section of the building, the foundation area of the original church raised in 1914. He shivered; there was a real chill down here. He passed several heavy wooden doors along the way, all of them securely padlocked. Then the corridor ended abruptly at an intersection, offering a choice of left or right. The passage to the right glowed with light and appeared recently used; the one to the left seemed less traveled; dustier, darker, more cobwebs. He went that way.

He passed several more padlocked doors, all in poor condition. Some hung precariously on their hinges. Then the passage ahead was pitch dark; he had reached the end of the electric lights. Zack didn't have a flashlight but he knew the police searching here before him would have had lights. But how thorough had they been, if indeed they had even come this way? There were a lot of nooks and crannies along this tunnel. Zack felt his way with his feet, sliding them along. It was well that he did for the floor suddenly disappeared. He reached carefully with his foot and found a step. A stairway! He might easily have fallen down it.

Zack worked his way slowly down the steps. When he reached the bottom, he stood for a moment in complete darkness. He knew there was no point in continuing without light. He smelled stale earth. The disturbed dust tickled his nostrils. He took another step but stopped abruptly. He was standing on something sticky. He reached down and touched it with his finger. It was cold and tacky, like an old coke spill. Then another odor came faintly to him, a smell of rot and decay. No surprise, he was in a catacomb. But it grew stronger, seeming to waft toward him from the darkness beyond. Zack didn't know what old bones smelled like; still, this seemed fresher somehow. Standing there in the pitch black, Zack suddenly felt extremely vulnerable.

THIRTY-TWO

After Zack had gone, all Libby wanted to do was sleep. She felt drained of energy, of substance, as if she were a shell covering a great emptiness. She slept soundly until she was startled awake by a noise. Her numb mind grasped that it was the thump of feet along the corridor outside her door. She sat up abruptly, her heart pounding. A feeling of terror swept over her. She sat very still. The noise came again and then high-pitched shouts and Libby breathed a sigh of relief. It was children playing a game in the hall that had awakened her. The sounds disappeared on down the corridor.

I've got to get past this, Libby thought. *I can't let last night ruin my life. I can't let the terror go on and on like the last time. Not with this child growing in me.* She lay down again and snuggled deep into the warmth of the covers. She thought about what she'd said to Zack that morning, her plea that he stay and finish the job. Had she been too frightened, too emotional to make the right decision? Should she have waited and thought about it more carefully? By asking him to stay she'd completely reversed herself, she'd undermined her entire reason for coming to San Francisco. Why had she done that?

She thought some more and then sighed. Sure, Zack would come home with her if she insisted. But he'd never be content to leave his friends and colleagues facing the danger that he saw as his own responsibility. He would try to put it out of his mind but he would fail, and he would be miserable, and some unconscious part of his brain would blame her.

Libby was tremendously afraid of this thing that prowled the city, this killer creature that so terrified Detective Harrar, a seasoned police officer, that he took his own life rather than face its fury. And now that she had insisted that Zack remain to face this same killer, she must accept her own responsibility. She had told Zack that facing this monster would require a team. Shouldn't she be helping, then? Would that make the difference?

Libby's head ached. She was too tired to think about it now. She stretched and rolled over on her side and fell asleep.

"He's gone," Commander Wilson said over the phone.

Marty O'Bannon shook his head in disbelief. "Waddaya mean, gone?"

"Kelly's barracks room is empty. There's nothing left there except a few pieces of furniture and his uniforms. Looks like he's done a runner. And by the way, he had no orders that would take him anywhere near your district station yesterday." Wilson paused. "Don't you think it's time to level with me?"

"Yeah, I do. We're looking for him in connection with this series of murders. There've been more since the Presidio killing. We suspect Sergeant Kelly is involved in some way."

"Well, that's just great. Things are just starting to quiet down here after the hullabaloo over our night patrolman shooting a burglar a couple of weeks ago. Now here we go again. Just because we're Park Police, people think we're not real cops and we shouldn't carry firearms. No matter that we're trained at the academy just like you boys. Now they'll say we're a bunch of crooks. Just great." After a moment of silence he said, "Sorry about the rant. It just gets my goat."

"Understood. What are you doing about Kelly's disappearance?"

"The AWOL report is in. We've begun a search but we have very little to go on. We tried locating his nearest of kin but there were none listed in his folder."

"Why doesn't that surprise me?" O'Bannon mumbled. "I'm going to issue an all points bulletin for him. Have you got a picture you can fax over?"

"I'll send one right over." Wilson hung up.

O'Bannon sat quietly at his desk, thinking. This Kelly had come up from Los Angeles. Wasn't that where Zack and his Indian buddy said they'd first hunted this serial killer? Another coincidence. But O'Bannon didn't believe in coincidence. Kelly could have been deliberately destroying those footprints at the murder scene at the Presidio, and he might have just placed that note on Harrar's desk when Marty saw him leaving the station.

O'Bannon picked up the phone and ordered an all points alert for Sergeant Sean Kelly of the U.S. National Police. It read: "About six foot four, 300 pounds, heavy set, brown hair, likely armed and dangerous. Do not attempt to apprehend. If found, report and maintain surveillance."

O'Bannon felt a twinge of excitement. This could be their guy. After all this time, after all this horseshit from the Mayor and the Commissioner, they finally had the killer on the run. Marty looked at the list of incoming calls on his cell phone; four of the last seven were from the Mayor. He pushed the green call button.

Eagle Feather studied the sketch. “We should show this to the bartender,” he said. “He’s the only one left who could possibly have seen this guy.”

“What bartender?” Susan wanted to know.

Snyder answered for Eagle Feather. “At the Adagio Hotel. If we accept the line of inquiry that hinges on the murder of Megan McMitchell, we have to consider that the man in the lounge the bartender saw with Megan the night the ultra runner disappeared might be our suspect.”

“And if the barkeep recognizes this picture,” Eagle Feather said, picking up the thread, “it would authenticate that whole line of inquiry. It would validate the link not only to Megan but to Harrar and to the priests; the whole nine yards.”

“But would it bring us any closer to finding him?” Susan asked.

“Maybe,” Eagle Feather said. “If we took the picture around to the two churches we might find someone who saw this guy.”

“It’s all we’ve got right now,” Snyder said with a sigh. He stood up. “Why don’t I make a few copies of this? Eagle Feather, you can take one over to the Adagio. Susan and I can try the churches.”

“What about Detective O’Bannon? Shouldn’t we show it to him?” Susan asked.

Eagle Feather shook his head. “He’d feel obligated to publish it and then we’d be right back to the risk that our suspect might see it. Besides, this isn’t evidence, it’s a hypothetical likeness.”

“We should wait to see if the bartender verifies this sketch before going to the churches,” Snyder pointed out.

Eagle Feather paused. “That’s true. I’ll call you after I’ve spoken to him.”

Twenty minutes later Eagle Feather walked into the lobby of the Adagio Hotel and went directly to the lounge. It was open and lunch was being served to a few guests. A woman was wiping down the bar. She smiled at Eagle Feather.

“What can I get ya’?”

“Just some answers to some questions. Is the regular barkeep here?”

“Yah, he’s in the back doing inventory. Hang on a minute.” She smiled and eased down the bar and through a passage behind it. In a moment she returned followed by a man in jeans and a collared shirt. Eagle Feather recognized him from their earlier meeting.

The man looked at Eagle Feather. “You again. Did you ever find that person you were looking for?”

“Yep, we did. Sorry to bother you again, but I got just one question for you.” At the bartender’s nod Eagle Feather brought out the sketch and held it up in front of him. “Did you ever see this guy before?”

Immediately the bartender said, “Yeah, he looks like

the Virgin Cuba Libra. He was sitting right next to Blue Cacao, the one you were looking for."

"You're certain."

"Pretty much. The guy gave me the creeps."

"You've been a great help. Thanks."

Eagle Feather called Snyder as he walked away.

"Jim Snyder here."

"Identity confirmed," was all Eagle Feather said.

Snyder put away his phone. "Here we go," he said to Susan. "The barkeep recognized him. Let's go visit some churches."

Susan smiled at him. "As much as I like going to church, I should check in with my department today. I'll let you handle the grunt work. Do you mind if I use your computer? I can do my work from here."

Snyder was disappointed. "Well, sure, help yourself. But you're gonna miss the excitement of the chase."

"I'll just have to live with that somehow."

Snyder caught a cab and rode it to Richmond. It dropped him in front of the administrative offices of the Star of the Sea Parish. Inside there was great confusion. The church had lost one priest and now another was missing, all in just twenty-four hours. People carried files between the offices. Policemen stood guard in front of both priest's studies and yellow tape decorated their doors.

Snyder touched the arm of a passing woman carrying files. "Is the church secretary here? I'd like a word with her."

"Do you need the secretary for the church or the school?" the woman asked.

"Uh, church, I think."

She nodded toward a frosted glass window where Snyder could see and older lady sitting at a desk. He rapped on the door and poked his head in. She looked up and there was redness around her eyes and dampness shone on her cheeks.

"May I help you?" Her voice was subdued.

"Yes, ma'am. I'm a reporter with the Chronicle doing an investigation into this matter in cooperation with the police. Would you mind looking at a sketch?"

"A sketch?"

"Yes, ma'am." Snyder held the likeness up for her.

"Who is that?" she asked.

"You've never seen this man?"

"I don't believe so."

"May I ask, when did you last see Father Gilligan?"

"You mean actually see him, like to talk to him?"

"That's right."

A tear squeezed out the corner of her eye. "Not for a couple of months, I'm afraid. I mean not to actually talk to him. I'd see him going by every once in a while but he never looked up or said anything. He took a vow of silence, you know. That was after..." She turned her head away, unable to continue. Snyder heard her quiet sob.

"I'm sorry, ma'am. You never see his face during that entire time?"

"No, I didn't. I'd get notes from him; I'd find them on my desk in the morning. The poor man must have had many sleepless nights."

"Do you know anyone here who might actually have seen his face during that time?"

"I think Nina saw him once. I remember she was quite upset by how ravaged his face looked from his grief and guilt, like he was a different man." The woman looked intently at Snyder. "Why do you ask?

Snyder ignored the question. "Who's Nina?"

"She's the cleaning lady. She comes in late afternoons and cleans until seven or eight at night."

Snyder looked at his watch; almost three. "What time might she be in today?"

The woman stifled another sob. "I don't know, with everything that's going on. She might not come in at all.

Or she might be here already, trying to help out."

"Can you tell me what she looks like? Then I'll stop taking up your valuable time," Snyder said.

The secretary almost smiled. "Oh, you can't miss her. She's quite large and her hair is flaming red."

"And she cleans in the sanctuary?"

"Yes, I'd look there."

"Thank you very much for your help. I'm sorry for your loss."

Snyder left the administrative offices and crossed over to the church. He found the sanctuary alive with people. The news had spread and parishioners and friends of the church had come to pray. Snyder walked slowly along the pews. He saw no one in the sanctuary who fit the dramatic description he'd been given. He left through a side door and found himself in a carpeted corridor. He heard the distinctive sound of a vacuum cleaner and followed it. He came to a meeting room where a very large woman was vacuuming the carpet. She had bright red hair. She looked up when Snyder entered the room and turned off the machine.

Snyder smiled at her. "May I ask you a few questions? I'm assisting the police."

"Sure, I need a break," the woman said. "But I won't be able to help you much.".

Snyder held up the sketch. "Do you know this man?"

She shook her head without a word.

Snyder tried again. "Have you ever seen this man before? Please think carefully."

Again she shook her head. "I don't know that man," she said. "But he does look a little like Father Gilligan, especially with the hood and all."

"Thank you. You've been very helpful." And Snyder hurried away, trying not to let his jubilance show on his face. As far as he was concerned, it was confirmed. Just the fact that the picture had brought Father Gilligan to her mind was enough for him. The priest was an imposter, he was sure of it. The killer had taken Father Gilligan's identity and likely murdered him. He'd been hiding here in the church all this time. Very clever! And now that they knew he'd been with Megan at the Adagio Lounge the night the ultra-runner disappeared, everything came together.

Snyder called Eagle Feather in great excitement. Eagle Feather sounded excited at the news.

"That does ties up a few loose ends, doesn't it?" Eagle Feather said. "We have the impostor priest whom we've connected to Megan who is connected to Harrar. Maybe now you should release the sketch to the police. I'll report to O'Bannon, although everything we've got is circumstantial. The cops will have to find some actual evidence."

Snyder called Susan to tell her the news. After she answered he heard a muted roar and clack in the background instead of the silence of his apartment. "Where are you?" he asked.

"Hi, Jim. I'm on the Bart. I'm on my way back to

the University. I received a message from the department that they have a teacher crisis. I've got to go back and help out."

Snyder quickly told her the news. She was silent for a moment. "It sounds like you don't need me any more. You've identified him; now all that's left is to find him."

Snyder's tried to keep his disappointment out of his voice. "Will you be coming back at all?"

He heard Susan's musical laughter. "Miss me already, do you? Yes, I'll call you in a day or two to see how it's going, when things are on a more even keel in my department. Good luck with the hunt."

Snyder took the phone from his ear. The joy was suddenly gone from his day. The excitement of his triumph vanished now that she wouldn't be there to share in it.

It's remarkable how quickly I can become depressed, he thought to himself. He knew he'd let himself become too attached to Susan and felt a growing anger with himself. *I'm an old fool, to think that a woman like that would want to stay with me*, he thought. He'd been seduced by her youth, by the compliment she paid him just by being with him. Susan was impulsive. She was that rare person who could genuinely enjoy each moment of life and move on to the next without regret. Snyder knew he should try to do the same, but he knew he wouldn't. He'd spent a lifetime alone pretending to enjoy his solitude but knowing it was only a pretense, a defensive shell against circumstances just like this. He hated the feeling of hurt, the heartbreak, the yearning, the shame he felt when a woman walked away from him. And so he avoided it altogether. He felt anger grow with Susan as well. Why had she done this to him?

Then Snyder did what he'd always done before: he turned his thoughts away and focused entirely on his work.

Zack stood in the cheery sunshine, greatly relieved. In the dark tunnel of the catacomb the foul smell of decay that surrounded him had grown stronger and he'd felt a surge of fear that threatened to turn into panic. He'd had a sense of imminent danger. His instincts shouted at him to get away from there, and so Zack had backed slowly up the stairs, feeling his way up each step. He felt he shouldn't turn his back to the darkness. His progress was slow and fearful until at last he came to the lighted sconces. There he turned and walked quickly out of the catacombs and out through the sanctuary into the sunlight and took a deep breath. Zack remembered the sticky substance and looked at his finger. A reddish-black film coated it. Zack felt sure that Father Gilligan, the real Father Gilligan, would never be seen again.

O'Bannon was on the phone and up to his neck in Quick-Notes when Zack walked into the homicide offices at the Richmond District Station.

"You're just in time," Marty said when he saw Zack. "I just got off the line with the Mayor. I told him we've identified the killer and are initiating a massive man-hunt."

Zack's face showed his surprise. "You have?"

"We've managed to accomplish a few things in your absence," O'Bannon chuckled. He went on to sketch out his suspicions of Sergeant Sean Kelly and his subsequent disappearance.

"And you believe he's the one we've been looking for?"

O'Bannon nodded. "Yeah, I think so. And even if he's not, he must know who is." He picked up a printed sketch of a man's face from his desk and showed it to Zack. "This is an artist's rendering of the guy," he said.

Zack stared at it. "Where'd you get that?"

O'Bannon told him about Snyder and the anthropologist from U.C. Davis who had compiled the likeness simply from what they had learned about the killer and his victims. "I've got to say it's pretty goddam amazing," O'Bannon concluded.

Zack took the sketch and sat down. "And this is the Kelly guy?"

"Pretty much," O'Bannon said. "Close enough for me. He's that big, for sure. And the shape of the face is pretty close, especially when you figure it's a portrait drawn just from the evidence. But this sketch is just the icing on the cake. I don't believe in coincidence, so when I see this guy at the Presidio and then leaving this building and then find that note on Harrar's desk...and then that thing in the park..." O'Bannon shuddered.

Zack grunted, turning the sketch this way and that.

"It all fits," O'Bannon went on. "Kelly had the opportunity and the perfect cover to commit all the murders."

"This sketch seems like it could be a lot of people," Zack said. "And isn't it pretty brazen to come stomping along obliterating the evidence right under your nose after the Presidio murder?"

"When hasn't this guy been brazen?" O'Bannon countered.

Zack was deep in thought. "How do we explain the priest impostor bit? Wasn't Kelly performing duties for the Park Police?"

"Remember, no one saw much of Father Gilligan," O'Bannon replied. "Kelly could've done that bit in his spare time at night, or for just a few hours every couple of days. Didn't everyone at the church pretty much leave him alone during that time? They never knew where he was at any given moment. And their only communication with him was written notes."

"Yeah, I gotta admit it fits," Zack said. Then he looked O'Bannon in the eye. "Marty, you were scared shitless by this monster in the park. Do you really think this man could have been that thing?"

O'Bannon shrugged. "Maybe." He sounded defensive. "Maybe I made too big a deal of the howls and all. It was real dark and the noise came suddenly out of nowhere..."

Zack raised his eyebrows. "And what did he use for a weapon to cause the neck wounds?"

O'Bannon shrugged again. "I guess we'll just have to ask him when we catch him," he said.

THIRTY-THREE

Once old man Henderson learned that the killer had been identified and was on the run, he insisted that Snyder publish his article and illustrate it with Susan's sketch, saying it was in the best interests of the citizens of San Francisco to do so, not to mention the Chronicle. They were newspapermen after all, he said. The time for a scoop is now.

The resulting piece was headlined: "SERIAL KILLER IDENTIFIED; SEARCH IS ON". It might be his best work, Snyder thought. In it he described the investigation from beginning to end; all the suspicions, the fears, and the process. He lauded the police, particularly O'Bannon, for their open-minded outside-the-box approach that ultimately allowed them to bring all the pieces of the puzzle together.

As a result of the piece O'Bannon went from scapegoat to hero overnight. The San Francisco Police Department was put on a pedestal and held up to all other large city police forces as an example. Every cop in the Richmond District wanted to be seen with O'Bannon now.

But there was no sign of Kelly.

Zack prepared to leave San Francisco. He doubted Marty's conclusion, but O'Bannon had taken the bull by the horns and with every cop in San Francisco engaged in the hunt, the killer, whether it was Kelly or not, would have to lie low. And after the Harrar incident, Zack's focus was entirely on protecting Libby. He called Luke Forrester right away, thanked him for his patience and received his congratulations. Quietly, behind the scenes, the FBI was being lauded as well on account of Zack - O'Bannon had seen to that. So when Zack mentioned he planned to stay another twenty-four hours to relax and enjoy San Francisco with Libby before returning home, Luke raised no objections.

But the city was not entirely at peace. Every business, bar, and boutique had a copy of the Kelly's sketch posted on a wall. Everyone had the killer's likeness etched in the back of their minds as they went about their business. No one went out at night if they could avoid it. The city streets after dark were eerily quiet.

But there still was no sign of Kelly.

O'Bannon began to wonder if the predator had left the city immediately after he killed Father Gonzales. The timing was about right; when O'Bannon had sent the Park Police captain looking for him, his quarters had already been emptied.

O'Bannon called Zack to get his thoughts.

"Wouldn't surprise me," Zack said. "That's what I think happened in Los Angeles. We had murders at regular intervals, then nothing. At least this time, we have a likeness."

"So if we start hearing about murders in Portland or Seattle, we'll can...?"

"Show 'em the sketch."

"What's your sidekick think about it all?"

"You're not gonna like what he thinks."

O'Bannon chuckled. "I never do, but tell me anyway."

"He doesn't believe Kelly is our man."

"He's got some other candidate?"

"Not one that's human," Zack said.

"Well, I think we can agree now that we're not dealing with a mythic creature of some sort." O'Bannon sounded annoyed. "He needs to give it a rest. What's he doing, anyway?"

Zack laughed. "You didn't talk like that after you came back from Golden Gate Park. As to Eagle Feather, when the newspaper article came out and everyone raised a great hullabaloo, he went off the grid. I haven't spoken to him since last evening when he said Kelly wasn't our man. That's the last I heard from him."

"Think he went home?"

"Nope. I think he's still on the hunt."

Now it was O'Bannon's turn to sigh. "Well, it can't hurt to have someone else looking for the guy. *We* can't find him."

Zack hung up and looked glumly at Libby. She was stretched out on the bed reading a sightseeing guide but had tuned an ear in on Zack's conversation. At his look she lay the open guide down on her tummy and looked earnestly at him. “You agree with Eagle Feather, don’t you?”

“I suppose. There are some things that still don’t add up. But they might possibly be explained by circumstances we just don’t know about. Like O’Bannon says, we’ll ask the guy when we catch him.”

“Is that why you can’t relax yet? You think there’s a chance Eagle Feather might be right?”

Zack smiled at her. “What makes you think I’m not relaxed?”

“Oh, c’mon!”

“Sure, okay, I am just a wee bit concerned. But not just about that. There’s something else I don’t think has occurred to O’Bannon. The killer is still loose and his next scheduled kill according to his previous pattern is tomorrow.”

Libby inhaled sharply and looked at Zack with round eyes. “Then they’ve got to catch him soon.”

“That’s what I’ve been thinking.”

“Shouldn’t you say something to Marty?”

“I should tell him what? Look harder? I think they’re already looking as hard as they can.”

“But we should warn- ”

“Warn the citizens that we might be chasing the wrong suspect? Start a panic? No, I don’t think that’s the answer.”

“We’ve got to do something!”

“For one thing, we can do all our sightseeing today and then stay here in the hotel tomorrow night, don’t you think?”

“So we’ll just take care of ourselves...” Libby stared at Zack with her mouth pursed petulantly. Zack knew the look.

“Okay, Libby. I’ll try to think of something to help. I’ll call Jim Snyder over at the Chronicle and see what he thinks.”

Zack picked up his phone. Snyder’s line at the San Francisco Chronicle was busy, in fact so busy that after half an hour and several tries Zack still couldn’t get through. He left a message. Ten minutes later his cell phone rang.

“Zack, you called?”

“I tried. What’s going on over there?”

“It’s nuts. I’ve never had such a reaction to a news article. The phone’s been ringing off the hook; people are coming in off the street. We’ve actually had to post a guard to keep people out so we can get some work done here.”

“Are they afraid?”

“Yeah, partly that, I think. We’ve had a zillion sightings. But people are intrigued, too. These serial killers always fascinate people. Half the people want to write the book, and the other half want to read it.”

Zack groaned. "It's gonna make O'Bannon's job that much harder. But here's why I called: do you remember what we expect to happen tomorrow?"

Snyder paused. "I kinda thought with this massive man hunt going on that it wouldn't happen. You don't think he'd dare..."

"Not if this were just any guy. But remember who he is...what he is. Think of how long we've looked for him; think of everything he's managed to do right under our noses. Are you confident he can't manage to make his kill, even under these circumstances?"

"What can we do?"

"Well, that's why I called. I was hoping for an idea. What's your anthropology lady think?"

Snyder was silent for a moment. Then he said, "Uh, she's gone, Zack. Duty called."

"Oh, I'm sorry."

"No, it's nothing. But I think you've hit on something. After all, it was by studying the killer's past actions and practices that she was able to create the sketch that helped us identify him. Maybe we could do a similar frame-up to figure out what he'd do, where he'd be..." Snyder was starting to sound excited. "I'll give her a call. I can feed her the info she needs right over the phone."

After Snyder hung up, Zack grinned at Libby. "There, my dear, I've done all that I can do. Now would the lady be willing to accompany me to experience the sights, the pleasures, the exotic sensuality that is the city of San Francisco?"

The moment he ended his conversation with Zack, Jim Snyder called Susan's office number at the University. He knew he was shamelessly using this opportunity to re-establish their relationship, yet in truth he believed that the analytical approach Susan had used before could be helpful again. The phone rang twice and he heard the standard message: "I'm away from my desk right now...". He tried Susan's cell number only to be presented with another automated message. Disappointed, he decided to try later.

Eagle Feather stood in the large empty room and looked around. The door to the barracks had been left ajar and since no one was around he'd simply walked in. He knew Kelly had lived here only a few months but either his needs were very simple or he had taken everything with him when he fled. A wooden dresser, a small metal desk and chair, and a bed frame and mattress were all that remained. A thin layer of dust coated the moldings and sills, a couple of sticky notes lay dried, curled, and forgotten in a corner where a wastebasket must have been, and a small slip of crumpled paper and a couple of toothpicks were jammed under the molding in places. There could not have been a carpet; the outline of fading on the floor caused by light coming in the shade free south-facing window would have been visible even after just a couple of months. Kelly could have had a chair or stool of some kind but nothing substantial. A peg or ball footed armchair plus 300 pounds of Kelly would have left a mark. And the fresh painted walls, likely done just prior to Kelly's occupancy, showed no fade marks or punctures from pictures having hung there.

Eagle Feather's slow scrutiny brought his eyes back to the entrance door. He pushed it shut and found another curled sticky note snugged up against the molding. He picked it up and smoothed it out. He could just make out a name, *O'Keefe's,* written in light pencil. A colleague? Not a friend, certainly - Kelly wouldn't have had any. By tilting the note to increase the light contrast he could make out a single number: "*3*". There were no impressions to suggest anything else had been written after the number. Eagle Feather studied it idly. Was it a time, maybe for a meeting? Maybe.

Eagle Feather walked over and picked up the other two sticky notes. One was blank, but on the other he saw the word "*bar*" followed by "*4*". He saw that something had been written before the word "bar" but it had faded so much he couldn't read it. Eagle Feather compared the two notes and smiled. Yes, the entire message might well have read: "*O'Keefe's bar 4*", the time and place for a meeting: O'Keefe's bar at four, and another one at three. Likely Kelly had been meeting someone at that location more than once and used these sticky notes as reminders.

Eagle Feather left the barracks room and walked over to the Park Police offices. He found a sergeant at the duty desk.

"I'm looking for O'Keefe's Bar," he said. "Is it in the neighborhood?"

The sergeant looked up and smiled. "It's just down the hill in Richmond, on Balboa Street," he said.

Eagle Feather called a cab and asked to be taken to O'Keefe's Bar on Balboa Street.

When Zack and Libby looked out the window of their hotel room on the morning of May 24, the marine layer had cloaked the world in a grey shadow, but by the time they emerged onto the sidewalk bright sun had already chased the fog back to its lair behind the coastal hills. They held hands like two teenagers as they walked along, their faces lit in eager anticipation of the day ahead.

Their itinerary was set. They would walk to Powell Street Station and board the cable car for a ride to Fisherman's Wharf. After a stroll in Fish Alley and a tour of Ghirardelli Chocolates they would find lunch and then walk out Hyde Street Pier to view the historic ships. If time remained, they would visit the Maritime Museum. At the end of the day it would be back to the cable car for a ride to Sutter Street and a short walk over to the China Town Gate. Then a dinner of Chinese food and a relaxed evening stroll back to the Adagio Hotel.

Libby and Zack planned to use this opportunity to abandon their worries for one whole day and enjoy themselves, something they hadn't done in a long while.

Zack hadn't heard from Eagle Feather for over twenty-four hours now but he wasn't concerned. He knew Eagle Feather could take care of himself; in fact, he was more worried that Eagle Feather *would* call with some bit of news that would make Zack feel he should abandon his plans for the day. But all of that fled his mind at the first clang of the cable car and the loud chatter of excited tourists as they all climbed aboard.

The ride was entertaining, the monologue of the driver informative, and the conversations of the tourists around them amusing. When they came to cross streets high up on the hill they could see vistas of sparkling blue water far below and a refreshing breeze danced in through the open windows. At Bay Street they climbed off and walked along with the crowd down the steep hill toward the buildings at Fisherman's Wharf. They mingled with the crowds that flowed across their path on

Beach Street and let themselves be gently swept along like a log in a river, turning this way and that to peek in a window or to make a purchase at a sales cart.

At one Libby's eye caught a headline on a newspaper. It was the Portland Oregonian, not a local paper, and it read, "SAN FRANCISCO WAITS IN FEAR ON SLASHER KILL DATE". She silently pointed it out to Zack. He plucked it off the pile and read the story.

"All of San Francisco waits fearfully for nightfall. The citizens of this great city have done the math and they know well that the Throat Snatcher, that killer with a penchant for plucking open the throats of his victims, strikes every nine days and is due to kill again in twenty-four hours. Few souls will venture out tonight, for by the time the foggy sun of that city has risen tomorrow this fearsome predator may well have claimed yet another victim. The San Francisco police, aided by the FBI and other federal agencies have launched a massive manhunt for Sergeant Sean Kelly, a US Park Policeman they believe is responsible for at least four murders. But few have faith that this persistent killer can be caught in time to keep him from accomplishing his ghoulish goal. A statement from the mayor's office..."

Zack looked at Libby and frowned. "I thought the panic might subside once people believed that the killer had been identified. Do you think the people here are as worried as this reporter makes them sound?"

Libby was also puzzled. "I haven't been in touch with the pulse of this city since coming here; I feel more like I've *been* the pulse. But I can understand how people's faith in the police might be shaken, since this murderer strikes so regularly and with such impunity." She looked at Zack. "What do you think about this Kelly guy?"

They walked on down Beach Street, but their mood

had changed.

"I'm not sure what to think," Zack replied. "All the evidence leads to him, or perhaps I should say he fits all the known evidence. He had the opportunity each time and with his U.S. Police uniform he could go almost anywhere without arousing suspicion. He was the only person there at the right time to deliver that note to Harry Harrar's desk. And he was caught trying to destroy evidence after the Presidio murder." Zack looked at Libby. "And now he's on the run. I can't blame Marty for his confidence in that conclusion."

"But you?" Libby persisted. "What do you think?"

"The truth is I've never met or even seen this Kelly person. I'd have some sort of feeling about him if I had, maybe." He smiled at Libby. "But for now I've got to go with what Marty believes. We have no other suspects."

"But Eagle Feather hasn't accepted it," Libby insisted.

Zack laughed. "You know Eagle Feather. He's not going to accept that this mystic killer is a white Irish glorified Park Ranger. That would insult his intelligence."

Libby walked along in silence. After a while she pointed at a store window.

"I want some taffy," she said.

Eagle Feather was sitting in a rear booth in O'Keefe's Bar, a shadow among shadows within the haze and gloom, sipping a bad coffee and keeping watch over the bright rectangle at the far end of this tavern cave that was the door to the street. When he came here from the Presidio yesterday, he had found the bartender and showed him the sketch. The man had recognized the likeness right away.

Yeah, he'd said, he's been in a few times. He always meets the same guy in one of those back booths. The other guy? Never actually saw what he looked like. No, don't remember him coming in, never saw him leave, either. The table girl served him so I can't describe him. But this guy? Yeah, seen him come in several times, great big guy who always looked like he was about to have a tooth pulled. Always went straight to the back. Never stayed long, maybe ten minutes, then he'd get up and walk out again. He'd have a couple of Guinness. Can't tell ya' anything else.

Eagle Feather had gone back to his room and returned this morning simply hoping he might get lucky and that Kelly would come back to the bar. But he doubted it. He was at another dead end. He knew what day today was and he didn't think the massive manhunt would deter the killer. The focus of the police had swung to finding Kelly rather than preventing another murder. And with Zack out of the picture, Eagle Feather figured he was on his own, unless...

Eagle Feather pulled out his cell and called Snyder's number at the Chronicle. Snyder answered after several rings.

"The Chronicle. Snyder here."

"Eagle Feather."

"Well hey, Chief. What's going on?"

"I'm just hanging out, drinking coffee. You?"

"I'm at the office avoiding the curious and the detective wannabes. I'm trying to find a way to give the cops a hand finding Kelly." Snyder told Eagle Feather about Zack's idea to use Susan's methods to help track Kelly.

"But I can't reach her. I called her all day yesterday, at work and at home, left a bunch of messages, but no dice. I tried her again this morning. Still no good." Snyder sounded a bit frantic. "I tell you, Eagle Feather, I'm starting to get worried about her."

"Our time is growing short," Eagle Feather said. "I'm still trying to track Kelly. I learned he has been meeting another guy here at O'Keefe's Bar. I'm hoping one of them will come back today. But we need more. Why don't you try to do that profiling Susan did, if you can't reach her? You watched her, you fed her the facts; maybe you can do the same thing."

"I dunno. She knows a lot more about it than I do..."

"What've you got to lose?" Eagle Feather pointed out. "Go ahead, try it. Then call me back."

"But Susan- "

"Don't worry about Susan. She went back to UC Davis, right? No one's gonna bother her there. She's probably just real busy. She took a lot of time off to help out a certain old fart, remember?"

After ending the call, Eagle Feather drummed his fingers on the table. This was getting him nowhere. He didn't really believe either of the men would come back here - not now. But who was this second man? He wished the bar tender had been more helpful. The men must have met up the day Kelly decided to run, probably right here. Did they go off together? There just wasn't anything to go on. Eagle Feather dropped some coins on the table and stood reluctantly. With time growing short, he'd need to think of a whole new approach.

THIRTY-FOUR

His plan was set. The pieces were in place and would soon go into motion one by one like so many falling dominoes. He need only wait. He didn't want to leave this city but overreaching his disappointment was excitement, a level of excitement he had not felt for a long time. Soon now - soon it would begin.

The text message was from George Henderson, the News Editor at the San Francisco Chronicle. It was brief. It read:

James Snyder at SF VA Medical Center Clement Street brain tumor critical requested you - George Henderson.

It was the second surprising text message Susan had received in as many days. The first had been that request to return to deal with a teacher crisis in the department. She had rushed back but when she arrived she had been met by shrugs and confusion. No one seemed to know about any crisis or any text message. Now here was this alarming message asking her to return to San Francisco. Jim had never told her he was suffering from a brain tumor, let alone a condition that could turn critical so quickly. Was it another hoax?

Susan picked up the phone to call the Chronicle.

She noticed she had a message and decided to listen to it first. A strangely vibrant voice filled her ear.

"Dr. Apgar, this is George Henderson. I felt I should follow my cryptic text message with a bit more information. I expect you will try to reach me but I will be out of town for the next several days. I had no idea of Jim's condition. He kept it to himself. He suddenly collapsed at his desk and his physician had the paramedics take him directly to the VA Medical Center where he was apparently receiving treatment. When he regained consciousness he asked for you. I hope you will not disappoint him. I'm sorry to be the bearer of such bad news."

Susan felt a surge of guilt. Might she have contributed to the urgency of his condition unknowingly? Perhaps she should not have been so...well, energetic. Susan knew about the nuerointerventional radiology at the VA Medical Center; it was leading edge stuff. Jim could not be in a better place.

Then Susan felt sudden anger. That bastard, she thought, to keep it to himself. Didn't he think it might concern me as well?

But she wouldn't refuse, of course. In her heart she wanted an excuse to return. She scooped up her purse and left a note at the department office saying she'd be gone a couple more days. She'd swing by her apartment and grab some clothes and if she left now in her Miata she should be able to reach the Medical Center tonight before visiting hours were over.

Snyder looked up to see the mail boy approach along the desks with the usual thick wad of envelopes in his hand. Snyder was used to a fair amount of mail in his work, but since his last article had been published it had really stacked up. He rolled his eyes at the mail boy and nodded his head toward the overflowing in-tray. The boy grinned back and dropped the new stack on top, causing a slow avalanche of memos and envelopes to slide down onto his desktop. Snyder grunted and nudged the encroaching pile off of his keyboard and as he did his eye caught a flash of pink among the white. He dug it out. It was a pink envelope addressed to him in a woman's writing. Intrigued, he slit it open. There was a letter typed on official UC Davis Anthropology Department letterhead, an invitation to join Susan at Building Eight of the VA Medical Center on Clement Street. Tonight. He read on. She would be there for a conference with her department just the one night. She could see him around eight that evening to spend some time with him if he wanted - but only if he wanted. She missed him. Love, Susan.

Jim Snyder felt a rush of feelings. He'd wronged her in his heart; he saw that now. She'd not deserted him. The day seemed suddenly brighter. When Jim went on with his work he began to whistle a cheery tune causing his colleagues at nearby desks to look up in surprise.

The fog crept up through the crowded Eucalyptus forest like a cold breath. Kelly shivered and pulled the hood of his sweatshirt up over his head. When he came here he'd been plenty warm. He'd brought the sweatshirt just for the launch ride. But Kelly wasn't complaining. When he'd learned the cops were on to him, not knowing what else to do, he'd run right to Donny, who much to Kelly's surprise had been a real prince. Donny slid another packet of money across the table to Kelly and told him he had a plan that would see Kelly safely out of the country and down Mexico way for a couple of months until things died down. He'd told Kelly to come directly here to this place, telling him how to find this spot deep in the eucalyptus grove up on Mount Sutro, a place no one would look for him. Then at dawn the next morning he was to creep down to Land's End where a launch would meet him and take him away, no one the wiser. And with the money in this envelope he'd live like a prince in Mexico.

Birds chirped high up in the trees and from somewhere far below came the constant boom of surf as the cold Pacific threw itself against the rocky cliffs. To sailors it's an ominous sound, but to Kelly it signaled his escape and his mind filled with images of tropical cocktails and affordable whores.

Zack and Libby were seated at a sidewalk table enjoying a sandwich when Zack's phone rang. It was O'Bannon.

"You see the papers?"

"You mean the dire warnings of another murder tonight?"

"Yeah. And they've even got a name for him, the "Throat Snatcher".

"This city enjoys its serial killers."

"Yeah, but my bosses don't. Can you come over to the district station? I'd like to bounce some thoughts off you."

"Marty, I can't do that. I promised this day to Libby. And then I'm taking her home. All that's left is for you to catch this Kelly guy - you don't need me for that."

"Zack, with all the help you've been, I hate to ask

this. Just give me an hour, okay? You've had experience with this guy and a few thoughts from you just might turn this whole search around. I don't have to tell you my whole career kinda hangs on what comes next."

"I've never known you to worry about your career before," Zack chuckled.

"That's not actually my concern, although it would be nice to have a pension when I walk away from here. To tell you the truth, I'm pissed off: at the press, at my bosses, at my colleagues who're supposed to have my back but are as fickle as bunch of teenage girls, and especially at this Kelly guy who's been dancing around right under my nose."

"You pissed at me?"

"Not yet, but don't push it. But seriously, Zack, if you can give me just an hour sometime this afternoon I'd really be grateful."

Zack looked over at Libby who'd been making hand gestures at him to go ahead. Zack shrugged. "Okay, Marty, but just an hour. How 'bout I come by at four?"

After Zack hung up, he asked Libby, "Why'd you do that? He doesn't really need me."

Libby's face was serious. "He wouldn't have asked you if he didn't think he needed you. And besides, you've spent a lot of time on this investigation. Here's your chance to help wrap it up."

Zack reached for her hand. "Okay, but I meant what I said. I'm only giving him an hour and then I'm coming right back to the hotel and you and I are having drinks at the lounge and a real nice dinner."

"It's a deal," Libby said and smiled.

Eagle Feather got tired of waiting and walked out of O'Keefe's Bar. He knew in his heart that neither Kelly nor the mystery man would be coming back here. He guessed that Kelly would already be well into his escape plan whether it was to hole up until things calmed down or get out of the city right away while he could.

But Eagle Feather wasn't as concerned about Sergeant Kelly as he was about this other man. He had a bad feeling about him. Guys like Kelly didn't have friends; he had too much to hide. What is it they said? "*To whomever you tell your secret you surrender your freedom.*"

So who was this other guy? And why couldn't the bartender describe him better? It reminded him of their search in the Tenderloin District when they'd questioned people about the man who was meeting Megan. They'd all described him from their feelings about him rather than by his appearance.

Well, he needed more than that. He called Snyder.

"What've you got from your profiling?" Eagle Feather asked Snyder when he answered.

"Like I told you, this exercise requires someone who has more experience with it," Snyder protested. "I fed in those same facts we used for his description which are all we know, really. But all I got is the obvious."

"Well, like what?"

"Well, like he favors the forest, the natural areas, the parks. He needs trees for travel and when he attacks victims. He uses the dark. He's incredibly strong: things like steep cliffs or tall trees that would be obstacles for you or me don't pose a problem for him. And he's fast, probably much faster than we would expect- "

"How'd you come up with that?" Eagle Feather asked.

"His victims were all athletic to some degree. One or two were young and quite active. One was even an experienced jogger. And the kid was on a bicycle on a steep hill. Yet none of them apparently came close to escaping."

"Okay. What else?"

"There's his brain development. As Susan suggested, he's a mix of animal cunning and human logic. It suggests he has better than average ability to anticipate and to plan, probably beyond what we might expect. He's a chess player. So whatever your average criminal might do in a circumstance like this, he might not."

"How do you mean?"

"For example, right now every cop in San Francisco is looking for him. Any wanted criminal in his right mind would run and hide, try to escape."

"And you think..."

"I think he might just go on about his business. I think he might kill again tonight."

O'Bannon was waiting for Zack at the watch officer's desk in the district station when he arrived shortly after four. He took Zack's arm and led him to an interview room so they could talk without being interrupted. As soon as Zack sat down O'Bannon pulled out some photos and slid them across the table to him.

"A fishing boat found this guy snagged on the north tower of the Golden Gate Bridge this morning. These are photos taken by the coroner. Notice anything?"

Zack stared at the photographs, sliding one under the other like playing cards as he compared them. "Looks like he's been in the water a while..."

"Yeah..."

"He's chewed up. Fish?"

"Maybe. Anything else catch your eye?"

Zack saw it now. He looked up at O'Bannon and spoke slowly. "There's a big bite out of his throat."

"Yep."

"Now I see why you wanted to chat. How long has he been in the water?"

"They think a week to ten days."

"Anywhere from the 15th to the 18th?"

"Something like that."

"Meaning this could be our ultra-runner."

"That's what I'm thinking. We're working on an ID now."

"Any idea how he got there?"

"Well, the currents are real strong in and out of the Bay through that bridge. I talked to some fishermen; they know the currents better than anybody. They say anything that washes out towards the north tower is likely to have come from the middle of the bay and north."

"So Alcatraz, Angel Island, maybe Belvedere, that kind of thing?"

"Yep."

"But no nearer to the city?"

"Nope."

"If this is the ultra runner, what was he doing in the middle of the Bay?"

"Yeah, well, that's the question, isn't it? We may never know the answer to that one."

Zack sat deep in thought. Then he looked up at O'Bannon.

"Let me walk through this with you. When considering the kill sites, we've seen a preference for heavily wooded recreational areas, all pretty much deserted at night." He ticked them off. "First Buena Vista Park, then Golden Gate Park, then the bunkers at the Presidio. Even the fourth kill" -Zack looked at his iPhone calendar- "on May 7 was in a place dark and deserted at night. The consistent factor here is no houses or structures where people live."

Zack looked up. "Have you got a map of the city?"

O'Bannon went out of the room and returned quickly with a guide map of San Francisco. Zack opened it and spread it out on the table. "There may be a pattern here," he said.

O'Bannon sat down and they both studied the map. Zack took a pencil and drew lines to connect the murder sites. "In Golden Gate Park we found the body just about here," he said, drawing an x with his pen just east of Lloyd Lake. "I'll start my line where he first killed at Buena Vista Park and draw it up through the Golden Gate Park site" -Zack began to draw- "and then to the site at the Presidio."

The two men stared at Zack's line on the map. It described a large 'L'.

"Where does Twin Peaks fit in?"

"From an old forest point of view, it doesn't fit at all," Zack said, and shrugged. "But just for fun, let's start the line at the Presidio and take it down through Golden Gate to Twin Peaks," Zack said, drawing it.

"Well, that didn't help," he said.

Both men stared at the resulting arc. Then O'Bannon took the pen and continued the arc southeast and around to the north to complete a huge circle that closed at the Presidio.

Zack stared at it. "Look at all the green places, the preserves. Your circle passes just north of Bernal Heights

Park and then it's all ocean until..." He put his finger on a spot. The arc of the circle passed directly through Alcatraz Island before coming ashore at the Presidio.

O'Bannon watched Zack's face. "Coincidence?"

"Maybe. Didn't your fisherman say the middle of the Bay or north?"

"Sure, but- "

"Wait," Zack said. He took back the pen and drew a straight line from Twin Peaks north through Buena Vista Park and straight up to Alcatraz Island.

O'Bannon scratched his chin. "I never realized how well those places lined up."

"But look what we've drawn," Zack said in a whisper. "It's a large bow. Like on the constellation Orion."

"Now what if we put an arrow in the bow," O'Bannon said. He drew a straight line east to west through the middle of the bow that paralleled the streets of San Francisco. It passed directly through Lincoln Park at Lands End.

"We may have found where his next kill will take place," Zack said quietly.

THIRTY-FIVE

Eagle Feather walked slowly up the sloping sidewalk on 8th Street toward Golden Gate Park deep in thought. He had decided it was time to follow his instincts, which told him that Kelly wasn't the killer. So it had to be the second man, the man Kelly had been meeting. A loud honk snapped him out of his reverie and he stepped back up on the sidewalk, waving the car on.

He went on with his thoughts. The second man must have taken the identity of Father Gilligan. That way he could remain in hiding yet stay connected to the outer world through the offices of the church and the confessional. He must have found Megan that way, and probably Sean Kelly as well. Recruiting Harrar would have been a different matter but the killer could have gained leverage over him from someone else's confession.

Eagle Feather thought about the kill sites. They were close at hand to Richmond. The Presidio, Golden Gate Park, even Buena Vista Park were within reasonable walking distance. It made sense for Inner Richmond to be the center of the spider's web. But once his web was destroyed, where would the spider go? He must have an escape plan. His new destination would be already secure and his transportation set. He must have anticipated that his retreat might be hasty. He would not be counting on standard transportation out of the city. That left out train, plane, bus, car, or ferry.

So what was left? Escape by water somehow, maybe on a private vessel. Even a small boat would suffice to get him up or down the coast undetected, particularly at night.

The killer wouldn't trust another person with information as important as his escape plan, Eagle Feather knew. So he wouldn't hire a boat. That could mean he had a small boat of some sort hidden away somewhere. It would have to be where it wouldn't be accidentally discovered, somewhere seldom frequented. Assuming he was correct that the center of the spider's web was in Richmond, the place to search would be the most desolate shoreline nearest to the district.

Satisfied that his logic was solid, Eagle Feather sighed and turned west toward the Pacific Ocean to begin the search.

"The last thing we should do is flood Lands End with cops," Zack was saying. "This might be our last best chance to catch this guy. We don't want to scare him away."

"That's just my point," O'Bannon said. "We *do* want to scare him away - from killing another person. We'll catch him now that we know his identity. It's inevitable. So meanwhile, let's prevent another murder."

Zack argued quietly, patiently. "You *believe* you know his identity. I'm not so ready to grant that. And what if you're wrong? With a huge police presence at Land's End you might drive him elsewhere to kill. Nor do I believe his capture is inevitable. I've chased this guy too long and too far to believe that."

O'Bannon sighed. "Look, Zack, I don't mind being the renegade cop, so long as I know I'm right. I don't even mind jeopardizing my career or my retirement for the cause - you know that. But I'm not ready to sacrifice a citizen of San Francisco - some poor joker who just happens to be taking a stroll in the park tonight - just to play mind games with this monster. I'm not ready to grant the bastard that much room."

"I agree. I'm just saying let's think this through, let's come up with a plan that won't tip our hand. If we're right about where he'll be tonight, and I believe we are, then we need to exploit our advantage. We won't get another chance."

"What do you propose?"

Zack's eyes gleamed. "I don't think it will be a random kill. All of his murders have been well planned as far as I can tell, with the possible exception of that kid on the bike at Twin Peaks. But I believe he killed that kid in that particular place mostly to throw us off the scent. I don't think he expected us to tie that one in with the others. He's gotten sneakier, don't you see? That kid was made to look like the victim of an accidental fall down a cliff. And he never expected us to figure out his next kill, the ultra runner. He somehow enticed that poor guy out to Alcatraz, then killed him and dumped his body in the Bay."

Zack looked at O'Bannon beseechingly. Do you see what I mean? He wanted us to think he was all done, finished, gone. He knew we were on to him and he began to cover his tracks."

"You think he's already selected his victim? You think he somehow knows that his victim will be at Lands End Park tonight? Just strolling down the path like a hotdog on a bun, ready to be chomped on?"

"Yes, I do. I think the arrangements have already been made. I think his victim is already planning to be there. That's how he's done it before."

O'Bannon was fascinated despite himself. "So how does that help us?"

"It helps us because we can be there, too. Let's put ourselves inside his brain. Given his past kills, we can expect he's found someone athletic, someone who'll give him a challenge. This person will go there to keep an appointment, or something of that sort, probably at one of the more public locations. That way the victim won't become suspicious. The hour will be late to isolate the victim as much as possible, but not too late. How will he attract the victim? It could be money or sex or something else that his quarry just can't resist. My guess would be sex. That would suggest the desire for a romantic time and place, say for instance a spot overlooking the Pacific with the moon just rising, that sort of thing."

Zack looked at O'Bannon. "You know that park. Where would you go to watch the moon rise over the water?"

O'Bannon didn't have to think long. "I'd say here, definitely." He put a thick finger down on the map. "This lookout point is the perfect spot. I took my first wife there when I was courting her." He glanced sidewise at Zack. "It gives a great view back toward the Golden Gate Bridge. When the moon rises, it comes up right over it. It's incredibly beautiful."

Zack grinned at O'Bannon's enthusiasm. "I think you're more of a romantic than you would like to admit."

"Maybe," O'Bannon grinned back. "But you learn to keep it hidden after a couple of wives."

Zack turned back to the map. “How do you get to this place?”

“There’s a trail there called the Lands End Trail. You get on it here” -he pointed to a parking lot off of Point Lobos Avenue- “or here...or here.”

“There’s a lot of ways to get in, it looks like. He’d like that, I think. But once on the trail...?”

“Going north on it you can’t get off again until here.” O’Bannon pointed to a spot where the trail met El Camino del Mar.

Zack studied the map. “If I were the killer, I’d think that was perfect,” he said. “My victim could be persuaded to come out along the trail expecting to meet someone in a very romantic spot where they’d likely be alone. Once there, our killer does something to scare his victim and start him running this way” -Zack moved his finger north along the trail- “where there’s no exit to the trail until you get all the way up here.” Zack moved his finger along the trail and looked at O’Bannon, his mouth set grimly. “And our victim won’t make it that far.”

“You may be right about all this. But how do we deploy? And if for some reason he doesn’t choose this place? Then what?”

Zack stared at O’Bannon. “Marty, we’ve got to take a risk or we’ll never get him. Look, we both believe Lands End Park will be the place. And in the park, is there a better, more likely spot than here for his kill? I don’t see one. I think we’ve got to chance it.”

O’Bannon still didn’t look convinced.

Zack tried again. “Suppose we try this: we go out

there early tonight, conceal ourselves here" -Zack pointed to a spot near the overlook- "and watch and wait. After the crowds thin, we'll see who comes along. And we'll be perfectly situated to move between the killer and his prey. Meanwhile, your men will move into position gradually during the evening here and here." Zack pointed to locations at both ends of the trail. "They can be disguised to look like sightseers or people out strolling or jogging. They should be in position by dusk ready to respond to your radio call. And just in case we're in the wrong place, put more of your people here and here." Zack's finger came down on two other places toward the outer perimeter. "That way, we'll have everything covered."

O'Bannon was quiet, considering the plan. When he spoke, his face showed the strain. "Zack, you know I experienced...that is, I heard this thing in Golden Gate Park the other night. I got to tell you, I'm not fully recovered from it. I think your plan is a good one; it covers all the bases. But what about the human element? I mean, when this thing comes close, when it makes that god-awful cry and his victim starts running down that trail, how will we react to it? I mean you, me, the men? How do you know we won't all run for our lives? It's that scary."

Zack grinned wryly at O'Bannon. "Sounds like you might be a believer after all." Then he said, "I'm not going to kid you. I don't know how any of us will react. But we'll have the only advantage we can get. We'll know that it's coming."

Libby's mouth set in a stubborn line. "No, Zack. I know I said I wanted you to finish this thing, but not like this. Not out there in some deserted place in the dark where every advantage goes to this killer. Let O'Bannon and his cops take care of it now. You've shown them how, now you're done." Her voice shook with her intensity.

"Libby, we'll be surrounded by cops. This time it will be the place of our choosing, not his. He'll be all alone; we'll outnumber him ten to one. We'll never get another chance like this."

Libby's jaw only set more firmly.

Zack tried again. "Look, Libby, to be honest, I don't think he'll show at all. He's that clever. Some cop, or something else will give it away. All it takes is one little mistake and it's game over. He'll scout the place first. And my money says he'll grow suspicious and fade away and we'll just be standing out in the cold and damp all night by ourselves."

"Then why go at all?"

Zack looked unhappy and a bit guilty. "Because it's my plan. I talked Marty into it. I can't leave him to do it on his own. And like you said, I may be the only guy who knows this killer well enough to figure him out."

"Or maybe he'll figure you out!" Libby was growing even more upset. "What then? What if he's one step ahead of you and figures out where you'll be? Maybe that's been his plan all along, to kill you."

"I've got to go, Libby." Zack spoke quietly.

Libby grasped at a straw. "Then at least take Eagle Feather with you. This monster may think twice about attacking you if Eagle Feather is with you."

Zack shrugged. "Sure, I'll bring him along, if I can find him in time. But he's not answered his phone in the last twenty-four hours. You know Eagle Feather; when he goes off on his own like that, he won't be found until he wants to be."

"Zack, I don't like it."

Zack tried to be soothing. "I know you don't. It's a rotten situation. But it'll be over after tonight. Either we'll get the guy, or he'll run off to another city. Either way, I'm done."

"Then go. Go now. Don't call me until it's over. I don't want to know." Libby turned away.

Zack stood and looked at her, feeling torn. He walked to the door and turned back to her. "I'll be back, Libby," he said. "I promise."

Susan flew along Interstate 80, her blonde hair flying behind her in the wind, enjoying the late afternoon warmth. The air flowing into the Miata was just beginning to develop a cool edge. It would become much cooler on the Bay Bridge, Susan knew, but she'd leave the top down and maybe just turn on a little heat. She loved driving like this, exposed to the early evening air. But her enjoyment was tempered by the reason for her journey. Her mind went over the shocking revelation from Henderson. How bad was it really, she wondered? Was the tumor operable? Was it cancer? If so, was the cancer still localized, or had it metastasized? Questions ate at her as she drove along. She glanced at her watch. She should be there around six, she thought. Visiting hours likely went later, to eight or so. They'd have plenty of time to talk. And with her connections, she could stay later if need be.

She flicked on the radio and tuned it to her favorite music station. The piece sounded like Brahms, with all that brass. She settled her head back against the headrest and listened.

Jim Snyder left the office early and walked slowly back to his apartment. He felt confused and anxious...and elated. He knew in his heart that his conclusions about the killer were correct. He believed the monster would kill again tonight, probably in dramatic fashion. It would not be just a killing but also a statement, a final parting sneer at the city and those who had attempted to capture him. Then he'd be gone. Snyder wondered what more he could do. He'd called O'Bannon and told him what he thought. The detective had been curiously undisturbed by Snyder's conclusions, as if his mind was elsewhere. Jim couldn't tell if he'd made any impression on him at all. Then there was Eagle Feather. Snyder knew *he* believed it. But he hadn't been able to reach him. And besides, what could one man do, even one man with Eagle Feather's abilities?

But another part of Snyder would not allow him to dwell on these concerns, because that part of him wanted to break out into song. His heart bubbled at the thought of seeing Susan tonight. How fantastic, how utterly unbelievable that she was coming back and that she wanted to see him! When she'd left and when she'd neglected his calls he was sure it was all over between them. It was understandable. Snyder was no longer young. How could he hold any attraction for someone as young, clever, beautiful...someone as completely desirable as Susan? After she'd left he faced bitter reality; he told himself how lucky he'd been just to have a short time with her. And then he'd turned his mind to his work.

But now! Now he saw he'd been wrong. For some inexplicable reason she still wanted to see him, to be with him. She was even taking precious free time from her conference to arrange to see him. Snyder wanted to skip as he walked along the sidewalk. A passing woman looked at him with suspicion. *I must have a silly look on my face*, Snyder thought. But he grinned widely anyway. He didn't care.

Snyder let himself in the lower door of his apartment and went up the stairs two at a time. When he unlocked the inner door he thought of the time he'd spent with Susan here: their chats, their intimacy, her bubbly good nature. He kicked his shoes off and shuffled into the kitchen to find something to heat up for dinner. He hummed a little tune as he dug through the fridge.

Zack met O'Bannon at the Merrie Way parking lot near the Lands End Trailhead off Point Lobos Avenue. They both broke into grins when they saw each other. O'Bannon was wearing a too tight jogging suit that accentuated his paunch and with his iPod earphones he looked a bit like an elephant on roller skates. Zack wore an ivy league sweater draped over his shoulders and a yellow Pork Pie hat and could not have looked less like his usual laidback self.

"Where's your gun?" Zack stared at the skintight suit.

Marty laughed and patted his belt pouch. "Had dinner yet?" he asked.

"No, come to think of it."

"May I suggest the excellent cuisine and ambience offered over here?" O'Bannon pointed to the food truck in the parking lot. Indeed, as they approached, the appealing aroma of grilled sausage and tomato sauce reached out to them.

They munched on their sandwiches and O'Bannon explained the set-up between mouthfuls. "My guys are in place already. Each is choreographed to appear at an appointed time in various places throughout the park. The wildlife observers with their binoculars will appear" -he looked at his watch- "any minute now, the Japanese tourists will come in a bus at dusk for the sunset, the jogger will be coming through a bit later, and so on. The idea is that if anything is afoot early on we'll know about it and maybe prevent something from going down before we're ready."

"After they make their appearances, where will they go?"

"Some will be at the Lookout Center over there, others will be ducking down out of sight in various places around the perimeter of the park. They'll wait for my signal to converge on the trail."

"Seems like you've got the place sealed up tight."

O'Bannon raised an eyebrow at Zack. "I better, or my career will be pretty short after this."

They munched their sandwiches and drank their Cokes quietly after that, absorbed in their own thoughts. Around them, it was turning into a spectacular evening by San Francisco standards. The marine layer had yet to roll in, although wisps of fog were drifting here and there. There would be a spectacular sunset followed by an equally spectacular moonrise over the Golden Gate Bridge, if the weather held.

Unknown to either man, Eagle Feather was in the Lands End Lookout Center just behind them studying a trail map of the area. The map was not as detailed as a topographic map would have been but it was sufficient to give Eagle Feather a sense of the terrain, from the steep slope below the thick eucalyptus forest down to the jagged rocks and the waves of the Pacific Ocean. The Lands End Trail was made of crushed stone and dirt, a relic from the heady days of Adolph Sutro and his baths and popular resort. It was now a rail trail created on the original roadbed of Sutro's train that had hauled tourists from one breath-taking vista to another along the headland.

But for Eagle Feather the importance of the trail was in the access it offered to all the coves and inlets where the killer might have hidden a motorboat large enough for high seas capability. He noticed that there were a number of branching trails that took hikers to the Maze or to the Sutro Bath ruins and other locations. But he saw no conceivable place for hiding a boat along this coastline, so jagged with hungry rocks. There were several coves that were deep and dark and hidden beneath towering cliffs but the rough rock-strewn waters in those places would tear the bottom out of any boat that attempted to launch from there.

Could he have been wrong after all? Maybe this wasn't the creature's plan. If so, then Eagle Feather was in the wrong place to intervene. Yet from a predator's point of view, this rugged area was a perfect place to find his prey, make his kill, and then hide in the crags or forest.

What would I do if I were the killer? Eagle Feather asked himself. As perfect as this terrain was for a murder, it was a poor location for escape in any direction other than the sea. There was an entire city full of cops searching just for him tonight and they were all between this place and safety in any direction he might go other than the Pacific Ocean.

Then Eagle Feather had a thought. There *was* a kind of boat that could slide over rocks without breaking, a sturdy vessel that could be easily hidden: an inflatable. Why hadn't he thought of that before? It changed everything. The boat could be folded up and tucked away in any one of these seemingly impassable slashes into the shoreline. A sturdy one with a large enough motor could easily make it through the surf. It might not be comfortable, but in a wet suit, it could be managed.

Eagle Feather felt a new urgency. Now he must find which of the many inlets the killer had selected for his escape. If he could locate it in time he could destroy the boat, or at least knowing its location he could lie in wait somewhere between the killer and his escape. Eagle Feather looked at the map again. To gain access to the cliffs, he would have to take the Sutro Baths Upper Trail that led to the observation point. There he would likely find paths worn along the tops of the cliffs. He looked at his watch. That was a lot of area to cover before nightfall over difficult terrain. Time to get going.

Jim Snyder tried to concentrate on the news program on TV but found his mind constructing scenarios for his meeting with Susan later that night, vivid images that for the most part weren't very realistic but sure were enjoyable. His reverie was interrupted when his eye caught a clip that showed Lieutenant Martin O'Bannon exiting the Richmond District Police building surrounded by press.

Snyder turned up the volume. The reporters were

asking O'Bannon what he intended to do about the killer loose in the city, rumored to be planning a murder that very night. O'Bannon was putting them off with phrases like "business as usual". That wasn't going to please O'Bannon's superiors much, Snyder thought. The indications seemed to be that O'Bannon was going home, and now the reporters were hitting back hard with phrases like "fiddling while Rome burns".

Snyder was puzzled. He was sure O'Bannon could not be quitting for the night, not this night. But Marty was allowing the reporters to think that. Snyder sat up and leaned in closer to the TV set. He realized that O'Bannon was up to something; he seemed to be deliberately misleading the press to get them to go away. He didn't want to be followed. So where did he intend to go? All of Snyder's reporter instincts screamed in unison. O'Bannon had a plan. That meant that he must have new information.

Snyder looked at his watch. Six-thirty. His rendezvous with Susan was at eight. He had plenty of time. He grabbed his safari jacket, pulled on his hat and rushed out the door. He headed to his office to get his police radio scanner. He'd soon learn where O'Bannon was going.

Susan reached the outskirts of Oakland and looked at the dashboard clock. Twenty minutes to seven. Good. She had time to grab a bite. She followed a down ramp toward an In & Out Burger sign. The music on her radio had turned to Wagner and her exit from the freeway was accompanied by the thundering horns in *The Ride of the Valkyries*. In the parking lot she sat and waited for the theme to reach its climax and then shut off her radio and went inside. She was hungry, she was worried and anxious, but she was also eager to see Jim Snyder.

Whatever he was going through, she knew she could help.

THIRTY-SIX

Sean Kelly peered up through the tall trees to the patch of sky, which was the entirety of his view from his thick-brush hideout in the eucalyptus forest and he saw that the blue-grey sky had become tinged with pink. He didn't have a watch; he'd been told not to wear jewelry or any metals that might reflect light. Even his gold earring had to go. It had been a long afternoon crouched in this place, chilled by mists some of the time then baked when the mists disappeared. He'd been told not to leave his hiding place for any reason and he'd been good, despite his cramps. He'd peed several times and defecated once and his hideout was getting ripe. When he saw the sky turn rosy, he was happy. That meant he didn't have to wait too much longer.

No one had come near this place all day, although he'd heard the sounds of children laughing and dogs barking and once the sound of men talking loudly as if flying by on bikes. But it had all been hundreds of yards away and he'd never been worried about discovery. But now he had a tremendous desire to stand and walk around a little, just to shake loose his tight muscles and numb legs. Shadows were beginning to grow long around him but still he hesitated to move while it was still light enough to be seen. He'd wait just a little bit longer until it was so dark that no one could possibly spot him through the trees. Then he could stretch.

Kelly went over the instructions in his head that Donny had given him. He was to stay put until he heard a low, long whistle. It would sound sometime in the very early morning. When he heard it, whenever it came, he was to start walking straight down hill until he reached the cliffs above the sea. That was where Donny would find him and lead him to his escape craft. Then he'd be gone and no one would ever find him. Kelly shifted his position and hunkered down again. He'd just have to be patient.

O'Bannon looked at his watch and then looked at Zack. The sky was rose tinted now and sunset wasn't far off.

"It's time to move to our position," he said.

Zack nodded without speaking and together they began to walk at a steady pace north along the Lands End Trail out of the parking lot. They followed it as long as it maintained that direction, but when it jagged back south, O'Bannon turned off onto a smaller path.

"The old roadway angles south then comes all the way back up north," he explained. "We can cut off the extra yards with this shortcut."

"Do you know this area well?"

"Reasonably well," O'Bannon said. "I studied the history of this place once, just the Sutro era, no earlier than that. But he was responsible for most of the paths we'll be on tonight. He was quite a character; made his money in the mines during the gold rush, then came here and spent it like water."

They had come to an intersection at a wide trail.

O'Bannon touched Zack's elbow. "We go left here. We're on one of his railroad beds right now. He used to take tourists along this route to see the spectacular views, and of course the route included his spa and resort areas." O'Bannon chuckled. They walked along at a steady pace while he talked. "The guy built his own railroad. It began at the ferry terminals down at the Embarcadero and it brought tourists all the way out here where they could transfer to his trolley or just walk along the shore. Then along came the Pacific Coast Railroad offering to buy Sutro's Ferry and Cliff House Railroad for a huge profit. So he sold. Then after a while he noticed that the PCR had doubled the ticket cost. This really pissed him off, so much so that he started to build a competing railroad right next to the first one that he'd built." O'Bannon waved his hand. "Most of what you'll see along the way was built by Sutro, but much of it is in ruins now. Only Cliff House is still operating today, but it's not the original building."

"Did it look like this back then?" Zack asked, looking around at the dense forest and windswept grasses.

"No, it was quite barren up here then. The city of San Francisco has done a lot over the years to make it more habitable and pleasant, including planting that eucalyptus forest. Now it's a great recreational spot, good for renewing the spirit." He looked sideways at Zack and laughed. "There's even a maze you can walk through and think weighty thoughts. It's way down at the tip of Lands End."

"Where are we going?"

"We're going out the trail beyond the golf course where there's a second junction with El Camino del Mar. It's one of only two places where people can access it until you get all the way out to the Lincoln Highway near

China Beach Park. The big draw here at night is the observation point where the land swings around to the east. That's where the great views of the Golden Gate Bridge can be found. That's where the people will be, the ones that the killer can choose from."

They came to a junction where a trail joined from the east.

"Where does that go?" Zack asked.

"That's the first of the two access points I mentioned. I've got men assigned to watch it tonight."

Soon they came to a fork in the trail.

"This is a loop," O'Bannon explained. "To the right it takes you along the golf course fairway and to another junction with the street. I've got people posted there as well. A couple of my men are even enjoying a game of golf until it gets dark." O'Bannon laughed and looked at Zack. "It's on the Department's dime. If I'm gonna piss off my bosses, I might as well go all the way." He pointed to the left. "That's where we're going. It's the more isolated part of the loop. Except for the side trail down to the maze I told you about, it stays out along the cliffs among the trees. That's where I'm betting he'll be."

"And where we'll be?"

"And where we'll be," O'Bannon confirmed. "I think we'll position ourselves near the last junction, at the far end of the loop. We can find a place to hide on the eastern side of the trail where we can trap him between us and the cliffs."

As they trudged along Zack thought about the risk O'Bannon was taking. It was all based upon their hunch, which in turn was based upon lines on a map connecting several landmarks which when connected described a bow and arrow. Marty was committing a huge amount of manpower all because of that drawing. If he was wrong..."

Then Zack had another thought. If he was right, it could turn bad in a whole different way. Zack felt for the Sig Saur 226 in his pocket. He found himself wishing he'd packed a heavier weapon.

Snyder huffed up the stairway to the news floor wondering why he hadn't just taken the elevator. Somehow he always thought the exercise would do him good. But there's no cure for old, he thought.

At his desk, he combed through his lower drawer for the police band radio. He flipped it. The volume was up high and there was a loud squeal and a crackling of unintelligible words. A few late working colleagues looked up from their keyboards to see what was happening. He smiled apologetically and switched it off and thrust it in his coat pocket. Then he checked his messages, found nothing important, and walked out.

Snyder checked his watch when he reached the sidewalk. Seven o'clock. He still had plenty of time. He flipped on the radio at a softer volume and walked down Fifth Street to a coffee shop he liked. He could have a cup of coffee out on the patio on this lovely warm night and listen to the reports. Maybe he could figure out what O'Bannon was up to. He had plenty of time to make his meeting with Susan.

Libby had promised not to intervene and she resolved not to think about what Zack was up to tonight until it was over and he had returned. She ate her dinner, a passable plate of lasagna, in the hotel lounge and fought the overwhelming compulsion to call him. The bartender seemed to know who she was and gave her special attention. He'd come out from behind the bar to seat her and he made sure her dinner came out promptly. Zack seemed to have made a friend here.

The lounge TV was turned to the evening news and all the usual mundane stories: the Bay Bridge needed a coat of paint, someone's pet collie had traveled three thousand miles to find its owners, the Mayor was pushing a bill to increase parking fines, a grey whale had washed up on shore near Half Moon Bay. The TV volume was set low and Libby let it all wash over her, until she heard a familiar name spoken. She looked up to see Marty O'Bannon being filmed leaving the District Station. Reporters surrounded him.

Libby signaled to the bartender to turn up the sound. He complied instantly and now she could hear the reporters' questions. They were asking O'Bannon why he wasn't doing more, asking where he was going, what his intentions were. And he seemed to be saying that there was little he could do right now. Was he actually going home? He certainly seemed to be indicating that he was; the reporters seemed to believe that. Their sarcastic questions were very pointed.

Libby dropped her fork. How could O'Bannon be going home? What about Zack? Was the man going to desert Zack? Was he leaving him on his own to hunt this killer? Libby had another thought that was even more disconcerting. Had Zack lied to her? Had he known all along that O'Bannon wasn't going to be with him tonight? Had he lied to Libby so she wouldn't be upset, so she wouldn't try to stop him?

Libby felt her heart pounding. She wasn't angry with Zack, she was afraid for him. He couldn't even count on Eagle Feather to help him. Hadn't Zack told her he had gone off the grid and was out of touch? Zack would be entirely alone out there. That was not their deal. Libby immediately pulled out her cellphone and called Zack but was redirected to his messaging service. Either his phone was off or he was using it. Libby left a message telling him to get right back to her, that it was important. But she knew in her heart he wouldn't, not if he was on a Don Quixote quest to tilt against something much more deadly than a windmill.

Susan pulled up to Building One of the VA Medical Center on 42nd Street at half past seven. Parking her little Miata was easy and she was soon climbing the steps to the main reception area in the large front lobby. She asked the young woman at the desk for Critical Care, Neurology.

"Is there a particular patient you wish to see?" she asked.

"Yes. His name is James Snyder."

"Oh, yes, Mr. Snyder. Are you Susan Apgar, by any chance?"

"Yes."

"I was asked to see that you received this envelope." The receptionist reached into a drawer and brought out a pink envelope with Susan's name scrawled in pen.

Susan thanked her and walked over to a couch in the lobby. She sliced open the envelope with her car key.

There was a short printed note inside.

"Dear Susan, if you are reading this you have come. Thank you. I am scheduled for a procedure tomorrow morning utilizing nuerointerventional radiology, which I hope will prevent the need for surgery. I would like to see you. I have stepped out for a short walk down the path beyond Veteran's Drive just past Building Seven. Please come meet me there and I will explain it all. Love, Jim."

Susan walked back to the desk. "Can you direct me to Building Seven?"

"It's just at the far end of this parking lot," the girl replied, smiling.

Susan thanked her. Outside the building she turned left and crossed the parking lot. She saw the entrance to Building Seven and just beyond it was Veteran's Drive. A short way along the drive she found a wide path that led away from the street. She followed it down an easy grade into thick trees, now dusky in the receding light of the late evening. The path angled right and worked down the slope then jogged to the left and intersected with a road.

Susan stood there, confused. Across the road and through the sparse trees she saw a large area of green that looked like a golf course. But which way had Jim gone?

Then she heard the sound of voices, a low hum of casual conversation that seemed to come from somewhere down the road to her left. It could be Jim walking along with another patient. She turned toward the voices. There were no streetlights along the road but there was still enough natural light for her to see her way. She walked briskly but the voices seemed always to stay just beyond her sight. She picked up her pace. Then she heard the voices to her right, down a wide path that led into the woods. A sign near it announced *Lands End*

Trail. Susan hesitated and then shrugged. What the hell, she thought, I've come this far. She found a penlight in her purse, turned it on and followed the voices down the path.

Jim Snyder climbed out of a cab in front of Building Eight at the VA Medical Center at eight PM on the nose. He paid the driver and walked eagerly toward the building. But his mood plunged when he tried the door and found it locked. The hours printed on the glass showed that it had closed at seven PM.

As he was turning away he saw a pink envelope taped to the far edge of the door panel. He looked closer. It was addressed to him. He pulled it off and stepped back under the security light to read it. It was from Susan. It said that she and some colleagues had decided to walk down to Lands End to watch the sun set. Would he join them? He could find them by following this road to a path beyond Building 7. Take that path to a roadway, turn left, and after 200 yards turn right on the Lands End Trail. He'd find them somewhere along that path. Love, kisses, and she couldn't wait to see him.

Snyder tucked the note in his jacket pocket and followed the directions. The path led him away from the light of the buildings and into the darkness. Snyder chided himself for not bringing a flashlight but after his eyes adjusted he could just make his way. He reached the road Susan had described and turned left as instructed. After a short distance he saw where the trail lead off to the right. The wide path was easy to follow despite the encroaching darkness and he moved along it quickly. In less than five minutes he came to an intersection. Her note had not mentioned this. As he stood undecided a sound came to him, faint but distinct. It sounded like

Susan's voice but he could not make out any words. He listened but it didn't repeat itself. Had it been the cry of a seagull? He was probably interpreting it to match his hopes. The sound had come from his right. Lacking any other indication, Snyder turned and walked that way, into the wind and toward the sound of pounding surf.

The Sutro Baths Upper Trail led along the top of the cliffs and then turned away and entered a stand of windblown trees. Eagle Feather took a narrow track that kept to the cliff tops.

The light was fading quickly and he knew that once dusk fell his search would end. He picked up his pace. The path took him to a rocky promontory then turned back to the main trail. He saw nothing unusual here. Eagle Feather found another informal path leading back to the cliffs. It took him down to some boulders littering a small cove and then climbed back again. Here short tough grasses clung precariously to the granite to form a spongy rug beneath his feet. He walked over the neck of another promontory and came to a second inlet, much larger this time. The sun was at a low angle now and its rays illuminated features that otherwise might have been in shadow: a mixed blessing. The sun was dropping fast. Again Eagle Feather found nothing out of the usual, just large jagged rocks scattered about as if a giant child had been playing there.

The narrow path traversed yet another promontory ridge and came to an area devoid of grass where many people had stood to gaze. He could see why. The Pacific was putting on a powerful display, hurling itself against large isolated rock needles and swarming around them and churning itself into a milky froth in the cove below. He was momentarily caught up in the drama and beauty of the spectacle, and then hurried on. No boat could possibly be hidden here.

When the path turned inland yet again Eagle Feather began to feel discouraged. He must stay close to the cliffs to see into the next cove. He left the path and followed a very narrow ridge made slick by occasional slaps of brine that became a spine between the two coves. It was treacherous and he worked his way carefully along it until the next cove opened beneath him in its entirety. Unlike the other inlets, this one angled north and its promontory spine arced slightly to form a protective barrier against the western swells. It was almost a beach. The rocks had been pounded to pebbles and the shore sloped gradually to the water. Scattered here and there were several huge rounded boulders.

Then something caught his eye, something protruding from behind some boulders clumped together at the water's edge, something that blended with the dark green seawater and the grey of the rocks but had straight lines not of nature. Something was hidden there, carefully camouflaged. Had he not climbed out along this narrow ridge he would never have seen it.

Eagle Feather knew he was looking at the killer's escape craft. He tried to call Zack but reached his answering service. There was no time to wait for his return call. Eagle Feather called Libby.

When her phone rang Libby snatched it up right away, expecting Zack. But it was Eagle Feather. She was not reassured when he told her that he tried to reach Zack but couldn't. Libby told him her own worries.

"He left here to help Lieutenant O'Bannon," she said. "But just now I saw O'Bannon interviewed on TV and he seemed to be going home. I'm worried that Zack is out there somewhere all by himself."

"I would be surprised if O'Bannon went home tonight," Eagle Feather said. "He may have said that to throw off the media. Did Zack say exactly where he was going?"

"No. In fact I told him I didn't want to know," Libby said, feeling a bit guilty.

"Well, if he contacts you, it's urgent that you have him call me."

"Where are you, if he asks?"

"I'm at Lands End Park, but he'll need to call me to find out exactly where."

After that conversation Libby felt torn. Maybe Eagle Feather was right: maybe O'Bannon did have a plan to hunt the killer and maybe Zack knew those plans and would be with him. But on the other hand, she knew Zack and his tendency to go off on his own. What really disturbed her was that Zack was not with Eagle Feather, that in fact Eagle Feather couldn't reach him.

Libby glanced at her watch and saw that it was after seven PM. It would soon be dark. And all she would do is worry if she didn't do *something*. She pushed the number for the Richmond District police station. When the desk sergeant answered she asked to speak to Marty O'Bannon.

"He's not here right now. May I know the nature of your inquiry?"

"This isn't an inquiry," she replied. "I'm the wife of a colleague of his who is working with him tonight and it's very important that I speak to him."

"Well, miss...?"

"Whitestone, Libby Whitestone."

"Well, Ms. Whitestone, Lieutenant O'Bannon is out of communication, literally. His phone is off and he is under radio silence. You can't speak with him, I'm afraid."

"Do you know if FBI Agent Tolliver is with him? It's most important that I reach my husband."

"No, ma'am, I'm afraid I don't know that. I'm sorry."

Libby was desperate. "Please, sergeant, it is critically important that I reach my husband."

The sergeant was silent for a moment. Then he said in a whisper, "Ma'am, Lieutenant O'Bannon's location can not be disclosed - there is a maneuver underway. I'm prohibited from telling you that he is at Lands End Park. I'm sorry." And the sergeant hung up.

Lands End Park! Eagle Feather had just called from there. Something must be happening there tonight. Did Zack know about it? Was Zack with O'Bannon after all or was he on his own?

Libby made up her mind in an instant. She pulled on her jacket. If he was there and he was in danger, then she should be there too.

THIRTY-SEVEN

The half drowned setting sun tainted the water of the Pacific Ocean with blood red and orange and the sky phosphoresced in a widening halo. The fog layer was drifting north away from them and O'Bannon couldn't help thinking it was an unusually perfect evening at Lands End. He turned to Zack where he sat next to him on a boulder with his long legs crossed, watching the ocean swells.

"All the tourists will be out here tonight to see this sunset," he said. "The killer will have his pick of victims."

Zack kept his gaze on the orange-tinted Pacific. "I'd guess that particular choice has already been made."

"I just hope we're in the right place."

"I have to believe we've got it figured right," Zack said.

O'Bannon nodded. "The golf course beyond this patch of woods makes that area undesirable to him. And the optimum location for watching this beauty" -he nodded at the sunset- "along with the moon rise that's gonna follow it, is Eagle Point Labyrinth beyond these thick woods right in front of us. If I were the killer, I'd lay hidden in these woods and wait for my victim to come down that trail over there."

"He won't be waiting," Zack said. "He'll be guiding. Everything about the other murders suggests that he, shall we say, encouraged his victims along a certain course."

O'Bannon nodded and grimaced.

Zack continued. "Your men aren't too close, are they?"

"Stop worrying." O'Bannon grinned. "If anything, they're too far. We may end up wishing they were closer."

Zack looked carefully at his friend. "You're okay with this, aren't you? I mean, after your experience?"

O'Bannon's face turned grim. "I'd be lying if I told you I was thrilled. He put the fear of God in me that night...or maybe I should say the fear of the Devil."

Zack looked away. "Nobody blames you. This is not your average serial killer we're after tonight."

O'Bannon changed the subject abruptly. "How's your wife with all this? First you tell her you're leaving, then you decide to stay, then you say you're leaving again. Now here you are. Her head must be spinning."

Zack sighed. "Believe it or not, I'm here now because she insisted. But despite that I really don't know if I'm doing the right thing for my marriage. Or for my career, for that matter." Zack grinned at O'Bannon. "All I know is know I'm doing the right thing for my friends."

O'Bannon grinned back at Zack. "To be honest with you, I'm not so sure I'd be here if you weren't along. But speaking of friends, where's the Chief?"

Zack shrugged. "I have no idea. He went to ground a while ago. He does that sometimes when we're on the hunt together; I don't know why. He seems to need to work by himself at times without interruption."

"So you think he's still working the case?"

"I sure hope so."

At that moment Eagle Feather was in the best position to appreciate the astonishing sunset but he was hardly aware of it. All it meant to him was that time was running out. He couldn't wait for Zack to call him back - he had to act now. Without further thought he carefully worked his way down from the spiny ridge. In front of him, storm-stunted trees clung to the steep slope that fell away into the inlet gorge. Clinging to tree branches, he laboriously lowered himself until at last he stood on the smooth stone beach below the cliffs. He made his way toward the mouth of the inlet, stumbling and slipping on the precariously wet and slimed stones. At the high tide mark the stones were slickened by seaweed and kelp and the footing became even worse. He thought about the tide and recognized that the killer would have to plan for it; otherwise he'd risk losing his boat to the ocean before he could use it.

Then it occurred to Eagle Feather that the timing of the tide might be a clue to the murderer's plans. He would have to make his kill before the tide was in. He must be on some sort of schedule.

Eagle Feather knew nothing of the timing of the tides. There weren't any tides where he lived. He grinned to himself as he thought about the dry sands of Navajo Land. But it should be a simple matter to look them up with his iPhone.

He'd almost reached the large rocks concealing the craft when it suddenly moved. Eagle Feather froze. He waited. He could not be in a more vulnerable position. Moments crept by but there was no more movement. Eagle Feather began to inch slowly forward once more. It moved again. The object nosed out from behind the rocks and then slid back as if pulled by someone's hand. Eagle Feather waited breathlessly. Apparently whoever was behind the boulder had not yet seen him. He calculated the distance he must travel to rush the rock, guessing it might take twenty seconds to close the gap. It would not be fast enough if the hidden person had a gun.

Eagle Feather had no weapon. He picked up baseball-sized stone at his feet. It would have to do. He prepared himself for his attack. Then the object moved again, out and back. Eagle Feather stared and suddenly laughed. The movement of the object had coincided exactly with the arrival of a wave. So there wasn't anyone back there after all. It was just an occasional large swell lifting and shifting the boat.

Eagle Feather scrambled quickly up to the rocks. No one was there, but there was a boat, a stable-looking rubber craft fully inflated and packed with supplies. It was maybe six feet long and had a powerful outboard motor pulled inboard at the stern. This tough little inflatable could take its owner anywhere along the California coastline, to any place he wanted.

An anchor rope was attached to the bow, securing it to the rock. It was about eight feet long, plenty long enough to allow the inflatable to ride out much of the incoming tide. It would certainly be difficult to board it at high tide, what with the unpredictable movement of the swells, but probably well within the capabilities of the man-creature they hunted.

The Pacific had almost swallowed the sun; there was not much time. Eagle Feather tore into the neatly packed supplies, tossing food and perishables into the sea. He found a 3.5 Very pistol among the supplies. He tucked it into his belt, thinking it might prove handy. There was also a clasp knife with a four-inch blade. He opened it and tested the blade with his thumb. Satisfied, he turned to the boat and began slashing.

He'd had enough. He just couldn't handle crouching in these bushes any longer. Kelly's legs were numb and his back felt like it had been hit by a pile driver. Shit. He wasn't going to suffer this kind of pain any longer just because some overgrown orangutan told him to. Look, the sky was greying now and those streaks of pink were almost gone. It would be dark soon. Besides, it was his own life he was risking, wasn't it?

But still he didn't move. Donny scared him; admit it. He seemed to be everywhere; he probably was somewhere out there just waiting for him to break cover.

Maybe I'll wait just a little bit longer, he thought - say until that patch of sky above is all grey-black. Then I'll get out and stretch.

The cab dropped Libby off in front of Lands End Lookout on Point Lobos Avenue near a large new-looking building. She walked north on the wide concrete sidewalk that ran between the building and the parking lot and looked for any sign of official police presence. She saw none.

At the far end of the parking lot was a circular observation platform that allowed views to every side through quarter-fed telescopes. Beyond it a sign indicated the Lands End Trail. Well, the last thing she'd come here for was to take a hike.

Libby walked around the outer circumference of the viewing platform and took another walkway that headed off in the direction of the bluffs. She came to a long set of descending steps and stopped and looked all around. There was no sign of police anywhere. Could the desk sergeant have misinformed her?

Back at the parking lot it dawned on her that finding Zack might be more difficult than she'd thought. If a covert police action were taking place here as the sergeant had suggested, they would be trying hard *not* to look like policemen. Any of these people around her could be policemen; there was no way to know. She knew that Lands End was more than a simple destination; it was a very large area of forests and trails. How could she possibly locate Zack? Libby began to regret her impulsive decision to come here.

The sun was quite low but visibility was still good. Libby decided that since she was here already, she might as well go ahead and try to find Zack while there was light. When it became fully dark, she'd give it up. She went back to the Lands End trailhead and studied the map etched in the wood sign. She selected her route and set off down the trail at a brisk pace.

The sun sunk with resplendent and satisfying drama into the sea until only a tiny red sliver remained. The sky turned iron grey and the loitering fog began to creep back from the Marin Headland. Expectant viewers at various observation points along the Lands End Trail watched until the sun had been fully extinguished in the West and then turned expectantly to the East toward the Golden Gate Bridge standing in stark silhouette against the glow of the city beyond, and they waited patiently for the moon to rise dramatically behind it. But the fog had crept unnoticed back along the bridge and was slowly swallowing the northern-most tower like a blackboard eraser cleaning away a chalk drawing. Dusk fell hard and those still strolling beneath the tall eucalyptus crowns further inland were left in near darkness.

For Susan Apgar, it was time to turn around and return to the hospital and wait there for Jim Snyder to return from his walk. Her tiny penlight was a mere firefly glow, quite useless for anything other than highlighting a spot a few inches in circumference. Daylight was fading sooner than she expected and she had come too far along the trail in pursuit of the low conversational voices that were always just around the next bend. The path was wide and level underfoot where she turned back but she found herself becoming disoriented in the growing darkness. She came to a divergence of paths. She didn't remember the intersection but she made the best choice she could and went on. But now the path looked increasingly unfamiliar. Her doubts grew and she decided she must have made the wrong choice and she turned around once again. But when she came back to the junction it didn't look right at all. Had she gotten turned around somehow? Was this the way back or...? The flicker of her tiny light darted here and there as she grew more confused. Maybe she should reverse her direction yet again. Then the thought came to Susan that she might actually be lost.

Jim Snyder found the darkness closing in like a blanket

and his cell phone did little to light his way. When meadows surrounded the path it was lighter and he could walk faster but then a tunnel of trees would close in around him and his pace slowed to a crawl. It was fortunate that the pathway was wide and firm or he would have to turn back. Jim was certain he heard Susan's voice just up ahead. He should have closed the distance by now. He was currently in a tunnel of trees that led on and on into the darkness. Jim was vaguely familiar with this trail system but he hadn't actually walked any of it since he was a kid. He knew that the trail must eventually bring him to either 34th Avenue or Lincoln Highway where there would be light. From there he could find his way back. Susan must know the Lands End Trail system quite well to continue on in the dark so confidently. He wondered if she knew that he was behind her. Maybe that was her plan, to rendezvous in the dark somewhere up ahead. Snyder's loins stirred at the thought and he picked up his pace.

Libby came to a junction with another wide trail that lead off to the left - to the Sutro Baths, the sign said. By now the sun had sunk to just a sliver into the Pacific Ocean and the shadows had grown long. Her trail wound on through short and wiry heather and it was not difficult to see the way. Libby had spent her life in the outdoors and now as the path before her grew dim in the dusk she paused. Ahead there were trees and she knew that once she entered the forested area it would become much darker.

In her small backpack she had a headlamp equipped with five LED bulbs. She put down the pack and took it out. The lamp would light her way sufficiently to continue, although the closing darkness would hugely reduce her chances of finding Zack. Yet she felt she had to try for something compelled her, a vague fear that Zack was in danger somewhere out here. After adjusting the headlamp over her long hair, she shrugged her pack on again and set out at an even faster pace.

A stand of tall trees blocked the quickly fading sun and darkness came suddenly but the strong beam of her lamp sent a bright tunnel of light probing ahead. The trail was wide and flat here and Libby moved at a good pace. The sound of surf pounding and booming on her left was loud and comforting. She was in a heavily forested area and she could see nothing but the light beam of her headlamp and thin black branch tendrils reaching toward the path. Then she was out of the trees and the path widened. The surf was very loud here and she saw that she was at an observation point, high up on the cliffs. A phosphorescent white line marked the breaking waves far below. Libby continued along the path avoiding the cliff edge. She had seen no one else along the path and it seemed to go on and on. Everything seemed longer and larger in the dark. Then forest again and the darkness was complete. All Libby's reference points were erased except for the light-whitened path beneath her feet and the booming surf to her left. She was in her own dark world.

And then it came: a loud terrifying sound that rose to a screaming crescendo of blood-freezing malevolent intent. It seemed to come from every direction, at once predatory and evil, a howling profanity unlike anything Libby had ever heard before. Not the mournful howl of a wolf or the yipping cry of the coyote, not even the woman-like screams of a mountain lion: this utterance was unearthly and cruel and brain numbing. Libby's muscles contracted, her breathing stopped, her heart fluttered. Fear consumed her - raw overwhelming fear. It hijacked her brain and left her shaking and helpless like a gazelle in the jaws of a lion. What *was* that? What creature could possibly make such a sound? It was a long while before Libby could move and then she shown her headlamp beam wildly in every direction. Where was it, what was it?

Her logic tried to reassert itself and Libby began to rationalize, telling herself that there must be an explanation for that sound; there *must* be. She slowed the frantic swing of her headlamp and became methodical in her search of the forest around her. She delved deep into her memory for any creature that could possibly issue such a fearful sound. A lion? A tiger? No, this didn't have the rumbling deep voice of those large cats. A gorilla? A large male gorilla loose in the woods, maybe. Libby had never heard a gorilla scream, but she instinctively knew that this blood chilling sound was more predatory than any that could be made by an orangutan or a gorilla. So what was it, then?

Every fiber of Libby's body warned her that she was in great danger. She must run away. But the sound had seemed to come from everywhere. If she ran now, she might run right into its jaws. Libby didn't know where to go to find safety. She remained there, motionless, still, like a deer in a thicket. She listened and she hoped that this thing was not hunting her, that it was hunting something else. She turned off her lamplight, missing its comfort but worried that it might give her away.

Libby understood now that the killer - that fearsome predator responsible for all the mysterious deaths in San Francisco - that *thing* was somewhere in the darkness around her, and she must not let it find her.

Libby struggled with her panic. She tried to slow her breathing. She tried to think of mundane things to trick her mind and to stop the throbbing flow of blood in her veins. Her sweat, her pheromones, all the scents issued by her pores might be used by this wild creature to find her. She drew into herself and stood statue-like on the pathway in full darkness, absolutely still. Time evaporated. Her full concentration was on the monumental struggle of mind over body. But she was succeeding. She felt increasingly calm, absurdly so in the face of such great danger. This is how prey in the world of predators behaves, she thought. This is how the spotted fawn in the thicket escapes the jaws of the wolf.

Suddenly she felt an iron grip on her shoulder: powerful, unyielding. Her mouth and nose were smothered under the warmth of a rough palm clamped hard across her face. She couldn't breathe. She struggled with all her might but was held fast.

Then a familiar voice whispered in her ear. "Shush. No sound. It's Eagle Feather. Don't - make - a - sound."

Relief swept over Libby and she stopped struggling.

She tried to look back at Eagle Feather but could see only his outline, black against black. She gripped his arm, trembling.

"What *was* that?" she breathed.

"Don't talk," he whispered. "Wait."

It was good that she held his arm, for the probing cry rose again, growing, building upon itself, an auditory embodiment of hate and lust, a slavering cry that obliterated all other sounds and petrified her brain as it had done before until it finally fell away leaving the silence of a shocked and still forest. But even in her fear she thought she heard a different texture to the cry, a different resonance. It seemed more distant now, its effect minutely less. It seemed to her that the creature was moving in a different direction. Was it looking for her, she wondered?

Eagle Feather whispered in her ear. "It's hunting someone. It doesn't know we are here."

"What do we do?" she asked. And then a sudden

panicked thought. "Where's Zack?"

Eagle Feather shushed her again and whispered, "I don't know. Follow me," and he tugged at her shoulder.

Libby gripped his arm and followed his shadowy form along the path trying to match the silence of his footfalls, her heart pounding. His ability to navigate the trail in the dark was uncanny. She gave herself up entirely to his guidance.

They crept on, two shadows in a black world. She thought she sensed trees around them and she heard the busy whoosh and boom of the surf but then it faded into a distant accompaniment to the night breezes that riffled the leaves around them like softly shuffled cards. The terror she felt now was not for the howl of the beast, but its absence. Hearing its cry terrified her but at least then she knew where it was. Now, it could be anywhere.

Jim Snyder was stumbling along the dark tunnel of the path guided only by the faint glow from his cell phone when the fog found him. It dashed any hope of moon glow to help light his way. Its cool vaporous breath chilled him and it swallowed the reach of his tiny light even more. His progress was snail-like. Snyder's list of regrets was multiplying: he wished he'd brought his flashlight, he wished he'd brought a jacket; he wished he'd turned around sooner.

The siren voice that coaxed him along had gone silent and his thoughts of love and sex had begun to turn to a desire for warmth and food. He shuffled forward in a routine of trial and error, of stumble and correction. He coaxed himself to be patient, to take one step at a time. Soon enough the lights of the road would appear through the fog and darkness. Believe and it will happen.

Then the howl sounded.

Snyder stopped and stood listening. He was frightened and fascinated at the same time. The rising screaming howl was menacing to the extreme: predatory, hate-filled. It was the ultimate expression of the greatest depth of violence that could possibly reside within any creature, all articulated in this rising cry. It sought, it commanded, it threatened and it condemned all within the range of one single primal utterance. When the last ringing echoes faded away Snyder remembered to breathe. So this is the beast, he thought; this is how it sounds.

Snyder's body trembled and his heart pounded faster than he thought possible. Curiosity and fear swept over him in equal measure. He knew that this was the same creature that had stalked him that night in his office, unseen but sensed by some long forgotten instinct that resided within him.

What could it be? Had Susan been right after all? Did some hybrid animal-human live and hunt in the city at night?

The sound had come from all directions, but Snyder didn't believe it was close by. It must be somewhere behind him, casting about, searching for its prey. Snyder knew he must get far away and he broke into a stumbling blind run. Branches slashed his face. His toe snagged and he fell hard and quickly scrambled back up again and ran on, mindless of pain. His breath came in gulps and his thighs burned. Somewhere up ahead must be the road, and light, and people, and safety. He ran on.

THIRTY-EIGHT

Sean Kelly woke with a start. For a long minute he couldn't remember this place. Then it all came back to him in a flash and he leapt up from the bed of leaves where he had been sleeping.

Stupid! Stupid! He didn't remember falling asleep. But it was dark now, no question about that; Sean could barely make out the brush and trees that surrounded him. High above an inkblot mesh of branches surrounded a black sky. He looked at his wrist out of habit before he remembered that Donny had made him remove his watch. So what time was it? He had no idea.

The thought came to him that it might be almost dawn. There was no longer the busy sounds of birds or the voices of people. The forest was silent. Then he had another thought. Had he slept through Donny's whistle? Was Donny waiting out there even now? Or worse, had the boat already gone?

With these thoughts came panic. No, no! He couldn't stay in San Francisco, not now! He would be caught and jailed, or worse.

Kelly thrust aside the branches that concealed his hideout and fought his way out of the thicket. He didn't know where to go, but he did know his escape was by boat. That meant the sea, and the sea was at the bottom of the hill - that much he knew. Sean walked down the slope toward the distant sound of the surf, as carefully and stealthily and quickly as he could.

O'Bannon woke with a start. His eyes flew open but there was nothing to see. All was blackness. He shifted his weight to sit up, ashamed that he had fallen asleep but as soon as he moved his arm was gripped hard.

"Shush. Quiet. We've got company," Zack breathed into his ear.

The night was absolutely still. There were no birdcalls, no scurrying sounds, only silence. Marty rose to a kneeling position and felt for his gun. He could see Zack in outline next to him as a patch of denser darkness. He glanced up at the sky. It was light in the direction of the city but toward the Pacific it blended back into blackness. The trees closest to them were barely discernible. O'Bannon's eyes were useless now; he would have to rely on his ears - and Zack.

O'Bannon felt a sudden surge of fright. Being here like this took him back to that night in the meadow next to the Doughboy statue, the night he had been so unmanned by the howl of that creature. He trembled slightly. He was glad that the darkness hid his fear.

He turned to ask Zack what he heard but the grip on his arm tightened. O'Bannon could hear nothing at all. He listened hard. Then it came to him, a stealthy sound; the slight crunch of dry matter under a carefully placed foot. He would not have heard it had the night not been so completely still, without even a breeze rustling through the trees. He felt the tenseness in Zack's body through his arm and heard the slight sound of metal against leather as Zack un-holstered his pistol.

Still they waited. The sound did not repeat itself. Whoever or whatever was creeping toward them had stopped as if to listen. Maybe the stalker had heard Zack whisper and so had become aware of their presence. Or did he already know they were there and hoped to catch them by surprise?

O'Bannon reached into his coat for his own gun. And then it came, that same dreaded cry, that snarling howling obscenity. It felt like it was right next to him. It surrounded him and transfixed him and entered into him. It chilled him through and through like the icy blast of wind off a glacier. Its message of hate terrified him and its reaching, grasping rapaciousness filled him with horror.

Susan forced herself to breath: in, and out, in, and out - until her panic subsided enough for her to think. She was lost in the dark in the woods, true enough. But she was on a wide comfortable path that even a child could navigate. Her penlight, though dim, was at least enough to prevent her from falling on her face. And she knew that the path she was on would eventually lead her to street lights and houses where she could hail a cab and get back to her car.

Where was Jim? He must be out here someplace. She'd heard his voice just ahead; it *was* his voice, she felt sure. But what direction was ahead, at this point?

The drone of conversational tones came again, right on cue, somewhere off in the dark just over that way. Relieved to have a direction to go in, Susan edged her way down the dark path toward the sound. She found it increasingly difficult to hear it over the boom of the surf as the path drew close to the sea cliffs. A mental map flashed into her mind. She guessed that she must be on the uninterrupted section of the Lands End Trail that would eventually take her to El Camino del Mar. Well, so be it. A long evening lay ahead of her but at least she knew where she was going. She picked up her pace with new confidence.

But then all her thoughts of direction and safety were abruptly blown away like chaff in the wind. A sound rose up and swelled around her and gripped her like an icy hand on her heart. A howl, a predatory cry imbued with intense hatred and loathing and lustful hunger rose and swelled with an intent that could not be mistaken. Susan was immediately overwhelmed with fear and horror. Her penlight fell to the ground forgotten, her body turned to stone. A deeply imbedded primal fear smothered all other thought and froze her like a statue where she stood, a helpless victim. The howl grew and grew until it reached its zenith and fell away and finally ceased. The last echoes reverberated among the trees until at long last the boom of crashing waves reclaimed her dormant awareness.

Susan knew immediately what had made that sound. She knew it was somewhere behind her in the forest. That thought awoke her and released her and she ran for her life. She ran like she'd never run before, for she now understood that the monster she had created so casually on paper for Jim Snyder was very, very real - and it was somewhere behind her in the darkness.

Zack was almost ready for the howl when it came, not a conscious preparation, but a mental condition brought about by months of expectation. He'd heard it before, this same cry. Then it was at a great distance, yet that was enough to help him prepare a protective shield against it in his mind. It did not ameliorate the effect completely for he was human and therefore not immune. He could never fully defend against the horror and consequent panic induced by the cry of this monster, no matter how well prepared. But Zack was conditioned just enough so that at the first iteration of the howl he was able to thrust himself into action. He drew his handgun and rose to his feet and charged in the direction he had heard the stealthy footfalls. The howl continued even as he ran, echoing within the fog shrouded trees like the booming of a bass speaker in a small room. Branches slashed at him, undergrowth tripped him, but his momentum carried him on. Then through the murky haze he saw a shadow.

The forest thickened and darkened and despite his impatience Sean Kelly had to slow to a more deliberate pace. He needed both arms to protect himself against the lash of unseen branches; his face already had welts from them. There was no hurrying through this crap, he decided. But he was anxious. His mind kept playing images of Donny and some boat captain giving up on him and roaring away through the surf. Goddamn it! How long had he slept, anyway?

Sean wasn't being real careful about the noise he made; he was more concerned about protecting his face as he crashed down the slope, and so he was startled when a man's growly voice challenged him from the darkness.

"Who's that?"

Kelly stopped in his tracks and listened. The challenge came again.

"Who's there? Answer me or I'll shoot."

Shoot? Who the fuck was this now?

"Uh, who's that?"

"San Francisco Police officers. Now who are you?"

"I'm Sergeant...uh, Mack of the U.S. Park Police."

"Whadda ya doin' here? We've been assigned this quadrant," complained the voice.

Sean tried to steady his heartbeat. "I'm lost, I guess." He heard the sounds of someone coming toward him through the trees.

"Where were you assigned?" the voice asked, maybe a little more conciliatory this time.

Assigned? What was going on here?

"I just got here. I think we're supposed to be down near the ocean somewhere." Sean edged away from the oncoming sounds.

The rustling stopped. A flashlight beam searched the trees near Sean. He scrunched down.

"Where are you, man?"

Sean didn't reply. He stayed hunkered down and waited. His hand closed on a stone. The approaching officer was still waving his flashlight around. "Hello?"

Still Sean waited. Then there was rustling going away again and a muttered, "Screw it." Sean breathed a long sigh. But he was alarmed. Something was up. Were they looking for him here? How the hell could they know?

He waited there a long time. Finally he rose and crept on down the slope, veering sharply away from the watchful officers. He knew he must travel silently now. Who knew how many friggin' cops were out here? Maybe that's why he hadn't heard from Donny; maybe the cops were just too thick all over the place. Nothing for it, he'd just have to creep on toward the sea cliffs and hope to find the boat down there somewhere.

Twice more Kelly heard whispers and the rustling of bodies moving in the woods. But he was lucky. He heard them in time to creep around those locations before they could hear him. He crossed the wide bike path or whatever it was and crept on down through the trees.

The sun was completely gone by now, the fog was swirling around, but Sean could tell by the chill and the salt taste on his lips that he was almost to the sea. The surf sounds were much louder. No point in taking chances now. Kelly slowed his pace even more, taking just one stealthy step, weighting that foot, then moving the other. Either the friggin‘ boat was down there or it wasn't, but getting caught now wouldn't help him find it, that was for damn sure.

Sean Kelly was not prepared for the snarling furious howl that seemed to rise up right next to him, a cry that clutched at him and reverberated in his ears and breathed around him like the worst acid trip ever. He felt the hate and the bloodlust and it froze him and chilled his heart. It seemed to last forever. It grew and grew and Kelly felt smothered and held by it like a bird in the hypnotic gaze of a cobra. He choked and swayed on his feet, and fear like no fear he'd ever felt washed over him. He waited to die, to feel the hot breath of whatever the fuck this thing was just before it took him in its grip. And then it faded. The call fell away and trailed off. For a long moment Sean stood and twitched like a headless snake. He breathed in and out and tried to gather himself. What the *fuck* was that?

He heard a crashing through the underbrush, something coming toward him fast. He heard it smashing through the forest, snapping branches, tearing through the brush. It was almost on him!

Sean sprang into action. He lunged away from the oncoming sound and ran furiously back up the slope. His feet found a wide path and he turned down it and ran as hard and fast as he could with reckless abandon. He tripped and fell onto the hard surface and jumped up again without a pause, not feeling the pain. His brain shouted, *Run for your life.*

The second howl had not come from behind him, that much was clear to Snyder. He halted his stumbling run, confused, terrified. He could not keep running forward, he realized; he might run right into this thing. But maybe there was more than one? Was there another one behind him? The first howl had seemed quite distant. Could that creature have gotten ahead of him somehow? Was it that fast?

Snyder stood still on the dark path, heart pounding, his body shaking. There was nowhere to run. But he couldn't stay here. He felt great pressure in his chest. He knew he couldn't run any further. While the last tremors of the triumphant predatory cry faded he sank to a knee on the hard surface of the path, breathing hard. He'd rest for a moment, he thought. Then he'd go on.

A smell enveloped him, a familiar one, an odor he had noticed in the Chronicle newsroom and in the staircase the night he'd felt he was being stalked. He had smelled a faint trace of it near the murder sites too, but hadn't known it, hadn't recognized it. He knew that the creature was near.

His eyes opened wide in a useless effort to penetrate the dark, his ears trained for every sound. He brought his other knee to the ground and he waited. His fate was now in the hands of this creature that stalked him.

Snyder thought about his life as he waited. It had been good, he decided. He'd have liked to have married somewhere along the line, he thought now, maybe have had a kid or two. But he never would've given up his reporting career; marriage would have been second to that. He grimaced. Probably wouldn't have worked out. He'd been right, he supposed, not to marry, not to hurt a person he loved. Maybe he'd done that much right.

Something stirred in the trees near him and there came a new burst of the putrid smell. It was here. Would the creature end things now? Maybe it would see him kneeling here, maybe it would see that he could offer no resistance. Maybe it would decide there was no sport to be had with him. Maybe it would consider him unworthy of further attention and go away.

Then Snyder's mind turned to Susan. He knew now that she had not invited him here. It had been a trick, a ruse by this monster to entice him to his death in this lonely wind-blown place, where no one would witness his murder. The creature had singled him out, maybe because Snyder had pursued him so doggedly. Maybe this was payment for his stubbornness. After all, he had been the one to keep the investigation alive when others might have given it up. Did monsters hold grudges?

Something brushed past him and out of the corner of his eye he caught movement. It was fast, incredibly quick. How could he ever have thought to outrun this thing? Warm fetid breath moved across Snyder's face. Something hovered and disappeared again, something darker than the night itself. Snyder thought of all the apocalyptic prophesies he'd reported on in the past: the end of the world, the arrival of the anti-Christ, that sort of thing. Was that what was going on here?

Jim Snyder had two final thoughts. He thought again about Susan and how grateful he was for those last days he had with her. She had been a bonus gift to an old bachelor at the end of a solitary, lonely life: an unexpected, impossible gift. He was thankful that she was safe a hundred miles away, caught up in her own pursuits, being her bubbly happy self.

His second and last thought came just as the foul warm breath was at his neck: *This is one hell of a story that I'll never get to write...*

THIRTY-NINE

The second howl was different. It was every bit as terrifying to Susan but in another way. The message it carried was one of triumph. This was an animal that had cornered its prey and would soon make its kill. The cry had come from behind her but not as far away as the first. The monster must have run down its prey on the very path she had just traveled.

Susan was terrified but despite her fear her analytical nature asserted itself. If she was correct and the thing now had its prey, theoretically it should not pursue her. The creature had established a pattern of just one victim for each hunt, a victim it apparently selected in advance. If this held true, she should be safe. But theory and logic didn't comfort Susan right now. She wanted to distance herself as far as possible from this creature for she also knew it was unlike other animals - it hunted for pleasure, not for food. It might not follow its previous pattern.

Susan's heart raced and her legs ached. She was young and healthy but she wasn't accustomed to running this hard for so long. She knew she couldn't afford to wear herself down. If she wanted to save her life she must preserve her strength and keep her wits.

The fog thickened and swirled around her in cottony swatches. Susan had lost her penlight but her eyes adjusted to the darkness just enough to see the path and to keep on it. When the fog was too dense she slowed to a brisk walk, even though her instincts cried out to keep running. Susan felt completely and absolutely alone in her world of fog and dark, as if she were the only person left on earth. All sounds were muted. The boom of surf sounded a muffled sustanato. Her damp shroud introduced a sense of timelessness as if she had unknowingly passed through a portal into another universe. But her damp fog world was treacherous and prevented Susan from hearing the running footsteps on the path behind her until they were too close.

At the sound Susan sprinted forward and ran as fast as she could. Her resurgent panic impaired her breath and her lungs heaved. The creature had changed its pattern after all and was coming for her! But Susan's body could not sustain the effort; she struggled but slowed. Then the footfalls were directly behind her and she was struck a blow that propelled her forward with such force that she was lifted up off her feet. She landed hard, face down on the unforgiving surface of the path and her breath left her lungs with a whoosh even as her head slammed against the ground. She had a momentary glimpse of a large man-like figure passing over her and continuing on down the path. Susan lay stunned.

It had passed her by! It could have taken her but it didn't! Susan felt tremendous relief. The release of adrenaline left her shaking. But the thing might still change its mind. She must force herself to get up, to get away.

But the sound of running footsteps came again. It was returning after all. It was playing with her as a cat plays with a mouse. Susan shut her eyes and waited.

Marty O'Bannon thought he was prepared for the howl. He'd heard it once already. It shouldn't be as bad the second time around. But it was. He was vaguely aware of

Zack lunging forward and he wanted to follow but there was another sound in O'Bannon's ears, an internal humming like a hive of giant bees and the night shadows, the sky, the nearest branches all doubled and then blurred until he saw nothing. So this is what it was like to be blind with fear, he thought. The sound in his ears took on a strange rhythmic beat and then O'Bannon realized the sound was his own racing heart. The beats gradually slowed and when they did, his vision cleared and the forms around him came back into focus. He could hear again. The howl had trailed off into a hyena-like sob and was dying away. He could hear crashing in the underbrush where Zack had gone.

Marty knew it was time to give the order to close the net and he found his radio and lifted it to his lips.

"All units close in on Lands End Trail between Eagle Point and Dead Man's Point. Use caution. I repeat, use caution."

O'Bannon stood up from his crouch; his knees were painful and his thigh muscles were tight. He put the radio in his vest pocket, pulled out his handgun, and willed himself to push his way through the underbrush in the direction Zack had gone.

When the second howl came, Libby had hold of Eagle Feather's hand and was following him at a fast walk through the thickening fog and darkness. At its first utterance, her grip tightened like iron and Eagle Feather stopped and stood still and Libby stood close to him. She listened to that terrible sound, much like the first, but different somehow. Again it came from behind them, but closer - much closer.

"It's found its prey," Eagle Feather said. "We're too

late to stop the kill."

Libby somehow knew that Eagle Feather was right. That was the difference in the primal cry this time: it no longer sought, it had found. The howl was tinged in triumph. Libby trembled uncontrollably.

But Eagle Feather's next words carried a tone of satisfaction. "He doesn't know it yet, but he can't get away."

Then Eagle Feather turned and walked back in the direction they had come, back toward that monstrous sound.

Libby wouldn't budge but she could not release her grip on his hand. "What are you doing?" she demanded. "I'm not going back there. Do you want to die?"

"He's made his kill. He won't kill again. Now he'll try to get away. This is the time to finish it."

"How?" Libby whispered.

Eagle Feather patted his jacket. "I've got what I need. This is my best chance." He spoke quietly into Libby's ear. "You go on. You'll be perfectly safe. Just stay on this path and keep walking."

Eagle Feather dropped her hand and strode briskly back the way they had come.

Libby stood frightened, undecided. She was desperate to put distance between herself and that terrifying monster but her belief in Eagle Feather held her. She watched him disappear in a swirl of fog - first a mere shadow cast upon it and then swallowed up by it. She should go with him, try to help in some way. Then her hand lifted unconsciously to her belly. No, she thought. She needed to think of her unborn baby now. No more brave and gallant actions for her.

Her mind made up, Libby turned and walked on down the path as quickly as darkness and the fog would allow.

The shadowy figure moved quickly. It detached itself from the foggy darkness of the trees and disappeared out of sight. Zack burst into the cluster of dark trunks and saw it again, just beyond, moving fast. He ran hard after it. In a few moments he felt the level path beneath his feet and his speed picked up. But the thing was fast, very fast, and Zack could not gain on it. But he did have one advantage: he didn't have to worry about staying on the path; he needed only to focus on the vague figure ahead of him.

But Zack was falling behind. With another great effort he increased his speed but the figure had gone out of sight in the fog. Without it to guide him, Zack now had to concentrate on the path itself and he slowed. He could hear the sound of footfalls ahead eerily loud in the fog and he tried to concentrate on them over the sound of his own feet. Then he heard other sounds: a solid thump and a woman's short cry and then running feet continuing. Zack almost fell over the figure lying prone on the path before him. The continuing footfalls told him that the person at his feet was not the figure he chased. He wanted to keep on running, but it was useless now. He took out his flashlight and shone it on the person lying motionless on the path. In its beam he saw long blonde hair and the figure of a woman in light pants and a sweater. She lay very still. Zack reached down and shook her by the shoulder.

"Are you okay, Miss?"

He heard a release of held breath and the woman struggled to a sitting position.

"Oh, thank God!" she said.

"Are you alright?" he asked again.

"I am now. I thought you were that thing returning." She looked up at him. "Who are you, anyway?"

Zack kneeled next to her.

"I'm Zack Tolliver. I'm with the FBI."

"Zack Tolliver? The FBI agent who's been tracking this monster?" She didn't wait for an answer but extended a somewhat shaky hand. "I'm Susan Apgar. I've been working with Jim Snyder from the Chronicle. We've been trying to track the killer."

"Apgar. Are you the lady from U.C. Davis? The anthropologist or whatever?"

"That's right."

"Well, what the hell are you doing out here?" Zack's concern turned to annoyance. This woman's dangerous solo venture had ruined his chance to catch up to the killer.

Susan ignored his question and rose to her feet. "Did you see it?"

Zack was grim. "I was chasing it, at least until I

almost tripped over you. It's gone now."

Susan sounded annoyed in her turn. "Well pardon me for being a victim in your path. It's hardly the activity I would have chosen for tonight." She paused, and then tried to explain. "I had a note from Jim Snyder to meet him here tonight."

"Snyder? He's out here?"

"Well, I don't know. I never found him."

Zack stood up and reached a hand down to help Susan up.

"I hope not. This creature intended to kill tonight. From the sound of that last howl I suspect it already has."

Susan had recovered some of her poise. "That must be why it passed me by. It was on me before I could react; it knocked me down but stepped over me and ran on. I don't know why..." and then in a whisper, "but I'm grateful."

Zack started to move off. "There's a police presence here. You'll be fine if you go back the opposite way. I've got to go on."

"Where are you going?" Susan asked.

Zack didn't answer. He left her standing there and ran ahead down the path at an easy pace. The fog eddied away briefly and he could see the stark white line of the pathway for a brief moment before it closed in again. The moon had risen and the Pacific shimmered with its reflected light out beyond the land. Then the forest closed in on him and he needed every bit of attention to stay on the path.

Eagle Feather slowed his pace. There was no reason to rush. The hunter had made his kill and now he would follow his escape route, confident of success. But in that narrow cove, trapped between the cliffs and the sea, he would find his boat in ruins. He would have to turn back inland. That is when Eagle Feather would corner him. And this time he would finish the job.

Then Eagle Feather heard the faint sound of running footsteps. He listened. Someone was running toward him along the path. Eagle Feather stepped off into the darkness of the undergrowth and concealed himself. Almost immediately a huge figure burst into view and rushed past him: giant, silent, crepuscular. Then it was gone.

Eagle Feather was fairly certain it had not seen or sensed him. But he was unsettled and confused. The killer should not be here. He should be moving in the opposite direction, toward the cove where his boat was hidden. Had he another plan for his escape?

Eagle Feather was stunned by his own complacence. Of course the killer would have multiple escape routes, not just one. He was escaping now by a different route and there was nothing Eagle Feather could do about it. Or...another, more horrifying thought came to his mind. Had he been wrong about something else? What if the killer's night was not done? What if on the eve of his escape he planned to kill not once but twice? Libby was alone on the path just ahead of this creature, right where Eagle Feather had left her to find her own way out. She was defenseless and the killer was bearing down on her. Even now it might be too late.

In a panic Eagle Feather leapt out of his hiding place and sprinted down the path after the shadowy figure.

Libby was lost. She was on the path but it seemed to go on and on through the dark and the fog with the roar and boom of the Pacific constantly sounding to her left. Had she gone too far? Libby tried to remember. She had been to Lands End Park before and had even walked this trail, but that was a long time ago. Even then, she didn't walk its entire length and it had been during the day. Now the path did not seem at all familiar. And all the while Libby's heart was racing and her body was wound tight in momentary expectation of one of those dreadful howls.

A wisp of fog sailed out of the way. Libby saw that the trail forked up ahead. One path seemed to stay along the cliffs, the other turned inland. Her immediate thought was to take the inland trail toward streets and lights and houses: safety. The cliff route would be dark and isolated and far from help. But as she stepped toward the right fork, she thought again. What if this inland path circled back? It might take her right into the arms of the killer. At least on the path that followed the cliff that wouldn't happen, although it might be hours before she reached city streets. One way led to discomfort, the other to potential danger. Libby chose discomfort and took the left fork.

Sean Kelly never slowed his pace. He knew now that the howling creature and Donny were one and the same. He'd sensed in Donny a cruelty beyond any person he'd ever met, and Sean had met some tough customers in his dealings. He remembered his fear in Donny's presence, how Donny had always seemed to be right on the brink, ready to burst out of his civilized exterior and become a raging animal. Kelly knew now that his instincts had been right, because that's exactly what Donny was tonight.

Had Donny ever really meant to help him escape? Kelly didn't think so, now. There would be no boat, no escape route. That had all been a ruse so that Donny could kill him and thereby remove the last link in the chain leading back to him. The entire plan was to bring him out here in the dark of night to become his prey.

Well, fuck it! He wasn't about to let that happen. He'd been in a lot of tough spots before and he'd always come through, hadn't he? Donny was about to learn he had underestimated *this* victim.

Kelly pulled up short. Ahead of him the path divided. One branch seemed to continue along the cliffs, the other turned back inland. No choice here. The last thing he wanted to do was keep running along these wild cliffs and into the shadowy trees where Donny could pick him off like ripe fruit. No, it was the city streets for him. At least there he'd have some kind of chance. Kelly took the right fork and settled into a steady run.

When Eagle Feather saw the fork in the path he knew he'd lost. There was no way to know which path Libby had taken. The ground was too firm for prints. But the creature would know. It would smell her and it would follow her. He stood at the fork, frustrated. There was no time to waste; every second increased Libby's danger, yet if he made the wrong choice…?

There was nothing to do but roll the dice. Eagle Feather chose the branch to the right, the inland branch, and began to run.

Marty O'Bannon came crashing out of the underbrush onto the smooth wide surface of the Lands End Trail too late to see which way Zack had gone. He stood still and listened hard. His radio crackled with the calls and chatter of his team coordinating the net that would close in on the northern section of the park. He probably should go that way. But which way was that? In the fog and darkness he'd lost all perspective; he had no idea which way was north. He heard the boom of the surf and knew that the Pacific Ocean marked the western edge of the park but his ear couldn't pinpoint the sound: it hung there in the foggy echo chamber and might be coming from any direction. He played his flashlight around for a few more seconds, then randomly chose a direction and started off.

He traveled at a quick walk. The strong beam of his flashlight kept him on the wide path. Then he began to recognize features along the trail, features he'd seen on his way in with Zack. He had turned the wrong way. O'Bannon swore and turned back but in that split second his light picked up something on the pathway. He turned around again and shown his light at it. A person lay there.

O'Bannon came and knelt by the figure. In the glare of his flashlight he recognized the pale features of Jim Snyder of the Chronicle. He appeared lifeless. O'Bannon reached his hand toward the man's neck to get a pulse. He gasped and jerked his hand back. Snyder's throat was torn completely open. Black viscous blood pooled on the path surface beneath him.

The path took a hard turn to the right. This was not good. It appeared to be heading back the way he had come and Kelly had no interest in going in *that* direction. He needed to go east, the direction the path had been going before, not south. Maybe the path is squirrely, he thought; maybe it will loop around and return to its former direction.

Then he heard voices ahead, male official sounding voices. He remembered the cops he had almost run into in the woods earlier. They must be taking part in a maneuver, maybe hoping to trap the killer. Maybe they had!

Sean turned abruptly and ran quickly and silently back along the path. It was familiar and he could run faster now, despite the darkness. But his eyes could not penetrate very far into the swirling fog and when Eagle Feather appeared running toward him there was no way to avoid him. The two men collided at full stride and went down together in a tangle of arms and legs.

Kelly's reaction was instinctive. His large hand went for the man's throat while he tried to gain purchase on the ground with his other hand, struggling to pivot on top of his opponent. He felt the man strain upward in the effort to throw him off. Kelly allowed the man's head to rise slightly and then with a surge of strength thrust down on his throat, slamming his head against the ground. The man lay stunned.

Sean wasted no time in leaping to his feet. But just before he ran off he delivered a vicious kick to the man's ribs.

"Cocksucker," he muttered.

Zack aimed his flashlight down one pathway and then the other. They looked alike; the only difference was one of direction. He thought of the Apgar woman with annoyance. But for her, he'd be close enough to know which path to take. He thought hard, trying to put himself in the mind of the killer. Would he take the path to the right, which seemed to turn back inland toward the city or stay out along the cliffs?

He made his decision. The fugitive would want to avoid city streets at all costs. Zack took the cliff trail and broke into a run, his flashlight beam bobbing in front of him as he ran. He knew the light could give him away but it allowed him to move faster and right now speed trumped caution. He came out of the low trees and into a barren rocky stretch. To his left the moon's rays glistened on tufts of fog over the shimmery ocean and breakers wove a white line against rocky outcroppings.

Then Zack's eye caught movement just ahead. He switched off his light and slowed his pace to a fast walk. He glimpsed a figure as it emerged from the shadows and became a moving silhouette against the moonlit terrain. Then it evaporated again. More glimpses convinced Zack that the figure was moving away from him. Not swiftly, though. Not like a man trying to make his escape.

I need to move carefully, Zack thought. It could be he knows I'm here and he's looking for an opportunity to ambush me.

But the figure kept reappearing and its pace remained unchanged. Zack saw that the distance between them was gradually shrinking. Then the path dipped into a hollow and stubby trees surrounded him and Zack's view ahead was momentarily gone. He quickened his pace - he didn't want to lose sight of the figure. Then the path climbed back out of the dell and he was out of the trees and the moon crawled out from behind its fog curtain. The path ahead was plainly visible all the way to a distant fin of rock jutting out into the sea.

But the path was empty.

Zack swore under his breath and broke into a crouching run.

The emerging moon lit Libby's way. The cliff path came to a treeless area and merged into a well-trampled earthen platform that overlooked the roiling sea beneath. A long vertiginous fin split the shoreline beyond and protruded, wharf-like, out into the ocean swells. At its apex it towered high above the waves and rocks. Moonlight whitened a narrow path that threaded its way along the crest. A worn wooden sign stood near the trailhead next to a jumble of boulders. Libby walked up to it and read its message: *Dead Man's Point.* Libby shuddered.

But the moon's emergence was welcome, for the resulting view offered Libby a reference point. To the east she saw the Golden Gate Bridge towers and realized she must be close to the very tip of Lands End. The trail she had been on bypassed the fin and swung on to the east, probably toward China Beach and El Camino del Mar, and civilization, and safety.

An involuntary sigh escaped her. She might just make it out of this place after all. With new resolve she turned to follow the trail, but then she stopped. A slight sound had come to her over the booming surf, the clink of stone hitting stone. Libby didn't hesitate. She dropped quickly behind the closest boulder.

The noise did not repeat itself. The fog drifted further away and moonlight brightened the terrain before her. Libby's view down the path was clear all the way to the line of trees. The barren landscape presented a dreamlike quality and at first the appearance of the creature that emerged out of the scrub forest seemed a perfectly natural thing.

It was a large man-like biped yet Libby knew instantly it wasn't human. It appeared to have no clothing; its body was shadowy as if darkened by hair or maybe blackened by the sun. It moved efficiently and with an animal-like grace holding its upper body still and erect as it walked. It carried its head tilted back as if to capture the night smells in its nostrils. As she watched, it suddenly brought its head close to the ground with startling swiftness and sniffed from side to side just inches above the turf.

Libby stayed perfectly still. She didn't dare breath. The thing was obviously following a scent - her scent! If this nightmare creature detected her presence it would be on her in an instant. She felt terror sweep over her and she fought it back. She had no doubt the creature was tracking her. When it breathed her scent into its nostrils she felt a horrible sensation as if it had seized an actual physical part of her.

But now it was distracted. It sent occasional glances behind it along the path it had come down as if it knew something or someone was coming. Then it stopped and stood still, sniffing the air intently.

And then it was gone. Just like that. It must have dropped to the ground somewhere just off the path but the move had been so fast that it seemed to melt right into the terrain. If she hadn't seen it standing there just seconds ago, Libby would not have believed it was there at all. Now she heard the sound of running coming along the path toward them. She waited in horror, fearing what was to come.

The sound of the footfalls grew louder. The foggy damp air amplified the crunching sound of feet on gravel. Then the sound quieted as if the runner had slowed and become cautious. There were no more sounds. The night waited breathlessly. Then a man came into view, a shadow among shadows, his movements wary and deliberate. He held a gun in his hand. It was Zack.

FORTY

The moon had broken out again, bathing the rocky prominence in surreal light. Shadows blackened and sharpened. Zack could see the path clearly now. He put away his flashlight and pulled his pistol as he ran. His eye was on the place where he had last seen the figure, in an open area beyond the tree line. When he came close to the place he slowed and released his gun's safety. He stopped just at the edge of the trees and studied the path beyond. The figure was nowhere in sight. It must have greatly increased its pace and gone on beyond the far ridge or it was hiding just ahead. Zack crept forward.

When the howl came it chilled Zack even though he was expecting it. His heart fluttered. The sound assailed from every direction. Even in his panic Zack realized that the creature must somehow be able to throw its voice and so misdirect its prey. Not to be fooled he kept his focus on the place where he had last seen it. Even so, when it emerged it was with a quickness that Zack could never have foreseen. It was on him in a breath. Zack fired his pistol even as he was hurtled backward and tossed through the air like a rag doll. His gun arced off into the night. Zack slammed onto his back with an impact that forced the air from his lungs. He lay gasping, unable to rise and could only watch as the man-creature came and stood above him and stared down at him with red hate-filled eyes. Then it raised its head and issued a long howl of triumph. The cry still hung in the mist-laden air when the monster looked back down at Zack and without appearing to move was instantly on him, pinning him to the ground like a butterfly on a display board. An incredibly fowl odor snatched away Zack's breath. Then he felt his head thrust back to expose his throat. Zack waited for the end.

Sean Kelly had briefly forgotten Donny in his haste to avoid the cops who were crawling everywhere like lice, but then the cry came again. It struck terror into his heart once more and he knew that his real worry was this monster that hunted him. He couldn't tell if it was behind or ahead but he did know he couldn't stay where he was. He ran on.

Sean burst out of the trees and into an unworldly landscape bathed in moonlight and before him was a sight right out of some horror flick. A man lay on his back writhing in his attempt to shake off the beast that pinned him to the ground with one large hand and pushed back his forehead with the other. Its gaping mouth, huge incisors glinting, hovered over the man's neck. Kelly stopped and watched in horror. The creature swung its head to look at him, staring directly into his eyes. Kelly saw then that it was Donny, his eyes red with rage, his features distorted, his body changed. It was Donny, but he was no longer human.

Sean knew he was a dead man and with that realization came freedom. All the years of dissembling, of fearing discovery, of living in terror melded into one brain-seizing rage and he snapped. Kelly charged at his tormentor. The creature's surprise and its reluctance to leave its prey gave Sean just the time he needed to reach it before it could rise, and he slammed into the beast with every bit of momentum and power in his huge body. The impact was that of a charging bull.

Somewhere Kelly heard a shot ring out. He had

Donny pinned beneath him for just a heartbeat but in the next moment he was thrust off with such force that all three hundred pounds of him flew through the air like a kid on a trampoline and then slammed hard against the ground several yards away.

Zack felt the monster's hold relax momentarily and he ripped himself away and scrambled and crawled out of reach. He saw a large man grappling with the creature but then the man was launched into the air like a sack of potatoes. The creature bounded to its feet and turned to face Zack. He climbed unsteadily to his feet and faced it. The monster glared at Zack with pure hatred. But in the bright moonlight Zack saw that it bled from a small puncture wound high in its chest. When it saw Zack's look, it followed his gaze down to the wound and a look of surprise came over its face. It turned toward the boulders and only then did Zack see the ash-white face of Libby peering from behind with a pistol - his pistol - in her shaking hand.

Zack's heart sank when he saw her. A cruel smile lifted the corners of the monster's mouth. It seemed to know that Libby was Zack's weakness; that it could hurt Zack more by hurting her. Zack knew he had no chance to intervene. The moment hung there, a nightmare tableau washed in moonlight and framed by fog.

The creature turned toward Libby. But behind it Sean Kelly had found his feet and without hesitation once again charged at Donny like a crazed animal. But this time the creature reacted quickly and spun around and caught Sean like a beach ball in its huge sinewy arms. Then grasping the big man by his waist, it lifted him high in the air and moved toward the cliff to throw him onto the rocks below.

Then Zack saw Libby rise to her feet and level the gun with both her hands. He saw flame dart from the pistol barrel and at the same moment a hum sounded by his ear. Instantly there was a bright flash and both the monster and its victim burst into flame. Then there was another flash and the flames became a brilliant pillar of fire.

Through blurred vision Zack watched the two flaming figures clutch each other like drowning men and then topple over and still holding fast to one another roll as one to the cliff edge and then over it and plummet down, a fiery ball that illuminated the cliff face as it passed by. The fireball bounced off the rocks at the bottom and went into the water with a splash and a great hiss of steam. An uncanny silence followed. Moments later a wave broke over the disturbed water and, like an eraser across a blackboard, wiped it clean.

Then Eagle Feather was standing next to Zack and together they watched the waves roll in one after another above the aqueous grave.

"What the hell happened?" Zack asked.

Eagle Feather opened his hand. A gun-like object lay on his palm. It was an unusual looking pistol with a slender handle and two thick barrels.

"It's a Very Pistol," Eagle Feather explained. "I found the rubber boat the killer was going to use for his escape. This pistol was in it. It's meant to send up large flares at night when a vessel is in distress." He slipped the pistol back into his pocket. "This little gun fires a very large ball of flame that burns exceptionally hot. I thought it might prove useful." He stared down at the black surface of the sea. "I guess it did."

Libby came and stood next to Zack. She held his

pistol in her hand. She looked shocked. She handed the pistol to Zack with a shaking hand. He reached his arm around her waist and pulled her close. "It's over," he said.

Policemen were coming along the trail from both directions and everyone clumped at the edge of the cliff. O'Bannon appeared. Everyone stared down at the sea in silence.

"I guess everything is in hand," O'Bannon said.

"For now," Zack replied.

"Is that it?"

"For now," Zack repeated.

O'Bannon looked puzzled. He opened his mouth but before he could speak Libby reached across and placed a finger over his lips.

"He means 'yes'," she said and slid her arm around Zack's waist. "It's all over."

Zack looked at her and his expression softened. Then they turned as one and walked away together along the cliff path.

EPILOGUE

(San Francisco Chronicle: Page 1, Section A)

City of San Francisco Relieved But Chronicle Laments Loss

"An unusual quiet filled the halls and offices of the San Francisco Chronicle today as the staff mourned the loss of journalist James Snyder even as the rest of the city heaved a great sigh of relief. The Night Howler, that elusive killer who had held the entire city in his clutch of terror for three months was shot and killed by members of the San Francisco Police Department late last evening. Police surrounded the killer at Dead Man's Point in Lands End Park, but not before James Snyder became his final victim. Snyder, a highly esteemed reporter, was found on one of the park trails where he had died from a large gash in the throat, the trademark wound of the Night Howler. It is not yet known what Snyder was doing in that location but the matter is being investigated. Mr. Snyder had been cooperating with authorities in tracking the killer in an on-going investigation known only to George Henderson, Editor-in-Chief of the Chronicle. This reporter has learned that Snyder was in large part responsible for the success of the trap set by the FBI and a unit of City Police led by Lieutenant Martin O'Bannon. The Night Howler serial killer was identified as Sergeant Sean Kelly, a U.S. Police Officer assigned to the Presidio where his rank and station allowed him to move freely about the city. O'Bannon is up for promotion and has been assigned to work with the Police Commissioner to eliminate corruption within the City Police that was exposed during the investigation."

Susan Apgar pushed herself away from the toilet basin. This was the third morning she had felt nauseous to the point of vomiting. She wondered what was wrong. Susan took pride in her health; she seldom missed a day of work from sickness. *Only for adventure and field trips*, she thought wryly, *but never for illness.*

The thought of adventure brought Jim Snyder to mind and a feeling of deep sadness came over her. She remembered the shock and anger she felt when she learned of his death. They wouldn't let her see his body on the path that night. But Susan knew what must have happened. She'd heard that thing and she'd felt it nearby and she knew that she was very lucky to have escaped death.

They had killed the monster and that assuaged her feelings to some degree. But she couldn't shake off a sense of responsibility. She had taken the creature too lightly. She'd seen it as an academic challenge, as field research, a fascinating anomaly in her area of interest. But she should have recognized the danger.

Susan remembered her attempts to validate the creature for an academic paper. She had identified its chronological place in the ascent of man and she'd established how and where on that timeline the division had occurred. She'd surmised on the basis of the same characteristics that she'd deduced for Jim how the creature might have survived down through the centuries - among Homo sapiens, but not of them.

But in the end she never submitted the paper. It was beautifully written, compelling, argued masterfully. But it was a career ender. She had not a drop of actual physical evidence and without it they would scoff and call her discovery another Bigfoot.

She wiped the vomit from her lips and reached for her toothbrush. *Jim has changed my life forever*, she thought as she scrubbed her teeth. She couldn't go back to her old ways of thinking now. How could she teach anthropology to her students from traditional assumptions when she knew them to be wrong? She reflected again on her paper. The creature had existed. The murders were not the work of a deranged killer, as O'Bannon had led the public to believe.

Then another thought crossed her mind that her toothbrush midcourse.

She'd been assuming that just one of these creatures existed. But there could be more, couldn't there?

Everything had gone as planned and he was pleased, yet deeply disappointed to have had to leave the city of San Francisco. But he had managed his departure better this time; not like Los Angeles where he left too many unanswered questions, too many clues. And he'd underestimated the tenacity of that FBI agent. He wished he had been able to include Agent Tolliver in his plans but the circumstances had not favored it nor was there the need to take such a risk. It was better to leave Agent Tolliver alive believing he had succeeded.

Where would he go now? In Oregon there were lonely mountains and old growth forests that had never been tamed. And then there was Seattle, a city with ancient roots and unexplored subterranean passageways, a lustful city where the elements let loose their fury and the winds and the mists of the ocean chilled the soul. Or perhaps he would go even further north into the deep forests of western Canada...

The choices were many. And he had learned a lot in San Francisco. He would be subtler next time, more devious. He would be careful not to arouse suspicion. He felt new excitement growing within him.

And Tolliver...and the Navajo? There would be a next time. And next time maybe he would be the one doing the pursuing...

THE OTHER,

a Zack Tolliver mystery from

R Lawson Gamble.

"The hunters noticed the circling birds against the rose-tinted sky above the rim rock and saw where the flat rays of the morning sun glinted on something that didn't belong there and the three of them walked that way."

What they find sends FBI Agent ZACK TOLLIVER and his friend EAGLE FEATHER in pursuit of a dangerous and powerful killer.

"I read your book a couple of weeks ago and have been meaning to write you to say what a terrific read it was. I normally don't read fiction, but it grabbed me in the first couple of paragraphs and I couldn't put it down. It was well written, interesting subject matter, great characters – it just kept moving right along and I just loved it." Pamela Dozios, Lifestyle Editor Santa Ynez Valley News

CPSIA information can be obtained at www.ICGtesting.com
Printed in the USA
LVOW06s1317110614

389593LV00002B/38/P